Across The Continuum Sea

I0654954

Stuart Johnson
Chronicles 5

Peter Apps

τ AUP UK
Terrestrial And Universal
Publications

Published in the United Kingdom

TAUP UK
Sheerness
Kent

enquiries@taup.uk

Author's Note

Because of the plot development, characters appear who are racist and in particular, anti-Semitic. Characters views are as much fiction as the notion that they come from different universes or that they discover revolutionary ways of exploring space.

It is a sad reflection of our times that I need to point this out.

Foreword

Stuart and his friends are explorers using a device that warps dimensions and as Stuart says, "The consequences are mind blowing."

One of the less desirable effects of travelling to parallel dimensions or alternative worlds is that mental links form between alternate minds. A Stuart on one world can reach to a Stuart on a parallel Earth.

The concepts have developed over a series of adventures and you would need to read whole series to fully understand or even accept their world.

For example, James has taken in Andy, a fifteen-year old teenager. That's not too unusual but Andy comes from Egypt and was born some five thousand years ago yet James rescued him from a space ship and that might be too much information to accept in one sitting. Demetrius was a slave living near the city state of Athens and that's another tale in its own right which has already been dealt with.

Intelligent lizards living on a world where all creatures are connected telepathically may strain the suspension of disbelief too far without a long explanation and it is not part of this story.

Don't be put off if this is your first Stuart Johnson tale though. The tale is complete, just be aware Stuart and his friends are more used to travelling by portal and take more for granted. As Stuart also says, "I'm an are-we there-yet type of traveller. The fun starts when we arrive."

Chapter 1

As he woke, Stuart shifted uncomfortably in the hard bunk waiting for the strident bell to begin the day. Unlike the vivid dream he had been enjoying, he would leap to his feet anxious to avoid punishments for being too slow. The dream ended with the image of being in a warm comfortable bed nestled into another man. He could still feel the warmth and smell the scent of his companion, relishing the memory which momentarily blotted out the reality of another day breaking rocks or pushing the heavy wheelbarrow to empty it into the pulveriser. Sometimes the grinding wheels looked so inviting, a few moments pain and then oblivion.

For now, he could savour his dream which, like all dreams had its weirder aspects. The man in his dream was Brian Chapman. He liked Mr. Chapman, finding a kind gentle side to him. However, when the Reverend Carter had suggested that Brian was a little too friendly with his young handyman employee, Brian had no choice but to immediately fire Stuart.

When Stuart was caught in a passionate embrace with the Reverend Carter's son, Alan, he had been arrested for moral corruption and sentenced to twenty years hard labour while Alan faced a long course of psychiatric treatment.

The dream also seemed to jump to different times and worlds by some device that Brian had invented. Impossible of course for all new discoveries had to be sanctified by the Crusaders, a shadowy organisation that dominated so much of his world's thinking. The idea of intelligent species on other worlds would be anathema to them, threatening the biblical story of creation and so evil.

The bell interrupted his musings and he leapt up to start the new day.

~~~

As he woke Stuart nestled even closer, wrapping his arms around Brian, pulling him tight.

"Another nightmare?" Brian asked softly.

"The same one." Stuart replied, "I'm in prison, serving twenty years hard labour for being gay. It's so real though."

"Is it like those jumps you've had?" Brian asked.

"Yeah, I've wondered but what can I do?" Stuart replied. "I wouldn't be able to find him and even if I did, what would I do, break him out of prison?"

"You've said before that we haven't developed the portal there." Brian said. "You could ask the alternate selves that we've met to see if they know anything. It might help if you tried to do something, even if it doesn't lead anywhere."

"There's another possibility." Stuart said. "I'm just worried that so many people know about us and it's just a weird dream about the problems we'd have if everything came out into the open."

"Is it?"

Stuart shrugged, "I doubt it. I've got this feeling that it's real and this Stuart is reaching out for help."

"So, splitting this conversation, how worried are you about people knowing about us?"

"It depends on how much I think about it," Stuart answered. "There seems to be two main reactions. First, it's so big and fantastic, it scares them off and second it's so big and fantastic they get as absorbed as we do. Our idea is that by being so relaxed about security no-one thinks that there's much to hide and I think it works. It's the cover story that's the problem, it's understandable and therefore they can factor in financial consequences. I've often wondered though, what made you move here? I'm glad you did but what decided you."

"The people." Brian replied. "They were cautious about a stranger of course but friendly. I visited a few times and what with the village being so isolated, it seemed to be the ideal place to do my experiments. Of course the quarry being part of the property was a big bonus. It has those World War Two bunkers so I had a ready-made base before I built my first workshop. Then I met you and it was the best thing that had ever happened to me. I can stay behind if you like."

"No. I'm fine. You know, I'm not even sure that I have jumped like that before. It could be someone showing me their life. All we know is that crossing universes links minds."

"True. I'm still worried about you though. If I leave you, will you be all right. Do you have any plans for today?"

"No. James is taking Zack, Andy and a mate of theirs to see Sheffield Wednesday play. Dave wants to spend the day with Dedi's folk studying and I suppose you want to go to Terzon to plan for that quasar study. If I stay here Demetrius will feel duty-bound to serve me so I think I'll just visit Mum."

"Are you sure that you don't want me to stay?" Brian offered, "We could do something."

"No, it's OK. Thinking about it, I've got an ulterior motive. If

2

anyone knows what's happening in the village, it's Mum. Let's see what she has to say."

"OK." Brian said, "James has also got an ulterior motive. He's checking on their friend Billy to see if he knows anything. He doesn't think that the boy does but he's going to see if he lets anything slip while he's excited and off guard."

"There's a couple of Terzon scientists who're interested in the jumps so I think I'll take them to the Lizard planet and see if we can come up with any ideas but not yet."

"I didn't think that the lizards said much about their telepathic abilities." Brian said.

"They don't but they're only hu …" Stuart chuckled, "I was going to say human but they're not. They can be human-like at times and want to show off, so they might say something. I know it's clutching at straws but like you said, at least I'm trying something."

While Stuart visited his mother, James' day out proved to be relaxing and fun. Being single, he was finding being the parent of a boisterous teenager a novel and demanding new experience.

It was as they were leaving the game that James got a real chance to talk to Billy as the other two hared off to the souvenir shop.

"Not buying anything?" James asked Billy.

"No," Billy replied, "I wish I could get a job and earn some money like Andy and Zack. They do weird stuff, don't they."

"How do you mean?" James asked.

"They say they just have to sweep the floor and keep an eye on computer displays but Zack got into an argument with Mr. Venables the science teacher and he wrote the formula that proved him right. I don't even know what a Higgs-Boson particle is. Are they helping you study them?"

James breathed a sigh of relief. It seemed that Zack had got a bit carried away with their cover story but at least he was sticking to it.

"He shouldn't be discussing our work like that." James said, "But he seems to like science. How about you?"

"Dunno." Billy replied, "I'm leaving school as soon as I can. I'll get a real job and help Mum out."

"That's thoughtful of you." James said.

"You were in the army, weren't you?" Billy said, "I might join."

It's an idea Billy, but it'll help if you stay on at school and get some good exam results."

"That's what Mum says but I still want to help out." Billy said, "I'd ask you for a job but it's too far to cycle after school."

"Demetrius is looking for help in the forge at weekends but he's not comfortable asking." James said, "Why don't you see if your Mom and Andy will let you sleep over and ask him."

"Mum wouldn't have to look after me and could rest at weekends couldn't she?" he paused, "You said it like 'Mom'. Is that American?"

"It sure is, boy." James drawled in a near perfect Texas drawl before adding in his normal voice, "I don't like Andy being this long in a shop. He's probably trying to haggle and it doesn't always go down too well. How about you choose a couple of things, my treat but I'll be able to keep an eye on him?"

Billy smiled gratefully and they headed for the shop. Andy's cover story was that his parents worked on digs along the Nile leaving the impression that they were archaeologists. The truth was that they lived in Ancient Egypt and helped create the digs so Andy was used to bartering goods, haggling came naturally to him but he was not always popular in 21st century shops.

However, when Andy had gone with James to buy a new car, somehow Andy had taken over the negotiations and James had paid a quarter less than he had expected.

"I didn't know that you knew about cars." James said on their way home."

"I don't." Andy replied, "Dad always said to look at the dealer, not the goods and that guy was hungry."

If James was breathing a sigh of relief that Billy had not penetrated their cover story, Stuart was becoming a little concerned about the gossip in the village.

"It's you and Dave." his mother said, "You go to the pub, have a little too much to drink then talk too loudly."

"I suppose we do get a bit careless." Stuart admitted, "But we do need to take a break at times."

"I bet Andy's mother was worried about his father coming home from market, drunk." Mavis said, "And I do know how Dave was wounded that time so there's nothing new in drunks causing trouble but it's no excuse. You've just got to be more careful."

She paused, "I know that I'm just as bad. I do show off with the fruit pies and just where did Joe Milnes grow that marrow of his? Don't tell me but you get the idea."

"OK we've got to be more careful." Stuart said.

"Ida Sallin reckons it's all radioactive from your experiments.

I think she means it's mutated or something but if anyone starts taking her seriously you could have problems."

"But you don't think we've got problems yet?" Stuart asked.

"You bring too much money into the village." Mavis said, "Your rural industry scheme is a great success and you've pushed the parish council into setting up that bus service. That's just a couple of the ways you help the village so no-one really wants to rock the boat."

She hesitated before adding, "The worst gossip is left for you and Brian, especially now that Andy and Zack are hanging around. Mr. Bradley tries to stir things up and a few half listen so be careful with them."

Stuart nodded, "I'm still happy with Brian and it's the girls that have to watch out for Demetrius... I mean young ladies, not actual girls."

"And Richard doesn't stray any further than Gable nowadays, does he?" Mavis asked.

Stuart stared, not knowing what to say.

"It didn't do him any good bottling up his gay side and it's better than laying into anyone who approaches him." Mavis said, "He told me after I found out that you're space travellers. The whole thing was just so difficult to take in and your dad had to deal with you coming out and all those new attitudes. I didn't like it but your dad had to handle it in his own way."

"It's still very broad-minded of you Mum." Stuart laughed.

Mavis shrugged, "I shouldn't say this to my son but when we're in bed together we swap notes on the good-looking young men we've met. It's quite a turn on."

"Mum!" Stuart cried out in alarm, "That really is too much information. I just hope you don't talk about me like that."

Mavis grinned, "Let's just say that we both think it's a pity that you're our son."

"For fuck's sake." Stuart exclaimed, "I don't need to hear any of this."

"Even if I liked you swearing in this house, I don't think that word would be timely, do you?"

It occurred to Stuart that his mother was winding him up so he took a deep breath and retorted, "I didn't think any of this conversation would be appropriate in this house."

"I have morning coffee with Tanya and Chloe when Terzon and Earth are in phase." Mavis said, "They're amazed at how uptight we are about sex so I suppose I've relaxed a bit and life with your dad is much more fun."

"Tanya and Chloe aren't their real names are they?" Stuart asked trying to change the subject.

"No It's the closest I can get to pronouncing them." Mavis explained, "And it's something else I didn't expect to be chatting about, intergalactic friends. They seemed a bit aloof at first but once you get used to them, they're lovely people. It was the first planet with intelligent life that you found, wasn't it? They're lovely people but so serious."

"They believe in logic over emotion."Stuart replied, "It makes sense."

"I agree." His mother said, "It's logical to admit that your dad and I enjoy sex but you can't cope can you?"

Stuart left his mother's house, still flushed at the unexpected turn of the conversation but satisfied that his mother was keeping an eye out for trouble in the village.

He felt happier when he met up with Dave as they headed for the quarry until Dave said, "I've done it with Sally at last. She came on to me and I let her control events. After, she lay on top of me and fell asleep."

"What is it with people's sex lives and too much information." Stuart exclaimed, "I glad she's getting over her bad experiences and feels she can trust you but that's all I need to know."

"OK, don't get all excited." Dave replied, "I just thought that you'd be pleased for us."

"I am." Stuart said, "But it's one of those days. If James starts discussing his sex life, I'm going to chuck something at him."

Dave looked at him, puzzled but didn't say anything more until their meeting with the Terzon scientist.

"You mean well but you constantly teeter on the verge of interference." the Terzon said, "You think that your image is asking for help. If you agree, then in truth you will be helping him to rebel against his people. That is taking sides in a civil dispute."

"You forget, sometimes I'm there, so I am on one of the sides whether I want to be or not." Stuart retorted.

"But not all the time."

"No." Stuart conceded, "That Stuart is me. He is what I am. Should I be punished for being me?"

"There's those that think you interfere too much and should be left to your own devices." the Terzon said, offering a rare smile, "However, the problems are usually thrust upon you. Neither do they often have ideal solutions. You'll also have an ally in your friend

Spock. He is fascinated by the opportunities you give to study the same humans in completely different situations."

"So you will help." Dave stated rather than asked.

"We will withdraw our help if we think that you're meddling in affairs that don't concern you."

"That's understood." Stuart said, "The thing is, I'm still not sure that there's anything anyone can do."

"We think that there is." the Terzon said, "Would you be willing to sleep on this planet for a time?"

"Sure why?"

"Your lizard friends can detect your brain wave patterns. They can even distinguish between your alternates." the Terzon explained, "We wait for this particular alternate to return and then, when you're awake try to detect the pattern again."

"How?" Dave asked, then thought for a moment, "We built a detector for a beacon that Stu left on alternative worlds, we could use the same technology."

"Similar," the Terzon corrected, "We have ways of separating extremely weak signals that are jumbled together. We use them to investigate the background noise generated by the universe itself. It's too crude on its own for this job, which is why we need the lizard's help."

"OK I get the general idea." Stuart said, "But we're going to be scanning billions of minds. Finding a needle in a haystack would be easy compared to this job."

"I think you're trying to say that the search will be long and difficult, if not, impossible." the lizard said, "You have another strange phrase… metaphor, two heads are better than one. Do you have one that says millions of heads are better than two? We have watched your activities and now we have a chance to join in. Most of us are excited by the prospect."

"Most, but not all?" Dave asked.

"That question felt as if you were teasing us." the lizard said, "I'll try to answer in the same style. I would say that there are those who would regard a great being as an intruder and yes Dave, you are getting us into bad habits but we like them."

"Damn these translators." Dave laughed, "I must control my thoughts more."

"It's not only your translators." the lizard said, "You and Stuart, especially but there are others who leave an imprint on the…"

The lizard paused, "There doesn't seem to be a word for it,

we've been content to say the place from where knowledge drifts but that doesn't seem right now."

He paused, "It's somewhere real but beyond our knowledge and by physically going to your other selves you have strengthened your imprint."

"I think we would say that we have strengthened the links between our alternative selves." Stuart said.

"I am speaking of the universe that I know and you don't." the lizard said, "We do not know much about your world of electric, portals and such things but here and now our worlds meet."

"OK but you think that the imprint or signal between our alternative selves is stronger and will make it easier to find each other."

"The one you seek is reaching out because of his distress, which makes his signal stronger still. It is so strong that it crosses into awareness."

"OK humans have always believed in what we call the supernatural or that our brain has the potential to develop these powers." Stuart said, "If I said that I'd tapped a tiny bit of that power and I'm more receptive to my alternate selves, would that do for a start?"

"For a start, yes." the lizard said.

"And when I make contact with an alternate self I trigger it in them."

"That is also a start." the lizard responded.

"And you can detect this enhanced responsiveness."

The lizard thought for a moment, "I'm not completely certain what you mean by networking but I could say that we could look for the enhanced networking links."

"Which you call our imprint." Stuart said.

"It would do for another early step." the lizard said.

"Just a thought," Stuart said, "Could you contact your alternative selves and ask them to look for the other me."

"It does not help." the lizard said, "We've found his imprint in our awareness but we cannot give his position in yours."

"So we don't have to wait until he jumps in again. You might have said."

"Yes we do have to wait." the lizard said, "The imprint is everywhere. It does not leave a trail that we can follow."

"When we read the alternate Stuart's brain pattern, it'll have an electrical response which is of this world so we can trace it." the Terzon said. "The lizards will be able to use their knowledge to identify the pattern amongst the billions that our equipment will pick up. I'm not sure why we have to wait for this other Stuart to jump."

"You use words: bearings, signal strength, point of reference. They have some meaning when the jumps happen but not now."

For Stuart the meeting seemed to drag on for hours and it seemed as if they spent most of the time going round in circles. Dave just seemed bored.

"What did you make of it?" Stuart asked as they trudged away from the quarry.

"Not much." Dave replied, "The lizards aren't big on logic and the Terzons aren't big on intuition. It's going to be fun watching them work together."

"It's not fun for me, I hate jumping out of my body." Stuart retorted angrily, "I thought that I was done with it."

"I know." Dave said, "It's a pity that they won't go away if you just ignore them. It was being so disorientated when they happened to me and I was never away for that long."

"Some of my jumps could have been fun." Stuart admitted, "It was the feeling that I was so out of control and it was always nagging me that I wouldn't get home. Anyway let's change the subject. Looking back, it seems to me that thinking about them made them stronger."

"Strengthening the imprint or whatever." Dave said, "James is taking the boys to the football again on Saturday. I'm going. How about tagging along as well?"

But it was too late to change the subject. Stuart stumbled and everything seemed to go black around him. As he straightened he was aware of a tired, aching body and that he was being supported by someone.

"Stand up, Johnson." a harsh voice snapped, "You're not dead yet."

Stuart was unsure how to react but he had noticed before that when he jumped into an alternate self his body would react to the surroundings. Without consciously doing anything he pulled himself up to stand at attention.

"The chaplain tells me that you are argumentative and unwilling to admit that you are a sinner of the most disgusting kind. Very well since you refuse to understand the basic decencies of normal life you will be further isolated from it. Twenty-eight days solitary confinement, twelve hours on the crank."

Stuart had time to take in his surroundings, a bleak office and although the man behind the desk was in civilian clothes he was flanked by two officers in black uniforms. What struck Stuart more than anything was that the set up had a vaguely eighties feel to it, even down to the dark blue overalls and white t-shirt he was wearing.

Relaxing and letting the automatic responses take over he was marched out of the room through a reception area and out into a corridor. He saw a sign reading 'Dartmoor 3' before being led through interminable locked doors and down flights of steps then directed into a bare small cell.

Stuart puzzled over a crank handle as the warder said, "That's not the first dizzy spell you've had, is it. Rest tonight. I'll allow you some food and you can start the crank tomorrow."

The warder left and Stuart was left in complete darkness. With nothing else to do he lay down on the floor and made himself as comfortable as possible. He did not want to stay any longer than he had to but he would tolerate it for a while if only to give the other Stuart a break.

~~~

Meanwhile, Stuart-2 also felt himself being held but it took a few moments to realise that he was in the open air and it was not a warder holding him up.

Feeling stronger he straightened up, looking around before focussing on Dave.

"So you've got your chance." Stuart-2 said quietly, "Go ahead."

"Sorry Stu. I don't follow." Dave asked, "Are you OK?"

"As if you care." Stuart-2 sneered, "How did you get me out? Someone must have drugged me?"

Stuart-2 looked at Dave again, "How come the Reverend Carter lets you dress in shorts? That t-shirt's a bit tight and revealing as well. How come?"

"Let me guess. You were in prison and now you're here."

Stuart-2 nodded.

"You've had dreams about a different life?"

Stuart-2 nodded again.

"Do I fit in with those dreams?" Dave asked and was rewarded with a hesitant nod.

"But I'm awake and I was before the governor when it started. I can't be dreaming."

No, you're not. Let me call you Stuart-2 and the Stuart whose life you dreamed about Stuart-1. Do you follow?"

Again Stuart contented himself with a further hesitant nod.

"I'm Dave-1 and I'm friends with Stuart-1. You know Dave-2 but you're not friends."

"You're calling everyone in my dreams One, and everyone who's awake, Two."

"Near enough. Now supposing World-1 and World-2 are both real: parallel worlds, alternate worlds; call them what you like."

"It can't be, I've woken up on a different planet. That can't be real."

"Do you know a Brian Chapman and is he interested in science?"

"Yes I do. He talks about bending space and all sorts of stuff that the Crusaders don't like."

"The Crusaders?" Dave asked.

"They're not in World-1 are they? Are you saying that he was serious and could build a space machine?"

"In this reality, Stuart and I are space travellers, time travellers and we've visited alternative worlds. You're here because our visits to parallel Earths has opened some sort of door, which lets us jump to our other selves. I've only done it once or twice but Stuart has done it more than he should have done."

"I'm Stuart."

"Like I said, we're used to this so you're Stuart-2. Don't be offended but I'm more concerned with Stuart-1."

"I'm not offended, just keep talking. I like your stories."

"I'm telling you the truth." Dave said.

"Yeah sure." Stuart-2 laughed, "And you don't care that I'm a pervert."

Suddenly Stuart was scared. Even if Dave was serious, no-one would tolerate such terrible perversions, or would they? He was in the open air able to enjoy a warm spring afternoon instead of being driven to wield the sledge hammer against unyielding rock. He was talking freely, in fact talking nonsense instead of merely reciting the standard interpretations of the bible as if he meant them. He had dropped his guard yet this Dave was so different not using the chance to beat him up. Of course, it was a part of a dream that his body never ached from the hard labour. He could vocalise his own thoughts but he had let his guard down too much and gone too far. Scared now he waited for Dave's contempt and anger, confused when it didn't come.

"Stuart-1 and Brian love each other." Dave said, "That's not perverted, that makes them happy. If you stay for any length of time I don't think you should sleep with Brian though."

Stuart-2 stared at him, beginning to accept that Dave was genuine. More than anything, the change in Dave convinced him that he was on a different world.

"You really don't care, do you." he said.

"No." Dave replied, "I'm with Sally. It's not been easy but we're making a go of it."

"The only Sally I know got herself pregnant. She refused to name the father so she was put into her brother's care. He had the child adopted and later, she committed suicide."

"My Sally's brother is in gaol." Dave said, "He abused her when she was as young as eight and he was thirteen. She's still screwed up because of him."

"He's a church deacon." Stuart-2 said, "He counsels unmarried girls who are in danger of lapsing. What you've just said explains a lot."

"A pig is a pig on any world." Dave muttered.

"And in any dream." Stuart-2 said, "I seem to be able to talk so easily. I haven't dared start a conversation in months."

"That's a physical response." Dave explained, "It's what that body's used to."

Stuart jumped as Dave's phone sounded then watched quizzically as Dave answered it, listening to the one sided conversation.

"Yeah, I know." Dave replied, "He's with me now and I've designated him, Stuart-2."

"That was well spotted, especially over that distance."

"Oh I see, it's Stuart-1 you've detected because you're so familiar with his brain patterns. It's still good going though."

"We call it luck when what you call a low probability event happens and our luck is usually bad, so let's enjoy a spot of good luck for once."

Dave chuckled, "At least we know where he is. I tell you what, I'll take Stu-2 direct to Terzon and we'll record his brain patterns then I'll take him for a swim. If they haven't swapped back by then, I'll start introducing him to the rest of the gang."

Dave hung up and turned back to Stuart-2.

"If you want the complicated version then you'll have to wait for our Stuart." Dave said, "The simple version is that he's done so many of these jumps that he's got a unique and powerful brain pattern. Putting together the technology and skills of three different planets, we were able to detect a surge in energy as you two swapped so we've located your world. Your body and our Stuart are safely asleep about five hours ahead of us."

"And that's simple?" Stuart-2 asked.

"Oh God, am I starting to sound like Stuart?" Dave groaned.

"Careful, you don't want a fine for cursing." Stuart-2 exclaimed then thought for a moment, "That's my world, isn't it."

"You're learning." Dave chuckled, "And we've got another problem, the terrible twins."

Stuart-2 glanced down the track to see Zack and Andy hurrying towards them. He frowned.

"I know Zachary." he said, "His father is a lay preacher. I didn't know that he had a twin brother."

"Just a bit of bad alliteration," Dave said, "They're friends and get into trouble together."

"Oh." Stuart-2 said, "Alliteration? You're not the Dave I know. I take it that you stayed on at school?"

"No." Dave replied, "I've just caught up a bit."

Before he could explain more, the two boys arrived.

"Hi Dave." Andy exclaimed, "OK if we go swimming?"

"Andy, you've heard about Stuart's jumps, well this is Stuart-2 and he's a stranger here." Dave said, "Will you take him to Terzon, they want to record his brain pattern. I take it you like swimming, Stuart."

"Yes but I haven't got a costume."

"We call it skinny dipping, what do you call it?"

"A sin, I think." Stuart-2 replied, "The Reverend Carter says that even shorts are immodest and too revealing."

"Andy's an alien, like you." Dave said, "I mean that you've grown up on different worlds. He's been learning our ways and he'll understand when you have problems."

"OK, where are you from, Andy?" Stuart-2 asked.

"Egypt about 3,000 BC." Andy replied matter of factly.

Stuart-2 looked at them feeling that he was the butt of some joke.

"A little too much information." Dave chuckled, "We don't see time and distance in the same way that most people do, Stu. It's what we call the space-time continuum. We can fold it and it's easier to walk to the next galaxy than to catch a bus to Howkbury."

"But no-one will mind if I'm alone with two boys. On my world, it's OK if you're married, but if you're not you shouldn't be alone together." Stuart-2 asked.

"No-one will mind." Dave replied, "Don't worry, if they do attack you, it'll only be in fun."

"Oh, I wasn't thinking about that." Stuart-2 said.

"I know." Dave chuckled, "All three of you, you respect each other's private space. Understand?"

"Yes Dave." Andy said, "I know your laws and we'll keep Stuart out of trouble."

Dave really was more concerned that Stuart-2 would be swamped by Andy and Zack's rumbustious energy but he also thought that he understood Stuart-2's thinking. From what he had heard it seemed that Stuart-2's world had an obsession about sexual conduct and it was reflected in Stuart-2's doubts. Dave hoped that a little innuendo might relax Stuart-2 without an embarrassing conversation on what was and what was not acceptable. He was more anxious to talk to Brian.

Brian happened to be home that day, working on his earthbound projects. He looked relieved at the interruption when Dave arrived but became as concerned as Dave when he described events.

"We know so little about these jumps." Brian said, "I'm worried about him of course but to be honest I'm happier that you're helping him instead of me. If you've made physical contact with the other world, then the jumps may stop. They usually do."

"We seem to be learning but a mental direction finder seems like science fiction even to me. I can't believe we just come down to a set of electrical impulses."

"No, I don't think we do." Brian said, "I think the brain pattern simply interfaces us with this world. There's still a part of us that we don't understand. Think about it. Something holds that pattern together when we jump."

"Our soul, you mean." Dave smiled.

"It could be." Brian replied seriously, "Don't worry though. We won't get beyond the interface. We've talked about this before and we don't get anywhere but what really worries Stuart is; getting stuck there and never coming back. It does scare him even if he seems to think that he's only stuck there while there's unfinished business."

"Yes but this time he's just asleep in a prison cell." Dave said.

"And Stuart-2 is relaxing." Brian said, "Stuart-1 doesn't have the mental stress that Stuart-2 has, so body-2 will relax more while Stuart-2 loses some prison conditioning."

"Could it be that simple?" Dave asked.

"I hope so." Brian replied suddenly looking worried, "I can't think what other business we might have. We'll have to wait and see."

In fact, it was nearly thirty-six hours before the two Stuart's swapped. Stuart-2 spent as much time as possible in Brian's spare room where he had been given a bed. It was on one of the rare occasions that he ventured to the kitchen and met James, Dave and Brian sitting with Demetrius that the change occurred.

Stuart collapsed to the floor his arms involuntarily moving as if turning a handle.

James and Dave carried him to a chair where he sat gradually becoming aware of his surroundings.

"I could only just keep the speed up." he whispered before leaning against Brian and falling asleep.

With James' help they moved him into the living room and laid him on a couch while Brian drew up a chair to sit with him.

He was more his usual self when he woke up.

"I was sentenced to solitary confinement and the bit I didn't get at first, twelve hours on the crank." Stuart said, "There was a warder and he was as kind as he could be. He even explained how the crank worked. It went through the cell wall and on the other side was a large wheel with a rope wrapped round it as a brake. I had to turn the crank against the rope and keep up a certain speed. There was a counter and after a certain number of turns I was allowed to rest for a few minutes, given water or food. If I didn't complete the number of turns by lights out I'd be birched and not fed."

"How many turns did you have to make?" Dave asked.

"One every three seconds for twelve hours." Stuart replied, "Add in the breaks and I'm at the crank for fourteen hours a day. A half an hour's prayers followed by another half hour of stretching exercises before and after and then lights out for eight hours. Two days. I felt suicidal. I can't go back."

Stuart was in tears by the time he had finished his tale.

"Please." he sobbed, "Don't let me go back."

"Take him to bed, Brian." Dave commanded, "Come on James, let's take a look at this world."

"Shouldn't we wait for Stuart before we go charging in?" James asked as they hurried down the lane.

"When this happened before, the jumps stopped if we started doing something about them. Let's establish a physical contact with Stuart-2."

"Good thinking." James said, "What do you suppose that handle was working?"

"Nothing." Dave replied, "It was a form of hard labour from

the early 1800s. It was just a punishment, nothing practical."

"I've never heard of it." James said.

"It's actually something I learned in school. The original device had a screw which prison officers could turn to make it harder or easier. That's why British slang for a prison officer is a screw."

"Interesting choice of subjects to learn about." James puffed as they increased the pace.

"Oh I know about floggings in the Navy, Roman gladiators and a load of other things." Dave retorted, "Now I wish I had learned as much about Louis Pasteur, Alexander Fleming and all those who made our life better but they were never that fascinating."

They didn't talk any more while they made their way to Resolution, their space station orbiting the sun.

"Is it safe to rely on the coordinates?" James asked.

"We're only sending a probe and I'll be happy enough to find the planet first. I can't imagine the Terzons being that far out though."

"It was pretty weird technology, there might have been some bugs." James persisted.

"We fetched Demetrius from ancient Greece, Andy was born in ancient Egypt and we rescued him from a five hundred million year old spaceship and you're talking weird?"

"Don't forget I'm a seventies guy." James chuckled, "Star Trek was too way out for me."

"Yeah, and I do agree with you." Dave said, "Picking out one brain pattern from everyone else in all the universes is pretty weird. I don't know how all the lizards worked together through the Terzons and our equipment but it seems they did."

"And you're going to rely on it." James said.

"What's your plan?" Dave asked.

"There isn't another one, is there?" James said.

"Come on, let's at least try it." Dave said, "Who knows, we could have the pleasure of telling the Terzons that they got something wrong."

Although James and Dave often argued they were good friends and worked well together. Like Stuart, Dave saw James as the boss once a plan was put into operation trusting to his greater experience and skills learned as an officer in the American Army. For his part, James admired Stuart for his ability to spot the potential of any situation and Dave for his loyalty and willingness to go along with anything no matter how bizarre.

They both held their breath as they completed their work and the bulk of the probe de-materialised.

"At least there's a planet down there and it looks like an Earth." Dave said, "Let's hover over the British Isles and listen in to the radio broadcasts."

They were quiet for a time until Dave said, "Heard enough?"

"Too much." James said, "I take it that the 'Good Christian Capitalist Family' seeks to maximise their loans while praying to God to keep them working hard and so avoid the devil's temptations."

"And if you're willing to rely on the government then you'd rely on the devil to support you." Dave added, "Let's not look around too much, I don't think we're going to like what we see."

"I agree." James said, "I tell you something else, back home I thought a bit that way. I don't think that I want to know about me on this world. You've seen more civilisations than me. What do you make of this one?"

"It's the Crusaders who make this one different." Dave replied, "They've polarised politics but their Chancellor is more of a king-maker than a dictator. The electronic intelligence that we're getting shows that he rarely speaks to anyone below Minister or Secretary of State rank. What laws he pushes for are aimed at making the West more capitalist to counter communism and more Fundamentalist Christian to counter Islam. Sunday observance is big while Saturdays which is Islam's day of prayer should be as non-religious as possible. Did you catch that court case? The guy actually got away with being drunk on Saturday because he was defying Islam. There's no health service anywhere because it smacks of communism. The press and the Internet is basically uncontrolled because state control would be communist though there is something about sanctification notes. There are plenty of blasphemy trials though, yet the sentences tend to be pretty mild. Stuart's sentence was harsh even by their standards but Alan was Reverend Carter's son. Corrupting him was an insult to the church."

"Before I met Stuart, I believed that homosexuality should be illegal." James said, "I assumed that it corrupted the services and so on. They seem to have the same idea and back them with the fundamentalist ideas in the bible. It's openly challenging their version of the bible that lands people in trouble. It's not only blasphemous but encourages the twin evils of Islam and communism."

"Their version of the bible, did you say?"

"Yes!" James replied, "They seem to have removed awkward

parts of the older versions to, and I quote, 'Make its message clearer'."

"The Crusaders offer suggestions on what constitutes Christian behaviour but some places more or less tell them to get stuffed while in others it's almost law." Dave contributed, "Stuart-2's already mentioned some things about me. I don't want to know any more about me either." Dave said, let's focus on finding Stuart-2."

It turned out that there were five prisons straddling a road. A high wall surrounded the entire complex crossing the road at two points. They watched a car approach, stop apparently at a gate in the wall, drive through and stop at the second gate before being allowed to continue on its way.

"Our regular equipment is mapping out the site." James said, "We've got the right prison, and following on from both Stuarts' descriptions we've got the solitary confinement cells. There's twenty of them and eighteen are occupied."

"Okay, is the cell bugged?" Dave asked.

"No. What do you want to do?"

Dave flicked a switch.

"Hi, this is Dave-1." he said softly, "You're Stuart-2 and we're going to try to help you. Oh and this is real, you're not hallucinating."

Stuart-2 focussed on the tip the of the probe hovering in front of him but did not react, continuing to turn the crank.

"We're going to see if we can make life easier for you." Dave continued.

All Stuart-2 saw was the probe disappear but moments later he fell forward as the crank freed and just spun round. On the other side of the wall the crank turned a pulley wheel. A rope hung from a hook in the ceiling wrapped around the pulley and led back up to the ceiling to a second guide pulley and back down to be secured to a second smaller shaft and crank. By turning this second crank or lifting the ratchet the tension in the rope could be adjusted. The large brake pulley was half immersed in a tank of water to cool it.

It was crude but effective and there was a similar set up on the other side of the room for the next cell. James did not protest as Dave shifted the probe to release the other crank.

Then they positioned the probe in Stuart's cell so that he could see it.

"Talk to me Stu." Dave said as gently as he could, "Try talking like we did when we first met."

"I tried to stay." Stuart-2 sobbed, "I sat in that bedroom and tried to make it real but I couldn't. This is real and from now on, I'm going to do as I'm told."

"I've seen what this did to our Stuart and I can see what it's doing to you." Dave said, "We're going to get you out of here."

"Please, if I get caught trying to escape then I'll be shackled as well in solitary confinement for life." Stuart-2 cried, "Am I going to be in trouble for breaking the crank?"

"Hang on, we'll be back soon." Dave said but despite his promise the oppressive loneliness of the cell closed in on Stuart again. He already depended on that strange object with Dave's voice to keep him company – and sane.

"I've released all the cranks." Dave chuckled, "James isn't happy but at least no-one can blame you."

"They'll blame someone though." Stuart-2 said, "You can't win with them."

"We'll see." Dave exclaimed, "We're going to rescue you but it may take time. We'll keep you company and help with that damned crank but we need you to hold on."

"Will you do something else for me, please?" Stuart asked.

"If we can." Dave replied.

"I need to use the toilet. It's that hole in the corner. Can you give me half an hour alone and without that spyhole opening in the door, please?"

"Our Stuart likes his privacy as well." Dave laughed, "Let me seal the door. I'll turn off the mike and aim the camera towards the door. When you're ready just come and stand in front of the probe."

Small things, unimportant to anyone else can be of immense important to an individual. For Stuart-2 there was a terrific distinction between solitude and privacy. For the first time since his arrest he enjoyed the dignity of carrying out his bodily business alone. For once, he relaxed knowing that no-one could burst in upon him yet he did not feel alone because of the reassuring presence of the probe. He washed and cleaned himself feeling human again as he stood in front of the probe. Dave could see a marked difference in his demeanour.

"I should get back to the crank." Stuart-2 said, "I've got to earn some drinking water. The washing water is full of disinfectant and burns your mouth."

"We can programme the probe to do it." Dave said.

"No, you'd better free the door and let the screws see me working"

"Good thinking." Dave said, "We'll try to be here as much as possible and we'll think of a way to get you out. You've seen the size of the portal, there's nowhere big enough to materialise it nearby."

"So you'd have to fight your way to this level. I understand."

Having seen Stuart-1's reaction to being in the cell, Dave knew that everyone else would be only too happy help keep Stuart-2 company. Dave was still manning the probe when shouting and the noise of banging doors filled the air. Suddenly the door of Stuart's cell burst open. A guard rushed in, pushing Stuart to one side and turning the crank rushed out again.

Thinking that Stuart had enough entertainment for the moment, Dave used the probe to look around. A prisoner wearing a yellow armband was spread-eagled against the wall.

"It must have been the trustee." a warder yelled, "We'll question him later. First reset the cranks... no, tighten them up a couple of notches."

"Are we going to let them?" Dave asked, "And are we going to let that guy take the blame?"

"How about non-interference?" James asked, "And Stuart might not approve but do you know what, I don't want to stop you."

A warder had already entered a wheel room and was checking the mechanisms. As he tightened the rope so Dave used a laser cutter and the guide pulley mount seemed to shear and crash down from the ceiling.

"Shit." the warder muttered and hurried over to the other crank to tighten that. Just like the first, the pulley came crashing down. Dave flicked the probe around, chuckling at the increasing consternation as every pulley sheared when it was adjusted.

The senior warder looked at the frightened trustee.

"What did you do?" he yelled into the luckless man's face.

"Nothing sir." he cried, "How could I, the doors were locked. I don't have a key."

"Strip search him." the warder yelled, "Search this..."

He faltered and everyone turned to see what was wrong only to also freeze and stare at the keys drifting away from the warder's belt. Suddenly they vanished. James knew that he should disapprove and that Brian would be aghast at such cavalier use of their equipment but even he could not help chuckling at the petrified looks of horror in the corridor.

"It would be irresponsible to make some ghostly groans and clattering of chains, so I'm telling you not to do it." James said.

"I don't have to obey you all the time, do I?" Dave said, "But I've got a better idea and I can say it's an exercise in precise probe control."

All that the warders and trustee saw was the keys appear then go sailing over their heads as if thrown and then caught at the other end of the corridor.

"Do you want a go?" Dave asked as the keys went flying back in the opposite direction.

"Too late." James laughed, "They've had enough. I wonder if they'll remember to lock the door once they're all through. Drop the keys on the floor and let's get back to Stuart. No more games unless they start taking it out on the prisoners again. OK?"

Dave caught the tone of James' voice and understood that he was serious.

"I guess we don't want them too scared to look after them, do we?" he said.

James shook his head and everything remained quiet until it was time for the warders to check on the prisoners again. One picked up the keys that Dave had been playing with and hurried away.

It seemed strange to Dave but neither Stuart-2 nor any of the other prisoners knew anything about Dave's antics except for the shouts and cries from the corridor. The crank still turned easily and Stuart-2 cheerfully completed his daily quota of turns in half the time allocated, and he really was more cheerful than he had been for a long time. The visiting probe had given him hope and had broken the mind destroying monotony of his life. Most importantly he had friends even if he did not yet fully accept who they were.

The final incident was when the chaplain arrived. Both Stuarts thought of him as a pompous, self-important little man while Stuart-1 added that he believed in the government line more than he believed in god's.

"Of course there's no such thing as ghosts." he pronounced as they entered the corridor, "You were right in the first place. That trustee must have done something, give him a good whipping in the morning then threaten him with another one in the afternoon if he doesn't explain his tricks. Do you really want me to proceed with this exorcism nonsense?"

Dave glanced at James who shrugged.

"Go easy on him." James said.

Dave grinned evilly.

"It'll just be another exercise in precision control of the probe's tools." he said.

The chaplain had no idea how it happened but suddenly the heavy, metal cross he was holding began floating upwards. Dave was impressed with how quickly the chaplain reacted as he recovered enough to try to hold it down with two hands. The cross still rose inexorably upwards and despite his best efforts the chaplain lost the battle, finally losing his grip. The cross floated to a steel cross beam, there was a flash and the cross remained still while Dave shifted the probe to watch.

Even James was laughing helplessly as the warders fetched a step ladder and tried to break the laser weld then looked in defeat at the chaplain.

"We'll see what the governor has to say about this." the chaplain spluttered, "Ghosts don't weld metal. Williams must know something. He might be a trustee but he's degenerate scum like the rest. Interrogate the prisoners, see which of them are in cahoots with Williams."

As he turned to leave so he seemed to trip over something and went sprawling. The warders rushed over to help him up.

"Okay. Enough games. We've got to feed the prisoners soon, and they're still bent over the cranks. How about a truce while we let them out for a little exercise and feed them?"

It was the warder, Officer Stevens, who had taken Stuart-1 to the cell who spoke. By answer, Dave lifted the stepladder so that it closed and took it to the door, standing it against the wall.

"You can talk to it?" the senior warder asked.

"No. Whatever it is, is listening to us. It only seems to react to reprisals against the prisoners."

"OK I've got to report to the governor." the senior warder said, "What do you suggest?"

"If we don't keep the regime going then the prisoners will be scattered through the system." Officer Stevens said, "Our poltergeist will have to attack the whole prison system to look after its friends so it needs to cooperate. We get the cranks going again as soon as possible but we keep them at the standard setting. We've got no choice until then, we either relax the solitary confinement or reduce the hard labour to something we can monitor while they're still in their cells."

He thought for a moment, "I suggest we relax the solitary confinement and go for the hard labour."

"Why?" the chaplain asked.

"I'm not sure." Officer Stevens said, "I'm just wondering if any of the prisoners are less broken than they should be. It might be an idea to keep an eye on them."

"You always did think too much," the senior warder said. "You can come with me and tell the governor all about it. I'll suggest you take charge down here."

Chapter 2

"What are you two up to?"

The voice was enough like Brian's for both James and Dave to look round guiltily but were relieved to see Stuart-1 grinning at them.

"Stu," Dave yelled. "How are you mate?"

"I'm fine." Stuart smiled, "There's nothing like a dose of Brian's tender loving care to get me back to normal."

He became serious adding, "And the other Stuart went away."

"How do you mean?" James asked.

"Of all us Stuarts, he's the strongest one I've met." Stuart explained, "I reckon that it took a lot of determination to hang out for as long as he did and he's just not as laid back as the rest of us. It was a strange sensation, I knew that he was trying to come back and somehow I was stopping him then suddenly I was clear. So again, what are you up to?"

James described events.

"So they think that they've got a poltergeist do they?" Stuart said. "That's safe enough. Find the start of the meeting and we'll listen in."

James was still fascinated by the probes. They could go almost anywhere in time and space and just observe. The tip of one hovered near the ceiling of the governor's office, almost invisible and no-one at the meeting even looked up.

"The Home Office isn't going to like this at all," the governor said. "If I mention ghosts in my report, we're all likely to be transferred and downgraded. We'll put the crank failures down to defective parts, recommend that we scrap the existing spares and order new ones in. Put Williams on light duties in the infirmary as a carrot. Make it clear that if he opens his mouth, the stick will be solitary confinement for life.

"Keep the prisoners in the solitary cells at night but put them to work in the quarry during the day. Tell them that if they behave it'll be included as part of their solitary confinement punishment but if they misbehave they'll start their punishment from scratch. Now Officer Stevens, do you think that you can persuade your ghost friend to release the chaplain's cross and is there anything else we need to do to get back to normal?"

When Officer Stevens took a team of officers down to the

cells he found the cross propped up against the wall waiting for him.

"I'm glad you approve." he muttered to no-one in particular while Stuart-1 and his friends headed back to Brian's house to decide what to do.

"You're blowing non-interference out of the window." Brian said, "Are you sure that you know where you're going with this?"

"No!" Stuart replied, "I don't like that Earth so I want to do something about it, even if I shouldn't. Now that he's found us and learned to contact us, I don't think that Stuart-2 will let me walk away from it so I'll have to do something. To make him safe I'd even relocate him to another planet but I don't think that he wants to do that. I feel a lot of concern for Alan but keeping both of them safe on that world would mean changing the whole political set up."

"You're not planning to, are you?" Brian asked.

"They're just my thoughts on the situation," Stuart said. "I'd like to plan a prison break if only to keep him out of my mind and keeping him out of my mind is the only objective I've got so far."

"OK," Brian said, "I can't argue with that. I'm not happy about using our equipment to create a poltergeist though."

"It's not a problem," Stuart said. "They're more interested in covering it up."

The following day, Stuart-2 had no such misgivings. He felt better than he had done in a long time. He still could not fully accept that he had met people from a parallel world but something had beaten the regime. He had rested physically and he had enjoyed conversations with another human being albeit via the tiny tip of a disembodied probe.

He saw Officer Stevens watching him as he trudged to the quarry and instinctively offered a brief smile.

"Johnson, here, now." Officer Stevens yelled and Stuart-2 ran to obey.

"What do you know of yesterday's events?" Officer Stevens asked.

"Nothing sir," Stuart-2 replied. "I heard a lot of noise but that's all."

"Did anything unusual happen in your cell?"

"The crank suddenly freed up."

"Nothing else?" Officer Stevens asked.

"Er, no sir." Stuart-2 replied.

"Officially everything that happened is down to faulty equipment and I'm not going to rock the boat," Officer Stevens said, "I just don't like mysteries. Can you tell me anything?"

"Only some weird dreams that would give you a worse mystery, sir."

"Tell me anyway."

"They're about friends on a parallel Earth who're going to rescue me, sir." Stuart-2 said, carefully gauging Officer Stevens' reaction.

"And they're just dreams?"

"I can't believe that they're real but things do seem to be fitting in with them, sir."

"My son has an injured leg." Officer Stevens said. "The insurance company says that skateboarding is not a sanctified sport so it was self-inflicted. He'll need sticks for the rest of his life unless we can raise the funds for the operations he needs. Ask your friends to help him, will you?"

Even as Stuart-2 nodded, Officer Stevens yelled, "Get to work or you're on report."

Stuart-2 was not put out by the sudden change in attitude. It simply signalled that Officer Stevens was back on duty. No prison officer should make himself vulnerable to a prisoner so mentioning his son should have been a bad mistake. However, he was worried about his son, desperate enough to seek help no matter how improbable the circumstances.

The quarry was as backbreaking as ever, the work as tedious as ever but Stuart-2 knew that it was not going to break him. The only thing he regretted was that now that he had lost the utter desperation he had felt, he had also lost the energy to reach out with his mind.

The senior warder approached Officer Stevens.

"Does he know anything?" he asked.

Officer Stevens shook his head, "No. He rambled on a bit about bad dreams but that's all."

Stuart-1 and his team were monitoring Stuart-2 and heard the exchange with Officer Stevens.

"The warder's son is seventeen and broke his leg in two places." James said, "There's no health service of any kind and the immediate treatment nearly broke them. The leg needs corrective surgery and then physiotherapy but it's way beyond what the Stevens family can afford."

"We've downloaded his files and Dr. Tobias is willing to treat him but he'll have to spend time, either on Terzon or on our Earth."

"And we should treat him because?" Dave asked.

"Officer Stevens may help." James replied, "We've located a

couple of sites where prisoners are out of sight for a time. It'll be a good place to land the portal."

"So a warder apparently gets a lot of money just as there's a prison break." Stuart said, "You're still not used to the computer age, are you James. The boy's miraculous recovery will be noticed if only because he changes his CV to say he's fit for manual work."

"I did think of that." James said, "It was just an idea and Dr. Tobias did look at the costs on that world. They'd have to mortgage their house twice over but wouldn't we get bogged down in a side issue if we helped?"

"Is it a side issue?" Stuart responded, "We've all been examining the material we've got from this world. It's paranoid and there's a basic assumption that if there's a fault then someone is to blame. The governor's report makes no mention of Officer Steven's contribution, and blames the supplier for the crank failures. He blames their failure to recover the cross at the first go on indecision on the part of the senior officer present.

"Stuart's solitary confinement was for arguing with the chaplain. According to their guidelines, he should have been sentenced to extra religious instruction. It would have meant less sleep time but solitary was over the top. From their point of view, Officer Stevens' record is not very good, it says that he's too lenient and forgets that the prisoners are there to be punished."

Stuart glanced at James and Dave ready to make his point.

"If Stuart-2's escape is recorded then I want the governor to get the blame and not Officer Stevens. It's not much to go on, but I think that the governor fiddles expenses. I'm not planning it but if we get him noticed then prisoners lives might improve."

"But that's interference." James said, "It's against your own policy."

"Yes it is but it will be minimal, if Officer Stevens cooperates." Stuart said.

"Ah!" Dave exclaimed, "You've already got a weird and wonderfully complicated plan. Let's hear it."

"We're going to kidnap Officer Stevens' son, and ransom the boy in exchange for his father's cooperation. He'll play the loyal employee and tell the authorities so that they'll set up a sting to catch us. The trouble is, we'll be feeding them the information we want to get Stuart-2 in the right place. When he's in position, we can get him."

"Let me guess. The governor will try to take the credit for the sting and when it goes wrong he'll take the blame." James said.

27

"And I'm hoping that we get Stuart-2 separated so that we take him in the next day or so instead of leaving it to chance."

"Now I think I understand." James said, "You're going to try to get Stuart-2 working in an isolated part of the quarry, create a diversion and when everyone is distracted, materialise the portal."

"That's what I said isn't it?" Stuart asked.

"Not quite." James replied, "The only thing I understood was that you want to feed information to make it happen quickly."

"Well, we've got there." Stuart said, "Are you willing to use your military training to kidnap the boy?"

"And you want us to be seen?" James said, "So it's got to seem real. How long do I have to plan it?"

"As long as you like." Stuart replied, "We'll use field warps to compress events at that end so I want the boy taken two minutes after that last conversation between Officer Stevens and Stuart-2. I want the ransom note delivered ten minutes after."

"So in their time, it's already started." Dave said.

"If we go ahead, yes." Stuart said.

"I agree." James said, "Dave's right, it is complicated but it does minimise the chances of them finding out who we really are."

With their ability to fold inter-dimensional space, space and time had completely different meanings. Although they would be operating in a different universe, adjustments for time and normal space were simple and it was Terry, Officer Stevens' son who first found himself involved in an inter-universal plan to free an insignificant prisoner.

Princetown was only a village, not rating the facilities of a town so Terry had to make his way to the post office every day to sign on and show that he was willing to work. It was the only concession made to his injured leg. Since the money received would not cover daily fares, others unemployed in Princetown were expected to walk the seven or eight miles to Tavistock to sign on then be assigned duties.

In fact, Terry enjoyed the excuse to get out of the house and afterwards he would sit on a bench, waiting for the work assignments that never came and watched the world go past. On that particular day his peace was disturbed as a van drew up, and two men in masks leapt out. Before he could take in what was happening, he was hustled inside the van which immediately drove off.

People knew Terry and were concerned enough to phone his father and the police. The van security was no match for Terzon computers and even the key specifications had been downloaded from the manufacturer. It had been stolen minutes before and was abandoned minutes later along a lane that shrunk to a footpath across the moors.

The luckless victim of the theft was compensated for his trouble by the extra set of keys left in the van and cash in an envelope to cover his expenses. Of the kidnappers and their victim, there was no sign.

Officer Stevens had just reported to the office about that time and was surprised when a slightly puzzled secretary handed him an unstamped envelop with just his name written on it.

Inside was a brief note which read, '*Do as you are told and your son's leg will be fixed. Don't do as you are told then he won't need legs.*'

He was more puzzled than alarmed but just then the phone rang and as his frantic wife gave him the news, the governor sent for him.

The governor did not waste time commiserating with him.

"Why should your son be taken?" he asked.

"I don't know but I just received this." Officer Stevens replied, "One of the staff found it on the ground as she arrived."

"What do you make of it?" the governor asked, a little more warmly.

"I don't know, sir." Officer Stevens replied, "Apart from the fact that they're in a hurry."

"Interesting," the governor said, "Why do you say that?"

"Because I thought that kidnappers made you wait, sir." Officer Stevens said, "You know build up the fear to make you more cooperative."

"It's a good point. Go on."

"I can't help wondering whether that business in the solitary cell area has anything to do with it, sir. Was there anyone of particular importance down there?"

"It's something to check but not at your grade. Leave it with me. Carry on with your duties as normal."

Officer Stevens headed for the quarry, looking for Stuart and beckoning him over.

Stuart already looked tired and it was only mid-morning.

"My son's been kidnapped. What do you know about it?" Officer Stevens asked.

Stuart-2 looked surprised.

"I did have a dream last night, sir," he said. "Something shook

29

me awake but there was nothing there. Then a voice told me to give you a message. Terry will be fine so cooperate with the authorities. Don't try to take sides. It doesn't make sense to me."

Officer Stevens looked surprised and then with half a smile he said, "That's because it's none of your concern Johnson, 6704091. You know that if you do try to escape then I'll do my best to stop you."

"It sounds as if they're counting on it, sir." Stuart replied.

"Get back to work, Johnson."

Officer Stevens considered what he knew. Johnson knew his son's name and all the strange events seemed to be centred around him but why? Johnson may be degenerate but in many ways he was a likeable lad, certainly not involved in a big conspiracy threatening to undermine the Western Alliance. He could not think of any prisoner in Dartmoor 3 who fitted that category so who would go to such great lengths to stage an escape?

Officer Stevens hated his job but he was trapped. As an ex-serviceman, he was recruited by the prison service with a very lucrative offer. By the time that he had put down a mortgage for a house, arranged health insurance for his family and other benefits, he was as much as a prisoner as were his charges. He was sickened by the treatment of the prisoners in his charge and that the punishments were out of all proportion to their crimes. He could resign but he would lose a well-paid job, risk eviction and the well-being of his family.

He was fully aware that all the decisions would be made by the governor, and that he was just obeying orders. Organising an escape was a capital offence and the ringleaders faced death by hanging, not solitary confinement as Stuart-2 had suggested. The truth was that he was so disillusioned with his job that he almost hoped that Stuart would escape along with a good few others.

He may be desperately worried about Terry and should never have asked Stuart for help before but enough had happened to make him wonder if his prayers were finally being answered. It was not enough to let him believe Stuart's stories; fairies at the bottom of the garden would be just as credible.

A message to report to the governor again interrupted his thoughts but one thing he was certain of, he was not going to report his conversations with Stuart. If it ever came out he would simply say that he dismissed them as the ramblings of a degenerate. No-one would blame him.

"They've left another letter." the governor said, "This time it was delivered to your house."

"Did anyone see who delivered it, sir?" Officer Stevens asked.

"It was a neighbour, a few doors along from you. Apparently her house was out of the line of sight of the surveillance teams and she found it on her doormat. She assumed that it had been posted in the wrong door and took it along. It's instructions are to keep the helipad clear and report who's in the infirmary to this email address."

"So the target knows he's going to be released and will fake an illness, sir." Officer Stevens said, "Or I'm being used as a diversion."

"You're saying it's one of the scum we took out of the solitary floor."

"I don't know, sir." Officer Stevens replied.

"One is a diversion and the other is a real escape attempt." the governor said, "They're not going to kidnap your son, and bring in a helicopter as a bluff but we'll play safe. Keep the solitary confinement group together and put them to work in section eight. There're a couple of huts up there, chain them together at nights and I'll arrange a rota to guard them. If any of them claim to be sick, we'll just have to ignore them.

"I'll pull as many warders as possible back from normal duties and arm them. If any helicopter does approach, we'll have a nice warm reception laid on. Here's a list of everyone in the infirmary. Follow instructions, give them their information and we'll see who we can bag."

Officer Stevens returned to the quarries moving the prisoners as instructed. Section eight was a gully with steep walls. A prisoner could just about climb the side but he would be spotted as he ran for the surrounding wall. Dogs would run him down and he would be lucky to escape being torn to pieces.

Officer Stevens positioned himself at the opening and looked around grudgingly agreeing that the governor was right. Landing a helicopter in such a cramped, boulder strewn area would be difficult and their target could be anywhere amongst the rocks, gullies and cliffs. The helipad was close to the infirmary, which was probably the most lightly secured building in the prison. An attack on that was far more likely to be successful.

He did not have long to wait as his radio crackled into life.

"We've got reports of an unidentified aircraft heading in our direction. All warders report to the armoury. Officer Stevens take control of the prisoners still outside."

31

It was a ridiculous order and a stroke of luck for Stuart-1 and his team. The 'helicopter' was a probe emitting the right radio signals in response to radar beams it detected. He had planned a couple of explosions to distract the remaining guards but they were unnecessary. Officer Stevens hurried off to take stock of the situation and Stuart-2's group were left alone.

James materialised the portal and Dave leapt out.

"Stuart," he yelled, "Stuart, come on."

Stuart looked up, recognised Dave and took in the circular wall with an open hatch. He still thought of the portal as part of a dream but Dave had appeared from somewhere.

He turned to the rest of the prisoners.

"You heard Dave." He yelled in his turn, "Come on."

Stuart-2 stood waving towards the portal while Dave looked on, momentarily confused.

"No." he shouted, "Just you, Stu."

Stuart-2 hesitated but then he stood waving again. Some obeyed and ran towards the portal. Others just stood. Dave was in danger of being trampled underfoot in the rush. Stuart-1 looked on aghast.

Just then Officer Stevens appeared around a rock face responding to the shouts. He hesitated as he took in the scene then called out, "Freeze. Stay where you are."

A couple running for the portal obeyed but the rest kept running leaving Dave to jump out-of-the-way. As Officer Stevens ran for the portal, Stuart-2 realised that he had done as much as he could and, also ran. All Dave could do was listen to the cries as the escapees charged through the portal only to find themselves weightless and floating helplessly out of the other end.

Stuart-2 was the last through and Dave slammed the door of the outer observation wall shut almost too late as Officer Stevens charged into it. Dave pushed Stuart-2 through the main portal hatch, followed him pausing just long enough to close the main hatch. Officer Stevens could only watch as the strange round room pulled back then vanished.

The final shock for the governor came when he phoned the Home Office to report the escape and he was asked to verify the names of those who were missing.

"We have no record of these prisoners," the governor was told. "Those numbers have never been allocated. It's odd though. Prisoner numbers should be issued sequentially and all the numbers you've given were skipped for some reason. Leave it with us and we'll investigate."

Officer Stevens made his report but heard nothing more until he was summoned to an obscure office in Whitehall. He was introduced to a Mr. Balfour who exuded an air of authority.

"Something strange has happened and reports suggest that you are our most reliable observer." Mr. Balfour said, "I am not suggesting that you are complicit in any way but you do appear to have some empathy with the er, source of the goings-ons. I am not with the prison service so I'm not investigating lapses in the regime. My brief is to look at the wider picture and suggest a response. Please relate events to me but include your insights and reactions and anything you may have omitted in your official report. I repeat, this is not a prison service enquiry, it is an enquiry into a national threat."

Officer Stevens complied.

"Are you seriously suggesting that these prisoners were abducted by aliens?" Mr. Balfour asked.

"No sir, I am not." Officer Stevens replied, "I have reported what I have seen as well as my conversations with Johnson."

"Ah yes, Johnson." Mr. Balfour said, "You say that your only reason for suspecting him was that he suddenly became more cheerful and was more relaxed."

"Yes sir."

"Very well," Mr. Balfour continued. "When pressed other warders have confirmed that you took the initiative. It was Governor Wallace who ordered that details of events be suppressed to protect his position.

"We found a strange indentation where you say that this round room disappeared and another one where the getaway van was found. It's going to take a lot of time and effort restoring the files that have been destroyed. Backups and everything are gone as well. That information is top secret and does not leave the room." Mr. Balfour said, "Let's assume that aliens are involved for the moment. Given their apparent abilities, in your opinion, do they pose a threat?"

"No sir." Officer Stevens replied, "They wanted Johnson or at least one of the prisoners who escaped and unless he had top secret information that could compromise us they've got what they want."

"Is there any news of your son?" Mr. Balfour asked.

"No sir." Officer Stevens replied, "It's a bit worrying."

"Only a bit?"

"If they're keeping their promise to treat his leg then he could be gone for some time. I don't know what to think."

"Whitehall will be far less worried if they keep their promise and your son is returned with a cured leg." Mr. Balfour said, "In any case it's difficult to consider an enemy that seems so er, skilled for want of a better word.

"The feeling in Whitehall is that whoever perpetrated this escape did enough to allow us to save face if we keep quiet. Again, it's unusual to have such a considerate enemy. Even if these prisoners show up again and claim that they've been on an alien planet, we're not going to argue. The alternative is to spend a great deal of energy reconstructing their files and looking for them when we suspect that the effort could well be futile."

"And if you do find them then they'll quietly disappear again." Officer Stevens said.

"You'd think so, wouldn't you?" Mr. Balfour chuckled, "It does happen but not in this case. We think that a full-scale surveillance operation would produce more useful results. We're also keeping a very close eye on you. Your reactions seems to have established some sort of contact with the aliens albeit an extremely tenuous one but it's the best we've got.

"We're satisfied that you did the best you could in very difficult circumstances and we agree that your role was to calm all the prisoners rather than prevent a highly organised escape attempt single-handed. You've shown an ability to adapt to highly unusual circumstances and you're to be promoted. Governor Wallace has been arrested for embezzlement and has been removed. You'll take up his duties immediately at least officially. We'll appoint a deputy who'll do the bulk of the work. Your real job will be to head a highly secret inter-departmental committee with powers to investigate any more other worldly events."

Officer Stevens stared in surprise.

"Why me, sir?" he asked.

"Because you're our only expert on dealing with alien cultures and through Terry, you have a link to our visitors. If they're going to contact anyone again, it's most likely to be you." Mr. Balfour chuckled, "Later we'll brief our Western Alliance allies so you'll be in great demand. Your salary will be substantial and you'll be able to charge other countries, consultancy fees. You'll be working directly under me and I'm answerable directly to the Prime Minister."

"One word of warning though. Interest will wane if there's no further activity so be prepared to find yourself as governor for real and at a greatly reduced salary. However, if there is more activity, then you may become our first secretary of alien affairs."

Stuart-1 kept an eye on events on the other Earth, satisfied that it would all settle down. He was pleased for Officer Stevens, hoping that he would introduce what reforms he could as governor.

~~~

Terry was in Dr. Tobias' clinic just outside of Stuart-1's home village. He might have been kidnapped but he could not deny that he was in a well-equipped hospital receiving five star treatment. He listened patiently as Dr. Tobias explained the procedures to repair his leg without really understanding. Cutting away damaged bone and growing new tissue to replace it sounded more like science fiction than fact but it was possible. The Crusaders readily sanctified medical research though the more cynical believed Crusader leaders were old and wanted the benefits. However, Terry had noticed other things, there were no compulsory prayers, no posters promoting health insurance, none of the almost obligatory price-lists that he had seen in other hospitals. He had asked who was paying for his stay and the answer had been unsettling.

"We don't worry about that sort of thing here."

So where was here? Kidnappers kept their captors in dark cellars, not bright, cheerful hospital rooms so it nagged him; where was he? When he tried to ask again, the answer remained unhelpful.

"We can repair your leg and then you can go home. You don't have to worry about the bills and the only thing we asked is that you don't attempt to contact anyone outside the immediate area, especially your family."

The idea that he might be able to walk again without crutches dominated so he had agreed.

Even when he was confined to his bed, two young lads visited him. They chattered cheerfully and played games so that he never felt alone. It was two days after the operation while he was still confined to bed that Dr. Tobias came to see him.

"It's going very well." Dr. Tobias said, "I'm afraid that your leg will be in plaster for at least two weeks and then there'll be months of physiotherapy. Sport will be out of the question for at least three months and then you can ease back in."

"How about sticks or crutches, Dr." Terry asked, "Will I still need them?"

"For a time but they'll be difficult to use on a skateboard." Dr. Tobias smiled, "We're expecting a full recovery. The physio will strengthen you generally so you'll be less likely to injure yourself again. Now you mentioned your diet. What's the problem?"

"There's so much of it." Terry replied, "You tell me not to worry about paying for it, but it's difficult. Dad can't afford this sort of treatment."

"Don't worry about it." Dr. Tobias replied, "It's all on us so make the most of it. Repairing bones takes a lot of energy and we're speeding up the healing. Try to eat everything we give you because it's geared to feeding the process."

"Thank you, Doctor." Terry said.

"You'll get tired very easily so don't try to force things but when Andy and Zack get here, try standing to get into the wheelchair. That'll be enough for today but you'll be surprised at how much stronger you'll be tomorrow and then the day after. By the way, they're good lads and know about our work. They're more likely to answer your questions without thoroughly baffling you."

Dr. Tobias was right and within a week, Terry was standing at the main entrance looking down the drive to the gate.

"The village is to the right." Dr. Tobias said, "You can try for it but let the boys take a wheelchair along and bring you back when you've had enough."

"Why did you kidnap me?" Terry asked, "You're not keeping me prisoner. I'm just not allowed to use a phone but I'd like to contact my parents. What's the big secret?"

"You were warned that there'd be restrictions." Dr. Tobias said, "We rely on trust so please don't abuse our hospitality."

"No." Terry replied, "I am grateful to you for fixing my leg."

"Our pleasure." Dr. Tobias replied.

~~~

If Officer Stevens and his son were appreciating the benefits from their encounter, it took time for Stuart to sort out the chaos resulting from rescuing so many more people than he had planned for.

"I'd bring them here to the Lizard planet but after those soldiers I don't think that you'd be keen on hordes of strangers arriving again." Stuart said to Dave.

"You're wrong," the lizard replied. "Or rather we're not keen but it's part of our project isn't it. We will see it through. They can stay."

"Stuart-2 should never have brought them." Stuart-1 snapped angrily, "What was he thinking?"

"You know what he was thinking because he is you." the lizard said, "You would not have left them either. Be careful, his trials have made him stronger than you. If he decides on a plan, you will have to work very hard to stop him."

36

"Great." Stuart exclaimed, "So now I'm fighting myself."

"You sometimes wish that we were human eating monsters set on destroying Earth." the lizard said, "Then you could come here with your weapons and destroy us first."

"I don't mean it though." Stuart exclaimed.

"No you don't. You just want problems to be easy to solve. Looking after visitors will teach us about dealing with the sort of problems you do have. You would say messy ones that make you feel as if you're wading through mud."

The lizard paused, "The one you call Stuart-2 wants to change his world. There's also vengeance in his mind, you would say heart."

"That would be too much interference, wouldn't it?" Dave asked, "Even for us."

"Ask your friend Spock to analyse the other world." the lizard said, "If they are nearing destruction then it would be your way to try to prevent it."

"You think that I should interfere?" Stuart asked in surprise.

"You do not force people into submission." the lizard said, "You create opportunities and those that take them prosper. Those that don't, fail but it is their choice. There is something else to remember. The other Stuart is close to his Alan and could become close to his Brian. He is strong enough to demand that you help them. You may have no choice."

Stuart was not happy but he had no choice but to wait for Spock's report.

"We agree with your lizard friend." Spock said, "The prisoners you freed have been badly damaged mentally. The lizards have taken it upon themselves to try to cure them."

"And what about the rest of the world?"

"As you know the Western Alliance practices a system called Christian Capitalism. In fact the system boils down to keeping folk as deeply in debt as possible so that they're terrified of losing their jobs. However, it is effective because it keeps individuals divided, at best discouraging atheist gatherings and at worst preventing any sort of organised opposition. The world is unstable and in a long slow decline. Your race is very volatile so at some time I would expect the trend to reverse and move to the other extreme, the leaders organising every aspect of daily life. Neither extreme is healthy."

I take it that atheist gatherings are anything that dislikes the present government."

"Those that attend are also called Muslim fanatics and communists."

"The main point is, it's not a failing civilisation." Stuart said, "So there's not much that I can do."

"You have helped civilisations get back on the plan intended for them, you have also rescued the survivors of doomed civilisations." Spock said, "We would not interfere and would concentrate our efforts on blocking this other Stuart but as the lizards say, you have never forced your will on others. We would not consider it interference if you could offer an alternative future and would understand that your counterpart is compelling you to take a more active part than usual. Do you have any ideas on what to do?"

"A vague one." Stuart said, "Divert an asteroid so that it makes a very close fly by but work the orbit so that in about a hundred years it would strike Earth."

"And what would that do?" Spock asked.

"Force them to work together over a long period to find a solution." Stuart explained.

"But their Brian would develop a portal and this Western Alliance would have a new weapon." Spock said.

"Not if he had outside help." Stuart said, "Officer Stevens has been promoted and given the job of looking for alien civilisations. I'm thinking of giving him some help."

"So they would have two reasons for cooperating." Spock said, "Maybe you should give them a third."

"Like what?" Stuart asked.

Spock gave one of his rare smiles, "You're the expert on meddling and there is something else we understand. You short-lived beings have to be in so much more of a hurry."

Stuart had a lot to think about as he headed home. He decided to visit Terry and found him sitting at a table, studying a laptop, flanked by Andy and Zack. Terry tried to stand but Stuart waved him down.

"What are you up to?" Stuart asked.

"Teaching Terry about this world." Zack said brightly then seeing Stuart frown, "He can't go out if he doesn't understand, can he? He tried kneeling when Reverend Carter spoke to him."

"We grabbed him and put him in his chair." Andy said, "He got worried when we told the priest that he just stumbled but it didn't seem to be against Ma'at to hide that he didn't understand."

"I agree." Stuart said, "But we try to avoid telling visitors too much."

"I know, in case they change their own civilisation to be like us." Andy laughed, "Mum and Dad still think that I'm apprenticed to a wizard."

He paused, confused for a moment, "They thought I was apprenticed."

"Maybe 'still think' is better." Stuart said, "Time travel's confusing isn't it?"

"We've never mentioned that." Zack exclaimed triumphantly, "We've just said an Earth far, far away."

"The Reverend Carter says that we were put on Earth six thousand years ago to consider our sins and we still ignore the teaching God sends." Terry replied, "Thinking that there are other worlds with life is a sinful distraction and that we should concentrate on making our own lives more virtuous."

"Why does he think it sinful?" Zack asked.

"Because it's sacrilegious to believe that men who don't descend from Adam could live but I don't understand how there could be two Earths."

"We've come across dozens and there could be millions." Stuart said, "Each one is slightly different and they all exist side by side."

"There was a TV programme about a priest who was cursed by the devil." Terry said, "Each episode he came across his family and friends in different situations. The priest had to try to show the virtuous way. Sometimes he succeeded and other times he had to kill the lost ones. One writer described it as a parallel worlds story and there was one big fuss. The series didn't last long either. It covered ideas that God did not want revealed to us."

"The parallel worlds part is right." Stuart said, "But do you see this as hell?"

Terry smiled, "Well there's an awful lot of sinful sex on the Internet, isn't there?"

"It might be sinful but is it evil?" Stuart asked.

"That's a devil's question designed to make me stray." Terry chuckled, "The priest invited Andy to tea but Andy's not going to get a lecture on his failings is he?"

"No." Andy interrupted, "We'll argue religion then watch the Lord of the Rings or something. He can't believe that I've never seen it before."

"I've never even heard of it." Terry said, "It may be banned at home though."

"What else have you been looking at?" Stuart asked.

"I've found an Eric Stevens, but he joined an aircraft manufacturing company after leaving the Air Force. The picture looks like dad and it says he's got a son and two daughters. The son's called Terry and is my age so I don't know. Do I have to go home?"

"We can't force you." Stuart said, "But you should go."

"Why? From what Andy says he's come from somewhere even weirder than me."

"We promised both your parents that we'd look after you but that doesn't mean that we look after you in the same way."

"And you'd have to go back see your parents." Andy said, "I had to."

Stuart did not remember the visit the way Andy described but let it pass for Terry seemed satisfied. It still left him uncertain on what to do but maybe he should have a word with Terry's father as well.

~~~

No longer Officer Stevens, Mr. Eric Stevens looked up as his secretary entered his office. He was still bewildered by his change in circumstances even if so far, he had little to do except learn about Whitehall procedures and allow Mr. Balfour to go over events and answer his questions.

"There's a Stuart Johnson and a David Hilford to see you sir." she said looking puzzled, "I would have remembered booking them in but I'm sure the appointment just appeared on the computer. There's also a note that I should inform security to monitor events now that they've arrived."

"Thank you, Mrs Murdoch." Eric replied, "Show them in please and inform security as the note said. Whatever they see, they're not to intervene."

"Yes sir." Mrs Murdoch replied looking even more puzzled."

Eric looked at Dave.

"I recognise you from the escape." he said, "You're lucky that only officers on the walls were armed. If I'd had my gun, I'd have shot you."

"If you'd had a gun we'd have changed our plans. Sorry about your nose though."

"Don't be." Eric replied, "It was put down to you punching me during a fight to stop the escape. I'd have got a medal if the escape had officially happened. You're looking well, Prisoner 6704091."

"Let's say that I'm a close relative of your ex-prisoner." Stuart-1 said, "My name is Stuart Johnson but I've never been arrested, at least on this planet. If you want a clue about where we're

40

from, I'm Stuart-1 and I'm from Earth-1. Your prisoner was Stuart-2, and your world is designated Earth-2. I assume that you are recording this conversation as I suggested. I've only come to ask you if you want to visit Terry."

"Do I have a choice?" Eric asked, "You don't want to kidnap me as well do you?"

"No." Stuart replied, "We've also come to collect some history books for Terry. He wants to know how our two histories diverged."

"Why did you want us to inform security?" Eric asked.

"Because your superiors want to know if we're hostile or not. Security won't intervene as you ordered but I'm expecting a phone call any time now."

Almost by magic Eric's phone rang. He picked it up. Apart from a hello and, some yes/no replies he did not say anything until he hung up and turned back to his visitors.

"Apparently you were spotted leaving an empty conference room. Security's checked the room and all they've found were a couple of crushed chairs and scuff marks on the floor."

"Sorry about the damage." Stuart said, "The portal's difficult to manoeuvre to within an inch or so at this field level. You've seen its size so you can imagine trying to park it."

"That's no problem and no, I can't imagine anything about what you do." Eric said, "My brief is to establish a working relation with you and find out what I can, so I should go. However, Mr. Balfour would like a word with you. Could one of you remain behind and follow on?"

"Dave and I will stay if you like but allow us to be cautious. There's an old tank the army was going to use for target practice on Salisbury plain. May we use it, please? There's a Major Smithson listening in on the CCTV. He can arrange it."

Eric's phone rang again. He glanced at them as he listened to the man on the other end of the phone. The interview with Stuart and Dave was making his job more secure which was a blessing for he was earning a higher wage than he could ever thought possible. The downside was instructions to visit another world to see what he could learn. He had seen the portal disappear, vague stories about other worlds but where was it all leading? He dragged himself back to the real world

"The tank's all yours." he said, "What else do you want?"

"Nothing." Stuart replied, "Just tell the observers not to get within three metres, sorry, ten feet while we cut it in half. You can try to stop us if you like."

Stuart picked up his laptop and placed on it on the desk. Eric could only stare in wonder as a 3D image appeared. He could see every detail, even the soldiers, for once armed with cameras instead of guns taking pictures of the area. He could even see their startled looks as an incredibly bright beam of light appeared above the target tank at about roof top height, accompanied by a loud crackling as superheated air exploded. If the beam was not alarming enough, the tank glowed cherry red wherever the beam touched it. The beam cut lengthways emerging beyond the vehicle with a small explosion. With a thud the two neatly cut halves fell outwards.

"You've got ray guns." Eric said.

"We call them pulsed lasers." Stuart said, "I want to trust you and your superiors but forgive me for showing you my teeth before you show me yours. Let's see if we've got anyone's attention."

They waited quietly until Eric's phone rang again.

"Mr. Balfour would still like to talk to you and he says that your warning has been noted. I'll get someone to take you through to his office."

Dave and Stuart-1 were taken to Mr. Balfour's office who greeted them warmly.

"I answer directly to the Prime Minister." he explained, "You are presenting us with a situation that we could never have imagined and are completely unprepared for. You are probably very wise in showing us your teeth as you put it because that tank is the most tangible and permanent record of who you are. It puts you beyond a communist or an Islamic threat.

"Publicly the Western Alliance is a democratic organisation protecting the free world from the twin threat of communism and Islam. However, in private the United States has the military strength and successfully keeps its allies bickering among themselves just enough to prevent unified opposition to its plans."

Stuart nodded as Mr. Balfour continued, "I have persuaded the PM to take a soft approach with you in the hopes that you may help."

"Help you and the PM, help the country or help the planet?" Stuart asked, "They might not all be the same thing."

"There's plenty that would say that they are or would at least disregard planetary considerations." Mr. Balfour replied, "

"How come, you're not one of them." Stuart asked.

"I'm a civil servant." Mr. Balfour explained, "Politically I should be neutral. Admittedly, many of my colleagues see neutrality as not taking sides over which party best serves Alliance interests but I did write a paper on how the three-way cold war was highly unstable and uncontrollable. The PM read it before he was elected and we became friends. Naturally his information should come through regular channels but we do chat.

"Now when the business of strange goings-on at Dartmoor came up most of the government saw looking into aliens and ghosts as political suicide. If the press had got hold of it, then anyone taking it seriously would have been ridiculed into oblivion."

"Some things are the same on all Earths." Stuart said, "I've come across it before."

"Quite." Mr. Balfour said, "It's not a comment I ever expected to take seriously."

"So you have a reputation for having outlandish ideas." Stuart said, "You got this job because you were the only one who had more to gain than to lose by making a success of it. If it goes wrong, it'll only prove how much of an idiot you are."

"Brutal, undiplomatic but true." Mr. Balfour laughed, "It's also the reason why Mr. Stevens was promoted. No-one would care if he slipped back into obscurity."

"How would you define a success?" Stuart asked.

"Professionally, re-establishing Britain's role in the world, privately, ending this constant sabre rattling. There's also Crusader influence. Their public face is preserving morals and advancing the Christian faith which is popular. Few candidates do well without their support which means towing the Fundamentalist line."

"We keep hearing about sanctification notes but we can't find anything about them."

"You won't because they don't exist officially. Good Christians do not want to be involved in anything unholy so they can ask for proof that a business, project or just about anything does not offend God. The Crusaders issue sanctification notes to show that a project has been blessed. Look! I don't like the Crusaders. I suspect that if you made a large enough donation then they would sanctify devil-worship. The Prime Minister has hinted that he agrees with me but it would be political suicide to say it openly."

"I see that but why do you think that I can help?"

"Going back to your unflattering image of me, then I need a stroke of luck to keep my career going."

"At least you're honest." Stuart laughed, "And you do have your stroke of luck. The only reason I'm talking to you is because your Stuart Johnson has a very strong mind. I'm only considering helping you because I need to keep him off my back."

"I'm relieved that you do want something from us." Mr. Balfour said, "I don't pretend to understand the technicalities of your situation but what do you need to attain your goal."

"Short term, we Stuart Johnsons are gay, I mean homosexual. Your Stuart needs to find his boyfriend. Long term, he needs to find an environment where they can be happy together."

"Anti-homosexuality is one of the few things that the three blocs agree upon." Mr. Balfour said, "It's an intriguing thought but he could unite the world against him."

"It wouldn't be my first plan." Stuart smiled, "Are you satisfied that I am who I say I am or would you like further proof?"

"How about something for the cabinet?" Mr. Balfour asked.

"You could inform the PM that at 0900hrs tomorrow a meteor will strike Salisbury plain creating a crater nearly thirty feet wide. You can also tell him that there will be a similar strike every day until we're asked to stop. Of course if we have to do it too many times then your allies will start asking questions."

"Thank you, just one should do it." Mr. Balfour asked, "Do you have anything against Salisbury plain? It always seems to be your target."

"No. It always seems to be army training grounds so it seems to be a good place to use."

"In that case, will you excuse me, please? I need to see the Prime Minister. I'll get someone to take you back to the conference room. I've had someone clear a space for your device rather than have you breaking any more furniture."

Stuart grinned as he nodded in acknowledgement.

Meanwhile, Eric Stevens was pleasantly confused. He was aware that he was on a different planet, delighted to see his son looking so well but not expecting such a monumental event to end up in the village pub.

He was amazed at his son's progress, he could stand comfortably, even walk short distances without sticks and seemed so relaxed. No-one asked for his ID; he found it strange that the pub was open during the day 'when decent Christians should be at work' and marvelled at the cheekiness of the boys who were caring for his son.

At the bottom of the pub garden, there was a forge and a young man was busily shaping metal on the anvil. The youth had removed his shirt and only had an apron to preserve his modesty, yet a vicar arrived and was unconcernedly chatting with him instead of remonstrating him for his immodesty. One of the boys grabbed his juice and hurried to join them without even kneeling for a blessing. For Eric, the scene was bizarre, alien and totally different from his own world. It was the moment that he accepted where he was.

While Eric was allowing himself to get a little drunk, Mr. Balfour was struggling with a far more hostile reception. He was seated in a comfortable armchair in the company of a group of men who formed the inner core of the cabinet, the most powerful elected group in the country.

"You're saying that we're now in the hands of a pervert who's threatening to bomb us into submission," the Home Secretary exclaimed. "The idea borders on blasphemy."

"I don't think that Mr. Balfour was suggesting anything of the kind." the Defence Secretary said, "It's a peculiar story, certainly. I think that I could enjoy complaining to my American counterpart about the lack of warning from their defence systems."

"If it happens," the Home Secretary sneered. "You don't expect some pansy to handle something like this, do you?"

"Mr. Balfour, did you find this Stuart Johnson to be as flaky as George is suggesting?" the Prime Minister asked.

"No sir," Mr. Balfour replied. "I'd say the opposite. It took a certain amount of courage to meet us as he did, in spite of his demonstration of power."

"He admitted to your face that he was a pervert and a criminal yet you still had dealings with him. He should have been arrested."

"I agree with Stevens and as he suggested, I try to suspend disbelief while dealing with them but arresting them for crimes committed in another universe is stretching things too far. The reality we know is that his people have already organised one successful prison break and that tank was a pretty good demonstration of their power. Arresting him would have been easy enough but I don't think that we could have held him." Mr. Balfour said.

"We are not going to arrest them." Prime Minister Shanks said. "I'd like a full report from Eric Stevens when he returns. Also, I'd like more information on how our Stuart Johnson influences their Stuart Johnson."

The Prime Minister shook his head, wondering how stupid he sounded. "If they are a threat then they are making a mistake by giving us time to react. We've only dealt with youngsters and I can't believe that they were working on that portal thing while they were at school. Who is behind them, Gentlemen? Who sends them out on these missions? They have technology beyond our wildest dreams and I'm willing to bet that here, any research on those lines meddles with God's realm so it isn't sanctified."

"You're not arguing with God's word, are you?" the Home Secretary asked. "I agree that those people are ungodly and should be stopped, but you sounded critical of the blessings the Crusaders offer to guide us."

"I'm saying that until we can get a grip on things, they have the initiative and heaven help us if they're hostile. If they're not hostile, then antagonising them would be a mistake. If this meteor crashes as predicted we'll let John have his fun with our American allies but if they do succeed then you realise that their influence extends into space and their abilities become even more alarming."

Chapter 3

The meteor left a fiery trail as it streaked in over the Atlantic. Ships south of Ireland reported sonic booms. CCTV cameras clearly showed the path as it reached land over Devon and towns as far apart as Andover, Salisbury and Warminster reported the explosion.

After the initial shock, the story reverberated around the world. TV broadcasters showed images of the damaged military buildings near point zero while everyone breathed a sigh of relief that no-one was killed. Mr. Balfour was in the same room with the same select inner cabinet as the reports arrived.

"Are they listening to us?" the Prime minister asked, "The trajectory was perfect for John and his dig at the Americans."

"It's possible." Mr. Balfour replied, "It should have been spotted as it overflew America but as we know, it may have appeared just South of Ireland."

"What do you say, George?" the Prime Minister asked.

"You should have arrested them when they were here." the Home Secretary snapped, "They won't give us another chance to stop them."

"They are aliens." the Foreign secretary said, "Dealing with them should come under Foreign Office jurisdiction. They are after all representatives of a foreign power."

"More foreign than usual, I'd say." the Defence Secretary said, "What makes you think that they'll deal with anyone apart from Balfour and Stevens?"

"No, Mr. Balfour can answer directly to me." the Prime Minister said, "George, I want a full background check of Stuart Johnson. My report says he was born and bred in some Yorkshire village. Find out what you can about it. John, find out who else is developing this sort of technology. You'll need to bring in the Department of Religion, Education and Science but do it discreetly, please. Mr. Balfour, does Mr. Stevens have anything to add?"

"Ah." Mr. Balfour began, "I think that the Foreign Office may find that the rules on diplomacy may be somewhat different in interplanetary negotiations."

"How so?" the Prime Minister asked.

"It seems that Mr. Stevens spent a considerable amount of time in the village pub, in possibly their equivalent of Mr. Johnson's home village. He put it down to relief at seeing his son so well and the very liberal atmosphere on that world but he became somewhat drunk. Now apparently he was put to bed and allowed to sleep it off. When he finally woke up this morning there was some discussion on whether he should be taken back to last night. He could sleep further but such a long night period would induce jet lag on a chronic scale. I gather that they settled on seeing that he got to work on time."

"Are you saying that they have time travel capabilities as well?" the Prime Minister asked.

"I'm sorry sir," Mr. Balfour replied, "I couldn't bring myself to ask."

"I don't blame you." the Prime Minister said, "I think that you and Mr. Stevens need to find out what their operating parameters are."

"I don't think that beings as intelligent as this will want to deal with a drunk." the Foreign Secretary said, "Despite Mr. Balfour's comments we need a top team to deal with them."

"Mr. Balfour, you seem to find that remark funny." the Prime Minister said.

"I'm sorry sir but Mr. Stevens mentioned that he wanted a dart board for his office. Apparently he needs to practice before he takes on Mr. Johnson's father again."

As the meeting ended, in another universe and on a different planet, Stuart began his own meeting with Stuart-2 and the other prisoners who escaped.

"I'm trying to set up a working relationship with your government." he explained, "I need them to trust us."

"Why?" Stuart-2 asked.

"I want to find your Alan for a start." Stuart-1 replied.

"Then what?" Stuart-2 exclaimed angrily, "You'll turn us into refugees. We won't be able to go home."

"Look if we go diving in and shift the balance of power then we're likely to start a war. You're more or less bullying me into helping but let me do it my way so that everyone gains."

"I'm sorry." Stuart-2 said contritely, "I don't mean to bully you. Why can't you just threaten them with that meteor stuff?"

"Because they'll resent it and when we move on they'll become even more extreme."

~~~

Later, yet another, more private meeting on Earth-2.

"George, we're going to lose the next election unless we come up with something radical. The opposition's talking openly about interpreting the bible too narrowly and talking more about controlling money lenders in the temple."

"Socialist do-gooders." George snapped, "People should be free to follow the bible's word, not get confused by phoney interpretations."

"And you'll have far more time to preach the true word when you leave the Home Office." the Prime Minister said.

"Do you have anything in mind?" the Home Secretary asked.

"Yes but don't forget our alien friends could be listening in." the Prime Minister replied, "I agree that we can't step too far from the Christian Crusade yet. What we can do is make noises and test the waters. Now I've been looking at versions of the basic bible and I came across a parable, 'The Prodigal Son'."

"Yes I know it." George replied, "It's left out of the edited versions because its message is too deep for today's youth."

"I'm wondering if it could be used to alter our policy a little."

"Go on." George said.

"Interpret it as saying that youngsters do transgress but it's a wonderful thing when they return to the true path. I know, it also encourages youngsters to rebel and defy their parents but the public mood is changing and there's a lot of talk about children being able to enjoy their childhood."

"You'll be getting calls from the Crusaders HQ before you've finished your first speech." George exclaimed.

"That's another bonus." the Prime Minister retorted, "There's increasing resentment about the treaties we've signed with America. They might be necessary to give the Western Alliance a chain of command. However, more people question how allowing an American organisation to decree what time our children go to bed or what sports are acceptable helps in the fight against Communism or Islam."

"You're right, it is radical." The Home Secretary said, "Are you relying on help from our alien friends?"

"No." the Prime Minister replied, "Or rather, I'm relying on a threat in the background. Officially everything that's happened has a natural explanation but sadly staff do slip up with security. The CIA should have enough clues to guess that something is happening."

"You mean that you're allowing doctored documents to be leaked to them."

"Good heavens, no." the Prime Minister exclaimed, "We're their ally, they wouldn't be spying on us. However, …"

The Prime Minister let the conversation tail off. In politics nothing was as it appears. To outsiders, what was the talk of aliens really hiding? Were the hints about aliens a smokescreen to hide a secret project or was the British government really in contact with them and keeping other countries away. The Prime Minister was trying to introduce a degree of uncertainty to the proceedings.

On the other side of the Atlantic, the Chancellor of the Christian Crusade was graciously inviting the President of the United States to sit. The Christian Crusade claimed to be a university dedicated to spreading the true Christian word. It was always quick to point out that its chapels were just meeting houses where like-minded individuals could meet and discuss their faith. In practice, chapels had the feel of a classroom where the 'mentor' would pass on the official Christian Crusade message.

Since it was a university and not a church, statements were not religious but a serious study of current affairs. It was an important distinction in countries that tried to separate church and state and it had enough followers to sway elections anywhere in the Western Alliance. The American President was in the unlucky situation that the CCU was in his country, in Virginia, not far from Washington. As a result of this close proximity, the President could be summoned by the Chancellor to 'discuss matters of mutual concern'. Such summonses were phrased as invitations but the President had an eye on too many votes to be able to refuse.

"It's so good of you to come." the Chancellor said in his usual obsequious fashion, "I've been warned that the British government is about to commit blasphemy and heresy on a colossal scale."

"So you've heard from George Rosswell." the President said, "He's lucky that he's not been fired."

"As a professor of the Christian Crusade University, we would be very concerned about him being persecuted for his efforts to promote the true path. What do you make of this alien business."

"There's not much to tell apart from strange events in one of their prisons and a meteor that appeared out of nowhere then slowed in a way that's puzzled astronomers."

"And this talk of aliens?" the Chancellor asked, "You weren't told of a tank that was cut in two? George told me about the meteor a few hours before it arrived so what is going on?"

"I don't know." the President replied, "Maybe I should invite their Prime Minister to Camp David for the weekend. I'd need a good reason though."

"Include a meeting with me. I wish to personally offer my condolences at such a shocking event and to discuss whether it could be a warning from God that he may be straying."

~~~

Under normal circumstances, the Prime Minister of the United Kingdom and the President of the United States would have thoroughly disliked each other. However, they were both pawns in a political struggle that only succeeded in making the Christian Crusade more powerful. They saw each other as potential allies and a fragile friendship was developing between them.

According to one version of events, aliens created a diversion in a prison to rescue one of their own who had been taken prisoner. They kidnapped local citizens to do medical studies on them and the meteor had been a warning not to interfere again. However fanciful these speculations seemed, why was the kidnapping of an obscure youngster covered by the official secrets act?

Yet when the pair spoke at the time of the meteor strike, the British Prime Minister did not seem worried. On the contrary he spoke with a confidence that the President had not heard before.

What the President did know for sure was that he was known as the most powerful man in the free world. However, the reality was that he was at the beck and call of an oily, smarmy little man who called himself Chancellor. Maybe the Prime Minister did have a way to break the Crusader's power. He could work with the Prime Minister on that. As soon as he could, he put a call through.

"Good Afternoon, Prime Minister." he said formally, "The Chancellor of the Christian Crusades has invited you to an audience. I'd like an unofficial word with you as well so would you care to stay at Camp David."

"Thank the Chancellor for me and tell him that my diary is full for the next few weeks. I may be able to arrange for you and me to meet but it would be very unorthodox and very private. Would you be interested?"

"How unorthodox?" the president asked.

"Very unorthodox and very undiplomatic."

"OK then what do I have to do?"

"Have your weekend in Camp David." the Prime Minister suggested, "Take some morning walks through the trees and prepare for one hell of a surprise. If you find an intruder but he says that the password is 'pomegranates' then he comes from me."

"Are you saying that your men can just walk in out of our high security areas as they wish?"

"They're not exactly my men but not even this line is secure enough explain further. It would be political suicide to mention who they really are."

As the Prime Minister hung up, he turned to his visitor.

"I'm not happy about this, but you're right, the country needs allies." he said.

"As I've told you the basic rule is that we don't interfere." Stuart explained, "However, piquing the right people's curiosity and suggesting a course of action is not interfering because you can all just walk away from it. Look at it this way, the sooner your Stuart stops reaching out and pulling me here, the sooner I'll be out of your hair."

"And you've certainly got the President's attention. He should have protested far more about my threatened breach of his security."

"Any luck in finding Alan Carter?" Stuart asked.

"He's at a Crusader's college in Kent." the Prime Minister replied, "Special Branch and the anti-terrorist people could detain him but they're already wondering what you're up to. Once they get him, it might be harder to get him from their clutches than the college."

"It's good of you to see me." Stuart said, "But am I causing problems?"

"I've briefed the head of MI5, Sir Ronald Cummings. I trust him because he also sees the risks on this three-way stand-off. I consider him and Balfour to be allies." the Prime Minister said, "It flatters his ego to think he's got something that the Crusaders know nothing about. It's even better that the Americans don't know anything either."

"It also terrifies him that I smash through any security he can set up. He's got a choice: either admit that he's powerless to stop me or accept me and see what he can discover from the inside."

"You're accusing him of spying on you when he's said that he wouldn't." The Prime Minister said.

"He's security, I bet that he checks his own grandmother out on a routine basis."

"You could be right." the Prime Minister chuckled, "Be warned though, George Rosswell, the Home Secretary, and the Minister of RS&E are against you. Sorry, that's Religion, Science and Education. MI6's main brief is to gather intelligence from abroad. They see you as a foreign power and want your secrets. From now on, don't leave Mr. Balfour's department without Sir Ronald's say so and you will be accompanied by PaDP officers."

"What officers?" Stuart queried.

Parliamentary and Diplomatic Protection officers. If it gets out that we're treating the idea of visitors from outer space seriously we'll either become a laughing-stock or the target of every paranoid country in the world, scared of what we might do. I know, you're not from outer space but you're not of this Earth and that's as much as I can take in for now. You want me at Mr. Stevens' office by nine o'clock tomorrow morning."

"Yes please." Stuart replied, "Only if you want to be the first time travelling, interplanetary visiting, prime minister, though. It'll be a first in any of the universes we visit."

"What will be unique is there won't be a single press photographer or reporter," the Prime Minister chuckled. "Just to undermine my ego even further you say that on your world I'm just an obscure manager in a power company."

"I'm afraid so."

"And you've assigned two schoolboys to look after myself and the president."

Stuart nodded, "Don't worry. Zack watched Christopher Columbus leave the Canaries on his first crossing of the Atlantic. Andy is still more in awe of King Narmer. He's not impressed that our leaders can't have their enemies impaled but they're both excellent chaperones for our visitors because they understand what's needed."

"And I have to accept that statement without believing that you are completely mad."

"I have trouble saying it without thinking it's insane," Stuart chuckled. "We twist dimensions and the consequences are mind blowing."

"And what do you expect this meeting to achieve?" the prime minister asked. "I know, you've tried briefing me before but I'll sleep better if I go through it one more time."

"We're coming to the conclusion that you're heading for a war that will destroy you all." Stuart said, "We've done some nosing around and suspect that the Crusaders and the Islamic Warriors of Saladin are seeking to unite long enough to destroy the *atheist* communist bloc as they put it. Russia would find itself surrounded. The Western Alliance would push in through Europe in the East and across the Pacific in the West while the Islamic League would push up from the South. Russia is seen as the major communist player and no-one seems to mention China, which is a completely unknown quantity. Its leadership seems to be undecided how to let things play out. One possibility is it waits until everyone else becomes so badly weakened by warfare that it becomes top dog or it comes in early in support of its fellow communist state and ensures communism is triumphant."

"And your assessment is that either way, one side or the other will resort to nuclear weapons," the Prime Minister said.

"On my world people used to say better dead than red." Stuart said, "That sentiment died out over time but here it seems to be as strong as ever."

"And you wouldn't agree with it?"

"No. It's only a glorious victory if there's someone around to remember it."

"And you want me to sound out the president with a view to opposing this religious alliance."

"That's right." Stuart replied, "If you get to understand one another it'll be picked up upon by the opposition. That'll unsettle them because they won't know how and all I'll be doing is providing you with a secure means of communication, which you should have anyway."

"Very well." the Prime Minister said, "The signs are that the people are getting fed up with the Crusaders influence. It's the small things such as it being illegal to drink alcohol on a Sunday but there are so many other petty restrictions. If I break the Crusaders influence and stand on a more liberal platform, then I'll win every election for the foreseeable future. The President will have his second term guaranteed and his party will be unlikely to lose for some time ahead. Are you happy with us accepting the credit like that?"

"It's a fact of my life." Stuart grinned, "You and the President rely on publicity. I rely on the support of my friends. It's time for me to go and I'll see you tomorrow."

"Very well. Please understand, this is all new to me so will you explain your transport network, please. I'll feel happier if I understand where we're going and how we get there."

"Give me a moment while I sort my thoughts." Stuart said then after a moment or so, continued, "We've got an assortment of metal tubes divided into three sections. They're also divided into three sorts: portals, probes and space stations."

The Prime Minister smiled so Stuart continued, "The outer sections of the portal are entry and exit and have various safety features while the centre section has a connecting corridor with the operating equipment wrapped round it. Probes are smaller because they're unmanned; one end is full of observation equipment and the other, terminals. When they're activated one end remains here, the middle section warps through multidimensional space and the other end appears at our destination."

Stuart glanced at the Prime Minister who nodded in understanding so again he continued, "We have two space stations, Endeavour and Resolution. Nowadays Endeavour is more of a laboratory and is shared with a planet called Terzon which is in another galaxy. Resolution is a transport hub. Again it's got three sections. The two outer ones have portals, one is connected to Quarry-1 on Earth-1 and so on. The other is used for exploring. The centre section is just an empty space. The idea is that if there's trouble, the section with the travelling portal can be blown up, followed by the centre section while we escape back to Earth. Earth-1 that is."

"And I'll be weightless while I cross Resolution to the home portal. I'll never complain about changing trains again." the Prime Minister smiled.

"No. We know your planet and strictly speaking, we're not exploring so we'll just use the home portal. You come through, I redirect it and you go back through. You'll be weightless for less time and you won't have to cross Resolution."

In London-2, the city on the alternate world, a slowly expanding but still very select few regarded Eric Stevens as the Alien Affairs Minister. The floor on which his office was situated together with the conference room, was known as the London Space Centre. Only two or three really knew why but rumour and speculation were seeping out to the major world players.

The only hard fact that was becoming common knowledge was that the Prime Minister often visited Eric Stevens instead of sending for him and that on these visits, the head of MI5 acted as his bodyguard. It caused a certain amount of inter-departmental jealousy and wrangling but the Prime Minister trusted him more than anyone because his reports could be as cautious of America and the Crusaders as of their main antagonists.

To the outside world, the Prime Minister spent less than half an hour with Mr. Stevens. However, the first time that he watched the portal materialise and Stuart step out to greet him, his visit became considerably longer and far more exciting.

Stuart glanced at the MI5 chief.

"Next time bring a high definition camera." he said, "Those lapel cameras do a fair job but it's still obvious when you're aiming it. Do you want to come through first?"

The Chief turned to the Prime Minister, "I should, sir."

"Why? You could end up on one planet and me on another."

the Prime Minister said, "We'll go through together and you can wait at the other end. If Stuart doesn't mind, I'd like a clearer picture of his set up."

Stuart shrugged, "I'll get Major Norton to brief him. He's our military expert and can explain the various methods for destroying Earth."

Sir Ronald Cummings, the Head of MI5 was already out of his depth. What disconcerted him more than anything was the complete disregard Stuart had for his intelligence gathering.

He followed Ian Shanks the prime minister through the portal to stand even more confused in the workshop Stuart and his friends used as their home base on Earth-1. They watched as Stuart stepped through the portal again then returned again followed by the American President.

Stuart could not help sniggering when he first heard the president's name, Michael Jackson. President Jackson was a descendant of Andrew Jackson, the US's seventh president. In a world dominated by the Crusaders, a 'nigger singer trying to sound white instead of staying loyal to his own race' did not get very far so the name was associated with the president. Stuart was aware of the innate racial prejudice on Earth-2 fuelled by the idea that white Europeans had 'carried the torch of Christianity for two thousand years' even if he detested them. However, President Jackson proved to be a quiet, urbane man who looked startled when the portal appeared in front of him.

"Good Morning President Jackson." Stuart said, "The password for today is pomegranates. Your security will be here in a minute so would you hurry please?"

President Jackson knew that he should turn and run or, at the very least, yell for help. However, he was expecting someone, Stuart was not forcing him at gunpoint and he was seeing something that the Brits knew about yet his staff were in complete ignorance.

Prime Ministers and Presidents, no matter how bumbling or ineffectual in the job need ambition, determination and ruthlessness to get the post. President Jackson was far more than that, earning respect for his skilful dealings with the Crusaders.

He was sure that the apparition before him was the source of the British Prime Minister's new-found confidence and willingness to defy the Crusaders. If he didn't step forward then the British would have an incalculable advantage over him and that was unthinkable.

He hurried over to greet Stuart and allowed himself to be

guided through an airlock which vaguely reminded him of a submarine even though at one stage he was weightless. He stepped out into the workshop, thoroughly disorientated, relieved to see Prime Minister Shanks waiting to greet him.

"Did you have a good trip, Mr. President." the Prime Minister asked dryly.

"Er yes." President Jackson replied, "Thank you. OK, where are we?"

The Prime Minister glanced at Stuart before taking a deep breath and replying, "We're on a parallel Earth. To avoid confusion it's called Earth-1. Our planet, countries and names are designated two."

"And you expect me to believe that."

"Stuart?" Mr. Shanks asked hopefully.

"We suggest that you remain for twenty-four hours." Stuart said, "That way your body clocks will remain in sync with your time zones. Don't worry, the elapsed time there will be just ten seconds. I also suggest you take a stroll down to the village and have a cup of coffee so that you can get your bearings. Zack, Andy, come here."

The two boys stepped forward.

"These two lads will stay with you and try to answer all your questions. It's Sunday here so there's no school."

"If it's Sunday, isn't everyone home with their families?" President Jackson asked, "Won't they be going to church?"

"No not here." Zack piped up, "The pub's open now for ramblers. Demetrius will be at the forge but you should sit out the front and watch the village. It's the best way to get the feel of the place."

"That's right." Andy said, "And use your first names. Come on."

While the two bemused leaders found themselves being dragged off by two excitable teenagers, Sir Ronald Cummings was introduced to James, an ex-officer in the Military Intelligence branch of the American army while Stuart sought out Dave.

"Fancy a trip to Canterbury-2?" he asked.

"That's not a good idea." Sir Ronald said, "You've got no IDs and on a Sunday … "

He trailed off seeing Stuart's grin.

"Let's just say that your computers have been updated." Stuart said, "I was thinking of visiting yesterday and my false ID would fool anyone. Coming Dave?"

"Yeah sure." David replied, "Any reason for going?"

"We've still got to rescue Alan." he turned to Sir Ronald Cummings, "You can come along as well if you like. I'm sure you're dying to observe us."

Sir Ronald knew that he was just being invited out of courtesy but he was intrigued. Old habits were asserting themselves and he was seriously considering having them arrested as soon they arrived on his own world but he was not stupid. He knew of the tank being sliced and could see that there was far more to their set-up than he had realised. If he thought of himself as the Sunday version of himself, he would be travelling back to Saturday where there would already be the Saturday version of him at home following his usual routine. The Sunday version would be in Canterbury having travelled back a day so there would be two of him. The other would be trying to explain time travel and travelling to an alternate Earth without breaching security. He also had the Prime Minister and President to consider.

He glanced at Stuart. How on Earth did he take it all in his stride so easily. However, the portal was an incredible weapon. If his country could build its own, then it could rule the Earth. He played with the thought of ruling many planets but that was just a little too much, at least for now. His best bet was to gain Stuart's confidence.

"I think that I may learn more here." he said, "Canterbury is full of pilgrims at the moment so security's that much higher. Maybe you should try later in the year."

"Think day out, not security operation." Stuart said, "We're not looking for trouble and we're not going to cause any. I'm going to buy myself an ice cream and enjoy some sightseeing."

If Sir Ronald was considering a radical new approach to surveillance and espionage then Zack was trying to protect his two guests from an outraged Ida Sallin.

"You people won't be satisfied until we're all radioactive." she yelled, "Can't you incomers find anything better to waste your money on?"

"They're visitors." Zack said, "And you're being rude."

"I don't need some brat teaching me manners." Ida exclaimed, "I'll be having words with your father. You want to keep away from that lot in the quarry, they're turning you into one of them."

"A scientist, you mean." Zack said cheerfully, "I hope so but for now I'd like to show our guests some nicer villagers. Come on."

President Jackson managed a polite 'Good Morning Ma'am' before being dragged on by Zack.

"Sorry about that." Zack said, "She's friendly with David

Bradley."

Uncertain how Zack's response explained anything President Jackson said, "I'm trying to remember that you don't have the Crusaders here. Back home they'd make sure that you were heading for a switch in the wood shed."

"Dad doesn't like her much." Zack said, "Do the Crusaders like watching boys being beaten then?"

"Probably." President Jackson smiled suddenly relaxing. With youngsters standing up to adults, no security and a sharp tongued woman who had no idea who he really was, the situation was just too bizarre to worry about. As he thought about it, he concluded that what was really surreal was that Stuart's problems had nothing to do with inter-dimensional affairs but a village gossip.

He allowed Zack to guide him to a table outside the pub while Andy hurried in to find someone willing to serve them. Despite Zack obviously knowing about Stuart's activities he thought that some innocent chatter from the boys might settle him.

"How else do you boys help Mr. Johnson" he asked, expecting to hear about idle chatter about other guests. He did not expect two young teens would be that closely involved but he was impressed that they could take all it all so calmly. He certainly should not have added, "Have you been through that portal thing?"

"I watched Christopher Columbus set sail in the Santa Maria." Zack announced proudly, "I managed a trip through to meet Andy's parents but I think Stuart really knew about it. Shit, there's Billy. I'll tell you more later but you're on a business trip to see Brian and taking a few hours off. OK?"

"Why not." President Jackson said, "You're not very formal here, you'd better call me Mike."

The Prime Minister was content to sit back and watch. He was more used to the idea of parallel worlds and understood that the president needed time to adapt.

Billy looked at the two men curiously but contented himself with a 'hi', feeling as he often did, that he was an outsider. Zack and Andy had got him his weekend job, James always seemed ready to talk to him and listen to his problems so he could not put his finger on what bothered him.

Now was a case in point, they had obviously stopped their conversation and the adults seemed to be following Zack's lead. He was a little uncomfortable as he accepted Zack's invitation to sit with them but he liked Zack and Andy. As soon as he could, he sought out Demetrius.

President 'Mike' Jackson was wondering why Zack needed to use the portal to visit Andy's parents and not listening to the chatter between the boys. He was not completely sure whether he was asleep and the village was a dream or whether he was awake and his life as president was a dream.

He stopped, it was the bustle of ordinary life that confused him or rather the way he was being caught up in it and not even the prime minister was recognised in his own country. The boys were speaking most disrespectfully to adults though he had to admit, their easy-going manner made a pleasant change but then, even that acceptance was pushed to the limits when the vicar arrived.

Both the Prime Minister and the President were ready to kneel but Andy leapt up, hugged him and dragged him into the bar.

"Doesn't anyone respect Sunday observance?" the Prime Minister asked.

"I don't think so." Zack replied, "At least not like you do. The vicar and Andy will play pool for a bit and then and when the regulars are relaxed with him, the vicar will chat with them. You two want to talk business. Where do you want to go? We could go to a desert island if you liked."

"I don't think that I could cope with a new place." President Jackson laughed, "It's a warm day, I don't think anyone can overhear us so let's stay here. Zack, what do you know about the Crusaders?"

"Not much." Zack replied, "Your bible belt got a lot more political and formed its own party. It didn't do very well so it became the Crusaders. It's got a sort of detective agency and got the dirt on politicians it didn't like. Then politicians got too scared to argue with it and it spread to other countries."

"I've heard worse explanations from American school kids …" he paused thoughtfully and added, "From my planet."

It had taken an effort but he had finally admitted that he had travelled to an alternate Earth. The Prime Minister already accepted it and he was more concerned with his political future. Some twenty years older than the president, he remembered visiting relatives in a village very much like this one, relaxed, slow moving and welcoming strangers.

The British people were becoming tired of the 'New Puritanism' and his party's popularity was waning. There was a tension in his Britain. People were expected to be cautious until they had seen ID cards or sanctification notes. It might well be part of the fight against terrorism but, for example, a baker was not going to discourage a new customer and what was the security risk in buying

60

a loaf of bread? The authorities would say that he should ask but increasingly, not asking was seen as resistance to the Crusaders.

The problem for national leaders was that the Crusaders sent well-known personalities a dossier on them asking them to report any inaccuracies. The dossier tended to be extensive, accurate and there were few people that did not have something that they wanted to hide. The Prime Minister had experimented with drugs at university and putting it as delicately as the Crusaders report, his libido needed more than his wife could supply so he had enjoyed some very 'unsuitable company'. He often wondered, which call-girl had spilled the beans.

While President Jackson was getting used to his novel situation, the Prime Minister was more at and was considering ideas on how to proceed. He turned to Zack.

"What are the chances of getting Chairman Chernekov here? I know it won't be easy but you do have time travel, don't you?"

Zack took out his phone, trying to ring Stuart but there was no reply.

"I'll go and find Stuart." Zack replied, "I'll see what he says. Will you be OK here?"

"I should think so. Andy can help us if we need anything."

"What's your game?" President Jackson asked when they were alone, "We don't need Commie interference."

"No we don't and that's why we're inviting him." Prime Minister Shanks replied, "But before I explain, let me ask you this; who runs your country, you or the Crusaders? Ask me and I'd say the Crusaders."

The President nodded, "Go on."

"I'm getting an idea of who their team is and I've found most of them at home except for your Major Norton. On our world he's well into his seventies. However, if we announced a dramatic breakthrough in rocket technology and a treaty that it would only be used for deep space exploration then we could offer Chernekov facilities on the research station we're building. We can always say that Russian research provided a key contribution to the original research."

"So you'll share the technology with the Russians but not us." President Jackson said.

"We won't share it with anyone." Prime Minister Shanks replied, "Once you or Chernekov has got it then you'd squeeze us out and that's not going to happen."

"Instead you squeeze us out." President Jackson rasped

61

angrily.

"No, because you've still got all the power and influence on Earth." the Prime Minister said, "It's a balance of power. You keep us onside on Earth and we give you space."

"OK but involving the Russians?" President Jackson said thoughtfully then added, "It's a balance of power again. You could play the two big nuclear powers off against each other. How does it beat the Crusaders?"

"Science not religion brings a new spirit of cooperation to the world's major players. We managed it in spite of the Crusaders' opposition and we've already made discoveries that go beyond the Fundamentalists belief in the bible."

"Which goes against my personal Christian beliefs." President Jackson said.

"Oh for God's sake, you're on a different planet." Prime Minister Shanks exclaimed, "Just how political are your beliefs or can't you really consider a more modern approach to the bible?"

"Modern approach." President Jackson repeated, "You mean that the basic message remains unchanged but the style was written by people without any conception of the modern world."

"You're getting there." the Prime Minister chuckled, "You can add that it's interpreted by people who have no conception of what we're doing right now. We prove that the Earth is billions of years old and claim that science shows just how big and wonderful God's creation is."

"The Earth was still created in seven days but it was God's days, not Man's." President Jackson contributed.

"Then depending on how the wind blows we either phase out the religious links altogether or keep enough to keep the voters happy."

"OK but are you going to go all commie again with free health care and the like?"

"Maybe I could sound favourable but since the lower paid would use it more than the rich they'd have to pay more in tax. It'll be easy enough to delay it until the economic climate is more favourable."

"And it never will be." President Jackson chuckled.

The Prime Minister shrugged, "I don't know. Privatising it was very unpopular. If we break the Crusaders ..." he trailed off, briefly wondering who may have overheard him, then continued more confidently, "Forget the official policy I spouted earlier. Introducing a new health service would be the biggest challenge that we could make to the Crusaders. If we succeeded, then it would break them. With the backing that we've now got it's possible."

"And will our friends here, allow it?"

"So far as I can make out, they have their own rules to follow. Even if they're listening to us, they can't interfere but they're still in the background and an unknown quantity."

The President might have replied but he had just spotted Chairman Chernekov walking down the road with Zack. There was something odd about the boy but Jackson couldn't quite put his finger on it.

Chapter 4

Time travel confused everyone, even Stuart and Dave. Plans involving it had to ensure that someone did not bump into himself or find himself dealing with a problem at the wrong time. Everyone else buys an item and then uses it. Stuart could use an item that he found years ago but who left it in the first place? As events unfold it could prove to be a future version of himself but what happens if events change slightly and the future version forgets?

Allowing Chairman Chernekov to see a recording of events a little before they happened was no problem. He already knew that something unusual was happening in the United Kingdom and like any politician, he would hate being excluded from their little summit if he knew of it. Once he was intrigued by the meeting, arranging his visit became part of a well-used routine. Zack's arrest, facing a month in youth custody was much more of a problem and it could prove disastrous if he was held too long. The longer the authorities had to confirm that there were two Zacks with identical DNA and fingerprints the worse it would be. Supposing that they sent for his parents and they arrived with Zack-2 in tow.

For simplicity probes were fitted with equipment and software to mimic a mobile phone network. Unbeknown to her, Zack-1's mother had once phoned him to bring him home for tea as he left a theatre after watching Macbeth. Maybe that was not so unusual but it was the opening night in the newly built sixteenth century Globe theatre and he had watched William Shakespeare bowing to the applause. Zack was a willing guide to anyone visiting Earth so Stuart allowed him 'field trips' that helped with his school work.

When Zack arrived at the quarry on his mission for President Jackson, he checked the log and found that Stuart and Dave were in the alternative Canterbury. James was trying to distract Sir Ronald from taking too much interest in their equipment so they were in the kitchen drinking coffee while James chatted about his time in Military Intelligence. Zack tried phoning Stuart again but could not get through though the phone's tracker marked Stuart's location. He should have called James but that would have got Sir Ronald interested. The portal was set up, only needing to be materialised and what could happen in a sleepy English town? He knew he was breaking the procedures that had been drummed into him but in his defence he was on an errand for two very important people, unsure about involving James and Sir Ronald and was in a hurry.

He remembered to add his name to the log before he hurried through to Canterbury-2 close to Stuart's location. He stopped and checked his phone as a police car drew up.

"OK son." a policeman called to him as he opened a rear door, "In you get."

"Huh," Zack replied more confused than frightened.

"Get in." the policeman said more sharply, "This is designated as a pilgrimage town. We don't need you flaunting yourself like that."

Zack glanced down, still confused and wondering what was wrong. The policeman lost patience, grabbed his neck and bundled him into the car."

"Very well." the policeman said, "You'll be reported for wearing immodest dress and inappropriate behaviour near a religious sanctuary. I won't mention resisting arrest and make do with disrespect to an adult if you behave from now on."

"I'm sorry." Zack said, "I'm a visitor and didn't realise."

"You sound English, Yorkshire?"

Zack nodded then seeing the policeman frown added 'yes sir' and was relieved to see the policeman relax.

"Then you should know. Is there something wrong with respectable trousers, shirt and tie?"

"No sir." Zack replied, "I just didn't think."

"And you allowed the gifts of Mammon to distract you from proper Christian reflection."

"Oh the phone." Zack exclaimed, "I was trying to find some friends of mine. Something urgent has cropped up."

"So tell me, what is so important that you have to be so disrespectful."

Zack realised that he made a mistake and was not sure how to put it right.

"It's complicated." he replied, "I only came out dressed like this because I was in a hurry to find my friends. If I could contact them, then we could sort it all out."

"Do your friends enjoy seeing you half naked indoors?" the policeman said, "What else do they enjoy?"

"Sport, talking about girls, Dave bends our ear about his son."

"Ah and how long has this Dave been married?"

"I'm not sure." Zack replied, "Look, are all these questions necessary?"

"I think we'd better go to the station and have a morality-counsellor talk to you. Give me your phone please."

"Can I phone my friends first and let them know what's happening, please."

"We'll see what the counsellor advises. The phone, now. What did you do to it?"

"I just turned it off." Zack replied, "It seemed more respectful."

Turning it off triggered an alarm but for now he was on his own and he was frightened, hoping James was listening.

Although less alert than he should be considering the task on hand, James was listening out for audio warnings. The system was set up so that it could be monitored for long periods by a single person, so it allowed for the monitor needing regular breaks. The alarm was not particularly loud but James hurried back to the control desk to check almost pushing Sir Ronald to one side.

"What's wrong?" Sir Ronald asked.

"Zack's gone to your world then turned his phone off." James exclaimed angrily, "What's he playing at?"

"Zack is one of the young men who accompanied the Prime Minister and the President." Sir Ronald said ensuring that he understood.

"That's right." James replied glancing at the log, "He's gone to ask Stuart something. Now why didn't he ring?"

"You're asking me why he didn't make an inter-universe trunk-call?"

"It still blows my mind when I think about it." James chuckled, "But the principle behind it is straightforward. We've got a probe hovering over your Canterbury and the software for a cell is quite basic. Our phones are modified so it'll only respond to our system. Normally we don't connect to the local system to avoid two phones with the same number but it can borrow an unused number."

James had not been idle while they had been chatting.

"OK." he continued, "I've shifted the probe around and done some radio direction finding. The phone's at the police precinct, station over here. Let's have a look... There's Zack changing in a cell."

James was navigating the probe through the station and had found Zack. He glanced at Sir Ronald.

"I'd say he was arrested for immodesty or showing disrespect." Sir Ronald said, "He's a lot more boisterous than we expect our children to be. Are shorts and vest really de-rigeur for young men."

"Zack recently spent a lot of time in King Narmer's Egypt." James explained, "It was normal for youngsters his age to be naked. It's not the physical consequences of warping space and time that we find difficult, it's adapting to the different cultures we encounter."

"And Zack's adopted Ancient Egypt's heathen practices." Sir Ronald said.

"We're talking about where Andy comes from." James said, "They were a highly spiritual people who valued truth and honesty. Compared to them, twenty-first century folk just give lip service to their beliefs."

"Interesting." Sir Ronald said, "I take it that you've hacked into the police computers while we've been talking and that's his file."

James nodded, "He's being held until they can arrange for a counsellor to discuss his behaviour. He's being held on suspicion of immodesty and disrespect of a superior order. What the hell does that mean?"

Sir Ronald smiled, "To be honest, it's one of those unworkable laws that seemed like a good idea at the time. It's popular when it applies to children being rude to adults. It's less popular when the public is told that it's disrespectful not to go to church."

"You don't sound too keen on the Crusaders." James said.

"I defend my country. I'll use whatever means I can to do so but here's something that does not get mentioned. The government's computer software is American. The companies involved need sanctification notes from the Crusaders so how do you suppose that the Crusaders know so much about our politicians? I've got paper files on George Rosswell and guess what? There was a computer glitch, the computer files disappeared so I can't cross-check my paper file's sources. So far as I'm concerned communism and Islam are threats and I have to tow the Crusaders line, the Crusaders and you are also threats and I can't do anything about them."

Sir Ronald paused, "Of the four, I'm beginning to think that you're the least threatening and the Crusaders are definitely losing support amongst the general population. I'd happily ban a political party full of socialist or Islamic agitators and they're certainly disrespectful of our heritage but we're not a dictatorship yet and public opinion counts for something. Five years ago, Ian Shanks would have never been elected party leader. He was, and then a snap general election was called and he got a clear majority. I don't know if it was a mistake or he was pressured into making George Rosswell

Home Secretary but he sounded out allies. Both Balfour and I agree that a foreign organisation has too much influence but until you came onto the scene there was little that anyone could do. Ian Shanks had already opposed the Crusaders more than they liked so I would expect some scandal to appear in the press just before a crucial election. I'd bet that George Rosswell would be the front runner to become the party leader and therefore PM."

"I see." James said, "Back in 1973 when I was in Military Intelligence I might have agreed with you about the disrespect laws but I guess I've seen how laws and regulations can be abused."

"As in Ancient Egypt." Sir Ronald said seeking some understanding.

"No, denying free speech would be completely against Ma'at." James said, "I was thinking of some supposedly more advanced civilisations that I've come across. The Crusaders are a good example of what I mean."

"So you understand why I see them as a threat to the crown. I agree that Zack has some special problems so I'll help you."

"Thanks, I'm open to suggestions."

"Since you're an American, I suggest you claim to be from the Crusaders. Claim that Zack was sent to one of their colleges because of his rebellious nature and he's facing even more rigorous training because he won't settle."

James smiled and produced an ID card.

"I was printing this while we were talking." he explained, "Their computers will confirm that it's genuine and I've got one for you if you'd like to come with me. I was planning something similar so it was nice to know that you thought it the best scheme and there wasn't some unexpected problem."

"I appreciate the display of trust in inviting me." Sir Ronald said, "You appear to have a visitor"

"Hi, Richard." James said, "This is Sir Ronald Cummings, he's studying our methods. Sir Ronald, this is Richard Johnson who's come to take over. We have translators and that's their primary job but they can also translate electronic signals. It means that we can send simple messages over the Internet. 'Help' is the simplest message of all."

As Richard and Sir Ronald shook hands, James explained the situation and minutes later Sir Ronald found himself stepping out from behind some bushes to study his surroundings.

Crossing a busy dual carriageway proved the most hazardous part of the journey but they found an underpass, so not even that was much of a problem.

The duty sergeant was friendly enough until James mentioned Zack's name.

"Are you the friends he referred to?" he asked, "Why is he so friendly with older men?"

James produced his fake ID.

"I wouldn't exactly call him a friend except in Jesus," he said, "though he is in our care. We're trying to guide him in his path but, shall we say, it's proving difficult."

"Very difficult, I would imagine." the police sergeant said in a much friendlier voice, "Does he have any friends who would be looking for him."

"I doubt it." James replied, "He shouldn't be out and about here."

"I've sent for him." the sergeant said, "And I've found him some respectable clothes. What was the point of him parading around in sports wear?"

"You tell me." James replied, "Youngsters have some funny ideas about rebelling."

James was relieved when Zack was brought in. He thought that he was holding up his end of the conversation but it was heavy going. He managed to merely nod gravely as he saw Zack dressed in what was almost a school uniform, complete with a tie.

"Thank you, Sergeant and God bless you for your good work." James said, "Zack, are you coming with us or would you like to get yourself arrested again."

"I'm coming with you, sir." Zack replied then dutifully followed James and Sir Ronald out of the police station.

"Nicely done." Sir Ronald remarked, "You nearly convinced me."

"I had some help." James replied before turning to Zack, "Why?"

"Their Prime Minister and President wanted to invite their Russian leader and I was trying to ask Stuart." Zack explained then added ruefully, "Now I know why their phones are on standby."

"So you weren't trying to phone them, you were using the tracking system."

"That's right." Zack replied, "I can't believe how stupid I was."

"Well there's no harm done." James replied, "Let's say it was the right idea but the wrong method."

"I bet I'm in trouble with everyone else though." Zack

muttered miserably.

"It depends on how you finish the job you started." James said, "It was a good idea to speak to Stuart first, let's find him."

Zack looked puzzled, "What job. I was looking for Stuart and fouled up."

"No, you wanted to fetch the Russian premier." James said, "You ran into a bit of trouble which is sorted so let's find Stuart. What do you suggest?"

"Can you track him?" Zack asked, "But we'll screen you so that it's not obvious."

Sir Ronald tried to say something but James shook his head.

"You might have a better idea." James said, "But Zack's will work."

"I know where he is." Zack yelled suddenly, "I forgot about the translators."

"Quiet Zack." James said, "People are looking."

"The translators feed information directly into our minds." James explained to Sir Ronald, "You can talk to each other through them providing you keep to very simple ideas."

"We also turn them off because we might think the wrong thing about someone." Zack giggled.

"Which puts a whole new complexion on impure thoughts." Sir Ronald smiled.

They strolled through Canterbury at a leisurely pace admiring the ancient buildings, catching glimpses of the cathedral that dominated the town but they deliberately skirted around the main pilgrimage areas. The houses became scarcer and on one side of the road woodland stretched away but on the other side there was a grim forbidding wall. James was relieved to see Stuart and Dave walking towards them.

"Hullo, I didn't expect to see you here." Stuart said, "Is anything wrong?"

"Not any more." James said, "Zack will fill you in."

To his credit, Zack included his arrest then stood waiting for Stuart's verdict.

"OK, rescuing Alan's going to be harder than we thought." Stuart said, "We could come crashing in and kidnap him but we need a more subtle approach."

"James and I could do it." Zack said, "He's got an ID card and sounds just like a Crusader."

"James?" Stuart queried.

"We got Zack out before they got him too deeply into the

paperwork." James explained, "They considered it to be a minor public disorder and were more than happy to save themselves the work. I don't know if we'd get away with it here."

"We would if I came with you." Zack said, "I'm accusing Alan of what's it called, - depraved conduct and you're investigating."

"That could work." Sir Ronald said, "How did you work it out, young man?"

"I picked up on a lot while I was under arrest and when I got my translator back, it filled in some background but it was seeing how the police treated James that made me think."

"James?" Stuart asked.

"I'll try it." James replied, "We've adjusted the records back at their University so I should outrank everyone here and I agree that it'll look good if Zack identifies Alan. I suggest that you three duck into those woods and get the portal here. If we come a'running, I don't want to stop until I'm inside."

"You will be able to recognise Alan won't you?" Dave asked.

"Yeah." Zack replied, "He's stayed in the village. He's been in space as well hasn't he?"

"Not this one." Dave said, "Ours has."

While Zack and James strolled up to the entrance of the college, the others followed James' suggestion and waited in the woods opposite.

Stuart expected that any problems would occur at the entrance when James produced his card but a man dressed as a monk hurried down the drive to greet him.

"You have an Alan Carter here under special guidance." James said, "But I'm investigating some unfortunate occurrences in his home village. I need to take him to the police station rather than hold an unpleasant interview here."

"That's very thoughtful of you, Professor." the monk replied, "Of course we'll accommodate a deacon of the home university. May I ask, who is this young man?"

"Shall we just say the victim of some terribly depraved acts. It's important that I identify the Carter boy before disrupting your training programme."

"Yes of course." the monk replied, "I'll send for him. May I offer refreshments. Would you like to come in and rest?"

"A blessing on your kindness but I do think that I'd rather enjoy His beauty out here."

"Of course. I'll be as quick as I can." and the monk hurried off, returning just moments later shepherding Alan along. James turned to Zack who nodded gravely. James took out his phone.

"My apologies for this intrusion but the sooner the paperwork is completed the sooner we can all resume God's work."

"No apologies needed, Professor." the monk replied, "I understand completely."

"It's done." James said, "A blessing on you and your colleagues in your efforts to spread the true word."

The monk bowed his head in thanks and guided them back to the gate.

"Don't look back." James hissed as they crossed the road, "There's Stuart in the trees and he's beckoning us. Come on."

The monk was watching James as he led the boys away. Something was not right. The boy that arrived with James was talking to Carter, almost calming him when according to the Deacon, he should be repulsed by the deviant. Why were they walking and why was not Carter restrained? Suddenly a thought struck him. The boy, Zack, wasn't needed. The identity check could have been done by computer. There was something wrong.

"Just a minute, Professor." the monk called out but the group ignored him.

Hurrying after them, he called for monks who were gardening nearby to help him and they set off at a run, catching up fast. The monks were seconds away when the group turned into the woods but they faltered as they reached the track for it was deserted. They listened for the sounds of the fugitives then searched around the bushes looking to see where they were hiding but found nothing except for strange indentations in the track. The portal had been and gone and woods were empty.

Back on Resolution Stuart strapped himself down behind the console while Zack stood with his feet tucked under loops to stop him drifting away.

"Don't look so worried Zack." Stuart said, "I've stood there while Brian's sat here, having a go at me for fouling up. You kept your head when things went wrong and I was dithering over rescuing Alan. You should have told James what was going on and he could have advised you. I prefer using the phone to the translator as well but James could have reminded you not to use it and guided you via the translator."

"I didn't think, I'm sorry." Zack said.

"James said that fetching Mr. Chernekov is your project but we've got to juggle the time lines a little so do you mind if I set the portals while you go and greet him."

"I understand." Zack said, "You're deleting my password. Yes of course I'll fetch Mr. Chernekov."

"I'm not deleting anything." Stuart said, "It's just that we're running a bit late with the time you spent in Canterbury but we can catch up if we juggle time around a bit."

Zack smiled, "I am sorry that I got arrested. It won't happen again."

"If you stick with us then it probably will." Dave smiled, "There was one place, it was a bit like that Earth but weirder. We made a mistake near one of their temples, the crowd turned nasty and soldiers had to rescue us. Anyway detaining someone was considered a very bad business so the room we were held in was more like a five star hotel complete with room service. The soldiers asked us who we were and then went and explained it all to the mob. It was odd, after that no-one could do enough for us and were so apologetic for jumping to conclusions. We were lucky and you were unlucky in our treatment, that's all."

Zack nodded

"Thanks." he said gravely then brightened up, "James said that he'd take me to the opening night of 'The importance Of Being Earnest'. I can still go, can I?"

"Of course." Stuart replied, "But that's not a school project is it?"

"Partly." Zack responded, "After speaking to William Shakespeare I suppose that I'm getting interested in the theatre."

"Stay close to James if you want to talk to Oscar Wilde then." Stuart grinned, "He might be willing to discuss more than the theatre with you."

"I know about him." Zack said, "I've learnt my lesson and I'll plan that trip very carefully."

~~~

Like most communist government offices Chairman Chernekov's office in the Kremlin was bugged but there were no cameras. Even world leaders have calls of nature and it was as he returned from one he found a strange little TV on his desk. It apparently showed President Jackson stepping out of an airlock to be greeted by Prime Minister Shanks then walking openly along a country lane with just two young boys as guides.

A message along the bottom of the screen said that the information was for him alone and he could learn more of events in the UK if he was willing to cooperate.

His first instinct was to sound the alarm but he hesitated. Like the American president he had received garbled reports including one suggestion that the meteor had been a missile attack launched by the Crusaders. Also, like the president he realised that if he did not cooperate he would be kept on the outside of... His thinking faltered, kept on the outside of what?

"Damn this report." he spluttered angrily, "How can I question the author if he's in Vladivostok?"

Although he phrased his frustration for the benefit of the microphones it was real enough and he was a little surprised when the answer flashed up on the screen.

"Write your questions down and hold them above the screen."

His first question was simple, "Who are you?"

The answer was puzzling, "Someone who's getting dragged into affairs on your Earth but who wants to be left alone."

His second question was more of an order, "Prove that this is not all a fake."

There was the thud of a file hitting the floor. Nothing had moved on his desk yet there was a file on floor. He picked it up and looked at it. The first page was a plan of his office showing all the bugs including one marked US. The next one showed a nearby office, again showing all bugs but all were marked as disabled. He looked at the plan again, it showed furniture with arrows indicating that it should be moved.

Whatever else, he had to check the American bug apparently behind a telephone socket. The shock-wave when one of the most powerful leaders in the world demanded a screwdriver, a hammer and a chisel was a mere tremor compared to when he marched out of his office holding the bug. When he demanded that the head of KGB be in his office within the hour, no-one dared argue.

No-one questioned him when he gathered up the files on his desk and stomped off to a nearby office. Neither did anyone consider it a good time to question him when he demanded that a couple of soldiers shift furniture and that he should not be disturbed until he was ready for the KGB chief.

More than any leader, he was managed by his staff and the shadowy organisations behind them. He had caught the lot out on a massive scale and they would treat him far more carefully in the future. Whatever else happened, the day had already gone well for him and he was prepared to relax hoping that subsequent events would prove just as useful.

He was not disappointed. His involuntary gasp as the portal

materialised turned to amusement when Zack stepped through, bowed his head and said as politely as he could, "Good morning sir. We thought that I would be less of a threat than an adult."

Sometimes situations are just too ridiculous to comprehend. Chairman Chernekov broke into a deep belly laugh almost doubling over as his emotions took over.

Finally, he recovered enough to splutter, "If you were a threat, my boy, I'd have been squashed by that machine of yours. What can I do for you?"

"I'd like to invite you to a meeting with Prime Minister Shanks and President Jackson on my home world."

"Your home world?" Chairman Chernekov asked.

"Yes sir. I can explain on the way. Do you have problems being weightless?"

"Not that I know of." Chairman Chernekov was giving into events though he felt like the straight man to a comic magician and was waiting for the punchline. The bug incident was a big boost in a way that he understood so he could afford a moment's tolerance.

"I won't be left undisturbed for long. I don't think that I'd have time to go anywhere."

"Is now a good time to mention time travel?" Zack asked, "I took a small detour and listened to Lenin. I couldn't stay long though because I chose a bad time. I think it's called Bloody Sunday and the gunfire got too close."

"For us it was a magnificent day." Chairman Chernekov said, "But still, since you're inviting me, shall we go. I have to see this through now just for my own satisfaction."

As President Jackson stood to greet Chairman Chernekov, he realised what was different about Zack. His clothes looked as if they had been issued by the Crusaders.

Zack pointed to a small device that had been left on the table between them and grinned.

"Chairman Chernekov learnt English on his way from the quarry and you two gentlemen might like to practice your Russian. If you'll excuse me, I'm going home to change."

Chairman Chernekov looked at his two hosts and speaking in English for the first time in his life and not understanding just how well the translators understood the vernacular asked, "Now just what the fucking hell is going on?"

Whilst the three world leaders responded to their unusual situation, Stuart was on the Lizard planet talking to Stuart-2.

"Alan passed out when he got here." Stuart-2 said, "The

whole thing was too much for him. The lizards are doing their thing and calming him though but he's been through some rough brainwashing and aversion therapy."

"As long as the lizards are happy with you all staying then he'll be better off here. I don't think that the Crusaders will have the same sort of power that they have now so you might find yourself in a more tolerant world."

"Thanks for what you're doing." Stuart-2 said, "Is there anything I can do to help?"

"No, we've got all the help we need." Stuart said, "Sounding like a Terzon, it's fascinating watching young Zack. He's not really an explorer but he borrows the portal the way I used to borrow Dad's car. He's also good with people, so is Andy and we're dealing with people problems more than anything."

"I've tried and I can't seem to reach out any more." Stuart-2 said, "You could walk away from this now but you're a people person as well, aren't you."

"So I'm told." Stuart-1 said, "It means that you are as well and you've got to decide what to do about this little group that you brought with you."

Stuart-2 nodded, "I know. After prison this place is just what we need and no-one's in a rush to leave. Some should be receiving treatment but I think that the lizards may be doing something."

"They probably are." Stuart-1 agreed, "As they say, it's their domain and we have to accept it just as they have to accept all our gadgets. Have the monkeys got you playing cricket yet?"

Stuart-2 nodded, "Something like it. They don't seem to understand about a team winning but they like making the balls as difficult as possible. Then they watch the acrobatics of whoever's on the receiving end, bowler to batsman or batsman to fielder."

"Fine." Stuart responded, "I'm heading home. Let's see if we've started World War III on your planet."

As Stuart approached the pub, he could hear that relations were friendlier than he could have possibly expected. The sounds of a Russian folk song and a remarkably musical backing wafted down the lane and when he arrived he could only stop and stare.

Chairman Chernekov had a deep baritone voice while President Jackson was providing harmony as a tenor. Andy was joining in as were a couple of members of the local church choir.

Only Prime Minister Shanks looked put out but he clapped politely along with the rest of the audience but looked startled when Chairman Chernekov moved on to a lively rendition of Dixie.

76

No-one seemed particularly drunk and Stuart guessed that their sense of freedom and the unexpected escape from their responsibilities had been just as euphoric.

They might have continued but Prime Minister Shanks spotted Stuart, breathed a sigh of relief and introduced him.

"I apologise for wasting the valuable time that you've given us." Chairman Chernekov said, "But it is a beautiful day is it not?"

"Yes it is." Stuart said, "Please relax and enjoy yourselves but have you made any progress on your problems."

"Some." President Jackson said, "We are all anxious to break the deadlock on our world but our fear is that in the long term we will start fighting for full control of the technology."

"Your Brian Chapman is the key." Stuart said, "None of it will be possible without him and if he's anything like our own then he'll be very reluctant to work with you for that very reason."

"First, I have to send American diplomats home as a reprisal for bugging my office and President Mike will have to deny it and send some of our diplomats home." Chairman Chernekov said, "Ah yes, you call it sabre rattling. We can allow our hawks to indulge a little while we save the world. What's wrong, Stuart? Shocked at my cynicism?"

"No." Stuart replied, "I'm more concerned when politicians believe their own propaganda. That's when wars start. I'm just surprised that this meeting was such a success."

"You mean that you've met three leaders who are willing to negotiate." Chairman Chernekov chuckled, "Hitler did not work his way up the political system, he created his own and I agree, he believed in his own propaganda. We three have all been good little party workers, beavering our way up the system so we'll work as a team. We'll all use today to push our own little view of the world but for now it's to our political advantage to call for more drinks and leave as friends."

"What do we need to make this work, Stuart?" Prime Minister Shanks asked.

"Brian-2 will need to work somewhere where he is comfortable. We've always used this village throughout all the alternatives and the quarry is ideal. We need to take the Crusaders out of the village so that he's not hampered by them."

"They would howl religious persecution and God alone what else. Any thoughts?"

"Investigate the church personnel there. One deacon abuses girls that he's supposed to be counselling. If you could find something against the Reverend Carter then all well and good. While the place is at full gossip, our team should move in. I met a sergeant in the American army on a different world. He might be a useful member but if I do that then I'd have to include a Russian as well, wouldn't I?"

Chairman Chernekov shrugged, "You either include us or you don't. I'll make sure that he's useful to you."

Chairman Chernekov had a lot to consider. Compared to the relationship between Britain and America, his country was the outsider yet the strangers were ensuring that he was being treated as an equal. So much had happened since the screen had first appeared that he was thoroughly disorientated when he returned to his office, forgetting that in real time he had only left twenty seconds ago.

He was still confused when the head of the KGB arrived. Fortunately for him, Chairman Chernekov forgot to be angry.

"I need someone to go to England for me, he needs to have a counter-revolutionary interest in other men and an understanding of physics, especially the concept of a multi-dimensional universe."

"Comrade?" the KGB officer queried, "What is a multi-dimensional universe?"

Instead of answering he pressed a button on his intercom.

"Contact the design councils involved in space development, I require designs for a space station to be permanently manned, beyond the orbit of Neptune. It will be built on Earth then launched and supplied by a revolutionary new space travel system on a daily basis. That's all they need for now."

He turned back to the KGB chief, "Will I have your complete cooperation on this project or will I investigate other lapses in your operations?"

"I should like to know what is going on." the chief replied, "How did you find that bug?"

"I'm sure that the young man you pick for the England task will also be expected to report to you. I expect to see your selection in three days. You may go."

Chairman Chernekov received the file on Viktor Levkova in two days and the young man was brought to his office the following day.

Viktor stood nervously in front of the desk though he was also confused hardly believing where he was.

The Premier turned to the guard, "Get those handcuffs off him and leave us, he's no threat to me, are you boy?"

"No Comrade." Viktor replied, "What's going on, I know who

you look like but who are you really?"

"I'm who I look like." Chairman Chernekov chuckled, "You are a student of astrophysics in his final year and you write cheap novels about a ship that can cross dimensions. The ship is wrong, you need a fixed point in real space to navigate but what do you know of inter-dimensional space?"

"Only the theoretical concept and that there could be parallel Earths. There's no practical development, such travel is impossible."

"If it were possible, what limits would there be on space travel, time travel or to parallel worlds?"

"My fictional ship bent space through the fourth dimension" Viktor said, "It provided a faster than light ship and a few accidents involving time. I think that a practical application doing what you want it to do would require multiple dimensions."

"Six or seven?"

"At least and your comment about a fixed point makes sense, maybe it would have to be some sort of tunnel that could pierce the dimensions."

Chairman Chernekov placed his hands on a sheet of paper and pushed the edges together until it bent into a loop. Careful not to let the loop collapse he picked up a pin and pushed it through the base of the loop.

"Like this?" He asked, "Warping space and providing a shortcut to two distant places."

Viktor nodded, "It would be a doorway through space."

"Did you take any interest in that meteor that struck Britain a few months back?"

"Yes Comrade but the data supplied was false. It suggested a controlled descent which was impossible."

"You were arrested for anti-Soviet activities five days ago." Chairman Chernekov said, "You are accused of spreading Western propaganda designed to undermine the morale of our youth and your defence is that you merely wish to end the persecution of people like you."

Viktor nodded.

"This office could well become more sympathetic to your cause and you could have a chance to be, not only a Hero of the Soviet Union but a hero to your kind around the world. Interested?"

"Very much so." Viktor replied, "But I don't understand. How does an imaginary concept for my books give me such a chance?"

"You're to go to London and meet some people who will explain. Intelligence suggests that you will fit in very well. At least, you won't be shocked by your new comrades and find it difficult to work with them. You will offer every assistance and if you need anything you will call this office. You will also call this office if you believe that you are being isolated or marginalised in any way."

The only possible answer was 'Yes Comrade' and that afternoon Viktor found himself in an aircraft heading for London staring with some disbelief at his diplomatic passport.

Meanwhile the American president was finding it difficult to match the Russian contribution for the project. He had found Sergeant Pernell and his CO confirmed that he was efficient but wasted too much time in unchristian activities, namely he had an interest in science fiction and he played unsanctioned computer games. President Jackson sent for him and he also suddenly found himself on a flight to London, wondering what it was all about.

President Jackson's real problem was with matching Russia's background work. His only way to get anything done was to approach an appropriation's committee who would immediately draw up a tender and offer it to suitable firms. As the designs developed so parts of the project would be tendered out to smaller sub contractors and so on. Secrecy was always a headache in such an environment and in this particular case, the level he wanted was impossible to achieve.

As for Stuart, he could not visit Brian-2 without raising too many questions so he adopted a trick that he had used before. The Terzons had a very warlike past and they retained knowledge of espionage and disguise. A doctor gave him an injection and Stuart's face puffed up slightly. Once his skin was darkened, he turned his attention to his hair. The result was amazing. The changes were subtle but effective. Possibly he could still be recognised as a tanned Stuart, but close up he definitely looked like someone from the Mediterranean. Even the doctor was impressed with the way the ancient formulas had worked.

He took a taxi from Howkbury station which pulled up beside Brian's house. He knocked waiting for Brian to answer and showing Brian a piece of paper before waving the taxi off.

Brian looked startled, glanced around and beckoned Stuart in.

"That looks like my work." he said, "Where did you get it?"

"That could be a very difficult question to answer properly." Stuart replied, "If I understand the situation correctly, you were working on a portal. Because you refused Crusader guidance, you couldn't give suppliers a sanctification note confirming that you were not intruding on God's domain."

"God's domain like hell." Brian exclaimed angrily, "You people don't have exclusive knowledge on God's work."

"I'm not with the Crusaders." Stuart said, "I am working with your government for the moment but there are less than a dozen people on this planet who know where this equation leads. We've got to keep it that way while you build a portal."

"While I what?" Brian retorted, "You've no idea how dangerous a portal could be, I'm not building one for the government to abuse."

"The government doesn't realise it yet but it's going to get spaceships. They work at a very basic level. You will have to build a full-blown portal in secret and maybe think about leaving Earth with your team."

"My team?" Brian asked.

"You haven't asked my name yet," Stuart smiled. "Could we leave that for the moment. The proposed list is Stuart Johnson, David Hilford who you may know and two you don't, Sgt. Charles Pernell United States Air Force and Viktor Levkova who's a Russian academic."

"I was beginning to believe you but now I think you'd better get out," Brian exclaimed. "Stuart's in gaol and Hilford's a drunken layabout looking for a fight."

"I did say proposed team and you might be right about Dave but he might just surprise you if he got the chance to use his talents properly."

"You could be right," Brian-2 conceded. "And Stuart? He's a good lad and shouldn't be in prison. Him and Alan Carter weren't doing anything really bad."

"Stuart's out of gaol and he's with Alan." Stuart said.

"Are you related to Stuart?" Brian asked, "I can see a resemblance but you're not from around here, are you?"

"Yes, we are connected." Stuart replied, "When we're together, he's known as Stuart-2."

"So your name is Stuart Johnson as well," Brian said. "I'm pleased to meet you."

"Sorry, I should have introduced myself sooner." Stuart said, "I normally look a lot more like him but I've used a dye to darken my skin and a doctor gave me an injection to puff my face out."

"You've taken a lot of trouble to visit me." Brian said, "Will it fool the church Mafia though?"

"Church Mafia?" Stuart queried.

"The Reverend Carter and his gang." Brian exclaimed, "This

village is very isolated, and they more or less control it, with the Crusaders' backing of course. I bet someone flagged that taxi down just to find out who you are."

"Yes of course, he has a doctorate in divinity from them, doesn't he." Stuart said, "I can't think why he's content with this little place though."

"Between him and Squire Bradley, they've got an excellent base. Carter offers 'spiritual guidance' to all the surrounding parishes in exchange for a tithe while Bradley runs the district council as well as funding the local constituency party. He's planning on standing for parliament backed by the Crusaders. It's a neat little empire which keeps them occupied."

They sat chatting for a while. Brian-2 who was obviously excited at the opportunity to discuss his theories but they were interrupted by a knock at the door. Brian answered, ushering in an arrogant young man who stared at Stuart.

"What's your business here?" The youth asked, without preamble.

"Hello Jason." Stuart replied, "Still your usual charming self I see."

"How do you know me?" the youth asked, "What's your business here?"

"I know another Jason Hardcastle." Stuart said, "He raped his sister, and is in prison for drug dealing. There were rumours about under-age girls but nothing stuck."

"I'm a parish deacon, serving the Lord through the Reverend Carter and insinuations like that show you to be under the Devil's influence."

"And I wouldn't let you counsel my daughter or my sister. My business here is my own and nothing that you need to concern yourself with." Stuart replied.

"The Reverend Carter guides his flock and protects them from evil." Jason intoned, "We concern ourselves with anything or anyone who may bring evil here."

Stuart turned to Brian, "I'll be staying in the village for a few days. I know it's an imposition but could I stay here. We can talk more about your research."

"Mr. Chapman has never married." Jason exclaimed, "It's inappropriate for him to have close contact with vulnerable youngsters of either sex. Besides, his research is proscribed for it seeks to lead man from the biblical truth."

"I'm not exactly a vulnerable youngster." Stuart chuckled,

"Don't worry, you're included in my plans but the time isn't right yet."

"You're not welcome in this village." Jason said, "You may stay until your taxi arrives. I'll phone for one now."

Initially Brian-2 watched the hostility between his two visitors with some concern but he was reassured by Stuart's calm contempt for Jason. He also had the feeling that Stuart was waiting for him to intervene.

"Stuart, you may stay tonight at least." he said, "I'd like to know more of your research and how it compares to mine. If I think that it's necessary I'll prepare a report of our conversation for the Crusaders. In the meantime, as with Lot and the angels, he is a guest in my house and I will not see him harried any further."

Jason stood uncertainly for a moment before he nodded and left.

"That's the thing about religious idiots, when you quote the bible back at them they get confused." he laughed, "We'll have time while he figures a reply."

Brian was not completely right for it was not long before there was another pounding on the door. This time it was Dave-2 followed by Richard-2, Stuart-2's father that burst in, both holding baseball bats.

"We don't like perverts disrespecting our church." Dave yelled, "What are you, a Muslim?"

"I'm many things." Stuart-1 replied, "I could even be offering both of you the sort job that you could only dream about."

"Yeah, doing what?"

"Come on Dave." Stuart said, "I'll show you. The two oldies can wait here and you can explain it all when we get back."

Daves were intelligent, athletic and full of energy which could easily turn into aggression. Dave-2 had found the release he needed by working for Reverend Carter but he was little more than an enforcer, a bully eager with his fists and relying on the Crusaders authority.

It was always weird for Stuart to treat people that he recognised as family and friends as strangers, and as with his own disguise found it easier to think of them all as cousins. However, he had met Dave on a number of parallel worlds and had a fair idea of what could jolt him out of his rut.

As they trudged up the track to the quarry, Stuart took out his phone. Dave noticed.

"There's no signal round here." he said then added, perhaps a little contemptuously, "There's no need for them in God's countryside."

"This one works." Stuart replied, "See it's got a signal and it's ringing. I just want to make sure that transport for Terzon is ready for us at the quarry."

Dave heard a reply. It sounded like 'Okay' and it seemed to have an American accent but he couldn't be sure.

"Where are we going?" he asked and Stuart was pleased to hear curiosity replacing the aggression in his tone, "Where's Terzon?"

"It's difficult to explain." Stuart replied, "Bear with me, you won't be disappointed."

"No!" Dave yelled, "You tell me now or we go back."

He was brandishing the baseball bat ready for a fight.

Despite his travels and adventures, Stuart had never been much of a fighter but he had several advantages over Dave-2. James had insisted that he learn a little self-defence, he was sensitive to other people's body language and he had learnt enough to protect himself. Most importantly he and his real friend, Dave-1 still horsed around in a companionable rivalry so he understood how this Dave would react.

Stuart-1 and Dave-1 both had another advantage, they were physically fit. They drank to socialise rather than spending their time in the pubs trying to blot out the world and ate healthily. Compared to Dave-1, Dave-2's reactions were slow. Even as he swung the baseball bat to threaten Stuart so Stuart stepped inside the swing and punched Dave as hard as he could in the solar plexus. The bat missed him and it was Dave's arm that forcibly connected with Stuart's shoulder. Dave-2 dropped the bat, wondering if his arm was broken.

"Do you want to play some more?" Stuart asked, picking up the bat and throwing it into a field.

Stuart waited until Dave recovered his breath then held out his hand to help him up. Dave was unsure how he had lost all of his advantages so easily and took the offered hand to stand.

"You can go back if you like." Stuart said, "I won't stop you but you'll miss a hell of a chance."

Dave's mind was racing, still keyed up for a fight. Once he was down, Stuart could have beaten him to a bloody pulp. If he had got the upper hand, then Stuart would have been left half dead. Instead, there was still the prospect of something, he was not sure what but if Stuart was that capable then what he offered had to be special. He nodded.

"I'll come with you." he said meekly.

The quarry was almost identical to Stuart 1's. Brian's workshop was missing, there were rocks and stones strewn around that had not been cleared. However, the bunkers left over from research in World War II were still there but Dave was not looking at the familiar features. He was staring at the metal disc with a bulkhead, containing an open hatch.

Stuart had once described an imaginary trip, with Bill the pub landlord to Brian

"Imagine taking him back a hundred years to buy a genuinely traditional guest ale."

"This is just imagination, isn't it?" Brian asked.

Stuart grinned as he nodded before continuing, "He knows the rumours about what we do though he doesn't know the details. He'll accept that something odd is going to happen but he'll be thinking more of covering it in his books, wondering if the barrel will tap OK and the rest. He'll be dealing with the side he knows and understands until he sees the portal."

Brian nodded.

"His attitudes will really start to change when he sees the portal materialise. We know that he'll spend ages studying it. Do you want to bet that he'll ask if it's blown up?"

It was Brian's turn to grin but he shook his head.

"OK." Stuart said, "That's when it starts becoming real because he can see something really weird. If he carries on, then I warn him that he's going to be weightless. He'll nod his head but it won't register until he floats out into Resolution."

Stuart paused.

"I read something once, earthquake victims are particularly prone to post-traumatic stress. The one constant in their lives is the solid ground below their feet. Suddenly it's not solid; it's betrayed them and that can be a terrific shock. It makes sense, babies fall over before they can talk and from then on, the ground is always there.

"Now going back to our theoretical trip. Suddenly Bill discovers that there's no ground, no up, no down and he's floating. He hasn't had years of training like an astronaut, there's been no blast of rockets to tell him that he's in space, just a warning from me. It'll make anyone think and become far more receptive to new ideas."

"I've never thought about it like that before." Brian said, "Are you sure?"

Stuart nodded and luckily Dave-2 proved to be no exception to Stuart's theory. From the front the portal was a tunnel stretching somewhere. From the side a metal ring and from behind shimmering air, resilient like a force field but with no sign of the rest of the tunnel which crossed dimensions to a space station.

Dave-2 looked helplessly at Stuart wondering what question would not make him seem like naïve idiot.

"Our transport?" he finally managed to ask.

Stuart nodded, "Be careful when we go through. You'll be weightless at the other end."

He knew that the warning was pointless, like everyone else Dave-2 did not take it seriously. Dave-2 hung on tightly as Stuart drifted effortlessly around guiding him through a portal and back, to Dave's relief, on solid ground. His relief was short-lived. He was no longer in the quarry and the view was nothing like his native Yorkshire.

"Where are we and don't just say, Terzon." he exclaimed.

"OK, we're on a planet in the neighbouring galaxy and the planet's called Terzon. Oh, that guy who's coming to meet us is called Spock and he's going to find you fascinating."

"Why?" Dave asked, "Is he a pervert or something?"

"No, he's an anthropologist. Since you're from a parallel universe, he wants to compare the way you've responded to the influences in your universe compared to the other Dave Hilfords he's met."

Dave stared, thinking about the unusual spring to his step then leapt up into the air.

"I can't jump that high. What have you done to me?" he asked.

"Nothing." Stuart said, "I told you that we're on a different planet and gravity's less."

"Hi, Spock." Stuart said, greeting the Terzon, "How're you doing?"

"I believe, fine thanks is a suitable reply." Spock said, "Especially since it's true, How are you doing, Dave?"

"Er, yeah, OK, I guess."

"Which I believe should be interpreted to mean that you're having a different day to the one you expected."

Dave managed a grin, "You could say that. Have I really travelled to a different planet?"

"You have, and Stuart's brought you here because he claims that it's got the best beaches and swimming in two galaxies.

However, I don't suppose that he's tried them all yet."

"Er, no." Dave replied, "He doesn't travel to other worlds just to go swimming, does he?"

"Interesting." Spock said, "A significant number of Dave's ask that question. The original Dave summed it up rather well. His mission is to travel to new worlds, meet new people then stir everything up so that they're never the same again."

Dave managed a cheerful chuckle then a thought struck him.

"We're not going swimming now are we." he asked, "I haven't brought anything to wear."

"Oh you don't wear anything on the beach." Stuart said, "People would just stare."

"Reverend Carter would say that such immodesty is sinful." Dave said, "But he'd say that Spock isn't a son of Adam so he's sinful. He's denounced science and science fiction enough times and a load of other things."

"Are we going skinny dipping or not?" Stuart asked.

Dave looked nervously at Stuart who added, "Let's just wander down to the beach and play it by ear."

Once on the beach, Dave blushed again desperately trying not to stare but no-one else seemed concerned. Still blushing, he stripped and tried to relax and still nobody appeared to be concerned.

"It just seems so ordinary." Dave said, "I really am on a different planet and that's some sort of space-port or airport or something back there."

"It's a research centre that deals with alien life." Stuart explained then grinned, "Oh and we're the aliens."

"Another sin." Dave chuckled, "Humans aren't the centre of the universe."

He glanced at Spock, "Sorry I meant Earthmen."

"I understand." Spock replied, "Please excuse me. Maybe Dave is not ready to go swimming with aliens so I'll go and write up my notes on my latest specimen."

Sometime later, Dave was physically exhausted and relaxing on the beach with Stuart.

"You've mentioned parallel worlds and that you're friends with me on another world." Dave began, "Your name is Stuart but the Stuart on my world is a poofter and jailed for corrupting others."

"I'm Stuart Johnson and Richard is my Dad." Stuart said, "Alan and I have got together on a number of worlds but me, myself, I'm hooked up with someone else."

"How come you look so different?"

"Terzon's had quite a history. My Dave knows all about it and I forget it's all new to you." Stuart replied, "It started off with loads of warring islands so it knows a lot about espionage among other things."

"And you're a pervert."

"No I'm gay. In this universe, no-one cares."

"You should get treatment for it though. It's not natural."

Stuart detected far less conviction in Dave's voice and remained quiet.

"Spock isn't a son of Adam and he's OK so if you are a son then you must be as well. We're all different, aren't we. Am I with anyone on your world?"

"Yep, Sally Hardcastle."

"That whore ..." he trailed off, "There was always something about her. She seemed lost."

"Jason raped her when she was a child." Stuart said, "Dave-1 is so patient with her and she's getting over a load of other stuff as well. At least on my world she is."

"And she's dead on mine because she couldn't get away from the bastard." Dave murmured, "I didn't know."

"Don't knock yourself out." Stuart said, "You have a pretty traumatic relationship on a lot of worlds because you don't know. My Dave, Dave-1 has a head start on most of you."

"And this Dave-1 doesn't care that you're queer."

"Do you think that it's important."

"If I go for another swim, are you going to stare at my arse while I run down the beach?"

"Probably." Stuart grinned, "There's nothing like a bit of window shopping."

"Just keep out of the shop," Dave growled as he stood up.

Stuart lay back satisfied. He could not imagine going anywhere without Dave-1 supporting him but this Dave was in a darker place than most and would need to adapt. However, his warning to 'keep out of the shop' was more banter than threat so it seemed promising.

More than anything, having to adapt so unexpectedly to a lower gravity would unsettle anyone. It all helped to make him vulnerable, preventing him from resisting new ideas and attitudes. Now that he was accepting them Stuart could plan the next jolt to his system and take him to the Lizard planet.

As Dave crashed down onto sand beside Stuart after his swim he asked, "Why me?"

"You mean, why do we need a layabout bully who's no good for anything?" Stuart replied.

Dave flinched at the description then nodded, "I suppose so."

"I'm never sure why Daves never just join the army but maybe you'd struggle with the discipline. Brians get driven to prove themselves and when they succeed want to settle down. Stuarts go along for the ride until something catches their or rather, our attention. You can see what needs to be done and want to get on with it. Your Stuart's still not over his time in prison. Your Brian will relax knowing that his theories are correct, and the others involved won't understand what's going on so you'll find yourself getting the project started. Other Daves have done it then happily followed their Stuart as he gets his teeth into actual exploration. Do you get the idea?"

Dave nodded, "Was that meteor anything to do with you?"

Stuart nodded and Dave was silent for a time before standing up and jumping as high as we could.

"That space station thing, I'd love to spend time on that. How would I get permission?"

"You just have. Come on."

Stuart stood up and pulled on his shorts but Dave was testing the gravity again and didn't notice. Unaware that Stuart had scooped up the rest of their clothes he just followed Stuart. No-one stared at someone returning from exercise in the buff and Dave-2 was too busy grappling with events to remember the sin of immodesty until they were almost back to the portal.

"Sorry." he stammered nervously, "Why didn't you say anything, Stu?"

"About what." Stuart asked innocently.

"I'm not wearing anything, of course." Dave spluttered but not reaching for his clothes.

"You've been swimming and you're moving on to some more exercise. What's the point in dressing for that short distance."

"You did." Dave said accusingly.

"The space station is a lot more private and I thought that you'd be more comfortable if I did. What you do is your choice."

On the face of it, it was a trivial incident, but for Dave, it was the moment when the conflict between his old life, and the one he was being offered, came to a head.

Others were on the beach and Stuart was right, he would have stood out more if he had stayed dressed but now he had to make a conscious decision and another problem was developing.

"That girl keeps looking at me and I'm er ..." he covered his crotch with his hands.

"Above everything else, the Terzons respect honesty." Stuart said, "If you find her interesting then let her see."

Stuart had not planned or expected this situation but it could not be better. If anything could persuade Dave to accept his new life, then a chance to chase the girls was it. Stuart smiled to himself, unlike on Earth-2, the girls here were quite likely to do the chasing so Dave could be in for a considerable amount of fun.

"Maybe I should just go over and let her see close up." Dave said.

"Good idea." Stuart agreed, ignoring the sarcasm.

Dave stared in disbelief then surrendered to the situation, turning towards the girl.

"I'll leave your clothes by the portal and someone will guide you back." Stuart said, "Have fun."

Dave was unaware of the full potential of the portal and the consequences of folding multiple dimensions, and he was still grappling with what he had been doing when he returned. At first, he did not notice that despite an afternoon of exploring a new world only a few minutes had passed since his departure. If it was not for an aching groin and a translator around his neck he would have said that he had dreamed it.

Richard and Brian had waited in frosty silence until Stuart had returned and then, a little later, Dave. For once Dave was thoughtful but eventually he turned to Richard.

"You're leaving and Stuart is staying with Mr. Chapman." he said, "I'm sleeping on the couch to make sure that there's no trouble."

"Careful Dave." Richard said, "You know what Reverend Carter says. Only married men can show that they're using their bodies as God intended."

"Mr. Johnson go." Dave said, "Tell Reverend Carter from me that he's a narrow-minded idiot who knows nothing about the world... universe... God's creation."

He trailed off looking to Stuart for help.

"I'd say God's creation sums it up." Stuart said, "Don't forget that you've been in a different universe today."

Brian and Richard stared at him.

"Easy Stu." Dave said, "You're amongst strangers here."

"Just for the record, Dave." Stuart said, "I've offered you a job. Do you accept?"

"For the record, I do accept." Dave replied, matching Stuart's formality.

"David, Reverend Carter expects us to monitor the morality of the village. You can't just abandon your duty." Richard said.

As Dave looked between Brian and Stuart, he understood.

"I've got a better idea about the sleeping arrangements. Stuart and Brian share, I'll have the spare room."

He glared at Richard as he spoke, challenging him to respond but Richard had his own problems. Trying to hide his own bisexuality, he had gone along with Reverend Carter's crusade against immorality. However, he had been uneasy at the excesses and doubted his stand more and more since his son Stuart-2 had been sent to prison. With all his own self doubts, Dave-2's sudden conversion completely unnerved him and he left without another word.

Brian, Stuart and Dave spent a companionable evening with Brian and Stuart going over Brian's research with Dave half listening and half mulling over his experiences. To his surprise, he understood much of the conversation, then remembered the translator that he was wearing.

They were all tired and went to bed early, Brian had enough rooms so they all slept separately leaving Dave unaccountably disappointed that his matchmaking had failed.

Chapter 5

With both Russia and America worried about being left behind, events were moving quickly. Both Sergeant Charlie Pernell and Viktor Levkova were already in London, enjoying the luxury of being guests of Her Majesty's government and still with no idea of what they were doing there.

Stuart allowed Dave-2 another day to get used to his new life before taking him to London.

"I saw my Stuart, that's Stuart-2 and Alan, yesterday." he said as they strolled down to the quarry, "They weren't as friendly as you are but I can't blame them."

"How did you get on with the lizards?" Stuart asked.

"You might have warned me." Dave-2 exclaimed, "That place is something else but it was okay once I understood."

"If you've got them on side they'll talk to Stuart-2 and Alan about you."

"Where's Alan-1?" Dave-2 asked.

"At a music conservatory." Stuart replied, "I see him and his boyfriend occasionally."

They left the portal in the room set aside for them and once in the corridor were escorted to a small meeting room where he was greeted by Eric Stevens who made the introductions. It was a relatively small meeting that settled down as Stuart-1 sat at the head of the table.

"Sorry about the disguise." Stuart said as an opening, "It's an improved version of one I've used before and will wear off in a week or so. Viktor and Charlie have never met me before so they won't understand what I'm talking about but Eric and Terry may find it confusing.

"Like Charlie and Viktor, Terry is also here to represent his country and you'll have all the facilities necessary to contact your respective governments though obviously, Terry's is already set up. Again, it's Viktor and Charlie who won't understand that I'm the outsider here. It's also them that will have trouble understanding what we're planning until we take a field trip later.

"However, I may as well spell it out even if you don't all accept it at first. We're going to build a space station somewhere out in the orbit of Pluto plus the ships needed to supply it. The ships will be built in America, the space station by the Russians and the technology supplied by the UK. Any questions?"

"When Comrade Chernekov assigned me to this project we discussed it. I wrote science fiction stories based on the concept of warping space. If that's why I was picked then I don't think that it's possible in reality." Viktor said.

"Viktor's right and this is a joke." Sgt. Pernell exclaimed, "Why are we really here?"

"It's no joke." Stuart said, "Would you say that your government is taking this meeting seriously?"

"Yes it is." Sgt. Pernell conceded.

"Okay, Viktor might be able to accept this project more easily because he's written one or two papers on the possibilities and written stories based on those possibilities. You won't remember but I've worked with a Sgt. Pernell before, which is why I asked for you."

"No I don't remember." Sgt. Pernell said, "But you said '*a*' Sgt. Pernell."

"Sorry, but the purpose of this meeting was to introduce you all. Dave here will be in overall charge during the start up of the project. I'd like Sgt. Pernell to act as adjutant while I'm sure that Viktor will want to work with the head scientist. Now if you're happy with the basic set up, I think that we should adjourn to one of my bases where it's more secure and we can continue our discussions."

"Where's this base?" Charlie asked, "Surely they can bug anywhere near here."

"Near is a subjective term." Stuart chuckled, "My idea of near is Mars. What's yours?"

No-one spoke, not understanding what Stuart meant.

As usual, Stuart allowed plenty of time to make the trip. Charlie and Viktor had to study the optical affects of an active portal and they all had to get used to Martian gravity. Dave-2 tried to act nonchalant as if he was used to different gravities but although he did well, he overdid it and went flying but finally they were settled enough for Stuart to continue.

"Just to be clear, you're on Mars-1, that's the one in my universe, not yours." Stuart explained, "You'll build the ship for your governments and it'll provide your governments with a real incentive to cooperate. Real exploration is by portal and you can't entrust that to any government."

"But you're trusting us with it." Viktor said.

"Not fully, at least not yet." Stuart replied, "When you use the portals, you will see time and space in completely different ways. My mother goes shopping in the next galaxy and a friend of mine, Dave, got into a fight with an Egyptian soldier."

He paused for effect, "It was about 3,000 BCE and he took a nasty sword slash to his shoulder. I'm surprised but I've mentioned parallel worlds once or twice and no-one's picked up on it."

"And governments would only see it as a weapon." Terry said and Stuart nodded.

"This is a damage-limitation-exercise or your governments wouldn't even know about a ship."

If Stuart's plans were slowly unfolding, others were also meeting to make their plans, one such meeting was between two emissaries, in a hotel room somewhere on the Mediterranean coast.

"My master is becoming concerned that non-believers are uniting against us." Abu al Khayr Naṣṣār said, "We're hearing disturbing rumours."

"I thought that we were non-believers as well." John Reynolds replied.

Abu al Khayr Naṣṣār smiled, nodding his head, "We're content to accept that the Crusaders are misguided for now. The bigger threat is from those that deny the existence of a greater power and my master fears that the ungodly are becoming stronger."

"The Chancellor is also worried that the evil empire is plotting something." Jon Reynolds said, "He's also concerned about strange events in England."

"As are we and that is in your domain. My master is waiting to see how you deal with it."

"Deal with what? Strange events in a prison, a meteor that follows God's will and not man's laws of physics and a group of youths with hardly a brain between them."

"But there is a link. The Kremlin is asking for designs for a space station, while the White House is suddenly interested in deep space radar. Rumours about events in the English prison involve aliens from outer space and the Russian member of the group has exotic ideas on space travel. My master is curious about one of them, a Stuart Johnson though I have no idea why, but I admit that the other members seem unimportant so why have they assembled?"

"We will let you know if there's a significant problem."

"My master feels that the Crusaders should deal with the problem before it becomes significant and we have to intervene."

"The Crusaders would never tolerate your interference in our affairs."

"My Master feels that if you are unable to control events in your domain then what you would tolerate is irrelevant."

"The time may be coming when Islam and Christianity must unite to crush atheistic communism once and for all. Christianity still lives in Russia and the people will flock to support us while many of its satellites support Islam and would follow you."

"And you agree that our differences will wait." Abu al Khayr Naṣṣār said, "My master may well welcome you providing that this strange secular alliance is controlled."

"It will be." the chancellor's delegate said firmly.

Stuart's meeting was far more cordial but to his continuing surprise, no-one had picked up on parallel worlds.

Charlie had asked to go outside and Stuart had obligingly supplied him with a spacesuit. Viktor tried examining the portal but with most of it folded through multi-dimensional space, there was not a great deal to see.

Terry and Dave-2 were content to try various leaps and jumps, getting used to the low gravity. Stuart's tactics had worked and Dave-2 was rapidly adapting to his new life confidently believing that he was ready for anything, but then Dave-1 arrived.

Everyone from Earth-2 stopped and stared, with Viktor and Charlie in particular comparing the two Daves. Stuart decided that there had been enough shocks and it was time for another meeting.

"Does anyone still doubt that you can build this station?" Stuart-1 asked.

"It's still a big project." Charlie said, "But I can go along with it. Now just what can this portal thing do? I mean does it really travel to parallel worlds?"

"Yes it does." Terry cut in, "I've spent months in their universe. Zack and Andy have told me all about their time travelling and we're on Mars."

"If you can warp one dimension then you can warp them all and the effects take some getting used to." Dave-1 said, "I'm reading law and when I want to study, I visit a farmer I know. I sit under a cedar tree overlooking the Nile, and, if I want a break, I can watch the fishermen and the river traffic. Dedi owes me for nearly killing me so he respects my wishes to be left alone. Okay, Stuart can contact me in an emergency but there won't be a regular phone service for five thousand years. It's quiet because reed boats don't even chug as they sail past."

"Is that why you're so tanned?" Dave-2 asked.

"Probably." Dave-1 replied, "The point is, Dedi has been dead for five thousand years but he *is* my friend."

"Which is what Stuart, er, One means when he says that we'll start thinking in a whole new way." Viktor said.

"Partly." Dave-1 said, "But there's something else. I used to think that being rich meant having a big house and people doing what you wanted. Nowadays, I could own a planet, populate it with slave girls and have a house the size of London but what would be the point?"

He tapped his head

"It's something the Terzons and the lizards have taught me. I'm rich up here, that's where it counts and I feel good about what I'm doing."

"So you don't want a diamond mine earning you millions." Terry chuckled.

"Three fields where I just pick them off the ground are enough." Dave replied, "I don't need any mines."

"And you're happy living in a cottage in the village?" Terry asked.

Dave nodded, "We're on Mars at the moment, according to Dedi I'm a wizard on a par with the king's vizier and on Terzon I'm just Stu's sidekick. The cottage is sanity."

"And you've got to trust us to become like you." Viktor said, "These other places you mentioned, Terzon and the lizard planet will brainwash us into being like you."

"No they'll decide whether you can adapt but they won't make you."

Dave-2 stood up then jumped, jerking his hands upwards as the ceiling approached his head with alarming speed. It was a weird illusion because for a moment, his brain had trouble interpreting the effects of the leap. Recovering he drifted back down wobbling unsteadily as he struggled to keep his balance.

"Okay, I'm on Mars." he said, "But I don't fancy staying in the village any more. Too much has happened."

"On most worlds the village is an excellent base so that's the next job." Stuart said, "Sort it out. Who's going to help?"

"I'm thinking about how I've behaved in the past." Dave-2 said, "If you can deal with that, then count me in. What do you intend doing?"

"Staying with Brian-2 for a few days and turning Dad, I mean Richard-2."

"What about Viktor and me?" Charlie asked.

"Does your pub let rooms?" Stuart asked and Dave-2 nodded,

"If any of Reverend Carter's acolytes stay then he can't have any other guests and the bar has to close."

"OK then, we book you in there and we persuade Bill to apply for extended opening hours. That'll put Bill on side." Stuart said, "At least, I assume it's Bill."

Dave-2 nodded, "He wanted to open a restaurant but Squire Bradley insisted that it was un-English."

"He's like that in every universe." Dave-1 said, "Stuart can handle him though. Bradley never pays his taxes."

While Stuart's developing team got used to the idea of travelling between worlds and universes, yet more meetings were taking place. This time, the Chancellor of the Crusaders was granting an interview with the heads of the CIA, the Secret Service and the FBI.

"The president's not had any meeting with the British prime minister." the head of the Secret Service said, "The only strange event is that it suddenly seems as if he can speak Russian."

"And what of this diplomatic spat about bugs?" the Chancellor asked.

"Intelligence suggests that the premier himself found it." the head of the CIA answered, "We deny it was ours of course and we've no idea how it was discovered."

"My own sources say that the Russian premier now speaks fluent English and has become involved in some sort of space project. Are these all insignificant coincidences?"

"No." the Secret Service chief replied, "And you could be right about British involvement. NASA now believes that the meteor that struck was making a controlled re-entry that went wrong but the Brits don't have that sort of technology. Hell, we don't even know how it's possible."

"Hell is more appropriate than you realise." the Chancellor smiled, "Our intelligence suggests that they're getting very ungodly help; help that threatens the fabric of our wonderful Christian Capitalist society. We must be prepared to eliminate this threat with every means at our disposal. The United Kingdom may well have to be sterilised to prevent an evil canker from spreading across the world."

"You're suggesting a nuclear attack." the CIA chief exclaimed, "The President would never allow it."

"The President may well be betraying us." the Chancellor said, "You can no longer rely on him to act for the greater good. You gentlemen must be prepared to act accordingly. In the meantime,

97

why has the President summoned an obscure Air Force sergeant and sent him to London?"

The CIA chief grinned contentedly to himself. Maybe he knew more than the Chancellor after all.

"You probably know from George Rosswell that the Prime Minister is running an ultra secret committee known by the few outsiders in-the-know as the Ministry of Alien Affairs. The Sergeant you mentioned, Sergeant Pernell, and a Russian, Viktor Levkova are attached to it. Also, attached to it is an English boy, Terry Stevens. He was kidnapped a while back during a prison breakout and wasn't seen again until a few days ago. Now the kidnapping was never made public and the British police have never investigated his disappearance. At the very least his details should have been circulated to Interpol and our FBI as well other agencies."

"Our information says that he's crippled." the Chancellor said, "What use is he to anyone except that his father seems to be running this very secret committee."

"Crippled?" the CIA chief exclaimed, "According to our reports he goes jogging in Hyde Park every day with another youngster that seems to have easy access to this so called ministry."

"Youngsters seem involved all the way through this conspiracy." the Chancellor said, "A boy was spirited away from one of our retreats in Canterbury, England. Minutes before another boy was pulled from a police station in the same city. Now they both come from the same remote English village but there's something even more strange."

He paused as the others appeared suitably intrigued, "At the same time that the boy was in the police station, he was also paying his tithe by helping to clean the church. We have a good man there, the Reverend Carter and he remembers him clearly. The two boys have identical fingerprints, look the same and their DNA could have come from the same person."

"I can understand you being interested in the boy taken from the retreat but why were you so interested in the other boy?"

"In both cases a man claiming to be Pastor Norton was involved. Facial recognition software has identified him as Major Norton, late of the American Army, Military Intelligence."

"Why is the army interested in these boys?" the CIA chief asked.

"Major Norton retired from the army in the seventies. He's over eighty and lives in Maine. The man calling himself Professor Norton could have been him when he retired."

"Are we dealing with advanced plastic surgery experiments?" the FBI chief asked, "Are these subjects that got away? Are they clones?"

"We don't know." the Chancellor replied, "Gentlemen, the real point is this; between us we should know and it is very worrying that we don't."

And in an observation chamber somewhere beyond Pluto two people were looking down on the entire solar system.

"The Royal Navy is picking up on a number of American warships operating in the Atlantic. They're well to the west of Ireland so we can't complain but it is unusual." Sir Ronald Cummings said.

"It's nothing serious." Stuart replied, "They're forming a contingency plan to attack our base in Yorkshire. They'll get a nasty shock though."

"How so?"

"The missiles will go off course and head straight for New York. I'm not sure of their exact range but they'll crash into the sea before they kill anyone."

"You frighten me." Sir Ronald said, "You could conquer the world and we couldn't stop you."

"True." Stuart grinned, "Either you all surrender or I drop a couple of asteroids on your head. How's your stomach now? Are you ready for a drink?"

"No thanks and your jokes don't help. At least, I hope that they're jokes. Are you sure that wall is strong enough? Where's Earth?"

"Let's do it the scientific way." Stuart grinned, "Hold your arm at full length and crook your little finger. Use the first joint to the tip to measure from the bright star to the left and down a bit."

"There's so many." Sir Ronald exclaimed, "Any one of them could be Earth."

"Exactly." Stuart laughed, "We do brainwash people you know. How can you go back and worry about those silly little international squabbles when you've seen Earth like this?"

Sir Ronald nodded slowly, "Other countries are still a threat but I can see why our approach should be different."

"Fair enough." Stuart said.

There was one more meeting, this time in China. Those involved were high ranking government officials and they also puzzled over the strange intelligent reports that they were receiving. For the Chairman, that a special British committee had American and Russian delegates but no Chinese, rankled. He was also aware of another missing delegate and he wondered how Abu al Khayr Naṣṣār's shadowy master would react. Maybe it was time to offer concessions for the Muslim population in Tibet.

If events were being scrutinised around the world, the heart of the project had other problems. At first villagers were alarmed at a sudden high profile police operation in their midst. The alarm gave way to nervous puzzlement when Jason Hardcastle was arrested for rape and even the Reverend Carter was taken in for questioning.

Crusader lawyers and missionaries were immediately sent to the village only to find that all accommodation had been taken up by the police.

For a lucky few, nervous puzzlement was briefly replaced with delight when self-proclaimed Squire Bradley complained about upright members of the community being harassed. Used to getting his own way he chose to confront the Superintendent Jenkins, the officer in charge outside the pub. He also chose to complain about the pub breaking opening hours.

"Police lawyers are looking into it." Superintendent Jenkins replied, "It seems that there are some archaic laws concerning inns supplying sustenance to travellers. My men appreciate the food and soft drinks he's serving."

"It's a pub." Squire Bradley spluttered, "It's purpose is to sell ale to the locals. It's got no business turning itself into some sleazy continental bar and what about the locals slipping around the back?"

"Our orders are not to interfere with village business." Superintendent Jenkins replied, "I must admit that I've never heard of 'don't ask – don't tell' but we're here to deal with specific problems and we don't go beyond that unless we have to."

"Well I'm making a complaint." Squire Bradley snapped angrily, "Do your job and stop undermining the moral backbone of the village."

"Ah." Superintendent Jenkins exclaimed, "As I said, my orders are most odd and come down from the Prime Minister's office. I don't know why he is so interested in you but it seems I'm to call the Inland Revenue and Customs & Excise to investigate your taxes, if I have to."

Superintendent Jenkins expected another angry outburst but Squire Bradley remained quiet.

"You'll be answering to the Crusaders for this." he muttered as he strode off with as much dignity as he could muster.

Officially, Superintendent Jenkins' superiors hated him for his outspokenness against Crusader interference. However, he was a highly successful *thief-taker* and was popular with his men. Secretly even his superiors agreed with his views even though they were under pressure to contain him.

As he neared retirement he relaxed, not exactly turning a blind eye to crime but more tolerant of minor indiscretions than he should be.

At first, he saw being hauled up to the Home Office for a series of meetings, as a precursor to disciplinary proceedings. However, he found himself being interviewed by higher and higher echelons of the government and other officers facing similar interviews being returned to their forces. Finally, he found himself enjoying a cup of tea with the Prime Minister.

"I can't tell you anything about the core project but it's of vital planetary... Sorry I mean, of vital national importance." the Prime Minister said, "Your job is to ensure that the village where the project will be based works as normal without any outside interference, especially from the Crusaders."

"Especially the Crusaders, sir?" Superintendent Jenkins queried.

"Especially them." The Prime Minister confirmed, "You will liaise with Sir Ronald Cummings who is head of MI5. His role is to tackle the usual spy stuff, sorry again, I should say counter intelligence. I'm afraid I've spent time with some highly informal people and picked up some bad habits."

Superintendent Jenkins grinned, "I think I prefer spy stuff. May I ask, why did you say planetary earlier?"

"No you may not ask." The Prime Minister said, "I dare say that you'll be told before you should but now's certainly not the time. You'll be briefed further but I want a very tolerant approach to policing. Can you handle that?"

Superintendent Jenkins was too intrigued to refuse. He read a letter the prime minister handed to him before handing it back and watching the prime minister sign it.

"That introduces the person in charge. He should mention pomegranates as an extra check."

A couple of days after the interview, Superintendent Jenkins found himself based in a sleepy Yorkshire village. Having orders to become accepted by the villagers placed him in a strange situation. As he watched Squire Bradley retreat, he nodded to a couple of his men who were enjoying their cups of tea and strolled round to the back door and entered.

One or two of the locals watched him warily while Bill the landlord smiled a greeting before pouring a whisky and soda.

"Off duty?" Bill asked.

"No, so it's just the one." Superintendent Jenkins grinned before turning to one of the locals, "Keith, that old wreck of yours isn't roadworthy, is it? Surely you can walk in for your pint? You're just rubbing our noses in it, leaving it out there."

"Quite right." Bill said, "If he walks, he can cut across Marley field. His wife does when she goes to the shop."

"Bloody coppers are all the same." Keith muttered before stomping out.

"Don't you worry about it." another customer said, "That Jason Hardcastle's going to get everything he deserves, at last. We all know what he's like but the Crusaders were protecting him. Keith's just an idiot. You've given him fair warning so next time, you do what you have to."

"Thanks." Superintendent Jenkins said, "The name's Tom by the way."

"You don't behave like an incomer so you're welcome but why are you here?" Bill asked, "It's more than just stopping that pervert, isn't it?"

Tom nodded, "I don't know what's going on but some pretty high up folk are interested in this village. My orders are to see that there's no trouble and village life carries on as usual, warts and all."

"How do you mean, warts and all." Bill asked.

"I believe that someone has a still." Tom said, "I've been briefed on it and other stuff as well. If the Howkbury police get wind of it they'll come charging in as usual but my orders are to say it's village business and leave him to it."

"It sounds as if someone from the village briefed you. Can you say who it was?"

"No, some things have to remain secret."

"That's all right." Bill said, "It's very strange though."

"Tell me about it." Tom said, "This is my last post before I retire and it's as well. I'm breaking so many rules, that in any other circumstances, they'd kick me out rather than let me retire."

"And you've no idea why." Bill said.

Tom glanced around the bar. Everyone was listening intently.

"No." He replied, shaking his head, "But there's definitely something strange going on."

Tom's timing could not have been better for the door opened and a young boisterous group entered. The regulars just stared and even Tom was startled for it was unusual to see two, possibly three sets of twins. Being a relative newcomer he did not realise that Dave Hilford was known as a bully and the Crusader's enforcer. The locals looked between the two Daves, wondering where the twin had come from and fearful that he might be as mean.

Then there was Stuart and his cousin. Stuart had been popular before his arrest. A few thought that he was a pervert who had deserved jail but most thought that he had been badly treated and no real threat. His cousin's cheeks were puffier and he was a little darker but standing together, the resemblance was remarkable.

Finally, there were the two Brians. No-one knew that much about Brian so he could have had a twin brother.

At first, it was less obvious but it dawned on the locals that the Stuarts and the Daves were intermingling like old friends and not as bitter enemies. Stuart-1 approached Tom.

"I'm Stuart Johnson." He said holding out his hand, "Have you been briefed?"

"I was told that a Stuart Johnson had been jailed and then escaped but I was not to question which one. It didn't make sense at the time but maybe it does now. Do you have a letter for me?"

"I do." Stuart-1 replied, "I think that you were present when he signed it and mentioned *pomegranates*."

"Very well, sir." Tom replied formally, "My orders are to liaise with you and you'll brief me as necessary."

"OK, I'm Stuart-1. The other one is Stuart-2." Stuart explained, "Similarly the darker Dave is Dave-1 and the other is Dave-2. The same goes for Brian but they're harder to tell apart. Basically anything to do with me is a one while anything to do with this village is a two."

"So you're not from around here." Tom said.

"No, and since you're fishing then I'll tell you that Sgt. Pernell of the USAF and Comrade Levkova who is a Russian scientist are also two's. Now, does that confuse you enough?"

Tom laughed, "Point taken. Don't ask questions."

"Feel free to ask questions." Stuart replied, "But as a young friend of mine once so wisely pointed out, make sure it's the right question. Let's all have a drink before the Reverend Carter gets here."

"Maybe we should wait until he's gone." Bill said, glancing nervously at the Daves.

"No, I'm thirsty now." Dave-1 said, "Besides, the last time Stuart offered to buy a round, beer was only tuppence a pint. Get them in before he changes his mind."

With the other Dave chuckling with the rest, Bill gave in and began pulling the pints. Tom drew Stuart-1 to one side.

"You realise that I'm condoning drinking out of hours." he said.

Stuart nodded, "There are some legal niceties about this situation that I don't understand. Dave-1 might understand the law better but I'll try. This village now has embassy status and for the purpose of this conversation I'm the ambassador for my home. You and your team are invited in for two reasons. One is to prevent the usual crimes, robbery, murder and so on. The other is to help prevent the village from being swamped by people interested in what we're doing. You do not have permission to intervene in anything that the Reverend Carter or the Crusaders consider morality."

Stuart paused beckoning Bill over.

"Tomorrow open your front doors at noon. We'll pay for those empty rooms to be converted into a restaurant as soon as possible, but it's summer and maybe you can rustle up snacks for any tourists. How does that sound?"

Before Bill could answer the back door crashed open and the Reverend Carter swept in. He was a large man able to use his size to intimidate people. Many locals stood ready to kneel and even Tom felt uncomfortable.

"Good. Now you've arrived, Abraham, the party can really begin." Stuart-1 said, "Brandy, isn't it?"

"When that policeman remembers his duty, you will be arrested for gross immorality and distracting Christian citizens from their god fearing work." Reverend Carter pronounced.

"Easy on the clichés, Abe." Stuart said quietly, "One of your henchmen is in jail, another is finding a higher calling and we're working on the third. Now most of the folk in here are farmhands taking a break before milking or just taking a quiet day off. My friends and I are celebrating the launch of a new venture so how about that drink? You'll need it in a moment."

"Why? Pray tell me." Reverend Carter asked, his red face showing his struggle to keep his temper.

Once again, the timing was perfect. Not even Stuart could have planned it, as Alan, Reverend Carter's son came into the bar, looked at his father but grinned as he saw Stuart-2.

"This'll be so embarrassing if I've mixed you two up." he chuckled as he threw his arms around Stuart-2 and planted a long, loving kiss on his lips. He turned towards his father whose face was becoming an alarming shade of purple as he stood transfixed, almost comatose, unable to take in the enormity of the challenge he was facing.

"OK lover-boys." Stuart-1 called out, "This planet's not ready for you yet. Try not to embarrass anyone."

Stuart-2 and Alan pulled apart, grinning. Stuart-1 turned back to Reverend Carter.

"Anyone who wants to, can attend your services. They may kneel and seek your blessing if they wish. They may offer their time or their money as a tithe if they wish." Stuart said, "If they don't wish then you will not force them."

"I... I... I..." Reverend Carter spluttered struggling to reply, "I... will not stand by and allow you to turn this village away from the Lord."

"I'm not turning anyone." Stuart exclaimed, "I'm not that religious myself but I don't believe that it revolves around keeping you in luxury while you use bully boys to interfere in everyone's lives."

"I am the Lord's shepherd." Reverend Carter thundered, "We need to pray for deliverance from the curse that has descended on us. David, help me summon my flock..."

He trailed off again as he stared uncertainly between the two Daves. It was too much: the rebellion was too great. His shoulders sagged and he stooped a little, suddenly looking ten years older as he turned to Alan.

"I can still forgive you and accept you as my son." he said, "Turn your back on your corrupters and come with me."

"I'm staying with Stuart." Alan said, "I do believe in God. I know the work that He has chosen for Stuart and I'm going to help him."

"How could you possibly know what God has cho..." The Reverend Carter faltered again. He was confused and intimidated by the unexpected resistance against him. Truly spiritual folk would think about praying for guidance but the Reverend Abraham Carter only thought of restoring his position in the village, and assumed that God would agree. Instead of God, he would turn to the Crusaders.

Superintendent Tom Jenkins was uncomfortable with events. Alan and Stuart-2's display of affection repulsed him, they were flouting the law and the whole situation flouted the anti-blasphemy and religious-respect laws. At the same time, they were the very petty-minded and intrusive laws that he had complained about in the past, saying that they prevented him from investigating real villains, like Jason Hardcastle who had the church's protection.

There was something nagging him, just what did Stuart mean by *this planet* and it was the second time that someone had said it. Was it just a turn of phrase or was it significant? He had no idea except that there was going to be trouble and he was caught in the middle.

For now the pub was taking on a party atmosphere. Admittedly after hours drinkers were hardly the Reverend Carter's staunchest supporters but Tom even heard a remark about that damned incomer getting what he deserved. Stuart-2's welcome seemed a little muted so the other Stuart was right, at least so far as the village was concerned. Alan and Stuart's relationship was pushing things too far but since they were standing amongst the other youngsters maybe their behaviour could be rationalised; they were challenging Alan's father.

Word was getting around that something was happening and the pub was filling but everything went quiet when a woman arrived. There was nothing physically striking about her but she exuded a confidence and a presence that brooked no nonsense.

"Are you too proud to hug your mother then?" she asked Stuart-2 then turned to Alan, "Are you my son or my son-in-law?"

Mavis stood, holding out her arms and Stuart-2 hurried over. Still not satisfied, she beckoned Alan over. Superintendent Jenkins could not shake off the idea that homosexuality was repulsive but he saw something touching in the unfolding scene. Mavis was not done yet. As they broke their embrace, she stepped over to Stuart-1.

"This village has a lot to thank you for." she said, "You've got the police to finally do something about the Hardcastle boy and you've worked miracles on Dave. I've told Richard that if he wants to save our marriage he's got to change his attitudes as well. He's not a bad man but that Reverend Carter brings out the worst in everyone."

She paused, "I've sent Richard into Howkbury to get a double bed for Stuart's room. Queer or not, he's the same Stuart as he always was, so if Mrs Bryson still needs her garden dug, Mr. Jones needs his shopping fetched then you'd all better remember it."

Stuart-1 looked on amazed. Most villagers treated his own mother with respect but this Mavis was something else. He had expected a far more hostile reception for Stuart-2 and Alan and had even allowed time to deal with it but Mavis had reminded the villagers that Stuart-2 was one of them and that would forgive a lot.

"Reet, will thar tell us abhat what thars doing here." Whitcomb Butler asked. Tom had trouble understanding the old boy's thick Yorkshire accent but he thought he had the gist of it. The pub went quiet and everyone turned to Stuart-1.

"Our cover story is that we're studying particles from the sun that can disrupt radio communications." Stuart replied, "The real reason we're here is far more exciting than that. Do you remember that meteor that crashed onto Salisbury Plain. I can tell you that it was controlled by us but that's village business, OK? It's not for any outsider."

"You can rely on us, lad." another said, "You sound like a villager, but you're not though."

"Dave-1 is connected to Dave-2 but they're not twins or anything." Stuart replied, "I'm connected to your Stuart so we're both connected to the village. I can't explain more, at least not yet but I'll explain as I go along. There's two more guys that I'd like you to welcome. That's Sgt. Charles Pernell USAF and Viktor Levkova who's a Russian academic interested in space travel and yes, there's a clue there."

"We'll look after them, lad," the local said. "You just carry on looking out for them incomers."

Stuart-1 was ready to go home. It was difficult treating so many people that he knew as strangers especially his mother. On one level he knew that he really was among strangers but on another level this was his home and it confused him.

It was now down to Stuart-2 and Dave-2 to settle the village. A group of drinkers who objected to being told when they could drink was one thing, but the Reverend Carter was going to have a lot of support as well. The one thing that he did not want to do was polarise the village.

That first day, it was the Prime Minister who had the biggest problems dealing with the developing situation as he dealt with the Home Secretary, George Rosswell in person, and the Chancellor by phone.

"Chancellor, I'm sure that you have spies in the village. They'll brief you better than I can." the Prime Minister said, "The project is a matter of defence and is being run by my office and I would be obliged if you would accept that."

"Normally I would." the chancellor said, "National defence should be first priority for any government. However, my priority is to ensure true followers are not dragged away from the ways of the Lord by deviants and non-believers. We cannot allow a cabal of non-believers, Muslims and Satanists to threaten his word."

"I entirely agree." the Prime Minister said, "I'm so pleased that you approve of our actions in ridding the church there of evil."

"Ah, yes, the Hardcastle boy." the Chancellor said, "As you say, he was being led astray but he was a dedicated member of the church and he did help shepherd the congregation into the light. Perhaps the Reverend Carter should have assigned him to duties with less temptation but he was serving the Church and the state should not intervene in those matters."

"The village didn't think so." the Prime Minister said, "We'd be justified in arresting more of the church's shepherds but for now, it's not in the country's best interest."

"That sounds suspiciously like a threat." the Chancellor said, "It does not do to make God's church angry."

"Not even you can control the Internet, or the media completely." the Prime Minister said, "You don't want it seen that the Crusader's shepherds are above the law. I don't want attention drawn to the village."

"My apologies." the chancellor said, "I misunderstood. Will you allow me to send a personal ambassador to the village. He may be able to help the Reverend Carter in guiding his flock more effectively and he could warn us all if the village ways become too ungodly."

"As a private citizen, he may come and go as he pleases." the prime minister said, "but he may not claim any special privileges."

"I believe that I can accept that compromise." the Chancellor said.

If interest was growing in Stuart's activities, then it was Lau Cheng staying as a paying guest in a cottage, who first discovered that security was tighter than anyone expected. Although Chinese, romantic liaisons between his ancestors and foreign visitors had given him Caucasian looks. A natural intelligence, together with his looks had led him into espionage with a history of highly successful missions. It was, therefore, a shock to find himself arrested.

It was diplomatically done, two MI5 agents, obviously armed, made him an offer that he could not refuse. He could have tried running or even protesting, but it would have blown his cover. His best hope was that he could bluff his way out of trouble. Steeling himself for a tough interrogation he was a little confused when he was taken to the local pub then politely but firmly invited to join the two young men at the heart of the mystery and offered a drink.

"Would you rather be called John Smith or Lau Cheng?"

Stuart-1 asked.

"John Smith, of course." he replied, "I don't know this Lau Cheng."

Stuart-1 switched to Cantonese and picked up a folder, written mainly in Chinese and handed it to Cheng.

"Don't force me to use a cliché." he chuckled, "Spy films are full of situations like this and I don't want to feel as if I'm in one."

Lau Cheng glanced through the file and relaxed. It was a complete dossier on him including his earlier missions. He had no idea how his cover had been blown, or why he had not been arrested sooner.

"Very well, I'd rather be known as Lau Cheng." He said in defeat.

"OK. We made a mistake not involving your country." Stuart-1 said, "Would you rather stay on the same basis as the other representatives or would you rather go home?"

"That file. If you know so much about me, why am I not being arrested?"

"You've got safe conduct until you return to China. I wouldn't travel much after that, if I were you."

Lau Cheng nodded, "I see. I should contact my government."

"I'll be honest." Stuart-1 said, "The biggest problem is that you're twenty odd years older than the other representatives."

"Very well. Am I under arrest?"

"No, of course not. Those two MI5 agents could drive you to your nearest embassy or consulate but if you'd prefer to make your own way, then by all means do so."

"Either way, I'm a marked man." Lau Cheng said, "I may as well be driven in comfort. You say that you would prefer a younger man as a representative. Is there a reason?"

"He may well spend periods weightless or under different gravities and we'd be a little concerned about your health. By all means send a woman, we're not deliberately sexist, it's just worked out that way."

Lau Cheng looked at Stuart-1 for a long time.

"I understand." Lau Cheng said, "My government is going to view your kindness with the utmost suspicion. No-one is as relaxed about security as you are. Their explanation will be that, if you know who I am then you'll feed me false information or you've turned me."

Stuart and his friends were also aware of Daniel Lone. His real name was Daniyal but he had anglicised it. Stuart thought of him as the Arab representative. He was left alone because no-one could detect any real malice in him. He claimed to be a writer seeking somewhere quiet to work: he watched from a polite distance as he sent regular reports, especially about the Stuarts.

Middle Eastern politics always seemed confused. Nation states depend on tribes, some of which were nomadic and ignored frontiers. Rulers seemed harsher but without them, whole regions degenerated into confused mêlées between fragile coalitions and ancient vendettas. On this world Islamic nations seemed to be controlled by a shadowy and sinister organisation. Not even Stuart or his team could find out much about it, because it encouraged its followers to remember their heritage. They lived in the desert without electricity and thus, without electronic surveillance, the most technically advanced intelligence organisations found themselves working back in the stone age with little success.

Brian was busily getting his papers out of storage and compiling them with the willing assistance of Viktor Levkova. With Dave-1's help, Dave-2 and Sergeant Charlie Pernell were overseeing the quarry development which was rapidly taking shape.

Viktor, Charlie and Dave-2 were also busily working on a spaceship design. Early on Viktor had insisted that the design work should be done on Mars.

"It's not enough to know that I can go there." he said, "It's the only place that I remember it's really happening. Anywhere else and it feels like I'm just playing some extraordinary game."

Stuart-1 spent time on Terzon. Certain key elements of the ship's generators were being built there. They were to Brian's design but were encased in a plastic that was impenetrable to detection devices on Earth. Extra circuits were also embedded in the unit. They had two purposes: to make it even harder to work out the module's function and to become white-hot and melt the whole module if it was tampered with. Without knowing which circuits were which, the modules were impossible to open without doing irreparable damage Left alone, they would work for years.

Stuart-1 was relieved that Brian-2's work was going well and he was already developing his theories. They would lead to the development of a portal on that planet similar to the one that Stuart-1 and Brian-1 used. Once plans had been finalised, Dave-2 and Charlie Pernell received reports about the construction of the spaceships and space station.

Stuart-1 had little to do even though an unexpected situation had occurred. The three leaders had got to like their summits in a village pub and insisted on a weekly meeting there.

Anyone who follows political lives will be aware that a political leader, be they prime minister, president or chairman always look far older and more tired after their time in office. Already the leaders that visited Stuart-1's world were bucking the trend and that was simply because they had time away from the office. Ian Shanks joked about having an eight-day week and from their perspective they did with the help of a little time travel.

The British prime minister bought stout walking boots and hiking equipment and spent his time out on the moors with just Zack as a guide. What Stuart-1 found odd was that President Jackson and Chairman Chernekov rehearsed with the village choir and held impromptu concerts in the pub gardens.

For once Stuart really could relax and watch. He even had time to chat with his friend Spock.

"Earth is a curious world." Spock said, "It's very volatile compared to our own and it does provide an interesting view of time."

"How do you mean?" Stuart asked.

"We've looked at your data on parallel worlds," he said, "and the lizard people are helping us to find other alternates. The results are fascinating."

"Go on." Stuart said.

"We've not found two alternatives that are identical yet." he said, "There are some that appear to be so but careful study shows up differences. There are plenty that need further study so we might still find something. However, it's difficult to explain but as you may know, universes are ordered or packed. I think that you once described it as one dimensional straws packed side by side and in layers in a three-dimensional box. It takes some imagination to expand the concept to explain how our three-dimensional universes are contained in a twelve dimensional matrix."

"Yeah, I do know." Stuart retorted, "I just look at the maths and follow the results. It's not ideal though. I still find navigation difficult."

"You may need to understand it more." Spock said.

"Why?"

"Within the matrix are clusters of universes. They are similar. We appear to be in one such cluster where your village is particularly stable and it depends on Brian finding it. Towards the edges of the cluster, Brians are less likely to develop their theories."

"OK!" Stuart acknowledged, "Does that explain why the

villages in the different alternates I visit are similar?"

"It's part of the pattern but not an explanation as to why." Spock replied, "That's being pedantic but we're observing and we have no way explaining our observations."

"I know the feeling." Stuart exclaimed, "I spend most of my time dealing with problems that I don't understand."

"And I have a new one for you." Spock said, "I don't think that you're going to like it."

"Try me." Stuart said.

"You believe that inside clusters, universes tend to influence each other through the links that individuals have with their alternate selves."

Stuart nodded.

"As a theory it's been impossible to prove or disprove." Spock continued, "But now we've discovered a universe where you don't exist. The lizards may have detected a Dave, but he's not in the village and they won't discuss it any further."

"We stop here." Stuart snapped angrily, "Stuart-2 was a threat to me and I had to help him. I am NOT getting involved with another alternate."

"In his despair Stuart-2 cast his mind around looking for help. He may have tried there before finding you."

"How?" Stuart asked, "You said that I don't exist there."

"We don't know." Spock replied, "It's very curious. Do you have any feeling that you're being led there."

Stuart shook his head, "No, I haven't. Are you going against your own beliefs and are hoping that I'll interfere?"

"No." Spock replied, "Would you object if we observed this new world though?"

"I wouldn't," Stuart replied, "but you should speak to Dave. He may not like what you find there."

"It wouldn't be our Dave." Spock replied, "He was influenced by your village and by you and I do wonder what I would be like if my world had not discovered reason."

Chapter 6

SS-Senior-Storm-Leader David Hilford strutted proudly into the restaurant where he was due to meet his mother. He liked his mother so he was unhappy with the coolness between them since he had denounced his father for betraying the Greater Reich.

His father considered himself to be part of the intelligentsia and so was entitled to question and examine instructions handed down from Berlin. David knew better. His father's job as a lecturer in agriculture was to ensure that future farmers of the Reich understood that their duty was to provide as much food as possible.

His father had invited his cronies around for a few drinks and they had settled in their living room. As David had entered the room, they were discussing the terrible slander that the first Great Führer had been incapable of siring children. His father was discussing the rumour that one of Dr. Goebbels children had claimed to be the Führer's son.

It was too much for David so he had contacted the local Gestapo office. He had been praised for his loyalty so he was believed when he had explained that his mother was not in the room when his father had spoken.

He had excelled in the Greater Reich Youth Movement (GRYM) not being crushed by the harsh training he had received, and willing to be equally harsh on those junior to him. Now he was an SS-Senior-Storm-Leader.

"Hello mother." he said, dutifully kissing her on the cheek, "You're looking well. How's business?"

"It's a living." Brenda, his mother replied, "Congratulations on your promotion."

"Thank you, mother." he replied, noting the lack of feeling behind her words, "I could propose you for party membership now. That would attract some useful new clients."

"I'll think about it." Brenda said, "What about you? Do you know where you'll be posted yet?"

"No, but I've got to report to a Dr. Darren Barker at the Ministry of Science. I don't know why."

"Maybe you're being assigned to security there." Brenda suggested, "When do you have to go?"

"After lunch." David replied, "We needn't maintain this charade for too long."

"I am pleased for you." Brenda said, "I'm not angry with you any more for denouncing your father. The more I think about it the more I realise that I never trusted his friends. If you hadn't said anything we both could have been arrested as well."

"I reported what I heard because it was my duty." David said, "I wish that you'd understand."

"Let's change the subject." Brenda said, "Work at the Ministry of Science is something even your dad could respect. Let's drink to your good fortune."

They were both uncomfortable with each other and the meal was a gesture more than a pleasure. Dave was glad when it was over, and he could forget the feeling that she was still angry but he had other things to worry about. Despite his claim that it had been his duty and he had spoken up for his mother, saving her, he did feel pangs of guilt. On that day they were suppressed by nervous excitement as he was shown into Dr. Barker's office, before standing at attention before his desk.

"Take a look at these names." Dr Barker said, "Do they mean anything to you?"

"No sir." David replied, "Well, except for mine of course."

"Who are the Crusaders?"

"I've no idea, sir." David replied, "Sir, I'm a loyal servant of the Greater Reich. I would not tolerate anyone who might oppose it."

"We know." Dr. Barker said, "Sit down and relax. I have a story to tell you. It's an odd one that could threaten the Reich if it's not a hoax. If it's genuine, then it's our duty to turn it from a threat to an advantage. A few weeks ago the police picked up a young man who kept asking when the Crusaders would arrive. He was puzzled that no-one had ever heard of them and he didn't seem to know anything about the Greater German Reich. He regarded the Great Führer as some sort of monster, and had never heard of the man who saved this country from a futile war and who guided us into a close union with Germany."

"Lord Halifax, you mean." David said, "Surely everyone is taught how he persuaded the government not to involve itself in Polish/German affairs."

"Apparently not." Dr. Barker chuckled, "You can read the full police report later but I want you to understand why you're here. Initially the police thought they were dealing with a drunk and some twisted anti-Reich feeling but suddenly the man collapsed to the floor, screaming in agony, clutching his head.

"At first, the police thought it was some sort of seizure but as he recovered he started acting like a completely different person. He was suddenly a loyal member of the Reich stating that he had been somewhere where the Greater Reich didn't exist but was controlled by those Crusaders I mentioned."

"He was mad then." David said, "What's it called, a split personality?"

"That's what the police thought but as a precaution he was sent to the Gestapo in case this Crusader thing was a real organisation." Dr. Barker replied, "Under interrogation he persisted in the claim that he had been somewhere else but he also produced that list of names. You and Brian Chapman are real people but the other three are not. The young man concerned is one Robert Downing. Before the seizure he called himself Stuart Johnson and he named his parents as Richard and Mavis. He also gave an address. Richard Johnson was killed in Russia three years before the young man was born and his mother, Mavis married William Downing. She comes from a small village in Yorkshire but moved to Manchester. There's a lot more that's included in the report but I want to get on.

"Brian Chapman was an obscure clerk in the Ministry of Economics. He was investigated for a connection with these Crusaders but nothing turned up, except..."

David waited expectantly then wondering if he was expected to say something, contributed, "My family comes from Yorkshire."

"Yes, you come from the same village that this young man mentioned and it is another coincidence. Chapman had piles of notebooks of what at first glance seemed to be science gobbledygook. However, it seems he was close to building a machine that could bend dimensions."

"Huh?" David exclaimed, "My apologies, I don't understand."

"He would be able to bend space-time to travel through space instantly."

David stared blankly.

"You've never read science fiction?" Dr. Barker asked.

David shook his head, "No, I can manage training manuals but I was never into reading for fun."

"I know." Dr. Barker said, "Books may give you ideas."

David frowned, suspecting some criticism of the system but Dr. Barker was moving on.

"Chapman and the Downing boy are to remain under arrest and you are assigned to look after them. Using my methods, you will help them to build this space machine."

It was a clear order but somehow a sharp 'Yes sir' did not fit. How could he possibly help in a rocket programme when he knew nothing about them but Dr. Barker was not talking about rockets. SS-Senior-Storm-Leader David Hilford had no idea what he was talking about.

Luckily Dr. Barker did not expect a reply as he continued, "Our rocket program has proved to be of limited use in colonising other worlds, which is why there's such interest in other means, no matter how unlikely. Orders for this have come from Berlin so be warned, you're under very close scrutiny from very high up. You also have protection from just as high, which means even the Gestapo must hold off. However, if the project fails then the Gestapo will be allowed to investigate just what this was all about."

David swallowed nervously. His first assignment as an SS-Senior-Storm-Leader would be nothing that he could have ever imagined. Despite an education limited to military training David was intelligent but he was already out of his depth. SS officers do not question orders otherwise he might have protested but his training required him to listen, ready to obey.

It was odd that the three chief suspects in a possible conspiracy would be kept together but if the project was genuine then the opportunities far outweighed the risk. For now, David had more immediate problems to deal with and he tried to concentrate on what Dr. Barker was telling him.

"I'm in overall charge, of course. You will not interfere with my handling. You're the trained soldier so that is your role. To look after them as I said."

"Oh, I see. I'm to act as bodyguard."

"In a way. You're only a lieutenant but you'll speak with the full authority of the SS."

"My rank is…" David began.

"Irrelevant." Dr. Barker interrupted, "Every agency, intelligence department and police department will want a piece of the action. No matter what rank tries to interfere, you will stop them."

David swallowed nervously again. Good National Socialists obeyed orders and respected authority.

"I hope I get written orders." he said.

"Of course and that's a good point." Dr Barker replied, "I'll phone the Reich Chancellery and have them delivered by special-messenger. In the meantime you can meet the others."

A little later David and Dr. Barker were in a helicopter flying

North.

"Feel free to ask questions." Dr. Barker said, "I know, that goes against your training so my order is, ask questions."

"Yes sir." David snapped back, "Where are we going?"

"To that small quarry near your village. For practical purposes you are to consider yourself as under arrest and confined to the quarry. It'll keep the local Gestapo happy and they won't be able to question you."

"About the Crusaders." David said, trying to understand.

"And about the latest incredible Nazi invention." Dr. Barker chuckled.

"Do you have Jewish blood?" David asked, "You don't sound that respectful of National Socialism."

"I don't have much to lose." Dr. Barker said, "I'm an obscure British scientist, not one of the best that Germany has to offer, and no-one will notice my disappearance if I'm part of the Reich's more ridiculous failures."

"So you don't believe in this space-ship then?"

"Honestly it's easier to believe in the Crusaders trying to undermine research." Dr. Barker said, "That's what my report said when I first studied Chapman's papers. I made the mistake of adding, 'but what if it's true'. That remark reached the Reich Chancellery and, for my sins, it caught the Führer's attention."

"But that's a great honour." David exclaimed, "You should be so proud."

"It's my death warrant." Dr. Barker said, "The Reich Chancellor won't want reminders of a foolish idea to contaminate his image. It's the price I'll pay for poking a little fun at the Greater National Socialist worthies. Unfortunately the Führer saw the Downing boy's story as a sign from our Aryan ancestors."

"But the Führer cannot be wrong, can he?" David said, "If he sees a sign then it must be so."

"And if it's not a sign then the evidence that it was not, will disappear so that future, newly commissioned officers will believe in his infallibility."

"Oh!" David exclaimed, "Is that a jokey way of saying that we'll be punished for failing to live up to the Führer's standards?"

"If you like." Dr. Barker smiled, "We'll be there soon. Your orders are to adapt to our operating methods and understand the circumstances that brought about our predicament. Oh, and by the way, we're hoping that you'll make the same sort of jump that Downing was supposed to have made."

"Do you really believe his story then?" David asked.

"I don't know what to believe." Dr. Barker said, "It's our job to find out but it's not something we can control, so we'll have to wait and see."

They were silent for the rest of the trip. David was trying to take in what he had been told. It occurred to him that he should denounce Dr. Barker for his disrespect of National Socialism. It would be difficult if he was answerable to the Reich Chancellery but it bothered him that his future was in the hands of someone so lax in his loyalty. They landed in a field near the entrance and approached the gate with their papers ready. The unsmiling guards and growling dogs were comforting in their familiarity. Even the twin barbed wire fences made him feel at home. There was a third inner fence, taller than average but looking more like a garden fence than a security fence.

"Make sure that you shut the gate when you use it." Dr Barker said, "We don't want anyone looking in, do we? Let's find the troops. They should be hard at work, so they won't be in the workshop. Let's try the kitchen. Come on."

According to David's limited knowledge, a scientist should be in a laboratory, studying the effects of his latest experiment. Considering Dr. Barker's behaviour, it would be interesting to see how he dealt with his errant underlings.

At least Robert leapt to his feet but his smile of greeting spoiled the effect and he hurried to pour out a couple of coffees.

"Hi Dave." he said as he handed one to David, "It's funny seeing you for real."

Brian glanced up.

"David Hilford?" he said, "Ever been off world? Ever met Stuart Johnson?"

"Give him a chance." Dr. Barker chuckled, "He started off today expecting to be appointed to some smart regiment. Instead, he's learnt about you two deadbeats and he's expecting you to be standing at attention and saluting."

Dr. Barker was quite correct. That's just what David was expecting but he was also expected to obey orders and Dr. Barker had ordered him to adapt so he smiled uncertainly and risked saying, "I feel as if I'm on another planet now."

"Well said." Brian laughed, "Robert, how about your contribution first. He's remembered a lot since he stopped being terrified by the bloody Gestapo."

"I remember seeing a calendar." Robert began nervously, "It

was about fourteen weeks ahead if I've converted it correctly."

"Don't sell yourself short, lad." Brian said, "They had the old Gregorian calendar. The months were most illogical, all different lengths. Anyway that was simple arithmetic. What's more important he's able to read my work and understand it, which is more than the so called experts were able to do. David, you're going to have to wear civvies. That uniform's terrifying the poor boy. Normally I can't shut him up."

"OK but is there any progress?" Dr. Darren Barker asked.

"I've just told you, yes." Brian snapped, "And it's down to Robert."

"Explain please." Darren said, "And please remember, it's all new to David."

"Robert suffered what is officially a seizure. During that illness he dreamed that he was on another world populated by people from this world and others who were figments of his imagination. What is odder is that in this dream Robert claims that he wore a necklace that helped him understand the world he was in."

Brian paused looking at David, "When he was first questioned he was confused and terrified and the bloody Gestapo can't see beyond rooting out treason. Here, he can sort out his memories because no-one's threatening to slam a fist into his face. Anyway he was, or will be, there for nearly eight hours. During that time, he learned to speak Swedish. He also learned about my notations and expanded versions of my equations. Suffice it to say, we can start building a portal as it's called there. Oh I forgot, most of his education happened on a third Earth that he was taken to."

"Why did you learn Swedish?" David asked.

"Because we went to the pub and there were some Swedish tourists wanting directions."

"Silly of me to ask." David muttered.

"No it wasn't, SS-Senior-Storm-Leader." Brian said, "It shows you haven't had all your initiative beaten out of you."

Dave angrily started forward then hesitated, with an effort, he remembered his orders.

"Please do not insult the SS." he said quietly.

"I meant no insult." Brian said, "But their training is to teach you obedience to the death protecting the Führer. This situation requires something different and this might help you take this project seriously. There is a possible world that does not like National Socialism, it can attack us at will and we cannot even find it. Is that a good enough reason to see if this device works?"

"Yes it is." David replied, "On that basis I accept your authority as head of this establishment."

Brian stared at him for a long time, appraising him.

"I think I see why the other worlds value you so highly." he said at last before turning to Dr. Barker.

"I shall have initial designs for a field generator by the end of the week. Allow time for its construction and calibration and then we'll know whether this is a complete waste of time or not."

At first, David felt like a complete outsider. He had no way of knowing whether Brian was developing something fantastic, was a misguided fool going nowhere or a saboteur trying in some way to attack National Socialist science.

Even Robert could help Brian but David had to accept a very junior role and found himself little better than a tea-boy. Then his orders arrived and he gazed in awe at the Führer's signature; orders from the Fuhrer addressed to him personally.

Things changed for him when he had to use them. He was startled when the security alarm rang. It was a loud strident bell that made everyone jump. He was not even wearing his jacket in deference to Robert's feelings though he had the presence of mind to grab a copy of his orders and march out to face two Gestapo officers strolling along.

"Papers." the leading officer snapped.

Smiling, David handed them over.

"These are copies that you can keep and verify." David replied, "Get out before I have you arrested and shot."

David's grin widened as the Gestapo officer's smug complacency gave way to confusion.

"We still have to verify that the prisoners are secure." the officer blustered.

David took out his phone and held his thumb over a button.

"Last chance." he said, "Get out."

The Gestapo agent looked at the orders once more, then turned on his heels and headed for the gate.

"Halt!" David shouted satisfied when the man came to a sudden stop, turned and faced him.

"Find out who the commanding officer of the guard is. Show him those orders and tell him to report to me in fifteen minutes. Dismiss!" The men hurried off.

Exactly fifteen minutes later the SS-Storm-Command-Leader (Major) arrived. David was now properly dressed and raised his arm in a salute.

"Heil the Führer." he snapped out.

The SS-Storm-Command-Leader acknowledged his salute.

"I'll have to verify your orders." he said, "How can I help?"

"Inform your men that anyone attempting to enter this compound is to be shot. If anyone does get in then those responsible are to be shot as well." David replied.

"It's not easy for enlisted men to defy the Gestapo." the SS-Storm-Command-Leader said.

"See that a copy of my orders are kept in the guard house." David said, "No-one sets foot in here without my permission."

"Write your own order to go with them." the SS-Storm-Command-Leader said, "It will be obeyed."

As the officer turned and strode back to the gate, David breathed a deep sigh of relief and headed back to the others, describing what had happened.

"Welcome to the team." Brian chuckled, "It took real guts to commit yourself like that and I didn't think you could do it. I just wish that you could become more involved in the work."

"I was just obeying orders." David said, "As you've said, that's what I'm trained to do but I'm just a junior officer ordering the Gestapo and senior officers around. If this goes wrong then I'm dead." he said, "If the Gestapo doesn't get me then that officer will."

Despite all his misgivings, he had taken sides against a senior officer and the Gestapo and both would seek a chance for revenge. As reaction set in, he started trembling before feeling giddy. He blacked out coming to in a dream, floating but looking down, or up, upon himself.

"What's up?" his body laughed, "Space-sickness?"

Briefly he thought that he was dead, that he was looking at his own dead body. However, it was breathing and it had spoken to him. Neither did his body's companions look like the spirits of Teutonic knights come to guide him to Valhalla.

He thought of Robert's story of being transported to another world, but why could he see himself, why was he floating why had it happened?

"Zack, go fetch Stuart-1." his alter ego said, "Tell him that there's something wrong with Dave-1. Andy, you know more about this than I do. What do you think?"

"I don't know." Andy replied, "We'd better not take him to Mars. We'd better take him back to Earth."

The explanation was gibberish so far as David was concerned. Although he felt different, he realised that he was breathing, so could he speak?

"Have you heard of anyone jumping to another place?" he asked.

Dave-2 suddenly looked relieved and Andy grinned.

"I've never done it." Andy said, "Is that what's happening to you?"

"I don't know." David said, "Is Stuart-1, Stuart Johnson? Have you ever heard of Robert Downing?"

"I'm just a visitor." Dave-2 replied, "Stuart is a Stuart Johnson but there's a lot of them about and I've never met this Robert Downing. What about you, where do you come from."

It occurred to David that as an officer of the SS he should be asking the questions and demanding that mere civilians especially boys should be standing at attention awaiting orders. He nearly laughed out loud. How can anyone stand to attention if they're weightless?

Ever since he had met Dr. Barker, nothing he had learnt during his time as a GRYM member then as a soldier meant anything. He could not bully and cajole underlings, he was treated kindly and he had to admit, he liked the more relaxed regime.

He would have carried out his threat and shot the Gestapo officer without a second's thought yet Brian had been more impressed with him for thinking on his feet and getting to grips with an awkward situation.

Being weightless was a shock and he was scared to move in case he just drifted off, out of control. He just was not in a position to exert his authority and if these people were anything like Dr. Barker or Brian then they would just laugh at him if he tried.

Luckily his musings were interrupted by the arrival of another young man about his age who spoke briefly with Dave-2.

"Hi Dave." the newcomer said, "At least I assume that you're a Dave Hilford. I'm Stuart Johnson and you're on the space station Resolution. Could you identify yourself please."

"SS-Senior-Storm-Leader David Hilford." David replied.

"SS?" Stuart asked, "That rings a bell."

"It should." Dave-3 exclaimed.

"Why?" Stuart asked.

"We're the Führer's bodyguard."

"Ah!" Stuart exclaimed, "Hitler's been dead for over seventy years and Nazism died with him."

"I should arrest you for treason." Dave-3 snapped, "At least… If I was home, I would. Where the fuck am I?"

"At least you sound like Dave." Stuart chuckled, "The best I can answer is that you're here. The real question is, why are you here? We'll start getting the answer if we chat to some of my friends. Are you up for another shock?"

Dave-3 nodded uncertainly. Gravity and a strong sense of up and down is one certainty that's learnt from birth. Suddenly being weightless was a massive shock that he could scarcely deal with.

At least his weight returned as he was guided through a steel tube complete with airlocks. However, a lizard rearing up from the long grass and staring at him, was startling. It was when it spoke in perfect English, asking to speak to Stuart alone, that Dave-3's sense of reality vanished again.

"You should kill this Dave combination." the lizard said.

"Why?" Stuart exclaimed, shocked at the suggestion, "You can't be serious... but you don't joke, do you?"

"He comes from a dangerous world. Your Dave would be trapped there and would understand. He would try to protect you. This visitor would return and help your enemies."

"Yes but that's no reason to kill a friend. The visitor is probably bad, he belongs to a bad organisation but it's no reason for trapping Dave in a bad place."

"You're right of course." the lizard said, "You are also wrong. This visitor is a Dave. They all need to face physical challenges and danger to reassure themselves. This Dave has already completed this rite. Now he's open to suggestion. He may find a better path or he might try to make a name for himself in his present one. You can help him decide."

"By killing him."

"He has to make the choice, and it is not certain. Your Dave already has, so he is a better choice there."

"I'm not killing anyone." Stuart said firmly, "It's bad enough that I've been the cause of others killing each other."

"You cannot change what's in another's heart." the lizard said, "I'm detecting something that I don't understand and it frightens me. You're right of course, you must prepare for something bad but now is not the time to act."

"And I can trust this Dave?" Stuart asked.

"He needs to find his new path and he may not succeed. If he does, then you will be able to trust him with your life. I know what you're going to ask and I don't know. I just know that something bad is finding its way here."

Stuart nodded, "I understand ... No, I don't understand but I trust your feelings."

"As I do yours and this new Dave's."

~~~

If SS-Senior-Storm-Leader David Hilford struggled with the sudden change of environment, Dave-1 adapted far more quickly. He had made brief jumps before, he was on solid ground instead of weightless and he was used to being in odd situations.

"Are you all right?" Robert asked.

"Yeah, I'm fine." Dave replied, "Someone walked over my grave. That's all."

"Of course he's fine." Brian laughed, "SS-Senior-Storm-Leaders don't have nerves. It's all in a day's work to threaten a couple of Gestapo officers."

"It's not." Dave-1 retorted, "I'd rather leave it to Over Storm Leaders."

"There's no such rank." Brian said suspiciously.

"I don't care which rank as long he's over me." Dave-1 retorted.

"Yes, so." Brian replied, "I didn't know SS officers were allowed a sense of humour. You know, for a moment I wondered if you'd jumped but you're in too much control. Just sit down and relax. You did well just now."

"I think that I'll take a look around." Dave-1 said heading for a door.

"That's the way to our rooms." Brian said, "Any trouble will be outside."

"I'm going to look for bugs in our rooms or do you want to argue with that as well?"

Brian shrugged and shook his head.

Dave found himself in a corridor with rooms on either side. Three had labels on the door and one had SS-Senior-Storm-Leader David Hilford written on it. Relieved, he entered, stopping to stare at himself in a mirror. He had to admit it, the black uniform and the crisp white shirt looked really smart but he needed to focus on other things.

He had recognised that he had jumped as soon he regained consciousness, taking in his surroundings without difficulty and responding, instinctively following the flow of the conversation. He knew from war films that no-one threatened Gestapo agents. He had been careless and flippant, guessing at a more senior rank. It had been a mistake and he had been lucky to get round it.

More importantly he had recognised a Brian, Brian-3 for now, and had learnt that they knew about jumps so they probably had a portal. No, considering the work that he was doing, Brian was close to developing one.

There was something else. There was something wrong with this Brian. There was a sarcastic edge to his voice. Maybe it had something to do with the regime that he was working under but it was unlikely. He seemed to sneer at that too. David detected an undertone to this Brian's attitude that he did not like.

The other youngster reminded him vaguely of Stuart but he seemed to jump and straighten himself every time Dave looked at him. Dave had only seen him for a short time but it seemed that Robert was used to being bullied, he had the same tendency to try to stay unnoticed. It may have been imagination though and time would tell.

It was the first time since joining in with Stuart that with no warning, he was completely alone in an off-world situation. He understood what Stuart had said about the nagging fear that he was trapped but Dave also remembered what he had said about having a task to perform, but what was it?

He was interrupted by a knock on the door.

"Come in." he yelled and Robert entered the room.

"Mr. Chapman sent me to see if you needed anything."

"No, I'm fine thanks." Dave replied.

Robert frowned.

"An SS officer would expect me to hang up his uniform." Robert said, "The Senior Storm Leader did."

"What am I then?" Dave snapped, "A ghost?"

"I've jumped." Robert said, "I know other Daves and you're more like them now."

"How do you mean?"

"I don't know." Robert replied, "You still marched around but it wasn't quite as much. I don't know, I just thought I saw something. I'm sorry."

Robert stood, looking fearfully at Dave.

"OK, don't worry." Dave said, "Maybe this jump of yours has just given you an over-active imagination."

"Yes SS-Senior-Storm-Leader. Thank you. May I fetch you a coffee or something?"

"No, but I need some fresh air." Dave replied, "You can walk with me and tell me more about your jump."

Dave stood up heading for the door. Robert coughed gently and handed him his cap, smiling gently. The smile turned to a frown as he adjusted the cap properly. Robert led the way, ostensibly to open doors for Dave but Dave felt as if he was being shown the way.

Dave recognised the quarry, curious about the wooden fence.

"There's more security beyond that fence, isn't there?" Dave said and Robert nodded.

"OK." Dave continued, "You're right, I have jumped but I have to assume that the rooms are bugged. Now tell me why you're not saying anything."

"I liked the place I visited. I've never met people who were so friendly. I want to go back for real."

"That's not possible." Dave said, "I don't even know how to find this place. Then I'd have to arrange for you to be alone when the portal materialised."

"You're saying I can go if it can be arranged." Robert said, "That's enough for now. I'll help you. Oh and I run laps around the quarry before everyone else gets up. It's the only time that I'm alone. That's about 05:30hrs."

"It's impossible then." Dave said, "I never get up that early."

Robert looked at him and grinned, "You're teasing me. You do time travel."

"OK, I'll do what I can but you know it might never happen."

Robert nodded, "I know. You're slouching. SS officers always look as if they're about to meet the Fuhrer."

"Isn't that insolence? Shouldn't I beat you up or something?"

"I'm sorry." Robert said suddenly very nervous, "You don't need my help do you?"

"I was joking again." Dave said, "And yes, I do need your help. I'll tell you something else, I'm glad that I've got a friend here."

Robert smiled, "I'm supposed to act as manservant. I don't like all my duties with Mr. Chapman but they could be fun with you."

"Your duties with me are confined to seeing that I'm properly dressed, I don't get lost and I don't say something wrong." Dave said firmly, "I know Brian's interests but the other Brians I know would be too scared of forcing you to even ask you."

"That's why I like your world." Robert replied.

They walked in a companionable silence with Dave relaxing and allowing his body to adopt its old habits. He actually found it easier to go with the flow and it gave him time to think. The more he discovered about this Brian, the less he liked him. Robert, reminded him of a trusting puppy responding to a little kindness.

But why was he here? Jumps only seemed to happen when there was something badly wrong. Brian had said something about threatening a Gestapo officer. Could that be it? The emotional tension from such a confrontation? For want of a better description, he could imagine the scene providing the 'energy' but there had to be something else, some reason for it to happen.

"I need to see what Brian, I mean Mr. Chapman's working on." he said, "It has to be without him suspecting I understand what he's doing."

"The Reich Chancellery thinks that he's planning a way of colonising space but his designs are for a multidimensional portal."

He smiled at Dave's startled expression, "I was wearing a translator and I was interested in how I got there. I can still see the schematics of how the field generators were configured. I've just got no idea of how to build one."

"So you understand multidimensional space." Dave said.

"No." Robert replied, "I got an idea of how the various warp fields were built up and I do know that Mr. Chapman's plans are for more than just travel in space. I've got vague ideas for other stuff but nothing I really understand."

"OK, has this Brian actually built anything?"

"He's building something now. It's one reason that he's so pleased with you, or rather the SS-Senior-Storm-Leader. He should be ready for a test today. If those Gestapo officers or anyone else was watching and it failed then they'd start thinking sabotage but they need a lot of calibration don't they?"

"Yes they do." Dave said, "You did well to pick up on so much. You'd get on with a friend of mine."

"Stuart." Robert said, "Yes I did."

Dave might had said more but Brian opened the door to yell for them. They hurried over.

"You may as well watch Senior Leader but keep out of the way. Robert, let's see if you have anything useful to contribute."

He led the way into the kitchen. To Dave's eyes, the device on the bench was a rickety Heath-Robinson affair compared to what other Brians would have done, however, like Robert, he waited expectantly.

As Brian worked the controls so the bench seemed to shimmer and fade until a component began to glow red-hot and exploded. Dave-1 found himself blacking out.

SS-Senior-Storm-Leader David Hilford also found himself blacking out suddenly back in the laboratory watching the smoke rise from the ruined equipment. He might have grabbed for a fire extinguisher but the satisfied smile on Mr. Chapman's face stopped him.

Just as suddenly Dave-1 found himself surrounded by his friends on the lizard planet. He breathed a deep sigh of relief when he saw Stuart. As quickly as he could, while everything was fresh in his mind, he recounted his experiences.

"I reckon that they've hit the resonance problem." he concluded, "That Brian's in a hurry and far less methodical. I reckon he knows more about the jumps than he lets on and he gets help."

"What makes you say that?" Stuart asked.

"I don't know. Maybe he was a bit too accepting that they even happened. He took it for granted that Robert had jumped and could be useful. I know it doesn't sound much but it was his attitude, his body language, I don't know. I know that I didn't like him though. What was my counterpart like."

"I'd say that he was enjoying himself." Stuart replied, "He liked his cadet training to become an SS officer but now he's ready for something else. He's as fascinated as you were when you discovered what we were doing."
~~~

And on Earth-2, in a luxurious hotel on the Mediterranean, the plotting continued.

"My master accepts that the situation is most puzzling." Abu al Khayr Naṣṣār said, "We're prepared to offer our help, Mr. Reynolds."

He paused but before John Reynolds, the chancellor's emissary could speak, he added, "Sometimes help is seen as a way of interfering or making political capital. Our offer is genuine, and we will not speak of it unless you do."

"And in return?" John Reynolds asked.

"And in return we ask that you be honest with us." Abu al Khayr Naṣṣār replied.

"Very well." John Reynolds said, "Our best idea is that the Brits have developed some super ray weapon and are deploying it in orbit. What bothers us is that we can't find any details of either the weapon, how it was launched, or how it remained hidden in orbit until the controlled re-entry failed. NASA and the Pentagon are investigating it but without success."

"And the group of youths in Yorkshire? The one called Stuart Johnson?"

"Given their general educational standard, it's highly unlikely that they're involved. Neither could their security cover a space project of this magnitude. We believe that they're a smokescreen to divert us."

"Very well." Abu al Khayr Naṣṣār said, "As a courtesy, I'm informing you that my master has sent his own observer to the village. He will not interfere in any way and he will have no diplomatic privileges."

"I understand." John Reynolds said, "It's not a problem and the Chinese observer is already there."

"There is one weakness in your assessment." Abu al Khayr Naṣṣār said, "It does not explain the odd behaviour of the British prime minister, the American president or the Russian chairman. It seems that they all lock themselves away in a room every so often for no apparent reason and they've developed extraordinary powers. They can speak in many languages and can detect the most obscure and carefully placed bug."

"Yes we know." John Reynolds said, "It's probably not a coincidence but stranger things have happened."

"Really! Can you me tell about them?" Abu al Khayr Naṣṣār suddenly smiled, "Forgive me. You made a good point but Yorkshire seems to provide a link to the various, er, projects. We're surprised that our observer needs no pass or ID and he claims that he can walk freely around their main site."

"That's probably right. There's no security of any description." John Reynolds said, "They'll take you to the main site that they're building and even pose in front of the construction works for you while they discuss their plans to study solar particles."

"No security could be that lax." Abu al Khayr Naṣṣār said, "Maybe it is a smokescreen for other projects, after all. My master thanks you for your frankness. He accepts that you have some unique problems in dealing with this matter."

Not long after, Abu al Khayr Naṣṣār was on a plane to Beijing where he was welcomed far more politely than usual.

The discussions were lengthy though Abu al Khayr Naṣṣār found an apparent slip by his Chinese counterpart interesting.

"Don't be misled." he said, "The security is highly efficient. They've caught and turned one of our best agents."

"Let me guess." Abu al Khayr Naṣṣār said, "He has easy access and they don't seem to care what he sees."

The Chinese representative nodded cautiously.

"I would approach their team leader and ask for China to be represented." Abu al Khayr Naṣṣār said.

"That is what Lau Cheng said." the Chinese representative acknowledged, "Why don't they just announce to the world that they have made a giant leap in the arms race?"

"Our best guess is that the United Kingdom understands the political consequences. The breakthrough, makes every other weapon and delivery system obsolete but maybe it is not fully deployed or is still in testing. The failure and crash landing a few months back made it known and now the United Kingdom has to use diplomacy to prevent itself being annihilated while it still can."

"And we lack a suitable nuclear capability so we're ignored."

"I may well instruct our observer to announce himself and ask to formally represent us." Abu al Khayr Naṣṣār said, "It may prove interesting. It would not hurt to follow your agent's advice."

"You suggest that he has not been turned."

"Anything's possible but his story is in line with our own observations. My master is willing to share information."

"As may we." the Chinese representative said, "We are cautious of allowing religious groups to slow the Long March of Communism but we can accept them. This new-found friendship between America and Russia is worrying. It seems that our Russian comrades are about to betray the cause. We may be in favour of a far stronger alliance than a mere exchange of information."

Abu al Khayr Naṣṣār returned home well satisfied. With the Crusaders undermining this new threat from within, and a growing alliance on the outside, he was confident the threat could be contained. His real problem was more disturbing.

His master was old and his mind was failing. To his followers, he was undoubtedly powerful and indeed, he still was. At times, his mind seemed clear and lucid and he fully understood the importance of the new weapon that the British had. It was puzzling that on these occasions, he seemed to speak more like an infidel than a holy man. He also seemed to have an odd obsession with one of the youngsters involved, by all accounts a particularly depraved non-believer.

When the time was right, would he, Abu al Khayr Naṣṣār be able to defeat him and establish a world fit for true believers?

If Stuart was just beginning to see the forces lining up against him, then Chairman Chernekov relished his Friday afternoons in a sleepy English village. He ignored the fact he was in a parallel universe and settled for a complete absence of worry for a few hours.

With Andy and Zack's help, together with Stuart's tacit permission he had compiled a dossier of intrigues and secret activity within the Kremlin. Whenever anyone tried to question his actions, he would pull the relevant file, quote from it then ask, "Do I attend to my business or yours?"

He was allowed to continue with his own business and, of course, none of the various power bases could admit that they had been compromised without revealing their secrets. In fact, they devoted more time to tightening their security, fearing that another faction had compromised them. It allowed the Premier to develop an almost mystical air of authority, which no-one dared challenge.

He also studied Russian history on Earth-1, intrigued by the changes that were attempted and irritated by the mistakes that were made.

President Jackson found it harder to maintain the secret. In desperation, he called in an old friend of his who ran shipyards. They met at Camp David.

"OK Chuck." President Jackson began, "These plans are top secret but can you build it somewhere out of the way, within three months and call it a submarine or something?"

Chuck spent time studying the plans then looked quizzically at his friend, "It's small enough and I can't see any problems. We could build sections simultaneously then do a final assembly but it's no sub. What is it?"

"If I said it's a spaceship and I don't want the Crusaders to get wind of it, what would you say."

Chuck turned back to the plans, "OK. My schoolboy physics says a spaceship is a tank pressurised to the equivalent of thirty feet of water as opposed to a submarine resisting an outside pressure a hundred times greater. The hatches and bracing makes sense if they're to keep pressure in but the hull seems to be over engineered for that sort of pressure."

"It's to give protection from radiation." President Jackson explained.

OK but what rocket is going to lift it?"

"You see those recesses?" President Jackson asked and Chuck nodded, "They'll contain a revolutionary new drive developed by the Brits."

"The Limeys." Chuck said, "I've heard scuttlebut about that meteor. Who's funding the ship?"

"You are." President Jackson grinned.

"I don't think so."

"OK but hear me out. In shipbuilding or aircraft terms, this design is as cheap a prototype as you can get. It's not much bigger than a tugboat, the design is simple, it doesn't need specialised materials or to tie up any highly specialised equipment. All you need to do is draft working plans to maintain the cover that it's a submarine for as long as possible. When word does get out, you'll be seen as a major contributor with a contract to build six of them."

"What about appropriations and competitive tendering?"

"I'll justify it as a national emergency. We had to move fast to prevent Britain doing an exclusive deal with Russia."

"OK, I've got one yard that's just not economic any more. The unions know it so I can warn them that if word gets out, the project will be transferred and the yard closed."

Chuck paused, "I can see how important this could be. I'd start work on all seven but I need some assurance that it's genuine."

"I'll see if you can attend the next project meeting." President Jackson said and could not help adding, "Ever been to Mars before?"

Chuck looked for the joke but didn't get it so he smiled uncertainly. President Jackson knew that the conversation had been too bizarre and had not registered with his friend yet. Chuck would willingly dismiss it as a diversion waiting for the real purpose of the visit. However, Chuck was still studying the plans, commenting on the designs and every minute he studied them, so they became more real and he would take the project more seriously.

"Why is it wrapped in hydrogen polymers, whatever they are?" Chuck asked at one stage, "That's unusual enough to get noticed."

"It's something to do with cosmic radiation as opposed to solar radiation. Believe it or not garbage bags would be effective but there may be other materials readily available. Anything rich in hydrogen is worth considering and we don't need the latest high-tech stuff either." President Jackson replied without thinking, "I heard Viktor complaining that the space station's layer wasn't thick enough."

"What space station and who's Viktor?" Chuck asked.

"You never heard that." President Jackson said firmly, "You'll find out but not yet."

"This really is why you fetched me here, isn't it? It's not some crazy psychological test to see how gullible or adaptable, I am, is it?"

"No, it's for real and outside of this room, no-one knows about it."

"NASA does, surely." Chuck said but the president shook his head.

"No. If you're in, you'll learn more at the project meeting."

Chapter 7

Prime Minister Ian Shanks had little to do except distance himself as much as possible from George Rosswell, the Home Secretary and confidante of the Crusaders.

The Prime Minister was aware that George Rosswell was trying to build a coalition to oust him but it would not achieve much until the Crusaders stepped in. In the meantime, he had one weapon that neither the other two world leaders nor George Rosswell had; honours. Among others, a police commissioner would receive a title for discreetly organising Superintendent Tom Jenkins' transfer, and a couple of newspaper publishers would receive awards for suppressing stories. In addition, a junior parliamentary secretary in Downing St, together with his counterpart in the Home Office would find themselves suitably honoured so that rapid promotion would follow. They provided a pipeline whereby information was diverted to the Prime Minister's office.

Without any massive research and development costs, he had to be running the cheapest space programme in history. With finances out of the equation, no legislation needed for air space or any other legal requirement then no-one else need be involved.

That was not quite true. He thought that immigration and customs should be informed but was UK-1 a separate country to UK-2 or were they the same country? The Prime Minister could imagine a farcical legal debate starting, which would not be at all helpful. He had seen a report of Zack's adventures together with the notion that there were two Zacks. He had suppressed it on the grounds that it would not be in the public interest to announce errors in the Home Office's database.

It was George Rosswell who found himself in trouble, caught between his loyalty to the Crusaders and his loyalty to his country. His country was Christian and it was the Crusaders who defended Christianity. However, he was aware that he was being marginalised. He had lost status in the cabinet but the truth was; the prime minister had more powerful allies and did not need him. The more he thought about it, the more he convinced himself that God had given him the task of saving the country from atheism. As Prime Minister, he would lead it into the light but who could he trust to help him?

While everyone else involved was busy building a spaceship, Stuart-1 had little to do. He might be helping a planet full of political intrigues and shifting alliances but it all had to happen at its own pace. In fact his biggest diplomatic problem was dealing with Zack's mother whenever they met.

"We're still so very grateful for what you've done for Zack." she said on one occasion. "I still can't believe that you trust him to look after all your important visitors. Are you sure he's not being a nuisance?"

"No, he and Andy are a great help," Stuart replied. "They put visitors at ease and of course show them around the village if they want a break."

"I keep worrying if he's doing anything dangerous but if I say anything he just giggles. Is he in danger?"

"I can only say what I've said before." Stuart said, "Yes there is a risk but we've got all sorts of safety checks and Zack is very responsible."

"That's not the way I see him. You should see the state of his room. You do travel don't you. Everyone thinks so. Even your mother does, doesn't she?"

"If it ever got outside village business then we'd have to shut down and leave." Stuart said.

"So you do travel and you take Zack. How did he get arrested?"

Stuart looked at her, startled, "What makes you think he did?"

"He came home one day. He was oddly dressed and upset. To be fair he thought you were angry with him but he did say something about having to change in the police station. He realised that he had let something slip and clammed up. I was worried but at his age, the police would have wanted me or his dad to go in, wouldn't they?"

Stuart nodded.

"Maybe you should know more of what we do." Stuart said, "After all you're still responsible for him. Can I get Mum to speak to you first? I trust her judgement when it comes to village business and she can decide how much to tell you."

Zack's mother nodded.

"I don't want to be a nuisance and you've got far more important things to deal with."

"Funnily enough, I don't." Stuart said, "Everyone else is busy but I've done my bit for now. I'll go and see her now."

As always Mavis, his mother was pleased to see him.

"Your Aunt Maria phoned this morning." Mavis said as they were chatting, "Apparently Caitlin's moving to California with her boyfriend and is so lucky to do all that travelling. I must be so disappointed that you're stuck in this tiny village with that man."

"Why 'my Aunt Maria' all the time?" Stuart asked, "Are you trying to disown your sister?"

Mavis smiled, "Maybe but I feel a little sorry her. Caitlin is her life but she hardly ever sees her."

"You don't see much of my sister." Stuart said, "I still don't know what she saw in that no good bum."

"Oh Sue's doing all right." Mavis said, "It's you who don't ring her or anything. They've both got jobs and Timmy's in play school. It's tight but they're managing. I'm inviting them and Maria here for Christmas. Timmy will love the nativity."

"What the real one or the display in the church?" Stuart asked, "Oh, I forgot, I'm stuck in the village with that man. It'll have to be in the one in the church."

"I would like all my family together, just once." Mavis said, "You and Richard will behave yourselves."

"Brian is family. What about Gable, Demetrius, James and Andy? They can't go home for Christmas."

"I'll manage especially if Demetrius helps. Just don't start arguing with your sister."

"I'll be the perfect host if you'll do something for me." Stuart said.

"Go on!" Mavis cautiously.

"It's Zack's mother." Stuart explained, "She's worried about him getting into trouble and pretty much knows about the portal. He's not quite sixteen so his parents have been good about letting him work for us. Do you think that they should know the whole story?"

"I've seen her stand up to Ida Sallin a couple of times." Mavis said, "She's definitely on your side and she'll keep you on side because you're Zack's best chance of university and a decent job. You're right though, she does have a right to know. Can you get tickets for the opening night of Grease?"

"Grease?" Stuart exclaimed, "That came out years ago."

"1978." Mavis said, "Can you do it?"

"If the theatre bookings were computerised and there were a couple of no shows then yes. I'll look into it. I take it that she likes the film."

"I can tell you all about it." Mavis laughed, "It's one of her main topics of conversation."

"In that case, maybe it's not a good idea." Stuart said, "She'll hate having to keep quiet about a trip like that. Just take her to meet Tanya and Chloe. Being weightless as you cross Resolution is enough of a shock for anyone."

"Tell me about it." Mavis shuddered, "I remember my first trip. Could the four of us visit somewhere a little exotic?"

"Dave has a friend, Dedi. He's the guy that slashed Dave and when he recovered, Dave visited to show that there were no hard feelings. Now Dedi makes him welcome and Dave visits to read his law books. He's not disturbed because Dedi owes him and the other villagers keep quiet because they've got a powerful wizard on side and don't want visitors driving him away."

"I'll think about it." Mavis said, "At least she'll understand why Zack is staying so tanned at this time of year. By all accounts we'll have to take James' new lady friend as well."

The weeks before Christmas that year were proving to be quiet. On other worlds their counterparts were busy but there was little for Stuart-1 and his friends to do. As an American, James felt homesick at Thanksgiving, missing his family and friends. That year, taking advantage of the lull he invited Billy and his mother to dinner. Billy often stayed with Zack or Andy so it was normal for him to sleep over. However, the next morning, Billy was shocked to see his mother coming out of James' bedroom.

Having been brought up in a world with little privacy, Andy was used to the idea that adults had sex. Typical, 21st century, Western teenagers believed that it was confined to their age group so Billy blushed furiously and it was Andy that broke the silence.

"Will Billy and I share *lots* of new brothers and sisters?" he asked.

"Enough Andy." James snapped, "Don't embarrass guests like that."

"I'm not embarrassing you. You're already embarrassed" Andy exclaimed, "It's what people do so I'm saying that you don't have to be embarrassed."

"Thank you, Andy." June, Billy's mother, said, "What about you, Billy."

It was Billy who was the most embarrassed. Still red-faced, but desperately wanting to be as worldly-wise as Andy, he could barely nod and mumble 'OK' in agreement.

Mavis' comment made Stuart realise that their security could be about to take another dent. Dave's partner Sally had no idea of what he really did and did not care. He went off to work every day, provided a good home while she tried her best to look after it. After the worst possible upbringing her idea of family life came from TV and magazines, and were oddly old-fashioned. However, husbands worked in offices not in space and she confined herself to complaining about silly village gossip.

June and Billy would be different. Billy was already friends with Zack and Andy, and suspected that there was something going on. June would be far more curious about the village gossip and would want to know more about it.

If anything gossip had died down since nothing new was happening. Strange visitors still arrived. Everyone connected with Stuart had an extraordinary ability to speak languages but it could just have something to do with *all them computers* they had at the quarry. Even the worst of gossips, grudgingly admired Dave for looking after Sally so well and the more elderly gossips were careful not to say too much in case they lost the new bus service that Brian had arranged. James' romance with Billy's mother was far more interesting. It was new and it was something they understood.

Stuart did not think that confirming what they did to Zack's mother would not change much. Her suspicions were fairly close to the mark so by confirming them, all they would do, would be to stop her looking further and, hopefully, it might even settle things more.

When he settled down with Brian one evening, there was something else on his mind.

"It feels all wrong over there." Stuart said. "It's almost as if something has control of the opposition and calmed it down. All the different countries and factions should be scrabbling around trying to be the one that discovers the secret. It worries me that someone knows what we're doing and is waiting for us to finish. It's worse that I don't know who or why."

"And you can't pull out?" Brian asked.

"No," Stuart replied. "The three leaders are getting on better than I expected. The world press is picking up that the UK is suddenly more of a world player again. It's also picking up that East-West relations have eased considerably. What's really going to shake things up is when they announce a summit in the New Year. Including the British Prime Minister is really going amaze everyone."

"Except for this opposition that you're worried about." Brian said and Stuart nodded.

"I'm worried about this new world, Dave jumped to." Stuart added, "Why did it happen? What have we got in common with it?"

"That's two concerns." Brian said, "Any connection?"

"You mean, is something pulling my strings again?" Stuart exclaimed bitterly, "How would I know?"

"I didn't mean that but you're obviously wondering."

"I suppose I am but it's not like last time." Stuart said, "I understand how and why Stuart-2 reached out. It was more or less understood that he needed help and he was determined to get it. The three leaders are fairly typical politicians and only see personal advantage in cooperating but they do understand how unstable things are. It's just this nagging feeling that things are not quite right."

"If you think that they're waiting for you to finish then all you can do is wait and see. Relax and enjoy Christmas and see what happens then."

"I wish I could." Stuart exclaimed, "Relatives I can't stand, Zack's mother going shopping with Mum and James' new girlfriend, I'm not going to relax much."

"Go on." Brian said, "I've got bits and pieces, just fill me in on the gaps."

"Let me see." Brian said when Stuart had finished, "Gable is from another planet, Demetrius from ancient Greece and Andy from even more ancient Egypt and was rescued from a space ship. You don't own a car but you do own a space station yet your aunt sees you as a loser and you'll have a load of relatives listening to village gossip. Why don't you ask your Mum if you can invite Spock?"

"Very funny." Stuart retorted, "Just wait until Andy and Zack tell Billy all about it. We'll be packing and running then."

"I agree that telling Zack's mother will only confirm what she suspects and seems to be happy with." Brian said, "Let Mavis arrange something with Richard. You needn't be involved. You can't do anything about James' liaison until he makes it official and she moves into the village. You can't do anything about work until someone makes a move. I suggest you forget about it all for now and treat your relatives as just another alien invasion."

"I like the way you describe it as work. It seems so ordinary."

"It's your life." Brian said, "You don't take it for granted, you stay pretty grounded and I'm proud of you. Get used to saying work over Christmas."

Stuart suddenly smiled, "If she gets too bad then I'll book Aunt Maria an Atlantic cruise; on Titanic."

Brian chuckled contentedly, relieved that Stuart seemed happier.

Other problems changed. James decided to have Christmas at

home and invite June and Billy again. They would stay until the New Year. Christmas would be easier for Mavis but having to deal with June and Billy seemed more likely.

"Andy's worried." James confided, "He doesn't mind them staying but he's worried about letting something slip."

Stuart shrugged, "If he does, he does. Kids can feel very important if they have this tremendous secret and you must see something in Billy. He looks up to you and would hate to let you down. If he does find out, then we'll do it the same way that we did with Zack. Keep an eye on him and see what the Lizard planet makes of him. I'll be glad when this Christmas is over, though."

Stuart's sister arrived first on Christmas Eve. Stuart was duly waiting with the rest of his family as they greeted her and they then introduced Gable. Stuart looked at Tim, her partner. He seemed different to how Stuart remembered him. *Purposeful and more confident*, Stuart thought.

"It's good to see you, Tim." Stuart said, "Dad, how about you, me, Gable and Tim disappear to the pub for an hour while Mum and Sue catch up. I'll feel ready to meet Aunt Maria then."

"You may as well stay there." Mavis said, "We'll bring Timmy down to the children's party when Maria arrives."

"Great." Stuart muttered, "She'll be able to humiliate me in front of all my friends."

"Where's Brian?" Richard asked, trying to change the subject.

"He'll be there. Demetrius was worried about neglecting us while he was so involved with the preparations, so they're having dinner at the pub."

"Who's Demetrius?" Tim asked, "He sounds like a servant."

"He is, providing we do things his way." Stuart chuckled, "He's got a thing for Ancient Greece and even universities listen to him. Mum doesn't have room for everyone, so you're staying with us. If you want anything, ask Demetrius."

"He sounds a bit odd." Tim said, "Will he be all right with Timmy?"

"If you stand on his toe then he'll apologise for getting in the way. If an intruder threatened us, then Demetrius would slice his throat open."

"Oh!" Tim said uncertainly, "How about you, Gable? What's your story?"

"I'm an archaeologist and I work with Richard." Gable replied, "If we're not away I stay in Stuart's old room."

"Where are you working at the moment?"

"Terzon." Gable replied then thought, "It's a bit out-of-the-way, I don't suppose you've heard of it."

Stuart was almost panicking. All Tim was doing was trying to get to know folk. After just a quarter of an hour they were desperately trying to maintain their cover, and Tim was supposed to be the easy one. Stuart was relieved when he found Brian and introduced him.

"I'm pleased to meet you, Brian." Tim said, "I must admit, you two don't look gay."

Tim was as nervous of meeting so many strangers as Stuart was of breaking security. However, Tim was alert enough to see Brian wince but remain quiet.

"I'm sorry. That came out wrong. Stuart was telling me about Demetrius and that sounded so strange that I ..." Tim paused, "It's coming out wrong again. I'm sorry."

"I can understand." Brian laughed, "We might be odd but we're harmless."

Tim had the good grace to laugh as well but then Brian added, "Demetrius is spending Christmas day with Dave and Sally. He'll expect us to be up early so he can get away."

"I thought that he was coming to us." Richard said.

"He was, but Sally was getting in a panic because she couldn't cook a proper Christmas dinner and Dave asked Demetrius for help."

"Can't he just go?" Tim asked, "We can manage, surely."

"That's not Demetrius' way." Brian said, "Just try going in the kitchen when he's around. You'll understand then."

"So do we dress and sit at the table for him?" Tim asked.

"No it's usually dining couches in the andron." Brian laughed, "Don't worry. It'll sort itself out. Just remember that he'll be mortified if he doesn't make you comfortable."

Just then Mavis and Maria arrived and a new round of introductions began. Maria looked at Stuart who braced himself, startled to see tears in her eyes.

"At least you're not too busy to speak to your mother." she said, "You look well, boy."

From that moment on, the next two days went well. Even with visitors expected to stay for over a week, nothing seemed to disturb their cover stories. They might even have got over the crisis that sprung up if Sally had not decided that all of Dave's friends should come to a party and even then, it was not her fault. Again with Demetrius' help, she did a splendid job and everyone was relaxing and enjoying themselves when Stuart's phone rang.

Those who really knew what Stuart did, knew that he received very few social calls and that he only carried one for emergencies. They were immediately quiet, alert waiting to know what was wrong. Maria looked annoyed, believing that Stuart was about to abandon them for more fashionable friends. Stuart listened then glanced around the room.

"There's been an accident." he said, "I have to go. James, I need your help."

He switched to ancient Egyptian before continuing, "Stuart-2 is having some sort of seizure. Dad, try to contact Dr. Tobias please. The rest of you, try to maintain our cover, or what's left of it."

Unfortunately, Maria wanted to make amends for her uncharitable thoughts.

"Tim's a nurse." she said, "He should go with you. Give Richard the details and he can phone for an ambulance."

"We have a doctor on call." Stuart said, "Dad can call him. Tim's on holiday, we'll manage but we have to go."

As James and Stuart hurried down the street, they heard footsteps behind him. He turned to see Tim running to catch him up.

"It'll take time for the ambulance to get here." he said, "Maria went on about me helping if I can and Sue said it was a good chance to get to know you better."

Stuart was trying to formulate a reply as he heard more footsteps and Zack joined them.

"Your mum said that Tim might need a guide." he said then continued in Egyptian, "I think she meant that I should distract him."

Stuart nodded, "Good thinking. Tim, Zack works for us and understands our equipment, be guided by him."

Tim nodded as they hurried along.

"Shouldn't we be driving?" he asked.

"I suppose we should." Stuart replied, "I was thinking that we'd all been drinking. I could imagine being breathalysed and it all taking longer."

It was not strictly true. The walk should have given him time to think and the portal would have sorted the time wasted. He need not have hurried off for the same reason but it would have been impossible to relax.

"What language were you speaking?" Tim asked, "Why do you use it?"

"It's Egyptian from about 5,000 years ago." Stuart said, "We're not completely honest about what we do and we use it

141

because only we understand it. I don't want you along but what sort of man would you be if you didn't want to help someone who's been injured."

"OK!" Tim said, "I'll try not to get in the way and I won't poke around. How's that?"

"Nowhere near enough but it's not your fault." Stuart retorted, "Let's see how it goes."

Stuart quickened his stride and stomped angrily ahead. Zack joined Tim.

"We shut everything down while all the visitors were here." Zack explained, "He's worried about what he's going to find and about how you're going to react."

"I'm only trying to help." Tim said angrily, "Now there's this big secret that I'm not supposed to see. What about this guy who's been injured. Doesn't Stuart care about him."

"Yes he does care." Zack exclaimed, "Just play it cool, yeah?"

James powered up the portal and Stuart stepped through. Tim looked on, amazed at the optical illusion and still not understanding what was going on. Zack tried to explain that most of the portal had vanished because it was passing through multi-dimensional space but it was not registering on Tim.

He was still concerned enough for the injured man but nervous of committing himself to a 'disintegrating' portal. Neither Zack nor James wanted to hurry him.

Finally, he said, "If you're sure it's safe, let's go but I'd better go first, Zack."

"Trust me." Zack said, "You'll want someone at the other end. Watch my feet."

By the time that he arrived on Earth-2, Tim was probably more dazed than Stuart-2. He recovered as he saw the patient lying on the floor, quickly checking his pulse and reactions.

"OK, he's weak but everything seems all right. What happened? Where are we and what's this all about."

"Stuart-2 may have been, er, shall we say, attacked." Stuart-1 replied, "Not physically but by someone trying to get into his mind. As long as there's no brain damage, then he'll be OK."

"I was thinking of a stroke." Tim said, "I don't know that other stuff."

"What about an aneurysm?" Stuart-1 asked, "We're prone to them."

Tim glanced between the two Stuarts.

"You mean one that's ruptured." Tim said, "I doubt it but they can happen without anyone realising it."

"I'm OK." Stuart-2 murmured, still weak, "Someone was being pushed in and he was fighting to stay out. I tried helping but I think that I hurt him. I want to sleep now. I don't want to go to hospital."

Dr. Tobias arrived just then so Stuart-1 shooed Tim back through the portal, breathing a sigh of relief when they were back in the quarry.

"If anyone asks it was a false alarm. An animal triggered an alarm and a passer-by panicked." Stuart said, looking at Tim.

Tim nodded thoughtfully but Stuart was uneasy.

As they walked back, Tim remained thoughtful until he said, "You must be rich if you can do all that."

"In what currency?" Stuart asked.

Tim looked surprised, "How about dollars. The Americans must be paying you a lot."

"Why?" Stuart asked.

"All this space stuff." Tim answered, "Or do you supply the military? How do you make money out of it?"

"We don't." Stuart replied, "We don't need any."

"Everyone wants to be rich." Tim said, "How about lending me a mill?"

"What sort of mill?" Stuart asked, for a moment puzzled by what Tim meant then daylight dawned, "Oh you mean a million pounds. Sorry, no can do."

"Why not? You must be able to afford it. A story like this, must be worth millions."

"Do you want a loan or blackmail?" Stuart asked.

"I wouldn't call it blackmail." Tim said, "We'd just be keeping it in the family."

"Look, I only let you come because I was worried about the other Stuart. Just remember I can give you a hundred million then leave you stranded on an asteroid with no way of spending it."

"You wouldn't though, would you." Tim said.

"For Mum's and Sue's sake, we've just been called out to a false alarm." Stuart said, "You haven't seen anything and we've never had this conversation."

Stuart was more annoyed with himself than anything. He had been relaxed at the party, enjoying his sister's company and pleased that his mother was having such a good Christmas. The call had caught him off guard, otherwise he would have been much more careful in dealing with Tim. He was also embarrassed now. Despite worrying about everyone else slipping up, it was him that had smashed their security. Worried, he tried reviewing things as they trudged on in a hostile silence.

Demetrius considered himself in an alien world and was content to explore it in his own fashion. Although he had no interest in going elsewhere, he understood what Brian and Stuart did and how they protected themselves. Anything left lying around disappeared into Brian's office, which was always locked. Their main computers were off world and there was nothing on the local ones that would give any information.

The quarry was shut down and only members of their team had the passwords to power it up again. They had equipment in the old wartime bunkers but it would take a thermal lance to get in.

What few papers and computer files could be taken by outsiders like Tim, were about designs for new medical scanners and obscure observations of solar particles.

Just then Zack caught up with him again speaking in Egyptian.

"He may have taken pictures over there." he said, "I think he took a couple in the workshop but he was hanging on too tight as we crossed Resolution."

"Thanks Zack." Stuart smiled, "And we were worried about you letting something slip to Billy. We've had other visitors so the quarry doesn't matter. You're good with image manipulation, you can make up some fake pictures. I'll explain more tomorrow."

"What are you two jabbering about?" Tim asked testily.

"Zack was just telling me about some pictures." Stuart replied, "He makes very convincing fakes then shows everyone how he does it."

They trudged on in silence though Stuart could feel the anger emanating from Tim.

Back at the party, everyone was waiting for news.

"False alarm." Stuart said cheerfully, "Someone out walking their dog thought they saw someone fall but it must have been a trick of the light."

"So you weren't needed after all, Tim." Sue chuckled, "Stuart should have given you a guided tour of the quarry."

"Oh I saw enough." Tim said.

No-one else picked up on Tim's mood except Stuart's mum. It was Sally's night and Stuart was determined not to spoil it for her. From her point of view, the night was a great success, even Dave's parents congratulated her. As the guests circulated, so the others were filled in on events. It was the following morning that everyone, including Mavis, seemed to gravitate to the quarry.

"I shouldn't have invited them." she said, "I knew that you were worried, Stuart."

"I didn't bargain on Aunt Maria being so helpful." Stuart laughed, "That threw me."

"How serious is it?" Richard asked.

"Bad enough." Stuart said, "The security software's scanning the usual sources and I've asked Zack to produce some fake pictures. If Tim shows a picture, Zack shows an identical one, then shows how it was faked. It'll raise our profile, no matter how much we cover up though."

"I was starting to like, Tim." Richard said.

"So was I." Stuart agreed. "Then all the bits we didn't like resurfaced. Still, it could have been worse. That SS officer version of Dave could have turned up in the middle of the party."

"What do you plan on doing next?" Dave asked.

"Survive New Year Eve's at the pub." Stuart said, "I'd like to keep our equipment shut down until everyone's gone. We can slip back to Stuart-2's incident then. That's what I should have done last night."

"Ah!" James said nervously, "June and Billy might be staying for longer. I could put them off but…"

He trailed off looking nervous, if not bashful.

"No you couldn't." Stuart said firmly, "And congratulations. Let's get it over with in one go. We're shut down, so I don't know if we could disguise things a bit, have an open day and demonstrate our research into solar particles."

"What about the portal." Brian asked, "Everyone knows that we've got a great big tube in here."

"Shove a tarpaulin over it and say it was a failure." Stuart said, "We'll fit a console in the airlock and if anyone pushes it, we'll show them how much we tried to insulate it. I don't know, we save worlds, surely we can manage a little show."

"So what now?" Richard asked.

"We go back and entertain our guests." Stuart replied, "I'm sure Aunt Maria's wondering where Mum is."

"You've really impressed her." Mavis said, "She picked up that I understood the *foreign language* as she called it and thinks it wonderful that I'm so involved. When I said that we needed to come up here, she almost shooed us out the door."

"Let's not push it though." Stuart said, "We'll stay shut down and catch up with time warps later."

It was Zack who wanted to speak to Stuart after.

"A lot of guys at school reckon Andy and I are a couple. You know we speak those languages and we're always going off together. Some are pretty nasty but Billy stands up for us. He even gives us space to … you know but we don't though. We could let him go on thinking that if you like."

"It's like June and James." Stuart said, "If you are a couple then we'll have to accommodate it. If you're not then you shouldn't have to pretend or be embarrassed or humiliated just to help us."

"We both like girls," Zack said, "but there is something. Andy's got those problems down there. Well, it does bother him. He knows he should never have children because of the radiation and it makes him shy. Back in his parents time, having sex didn't matter but it was a big deal if a man couldn't produce children and it does affect him."

"And you?" Stuart asked.

"I could get a girl friend." Zack replied, "I'm sure Melissa Goldsmith's interested but I'd feel kind of guilty if I do anything about it and leave Andy alone."

"Thanks for telling me." Stuart said, "If you can get with Melissa then do so. We'll look out for Andy."

Zack nodded his thanks and hurried off to catch up with James and Andy. Stuart felt happier. On the whole, they had made good choices with their friends and there was only one family member who might cause trouble. Brian was waiting for him and took him into the office.

"Tim's shut himself in their bedroom while Sue's gone off in a huff." he said, "Maybe it was as well that I stayed behind, he tried to get into my office during the night."

"I need to use the computers and see what else he's been up to. I'm beginning to think that I liked him better as a doped up kid." Stuart said.

Brian smiled as he nodded in agreement.

"He certainly was in a bad mood." Brian said, "How's everything else?"

"Not bad." Stuart replied, "James is less modern than he claims so I reckon he'll be proposing to June soon. Honestly though, I think that we'll cope. Stuart-2 claimed that someone was being pushed in. That's a new development if he wasn't just panicking. I hate waiting until everyone's gone before I investigate but I can't see any way round it."

"See what Tim's up to." Brian said, "Somehow I think that the other thing will be pushed onto us. You know, Sue's taken quite a shine to Demetrius and young Timmy adores him. The three of them have gone round to Dave and Sally's place so that Aidan and Timmy can play together. I can see something happening between Sue and Demetrius. In other circumstances I'd say that it was a good thing."

"It'll never work though." Stuart exclaimed, "Demetrius even hates going into Howkbury and sis will be getting withdrawal symptoms if she stays away from London much longer."

While they had been talking, Stuart had worked on the computers.

"It's alarming what I can find out even without Terzon technology." he said, "With it, it's a doddle. He's been googling parallel worlds and warp drives. Most of it takes him straight into sci-fi. He's found one or two papers including one of yours. Oh here's a turn up; he's found one by a Viktor Levkova. I never checked to see if he existed in this universe but apparently he does.

He's also been texting two women. God, I couldn't say half that stuff to you when we're in bed. Oh and guess what? Sue doesn't mind because she lost interest in sex when Timmy was born."

"That's not the impression we've got." Brian chuckled, "I never worried about thin walls before they arrived."

"So he's a louse after all." Stuart said, "And I think that I might kill two birds with one stone."

"Careful." Brian said, "What do you have in mind?"

"I don't know yet except give him the scare of his life. He won't hurt Sue or talk about what he's seen, but maybe you shouldn't know what happens."

"No, I'd rather not." Brian agreed, "You know, I complain that you and the boys use the portal as casually as riding your bikes but it's quite something that you can. You're right as well, we gather masses of data about the fields and warps that we use."

"Yeah but I've just got a better idea." Stuart said, "When they're back in London, I'll clone his phone and text Sue and these other two, and they can all meet up together. Sue needn't know that I was involved and can sort it out for herself."

"That sounds better." Brian said, "Now if we're on holiday I don't intend skulking around in here all day. Set the security then let's head down the pub for lunch."

"OK. Let's pop in and see Mum and Aunt Maria first. There's nothing here so we can leave Tim to sulk all day."

Both Stuart and Brian were quite cheerful as they strolled into the village. Stuart even enjoyed chatting to his Aunt Maria until his phone rang.

"Sorry to bother you but Dave's behaving oddly." Sue said, "He's demanding to speak to you but he's calling you Stuart-1. Sally's getting a bit worked up but Demetrius says that you'll know what to do."

"OK, it's only a bit of stress. He's working for us all day and studying law at night. He says that he feels split in two at times. I'll be right round."

Stuart switched languages, "It's a jump. It was the best story that I could think of."

"Go." replied Mavis, "We'll deal with Maria."

As he hurried out the door, he heard Maria say, "What is going on? How come he gets all these crises?"

When he arrived, Dave was sitting comfortably drinking a cup of water. Sally was fussing over the children and only Sue noticed when he murmured, "Heil."

"OK, I'm taking Dave for a walk." Stuart said, "He needs fresh air more than anything. He's still not used to not being a drop-out."

Sue caught the humour in Stuart's eyes but Sally said, somewhat huffily, "He never was."

"Come on, Dave." Stuart commanded.

Once out of earshot, Stuart asked, "The SS officer?"

"Yes," David replied, "What's going on? I didn't know that I could think myself here."

"Neither did I." Stuart replied, "Stuart-2 had problems as well. Do you know anything about it?"

David was silent for a time.

"Brian Chapman is doing something and it's more than just building a portal. Can machines control minds? I mean let you jump like this?"

"We've used a combination of machines and er, specialist people to find people across the universes but to cause a jump? That's another step."

"And Chapman's taken it." David said, "I'm loyal to the Führer, I don't think that Chapman is and I'm worried."

"Supposing I said that what you do on your world is your affair but if you try to control other worlds then I'll oppose you."

"I understand." David said, "I should point out that any resistance to the Reich would be ruthlessly crushed but it doesn't sound quite right here."

"No, I suppose not but for now, we're on the same side so what's the story?"

"I don't think that Chapman is interested in the portal. He's building generators on the kitchen table and even without Robert's help I don't think he'd find it difficult. He's said a few things when he's annoyed and off-guard but at first I thought it was a daft way of talking about two projects because he talked about the other Brian's work. Then I found myself travelling, jumping you call it. Do you ever call your portal a TDT, a trans-dimensional transporter?"

"No. I've never heard that name." Stuart replied.

"He's barred us from the lab and he spends most of his time in there but I don't know what he's doing but he sometimes comes out of his lab terribly confused. He was rambling once and said, 'I got him because his boyfriend was dead. It's so easy to make them accessible'." Dave-3 shrugged, "He realised that I was listening and clammed up. Other times, after he's been in his laboratory, he stumbles out and just rambles. I'm sure it's Arabic or some barbarian … sorry, you wouldn't call them barbarians would you? Could he make someone vulnerable so that he could grab his knowledge?"

"On some Earths, I've been killed or injured and Brian's come close to a nervous breakdown." Stuart replied.

"So if he found a way of killing you, your Brian would be so upset that his mind would be open." Dave-3 said, "My Brian could get his knowledge. Is that possible?"

"Are you suggesting that last night's business was an attack to kill Stuart-2?" Stuart asked, "Brian-2 is not that advanced with his work."

"Could he be looking for you but getting confused because you're not always on Earth-2? Would that make sense?" Dave-3 asked.

"Anything's possible." Stuart said, "Earth-2 is a lot closer to your world, in a multi-dimensional sense it needs fewer field warps. Mentally it makes little difference but if he's using warp fields to boost his mind … Sorry, I'm thinking aloud."

"That's OK." Dave-3 said, "He went in there last night and sent for Robert. Later I felt really strange, almost as if I was going to make a jump but couldn't quite make it. Then I heard Robert screaming and the feeling stopped. I reached the lab just as they were coming out and Robert was white and trembling. He answered when I spoke to him but Brian told him to go to bed. He was still shaken this morning but he did seem better though. Chapman muttered something about it being a pity that I've got no reference point and stomped to his room. I've spent today holding Robert and wanting to talk to you."

"OK, please don't be insulted but you don't seem very SS like. In fact, you seem like a very kind, caring person."

"Ever woken up to see your body floating above you and you weightless?" Dave asked, "It's one hell of a shock. If I'd been sent to the Russian front, I wouldn't have questioned my training but I suppose that I'm just starting to think your way."

"That's cool." Stuart responded, "Daves do respond to the portal like that. Your reaction is extreme but it's OK."

Dave staggered and looked around, grinning as he saw Stuart.

"How did he cope with Sally and Sue?" he asked.

"Just complain about feeling tired and stressed because of studies and work." Stuart replied, "How about you?"

"Nothing, I was holding Robert and he seemed terribly upset. I think that Brian was in the laboratory and that's it."

"Tomorrow's New Years Eve then my lot's leaving on the 2nd. Then it's just James' guests and a planet developing mind control. We should have moved a long time ago."

"And that would have stopped a planet developing mind control?" Dave asked.

"You know what I mean." Stuart snapped angrily, "We've got problems piling up and I've got to wait until a load of visitors go home. Too many people know about us now."

"Tim's the only outsider." Dave said quietly, "You can handle him and then it's just village business again."

"Maybe, what's really worrying me is young Billy." Stuart said, "He's going to get very resentful if Andy shares this big secret with Zack but excludes his new brother."

"You mean it could cause more trouble not telling him." Dave said, "You trust Zack and Andy with a lot and it makes them feel very grown up. Maybe Billy would respond just as well."

"Yeah, OK." Stuart exclaimed, "James is the oldest one amongst us. Don't you ever feel that we should still be at training school and the whole set up should become more professional."

"Passes at the gate, armed guards patrolling around and an immigration desk beside the portal, you mean." Dave said, "How about us doing weapons training and we go charging through, guns at the ready?"

"OK, not that." Stuart conceded, "But we should do something. At least government sites wouldn't have three kids taking it all for granted."

"Zack has settled down at school and all his homework's up to date." Dave said, "We just bunked off until we could leave so are we going to discuss responsible attitudes?"

"OK but will you and James check the blocks in the computers. Just make sure that they're restricted to places we know are safe."

"He worries about Andy, and does it regularly." Dave said, "We do drop our guard but the basic security is still ticking away in the background. The worst Tim is going to find are plans for an advanced medical scanner unless he can break through Terzon technology."

"And Billy becomes a laughingstock with his wild stories." Stuart said, "OK I get it. Let's just get the next few days over with."

Stuart might have relaxed and begun to enjoy his holiday again but when they got back to Dave's, Sue was still there waiting for him.

"Right! Sally and Demetrius have taken the boys over to the playground." she began, "Tim's been in a foul mood ever since you all got back last night. Dave had his funny turn, you all speak this weird language so what's going on?"

"We're all a bit stressed." Stuart replied, "We're getting ready to launch a new medical scanner with Dr. Tobias and ..."

"Stop right there." Sue interrupted, "You're lying and I want the truth. What's going?"

Stuart tried again, "We do secret work. Tim stumbled on some of it and couldn't understand why we're not making millions. He wouldn't accept that there was still years of testing."

"That sounds like Tim." Sue conceded, "He's always after some dodgy deal. Are you going to tell me what it is or is he? I'd prefer a clear answer and not a drunken one when he's just rambling."

"If I get Mum to talk to you and even maybe show you, will you leave it inside the village?"

"That old village business crap. I don't know. It's not drugs is it?" she paused, "No, that's more Tim's line. Mum would have nothing to do with it. OK. Today."

"It's going to be difficult with Aunt Maria around." Stuart said, "I never thought that I'd feel sorry for her but she does so miss Caitlin."

"Caitlin's a selfish cow." Sue exclaimed, "I saw her a few times in London and I don't think that she even remembers her mother's birthday. You've made more of an effort with her than she ever did."

She thought for a moment, "If Mum's happy with what you're doing, I'll leave it, if it's that secret."

"Thanks sis." Stuart said, "How are you getting on with Tim?"

"Don't tell Mum." Sue replied, "You neither Dave, or I'll cut your balls off, I'm thinking of leaving him. He's got too many strange deals and too many secret calls. There's been a couple of nasty looking guys calling at the flat and it's scary. He's kind enough and he dotes on Timmy but it's not enough."

"It's between us." Stuart said.

"I wish I could come back to the village but I'd never find a job or be able to afford the rent." she said, "I've had enough of London and Timmy loves it here. He wants to go out every day to look at the animals. "

"I could buy a cottage and let you have it." Stuart said, "Bill needs reliable staff with the restaurant so busy. The clinic needs staff. It's out of the way and a lot of outsiders don't like the roads round here."

"You could buy a cottage?" Sue asked, "How come you're so rich?"

"Our secret work." Stuart said, "And I don't want Tim to know."

Sue nodded thoughtfully.

"Who'd have thought that my kid brother would have turned out so well." she suddenly grinned, "Thanks Stu. By the way, just how rich are you?"

"I don't know." Stuart replied, "How many noughts are there in a billion?"

"You wish." Sue chuckled, "Seriously, could you help? That place a couple of doors down has got a 'For Sale' notice up. It would be ideal."

"Pop round to Mum's." Stuart said, "Ask her to phone the estate agent. If anyone can get a viewing this afternoon, she can. Dave and I will keep Tim out of the way. Otherwise, you'll have to make another trip up here in the New Year."

Sue looked at him quizzically but hurried off.

"So much for not telling your mother." Dave chuckled, "I can't believe how easily that fell into place."

"Easy?" Stuart exclaimed, "Diamond mines on an asteroid, security taking another hit and a bit of emotion reading via the translator. I didn't need any of it to see how Caitlin had rubbed a nerve though and Sue opened up."

152

Dave nodded, "OK you sensed that things weren't right between them but you wouldn't have done anything if Tim hadn't rubbed you up the wrong way."

"I wouldn't have checked his phone." Stuart agreed, "I should have relied on the keywords like I usually do but I wanted to make sure that Sue was all right."

"Anyway, you've got time to consider this weird new world." Dave said, "Any thoughts?"

"Only that on that world Brian is more interested in the jumps and he's trying to control them."

Stuart paused, "Stuart-2 got his attention but possibly he's getting Stuart-2 muddled with me. Something like that. Now that you've jumped there twice, I reckon we'll end up there."

"You didn't want that." Dave said.

"Despite everything, it's been a good break. I'll tell you something though. You're more part of this set up than I am."

"Hardly, I'm just the back up." Dave said.

"No. Don't ask me why but you are the most stable, constant part across the universes. You can start off by coming at me with a baseball bat, your fists, anything but as soon as you go through the portal, you adapt. Me I don't even have to exist for it all to happen."

"That's a cheerful thought but I get it." Dave chuckled, "We wouldn't get into so much trouble without you, though. You reckon that Brians drive themselves to prove themselves. Do you reckon that this new one's got a bit twisted?"

"Anything's possible." Stuart replied, "We'll just have to see what turns up."

Chapter 8

It's not that unusual to be 'on-call' during a holiday. For Stuart, the biggest problem was that he was just not used to working around people who had no idea what he did. He sat quietly with Dave until Sally got back with Demetrius and the children, and Stuart wondered who had been more excited, Demetrius or the children.

Although not his first winter, Demetrius could still be excited by snow and played as happily as the children. Sally saw a proper family scene with Demetrius in the role of kindly uncle and accepted him. She saw Stuart as the boss who made Dave work odd hours, got him injured and made him ill and so, liked him far less. However, it gave him an excuse to make his goodbyes and head back to see what his family was up to.

"Sally says that she'll look after Timmy for as long you like." he said, "What's happening?"

"The estate agent won't consider an appointment until the new year." Mavis said, "John Davidson has been transferred to Cornwall. It's a shame really, they're nice people and they've spent thousands modernising it. I think Sue will like it though."

"Yes but what about the solicitors?" Maria asked, "You'll have to have a survey, insurance, all sorts of things. It'll take months to buy."

"Let's visit and see what Vicky says." Mavis suggested, "I bet David Bradley's sees it as another holiday cottage to rent out and has made an offer. We should at least try to stop him."

This was definitely his mother's territory so he and Brian headed to the pub for a meal.

As they chatted Stuart said, "I know that you disapprove but without the portal, I wouldn't have known about Sue's problems, let alone been able to help."

"And you're going to use it to speed the purchase up." Brian said.

Stuart shrugged, "It's the goons turning up at the flat that I don't like. I'm tempted to give her a panic button that'll get us there in seconds."

"Make it a modified translator." Brian suggested, "As long as she's wearing it, you'll be warned if something scares her."

"You approve?" Stuart asked.

"Not so much approve as understand." Brian replied, "You'll

help an individual with the same energy that you'd help a planet. That's what I mean about you being grounded. It wasn't beneath your dignity to fetch super-grease from Terzon to fix Mrs Bryson's gate and spend an afternoon painting it for her."

"I should have just replaced the hinge." Stuart chuckled, "The screws just wouldn't turn though and she was fussing around in case I gouged the wood. A proper handyman might have fixed it but I would have needed a laser cutter to take off the heads or a sonic vibrator to shake them loose. In the end, I settled for those grease packs that trickle in then swell slightly. Still, she gave me fifty pence for all my trouble so it was worth it."

"That's what I mean." Brian laughed, "You'll take as much care of a squeaky gate as a planet dying of plague."

"Squeaky gates are new territory and difficult. I know what I'm doing with dying planets even if they take longer but I'm glad you approve."

The conversation drifted on until they were ready to go home. Stuart immediately checked the computer logs and discovered that Tim had spent all day in his room or, at least, around the house using the Internet.

"He's emailed a couple of newspapers." he said angrily, "He's using those papers by you and Viktor to justify his claim. No-one's replied yet and one was unread so I've deleted it. I'm diverting all his emails to me but I'll forward all the harmless ones."

"How do you do that?" Brian asked but paused, "OK I don't want to know and the Terzons won't approve of their technology being abused like this."

"I'm not meddling." Stuart said with a grin, "He said that he wouldn't interfere and I'm helping him to keep his promise."

"OK I'll accept that but I don't think that the Terzons will."

With Tim being carefully watched electronically Stuart could relax again and there were no more incidents until the New Year's Eve party. Even Tim made an effort and everyone was enjoying themselves when Stuart approached his Aunt Maria.

"Congratulations." he called out over the din, "You've won a competition."

"I don't do competitions." she replied.

"You must have forgotten about it because the prize is an all expenses-paid trip to California. You'll even have your own personal assistant to arrange everything for you. There's a list of events already lined up in the envelope."

Maria sat reading the documents in the envelope with

155

increasing amazement sharing them with her sister who looked approvingly at Stuart.

"I can't wait to tell Caitlin." she finally said.

"You're going to be busy." Stuart said, "And you're always saying how busy Caitlin is. Maybe it would be better if your secretary contacted her secretary to set up a meeting."

Maria stared at Stuart before understanding then laughed happily. Caitlin would have to be very nice to her mother if she wanted to attend any of the functions that Stuart had booked for his aunt.

"How about helping me out?" Tim asked when they were alone as the crowd surged around them.

"Sorry." Stuart replied, "I'm not helping you."

"I'll go to the papers and tell them everything." Tim said.

"Go ahead. Tell them everything and give them the proof you've got."

Fury clouded Tim's face and he swung a clenched fist at Stuart's face. Stuart had not drunk much, and was now more cautious around Tim. He stepped sideways out of the way. Tim stumbled, completely off balance. Stuart caught him before he fell to the ground.

"I'll buy you a drink," Stuart said, "then you go and look after Sue."

"Fuck you, you fucking queer." Tim snarled, "What do all your friends reckon you do at the quarry. What would they say if they knew."

Bill arrived as James grabbed Tim.

"Time to go home, sir." Bill said, "You've had enough."

"Do you know what they really do up at the quarry?" Tim yelled.

"They can be spacemen for all I care." Bill replied, "I'd like you to leave now."

"Tim, will you behave yourself. Come here and sit down, now."

It could have been Stuart's mother speaking but it was Sue glaring angrily. Tim might have argued but Bill the landlord had completely deflated the drama of his impending announcement so he meekly obeyed Sue.

Bill was doubly pleased with himself. Tim's reaction had confirmed that the gossip about the quarry was true and he had stopped a fight before it had got out of hand. In the general noise and bedlam of a New Year's Eve party, few customers had even realised that there had been trouble.

New Year's Day was quiet and Stuart breathed a deep sigh of relief when their guests left the following day. At last, he could stroll down to the quarry without looking to see who might be following him. His relief faded when he saw Zack and Andy waiting at the gate with Billy.

"We want to talk to you." Zack said.

Stuart let them all into the workshop and made himself a coffee as Billy was shown around by Andy and Zack. It gradually dawned on Stuart that Zack and Andy were talking about how they cleaned and swept, and were trained to monitor the equipment they used.

"Yes but what does it all do?" Billy asked, "I know I'm only here because we're moving in with Andy and James."

Stuart thought for a moment.

"How's your school work, Billy?" he asked.

Billy shrugged, "It improved last term. My mates say that I'm turning into a geek like Zack and Andy. I mean, my old mates."

"And you're not getting into any more trouble?" Stuart asked.

"No, it's more fun watching Zack and Andy wind up the teachers. They learn all that stuff here, don't they?"

"And can you keep a secret like they do?"

"I think so." Billy said.

"OK, Zack, I'm visiting Earth-2 when Dave and James get here." Stuart said, "They aren't arriving for a couple of hours because I wanted to check Resolution. If you boys can do that and monitor the portals, I can get on with some other stuff. Don't worry Billy, you'll be consigned to hoovering up dust and cleaning filters but you might find even that interesting."

"Are you sure, Stuart?" Zack asked, "We did explain that a lot was secret."

"Where's your phone, Billy?" Stuart asked in his turn.

"At home." Billy replied, "Andy made me leave it behind. I haven't got anything else."

"That's not strictly true." Stuart smiled, "You've got three one pound coins, a fifty pence piece and some coppers in your back left pocket. We do have advanced security here so be warned, it can strip you naked on screen. Those files are deleted provided nothing needs attention."

Stuart paused, "And don't look so worried. It's Andy who shouldn't have a pocket full of chocolate who could be in trouble."

Andy looked guilty then grinned.

"It's just a snack. I didn't think that you'd let us use the portal, today." Andy said before turning to Billy, "Zack and I are going to strip down to shorts that don't have pockets. You stay dressed until you understand why pockets are a bad thing. Shirt sleeves and trouser legs do funny things as well so unless you want them all zipped up it's easier not to have them."

Billy nodded, not really understanding but he dutifully emptied his pockets and stood waiting. Zack and Andy stood, also waiting for Stuart.

"I'm the boss." Stuart said nonchalantly, "Underlings get to do the work so start cleaning. I go through when everything's ready for me."

Andy and Zack stared at Stuart for a moment before breaking into huge grins and hurrying to a console.

"We've never booted up from cold before." Andy said, "How about you work the controls and I follow the manual?"

Stuart watched curiously as Zack and Andy powered up the portal. He guessed that they had watched some film for Andy read out the instruction, Zack set it up and called, 'Check'. Stuart knew that he was never that formal but as long as they were taking it seriously, he was content.

Eventually, Billy hurried across, looking bemused, still unsure what was going on.

"They say that it's all working and they've set the coordinates for Resolution." he said, hoping that he made sense.

"So what's the hold up?" Stuart asked.

"I think that they want you to check."

"Why?" Stuart teased and as Billy stood uncertain how to answer, he added, "If they really need me to check then I will but tell them to double check everything then go."

Billy felt even more confused as he relayed Stuart's message. Both Zack and Andy glanced at him and definitely seemed nervous as they checked their work, glancing across at Stuart when they were done. Stuart ignored them, apparently more interested in his own work on a monitor reading and sipping his coffee. In fact Stuart had been monitoring their progress and although everything seemed fine, he was tense, desperately trying not to hold his breath as the boys prepared to de-materialise the portal.

It was Billy who shouted in alarm.

"What have you done to it?" he cried out, "Has it blown up or something?"

Zack jumped at Billy's yell but quickly checked the readings before calling out to Stuart, "It's ready for you to go through and fire up the main one."

"You're doing fine." Stuart called back, "The other one is preset. You'd have to work really hard to mess that up."

Stuart was more interested in the interactions between Billy and the other two. James had said that Billy was easily led, while Zack and Andy had a wonderful opportunity to show off. Instead, they had behaved well, setting a standard for Billy to follow. Hero worship often implies a childish fascination but it also described Billy's developing love of James, the first man to take him seriously. Billy would rather die than let James down so he was determined to fit in.

Until the leaders on Earth-2 were ready to announce their new collaboration, Stuart had little to do. Earth-3 loomed menacingly in the background but there was little that he could do about that either. The Terzons and the lizard people were trying to find Earth-3 in the same way that they had found Earth-2 but it was proving harder. The lizards tried explaining that since he had jumped much less than Stuart, Dave's imprint was much weaker but the explanation did not mean much to anyone.

As he watched the main portal materialise, Stuart breathed a sigh of relief. He was in no rush and sat quietly reading. Billy would be in shock as he came to terms with being weightless and again, it would be interesting to see how Andy and Zack dealt with it. His own console was still mirroring Andy's and Zack's activities so he settled back to watch. It was nearly an hour before there was any activity and then it was training simulations that were selected.

Finally, Dave and James arrived, with James looking around for the boys.

"They're up on Resolution." Stuart chuckled, "It hasn't blown up, Billy doesn't seem to have broken his neck and they've just simulated landing a probe on Ganymede."

"Andy told me that they just wanted to show Billy around." James said irritably.

"That's all they wanted." Stuart said, "I sent them up there. I'd forgotten how slow Earth is compared to Terzon. Earth-2 is still waiting for the ships to be built. There's time and I want to figure out who I can trust, once and for all."

James nodded, "OK but was sending them up there unsupervised, a good idea?"

"You know the security. Resolution's got body heat sensors and motion detectors. Billy didn't move from the portal hatch for a good fifteen minutes. From the movements I guess that Zack and Andy did some acrobatics in front of him and then he took a slow flight across the playroom. He took more flights so I guess he was getting used to it. I reckon that they all needed to get their breaths back because they shifted to the console and started doing probe simulations."

"Sorry about that." James said, "Andy was torn between looking after Billy and coming here."

"OK, I've been thinking about it all. They'll all be able to apply for a driver's licence in a year or so. They'll be able fly solo in a few months though they can't get a full pilot's licence so I'm less concerned about their age. The point is that legally, they're coming up to an age where they're expected to be responsible and the portals are monitored." Stuart began, "When we're somewhere strange we use a buddy system in case someone is hurt. I'd like to extend that and have each boy shadow one of us as much as possible. They log in their hours of training. We'll work out some training journeys and missions and impress the dangers upon them. We've talked about this before but we've got to deal with safety aspects more."

James nodded, "It's a good idea. One training trip could be visiting Andy's parents. They should be able to handle that one alone."

"Any thoughts, Dave?" Stuart asked.

"No, but maybe things aren't as quiet as you think." Dave replied, pausing for effect, "You see I had a long chat with that SS officer last night."

Stuart and James stared at him while Dave sat back, pleased with the effect that his announcement had created. Finally, Stuart's curiosity got the better of him.

"Go on." he commanded.

"Brian-3 is definitely up to something. He spends long periods in that lab of his and at times, Dave-3 feels very odd especially if he's dozing. He's had some strange but very consistent dreams where he's in a tent but it's very fuzzy. Now that he understands more, he calls them partial-jumps. Last night, I was in bed, I was warm, comfortable, just thinking about things and suddenly he was there."

"Where?" Stuart asked, "In your head, in the room, where?"

"He was just there." Dave said, "I had a picture in my mind, of me looking in a mirror and being dressed like him, but that's all it was, a picture. I kind of thought to myself, *what the fuck is going on* and seemed to get the reply, 'I don't know, you're the expert'."

"Hallucinations with a sense of humour." Stuart muttered, "That's new."

Dave chuckled, "Anyway we chatted and as the lizards would say, this is not of my world so I don't know how else to describe it. Brian-3 was out there but he was on his way somewhere else. Don't ask me to explain that either. I think he detected us after a time and seemed to get closer. Dave and I decided to break the link and it was easy. I got up and went to the toilet so I was wide awake."

"What do you make of it?" Stuart asked.

"I don't know." Dave replied, "I felt comfortable or good when I was talking to him but I started to feel uncomfortable or bad when Brian-3 approached. Anyway we've thought of an experiment. Every evening, I'm going to shut myself away and think of pomegranates. He's going to do the same. If we're in tune like that, could we form a link that could be detected."

"Your combined imprint?" Stuart asked and Dave nodded.

"It's an idea." James said, "At least we'll be doing something."

"OK, I was going over to see how they were doing on Earth-2 but the probe we set up is pretty stable. I'll just phone."

Earth-3 was a mystery more than a threat so far as Stuart was concerned so he was still more concerned about their activities becoming too widely known. Much to his relief, village gossip had passed Maria by and she seemed unconcerned or unaware of his activities. Billy would be closely watched and plans were in hand to discredit him if necessary so Stuart was content to relax and let the others get on with things. Although he was unaware of them, meetings were still shaping events including one in his own London, where some nasty members of the underworld had caught up with Tim.

"I need to talk to Mr. Allen." Tim said desperately, "I've got something that's worth millions. I can give him names, addresses and more."

The two thugs looked at him uncertainly. Since Tim could not pay what he owed, then he would have been lucky to have walked again after the encounter. Tim sweated profusely waiting to see if he had got through to them but there was little point in threatening Tim. It took less energy to punch him hard in the solar plexus and, as he doubled up with pain, scarcely conscious, bundle him into the boot of the car.

Mr. Allen was a loan shark, drug supplier and fence. Oddly, he was known as a soft touch on the estates where he did legitimate business. Mothers wanting to buy their child a birthday present might receive the cash then be told, 'Sorry, I've lost the paperwork. Forget about it', an honest business man falling on hard times would have very favourable interest rates. The pay off for Mr. Allen was that he kept below the police's radar and he had legitimate businesses to process his other earnings.

It was as the borrowers became shadier so the terms became harsher and Mr. Allen had very little sympathy for Tim's get-rich-quick schemes and gambling. Tim had got by through his access to drugs in the hospital. He did not actually steal any but pointed out flaws in security and more importantly the ordering system.

Recently security had been tightened up and the computer systems had been upgraded. Tim was close to being found out and was panicking while interest on his debts to Mr. Allen was mounting rapidly. The best that Tim could hope for, was a bad beating and the 'chance' to work off his debts. For now, it was important to convince Mr. Allen that he was not stalling or trying to escape.

"I know I disappeared over Christmas," he said, "but I got a whiff of something and I think you'll like it."

"Go on." Mr. Allen said.

"Sue's family lives in Yorkshire and her brother is doing research into something. I thought that they were just nutters up there until I found out what they were really doing. They're rich and sent an aunt on a holiday, which must have cost a couple of million. You can check that."

"And what are they doing?" Mr. Allen asked.

"It's do with space and the NASA must be paying them millions. You've got to see for yourself otherwise you'd think I was playing you for a fool and I'd be dead." Tim said nervously, "It's that amazing."

"It's certainly a better story than I usually hear." Mr. Allen said, "I can wait before I deal with you, but why would it interest me?"

"Because they need to keep it all secret." Tim said, "They'd do anything to keep it that way."

"Except let you in on it." Mr. Allen murmured, not convinced.

"I had nothing to scare them with." Tim replied.

"What else do you have to offer." Mr. Allen asked.

"I'll give you all their details, you check it out for yourself, and if it's as good as I say it is then we're quits."

"Take him downstairs." Mr. Allen said, "Don't hurt him but he's not to leave."

Meanwhile, the person most affected by their activities was still Billy. Neither Zack nor Andy had warned him that he would be weightless as they charged out of the portal. He was terrified and completely disorientated as he drifted out into the vast central cavern of Resolution. Zack grabbed him, pulled him back to the wall where he grabbed a handrail and hung on.

"What's happening, guys?" he asked fearfully.

"Everyone's a bit scared, first time." Zack replied, "You're in deep space so you're weightless."

"Quit kidding. What's happening?"

"Come on Andy." Zack yelled, "I'll race you to the other side and back."

They both launched themselves across the station with Andy succeeding in adding a loop to his flight so that he swung over to land on his feet and leap straight off. Zack had to cushion the landing with both arms, grab a handrail and pull himself round before launching himself again.

"How do you control that flip?" Zack asked as they anchored themselves beside Billy.

Andy shrugged, "Dunno, sometimes I land at awkward angles. How about going for a flight Billy?"

"What's going on and forget the space shit."

"I tell you what." Andy said, "Forget about where we are and get used to being weightless. Once you're used to that, we'll explain a bit more."

Billy nodded, still nervous but let go, then kicked. He drifted away from the wall spinning helplessly. Andy managed to grab one of his legs while Zack grabbed an arm and they gently pulled him back.

"OK," Zack exclaimed, "It's like any other jump while you're pushing. You press down and have some grip so you can control it. The difference is that you can do it very slowly so you can really control it. Try again."

Billy managed to cross the cavern, yelling triumphantly as he grabbed a handrail. It was later when they were all tired that Billy mentioned what was really on his mind.

"You don't mind Craig Nelson calling you queer because you're doing all this stuff. You don't hang out with Stuart just because he's gay."

"We do mind." Zack said, "We'd love to shut him up but he's got relatives in the village."

Billy looked puzzled not understanding the significance.

163

"They're incomers." Zack explained, "They'd rather mix with their snooty friends than villagers, so they don't know what goes on here."

"Ah! If Craig thought that there was something more, then his relatives might start nosing around."

Zack nodded, "It's not so bad. We get to do stuff. If we started worrying about Craig, then Stuart or James might think that we're just a couple of kids that couldn't handle it. They'd stop us using the portal so we couldn't go camping on the lizard planet or visit Andy's parents."

Some work did go on, though. Dave spent time on the lizard planet and even the lizards were intrigued by his account of chatting to his alternative self. The Terzons were fascinated but there was no way of controlling events to duplicate the incident. Although he visited the lizard planet every day for a week to try his experiment, nothing happened.

The night he went home and was tucked up in bed, he felt the other Dave and his trademark greeting, 'Heil'.

"Hi." Dave thought, "Where have you been?"

"I'd tried visiting but it was too rough."

"Huh?" Dave-1 queried.

"I can't describe it. Something pushed me back. I heard pomegranates though but it was a long way away."

"Is your Brian still working in the lab?" Dave-1 asked.

"Yes." Dave-3 replied, "He goes somewhere. At least I feel him passing by."

"OK and thanks." Dave-1 thought, "I hope we meet properly but we should break before your Brian comes nosing around."

"My turn to wake up. Seig Heil." and Dave was alone.

The lull in their activities seemed to continue. Incidents occurred, such as Dave's experiences but by and large they continued to relax until one day about a week later, Dave and Stuart were asked to go to the lizard planet.

"We've found their imprints." a Terzon scientist said, "More specifically your imprint, Dave. We then found a noise, which is the only way that the lizards can describe it and located their planet. It's confirmed that Brian-3 is attempting to control mind-jumps and he regularly visits Earth-2."

"I had a feeling that we'd discover something like that. He doesn't jump to Brian-2 though, does he?"

"No, so there's still a mystery for you to solve. How do you intend to proceed?"

"Ask you to see if you can learn more." Stuart said, "Earth-2 is managing without me. There's more and more talk of multinational space research and the three leaders want to allow time for the public to get used to the idea. It's their world so I'll go along with it."

"That is wise." the Terzon acknowledged gravely.

If Stuart was content for things to remain quiet, it was Brian who had an unexpected adventure. It began as he was leaving the house to walk up the lane to the quarry.

"Excuse me, Mr. Chapman." a voice called out, "Could I have a word, please?"

Brian turned, to see Mr. Allen standing beside a sleek limousine.

"Certainly." Brian replied affably, "What can I do for you?"

"I'd like to discuss a business deal with you." Mr. Allen said, "Perhaps you'd like to show me around your laboratory."

"No, I'm sorry." Brian replied, "I'm not interested."

There was a hard edge to Mr. Allen's voice as he said, "You misunderstand, we will be making a deal. You're not in a position to go to the authorities or cause trouble so you need someone to protect your interests."

"Ah!" Brian said, "I understand now. Just out of curiosity who put you onto us?"

"I believe you know Tim Richardson." Mr. Allen replied, "He paid off his debts to me by facilitating this meeting."

They all jumped as the front nearside tyre on Mr. Allen's car burst with a loud bang. They were still looking as smoke curled up from the rear tyre, which also suddenly burst.

"I don't need to go to the authorities." Brian smiled, "Not while Demetrius protects me. Would you like him to phone the garage for you?"

Mr. Allen's two henchmen instinctively reached for their guns but they hesitated, uncertain about what had happened. Mr. Allen was just as confused as he looked for an open window from where the shots had been fired. Only Brian was unconcerned as he awaited a response from Mr. Allen.

Mr. Allen nodded, still uncertain. Apparently Tim had underestimated Brian but where had the shots come from? Why did it look as if the hole was burnt into the tyre? Another thought struck him; why had he not heard anything? Even a silencer should have produced an audible plop at such close range. Looking for a chance to recover the situation he accepted Brian's invitation to come into the house for a coffee while they waited. It did not help his composure to be greeted by Demetrius, who wore a sword held by a strap around his shoulder.

"You should visit his forge." Brian said conversationally, "He makes top quality goods."

"Maybe he does." Mr. Allen said, "And I'm getting fed up with these games. We're still going to do business and you will regret causing those punctures."

"You never introduced yourself properly, Mr. Allen." Brian said, "But I do know who you are now and what you are. Tim has already been released and the contents of your safe have been sprayed with a purple dye. You'd better wear gloves before you handle anything."

Brian paused, then laughed, seeing Mr. Allen's increasing confusion, "I'm sorry but this scene is straight out of a third rate detective novel. The point is, you've done a bad job of threatening me."

"You're bluffing." Mr. Allen snapped angrily, "No-one knows I'm here. You couldn't have known I was coming so how could you have done it all in the last few minutes. How did you know about me holding Tim though?"

He leapt up, his hand reaching towards his pocket but stopped as Brian said, "Look at your chest."

He glanced down to see a red spot directly over his heart.

"Remember the tyres." Brian said softly.

Mr. Allen sat back down again glancing around but only saw Demetrius, standing, expertly wielding a drawn sword.

Just then Stuart and Dave arrived. Brian was startled by how they were dressed: black trousers, black shoes with crisp white shirts and ties. Dave took a notebook from his back pocket looking at Mr. Allen.

"Name?" he snapped out using a strange, possibly German accent.

"What's it to you?" Mr. Allen asked.

By answer, Dave slapped his face hard.

"Name?" he repeated, "Or do we take you in. I promise you, ve haff ways of making you talk."

Brian's coughing fit briefly interrupted the proceedings as he desperately tried to suppress his laughter. Mr. Allen tried to reach for his gun believing that Dave was blocking the laser guided weapons but Dave did not need backup. Mr. Allen found his arms grabbed and twisted as he was lifted out of his seat and pushed against the wall.

"Name or I break your arm." Dave rapped out sharply.

"Ronald Allen. You're not the police so you'll regret this." he replied. Like Brian, Mr. Allen felt as if he was in a bad, cliché ridden film and one he did not particularly like. He was in an ordinary house talking to someone who seemed more concerned at being hospitable than causing trouble yet he was being threatened by a laser guided... A laser guided what? He had no idea and what about the swordsman? There was a glint in Demetrius' eye that Mr. Allen understood. He was not going to argue with him because at such close quarters the drawn sword would be more effective than pulling out a gun.

"No, we are in charge here and do not tolerate interference." Dave said, "You haf already been fined for your insolence and you have a choice. Leave now or we'll punish you further. You can phone for a taxi while you walk out of the village."

"What about the car?"

"What car? You don't have a car."

Mr. Allen's confusion just got worse. Even as he had pulled up outside the house, he agreed with Tim's assessment that Brian would be a push over yet all his advantages had vanished. His two henchmen should have been able to deal with any trouble but they just stared at the red spots on their chests. They might still have reacted but they relied on their boss's confidence and they sensed his increasing uncertainty. Brian's living room stretched the length of the house. They would have noticed a breakdown lorry arriving yet while they had been distracted by events inside, the car had simply disappeared.

"Are you leaving?" Dave asked and Mr. Allen meekly nodded.

With his arm still being pushed up his back and Dave's other arm wrapped around his neck, he found himself being pushed past his henchmen then out of the door. Brian could not help himself as he politely offered his hand to the henchmen. Lost, without a clear command they meekly shook his hand as they left.

Dave returned, looking around then muttered, 'Seig Heil' before stumbling and bursting into fits of uncontrollable laughter. As he recovered, they all sat down but Brian could hardly contain himself.

"What on Earth happened?" he asked.

"You can focus and send messages via the translator better than any of us." Stuart explained. "We got your signal that something was wrong, slipped a probe back to the start of the conversation and got the idea. It's taken us most of the day at our end but we managed to identify him and check him out. We also caught the idea that you thought you were in some corny thriller and it seemed like a good way of handling it. We sent you brief text notes back, which is why you assimilated it easily."

Brian nodded and Stuart continued, "We used a probe to blow the tyres and phoned Demetrius to put the sword on. The only thing the sword did, was to add to the sense of unreality. They would have understood if we'd come in guns blazing so we wanted them dealing with completely unknown quantities."

"Yes of course." Brian exclaimed, "I get it. They might have simply come back with more men."

"That's it, and they might have talked." Stuart agreed, "We used probes for the red dots and we could have stunned them if things had got out of hand. We were thinking of doing that then dumping them out on the moors but Dave-3 turned up."

"Huh?" Brian queried, "You don't mean in the flesh, do you?"

"Brian-3 is doing weird things with our er, imprint." Dave said, "I've told you how we can talk when he's doing his stuff and we're dozing. You also know that when the link's established we can jump."

Brian nodded again.

"Okay." Dave continued, "We jump anyway when there's some sort of problem at one end or the other, and I was getting ready to tackle gunmen."

"I see where this is going," Brian said, "but go on."

"I can't explain it." Dave said, "I remember events as if he was in the room as well and we worked as a team. He's a really nice guy by the way and came up with the plan we followed. It seems that the Gestapo and the SS don't like each other and he was quite happy to ham up a Gestapo officer. The clothes were wrong but he agreed that looking like Earth-1 security guards would work better.

He also agreed that it would help if we were a bit theatrical and the idea was to make it bizarre rather than confrontational so I mentioned some clichés we get in war films.

"He was surprised that we could time travel but we used it to go shopping in Sheffield in the real time we had."

Brian laughed, "It makes sense now. So where's their car?"

"Back at his office with the tyres replaced." Stuart replied, "They didn't see us because of the hedge but we fixed generators to it and sent it back."

"Was all that really necessary?" Brian asked, "I'm not

complaining but it was over-the-top."

"It was meant to be." Stuart said, "If we'd just sent them packing they would have understood and come back looking to save face, revenge or something. Now, they've got to explain laser weapons, disappearing cars and a well-trained SS officer. How do I put this? Our assessment is that his assessment will be that we're backed by a super powerful organisation. Dave is obviously a professional soldier, we've got the latest weaponry and he'd have to take on this shadowy organisation. To do that he's got to figure out what we've got and then match it."

"If he says anything, all he's got are a few bruises to his arm to show for it." Brian said.

"If he does say something then he'll have to explain how his money has become unusable and how he lost a prisoner." Stuart said, "If he keeps quiet he'll save face amongst the other, what, gangs? I don't know how this gang business works but I bet there's folk that shouldn't learn how badly he's been defeated."

"I can see another bonus." Brian said, "Dave-3 did sound officious. If Allen thinks that this shadowy organisation has anything to do with the government, then he'll want to avoid it."

"After I explained that Tim might try to involve others, Dave-3 reckons that we should just have made them all disappear," Dave chuckled, "but we just want them quiet, not stirring up investigations into their disappearances."

"Right!" Brian said sharply, "What's this business with Dave and Dave-3? That's far more important. Dave, are you all right?"

"I think so." Dave replied, "He's gone now. I suppose the crisis is over. I guess that I was getting worked up and that drew him in. He was surprised that it was daylight so obviously, he did a little time jump."

~~~

Back in London, Tim was startled as his cell door opened and he saw the tip of a probe. Guessing that Stuart was involved, he allowed himself to be led out into the street and the probe disappeared. He had been missing for a couple of days and it was the last straw for Sue. He found her packing.

"I'm going home." she announced, "Stuart's buying me a cottage and found me a job. Oh and a messenger dropped a package off for you. Yes, I did open it. It's ten grand and a note saying that a deal had fallen through and Mr. Allen was not very pleased."

She handed it to Tim, "I haven't taken any of it. Just take it and go. I want us all to be gone before this Mr. Allen comes

169

around."

She closed the suitcase with a snap and carried it to the door. Tim's attempt to cash in on the portal had ended disastrously. What no-one knew was that Mr. Allen was too scared of the mystery organisation to do anything about Tim who simply grabbed his passport and headed for Spain.

~~~

Back home there were other problems but Dave's jumps was the one that concerned Stuart the most. However, Dave was not at all worried.

"It's weird but I can live with it." Dave said in answer to Stuart's questions, "I trust him and believe me, I know him better than anyone else. I really believe that he's seeing the world in a whole new way and likes it. I don't think that he likes all the things that he's done and meeting us means that he can't put them down to duty or something, any more. There's something about his father and being very confused. He did something that was his duty but his father was putting them all at risk. Good Nazis only do things out of duty so he couldn't admit to being concerned for his mother so did he do the wrong thing for the right reason or the wrong thing for the right reason? Either way, it's bothered him and now he can talk to me. It's when I feel his Brian that I get the creeps. Sorry, Stu. It seems wrong saying that about Brian."

"He's not my Brian." Stuart replied, "Think Brian-3 or something if you need to keep it in perspective."

"How about visiting Dave-3 for real?" Dave asked.

"OK, we can try but I think his Earth may be out of range from here." Stuart replied, "Would you mind if we waited until we find out what other hassles we have."

"That's fine. Was I a bully at school?"

Startled by the question, Stuart did his best to answer, "Maybe if someone needled you but you didn't nick some kid's lunch money. Why?"

"It's something I get from Dave-3. Kids need to be toughened up to prepare them for life or something. I'm not sure. He seemed surprised that Zack and Andy aren't scared of us – no, wary. I mean he's pleased not surprised that they're not wary. I understand what I'm sensing but I can't find the exact words. I also get a little bit of envy because he likes our attitudes. He still wouldn't consider betraying the Reich but he's wondering if it's the life he wants any more. He's getting more comfortable with the idea of walking away from it."

Although Stuart was not idle, the break seemed to be continuing. Since Tim had his own problems and was no longer a threat, Stuart kept a quiet eye on Billy, glad to find that he was keeping their secret. Billy was happy with the way that his family life was developing. He was no longer the outsider at school, his mother no longer had to make do in a series of poorly paid jobs and he loved his new family. He also loved the physical and practical aspects of working for Demetrius at the forge, and after being given a translator, learnt all he could about the Athens of Demetrius' time, helping with translations.

In its own way, his new life was as exciting as Andy's and he wanted to enjoy it to the full so he was not interested in the portal. He learnt the language that Andy, his new brother, shared with the others so he felt included and inclusion was all that he wanted. The portal provided uncertainty, and uncertainty was a reminder of his old life.

His mother became accepted in the village so she heard the gossip and like the rest, only partly believed it. If June had not been a strong, independent minded woman, she would not have coped in the drink and drug ridden squalor of the estate where they lived. It was almost a fairy tale fantasy to be whisked away by a handsome and wealthy man, with whom she was falling in love. She was intrigued by the gossip but it only added to James' mystery and allure. James had no doubt that once she had settled in, then she would be an equal partner, needing to establish her independence in some way. To be fully independent she would need to do something well away from James' work.

It was the developing relationship between his sister, Sue, and Demetrius that Stuart found the strangest. He was not worried; they were just so different. What he did not realise was that Sue had enjoyed London's social life but had come to realise that it was going nowhere. Falling pregnant had been a shock but for all his faults, Tim had tried to look after them. However, he would never settle, always risking their security for a gamble or a dubious deal. Demetrius was everything that Tim was not, loving, sensitive and, most importantly, steady.

If Stuart had any concern, it was that so much of their security depended on Zack's and Billy's mothers seeing a better life for their offspring. However, their hi-tech security had also stood them well. Christmas had not been an unmitigated disaster and they were still protected by the village's cautious attitude to outsiders.

It would all develop over time but for now Stuart was satisfied that they could continue in the village and he could focus on 'work'. Events on Earth-2 were still proceeding without interruption much to Stuart's surprise because he had expected some sort of attack from the Crusaders' allies.

According to Sir Ronald Cummings, George Rosswell was trying to build a power base but he had a problem. Talk of alien intervention went against the Crusader's fundamentalism so he needed to suppress the idea. He could play up the Prime Minister's increasing sympathy for communist notions but improved welfare was proving to be very popular so he was not getting very far but he was active.

On the outside, the Warriors of Saladin were trying to build their own alliance, involving nations and organisations that normally hated the sight of each other. However, for the time being, they seemed content to send agents to monitor events at the quarry.

That the agents were made welcome, confused everyone, Sir Ronald included but he did not complain. Less than half a dozen people knew that security centred around super advanced equipment from another world, so intelligence agencies around his world wanted to know the secret of his success. Despite his innate suspicion of anything he could not control he reluctantly accepted that, had the team from Earth-1 been at all malicious, he could not have stopped them. Consequently, he accepted the inevitable and contented himself with watching them as closely as possible while unhappily aware that they were probably watching him even more carefully.

So far as Stuart was concerned, it was time to find out about Dave-3's world.

Chapter 9

To a great extent, Stuart was visiting strange new territory. The Terzons had mentioned clusters of universes and he was visiting a different cluster. For Stuart, visiting a parallel universe was everyday while most people would struggle with the concept. Travelling to another cluster was an extra step, enough to make him nervous and curious at the same time. Dublin was a little closer than London from where he lived. To reach Dublin though, he would need his passport and would have to cross Irish Sea so London was a far simpler journey.

It was not only the *travelling to another country* feeling, it was that it was a Brian who seemed to be the enemy. Worse still, it was the method he was using and what his aims were. Was he trying to conquer a world and if so, which one, Earth-3 or Earth-2 or even their own, Earth-1?

Stuart had always tried to avoid mental jumps, yet Brian-3 seemed to be creating them. Stuart did not know how they happened nor did he understand much else about them. All he knew for certain was that they happened when there was some sort of crisis at one end or the other. He also knew that time had little meaning because they could happen before events occurred in their proper sequence.

Brian-3 could have caused or influenced previous jumps so Stuart needed to find out what was going on. He also needed help so his first trip was a clandestine visit to Earth-2.

On Earth-2, of the three national leaders involved, Chairman Chernekov had benefited the most from inter-dimensional contacts. His staff and the various agencies they spied for were desperate to plant an undetectable bug in his new office and were failing miserably. It confused them that it was now the most secure room in the Soviet Union and, probably the entire world. While they were happy that America would have just as much trouble bugging it, they were unhappy at being unable to keep an eye on the Chairman. They would have been even unhappier had they known that their efforts were thwarted by a fifteen-year old boy called Zack who arrived regularly to do sweeps. He still felt bad about getting arrested in Canterbury-2 so he felt obliged to ensure his project of looking after the premier was properly done.

His favourite arrival point was a park across the road from the Tsar Bell and Tsar Cannon. The two monumental castings fascinated him, the cannon in particular with its 89cm bore, and one trip he planned was to discover whether it was ever fired. Despite his Western clothes, he strolled into the Kremlin, showing his papers to suspicious guards. Then he was shown around by Chairman Chernekov and as they strolled through the museums and public areas, so startled and delighted tourists found themselves talking to one of the most important men in the world. Always the politician, Chairman Chernekov knew that it was a potent display of his new-found independence. It was also a display of supreme confidence, which did not go unnoticed by foreign observers.

Zack was a mystery that no-one could solve. His doppelgänger had been found in a village in England that was already the centre of mysterious going's on. His papers were faultless and he was always expected by the premier yet once again various agencies found themselves powerless to do anything about the Chairman's activities.

One other mystery bothered them. Being an old building the Kremlin had high ceilings so the premier's office could accommodate a portal though no-one knew that one materialised. The mystery was, why did the premier insist upon an open space without so much as a carpet to adorn it and why was the floor in the bare area becoming increasingly scuffed and scratched?

It was on one of his routine visits to check for bugs that Stuart joined Zack. Premier Chernekov looked surprised but greeted him warmly.

"My dear Stuart." he said, "I assume that this isn't a social visit."

"No." Stuart replied, "I'd like a base where I can investigate another world."

"Highly secret of course." Premier Chernekov grinned.

"Definitely." Stuart replied, "I had thought of just setting up in Antarctica like we did before. It could be well hidden but this time I'd like backup to be available."

"I'm flattered that you'd come to Russia." Premier Chernekov said, "How about Tunguska? You could be scientists studying the 1908 event and the nearest military base can be ordered to offer every assistance."

"That sounds ideal." Stuart replied, "It should only be for a week or so. How are you doing?"

"Once the space project is announced, my position will be secure." Premier Chernekov replied, "My enemies are beginning to mutter about having me removed but it is not serious yet, though young Zack will have to confine himself to this room. There's too many who want a piece of him now."

Stuart nodded.

"What do you need, Stuart." Premier Chernekov asked.

"A compound where no one can see in, living quarters would make life easier. Power and a lorry or something for the backup I mentioned."

"What about satellite detection?"

"We can hide from them. We just don't want close up scrutiny."

"Should we know about this other world?" Premier Chernekov asked.

"Not yet and hopefully never." Stuart replied.

Premier Chernekov stared at Stuart who began to feel uncomfortable.

"You're a capitalist lackey." he finally said, "Why don't you see it as your duty to destroy Soviet Socialist Russia?"

"You know the answer." Stuart exclaimed, "We do not interfere. Well maybe we do but if you or anyone else told us to stop then we would. Imposing your will doesn't end differences but merely suppresses them. Sooner or later they burst out again."

"That doesn't answer my question. Why don't you want to impose your will? Why aren't you a conqueror descending from the skies to enslave us?"

"Why? I'm an explorer. I don't want to be tied down running an empire."

"It sounds good to say it." Premier Chernekov said, "But to mean it?"

"If you don't know me by now then you never will." Stuart said irritably, "I can leave you all to it if you prefer."

"So you can be insulted by the suggestion." Premier Chernekov said, "Forgive me, but you seem just a little too laid back and at peace with the world. I wondered just how genuine your feelings are and I do look out for my country. Give me a week and you'll have your base. How close do you want the back up to be?"

"I had a similar set up on a US base once." Stuart said, "That was on a completely different Earth but I had a full-blown general acting as liaison with the president. I'm just not sure what's practicable here."

Premier Chernekov thought for a moment.

"Colonel-General Vinokurov is running the space station program and has seen the reports from Viktor Levkova. I could transfer him to you and you could offer him the same openness that you show Viktor."

"Not quite the same openness." Stuart said, "I won't let him jump the research that's being done on your planet though I'll expect that he'll try."

"You have a radical approach to espionage." Premier Chernekov chuckled then added seriously, "Before your intervention, my advisers agreed that the political situation was becoming increasingly unstable and they could not find a solution. In fact, they considered a pre-emptive strike to be the best chance of survival. Colonel-General Vinokurov was one of those advisers but did not think that the situation was that desperate yet. He fully understands the implications of the space station and more than anyone sees it as the last hope for peace. I think that he'll be a friend to you."

"Fair enough, and thank you." Stuart said.

Premier Chernekov picked up his phone, "Find out where Colonel-General Vinokurov is and let me know. Tell him that I'd like him in this office as soon as possible."

He hung up and they waited in silence until the phone rang again. After Premier Chernekov had hung up again, he turned to Stuart.

"We're in luck. He's in Moscow and is on his way. Zack, my boy, why not prepare some tea while we wait."

Zack cheerfully went to a table holding a massive samovar. He then fetched an ornate cup and set it before the premier before calling Stuart over.

"I've poured some in this cup and added water from the samovar. Taste it, then add more water until it tastes okay. You might want to add some sugar after but you can try the other stuff if you like."

Stuart was quite happy to allow Zack to teach him the art of Russian tea making until Colonel-General Vinokurov arrived. As was now the accepted custom, the general knocked then waited until Premier Chernekov let him in.

Colonel-General Vinokurov stopped, stared at the portal then looked at Zack and Stuart.

"Welcome Igor." Premier Chernekov said, "Come and meet the source of our great venture. Stuart, your problems may seem more real if we visit your village pub. I'd suggest Mars but I still suffer from balance problems."

Colonel-General Igor Vinokurov looked on bewildered and

Premier Chernekov laughed.

"I'm not mad. I have been to Mars and I do suffer from space sickness. You are about to assume duties and responsibilities that nothing you have ever done before, could prepare you for. Are you ready, my friend?"

Still, Igor looked uncertain.

"Stuart, we'll go through. Zack is an excellent guide so he can bring Igor along. I do know that he will need time to accept it all."

Stuart was happy to go along with the arrangements. He agreed with the premier's opinion of Zack for the boys loved to show off their knowledge and show that they were part of the team. As James said, it was something that they could do without blowing up the universe.

Premier Chernekov was well into his second whisky when Zack and Igor arrived. Despite his years in military service, Colonel-General Igor Vinokurov was visibly dazed, almost trembling as he sat down.

"I must return." Premier Chernekov said, "I have an appointment with the Israeli ambassador at four and if I stay then I'll forget the briefing I was given this morning. I can find my own way back and I'm sure James will work the portal for me. Colonel-General Vinokurov, I believe that your mystery is about to be solved."

Igor was not really accepting what had happened to him let alone understanding what was needed of him and he looked startled when Billy and Andy arrived. He recovered quickly then looked at them thoughtfully.

"Hallo you two." he said reaching for his wallet and taking out a picture, "I wondered if I'd ever see you again but I kept my promise."

He looked around, "this is where we took that photograph, isn't it?"

Billy in particular looked puzzled but Andy was a seasoned portal user. He studied the picture, carefully.

"I don't think that we've taken it yet." he said, "The sun's not in the right place."

Billy and Igor looked equally puzzled while the others waited.

Finally, Billy said, "I don't get it."

"Zack's always got a camera with him," Andy explained, "He's going to take it."

"Time travel?" Billy asked, "He told me that the pictures of Santa Maria and Christopher Columbus were real but he was only kidding right. They're fakes. He's got all that software for image manipulation."

"The originals aren't fakes." Stuart said gently, "It looks as if you're going on a training trip." Stuart continued, "You should find it interesting."

"Do I have to?" Billy exclaimed, "I don't like that space station thing."

"Well, you could let all space and time unravel." Stuart said, "Well, not really, we'll manage something but it would help if you went along with it."

The decider for Billy would be that James would know that he had chickened out so very reluctantly he said, "It's okay. I'll help."

Despite having become a Colonel-General through his ability and intelligence, Igor was struggling to accept events. The arrival of Billy and Andy had reminded him of an odd incident the day before he had been told about the space station that his country was building.

The incident had niggled ever since though he had resigned himself to never finding the answer. He now had the chance but only if he could accept his present surroundings and he needed to solve mysteries, even niggling ones.

Later that evening, Stuart settled down with Brian.

"It's not Billy and Andy's fault," he said, "but kids seem to screw up the time-line. I still think that I should stop them."

"You've said yourself that they've never tried overriding the blocks in the computer. They're proud of being part of the team and they make excellent guides." Brian said, "I know you had trouble with the Darrington boys but it's probably coincidence that you're dealing with another batch."

"I hope so." Stuart said, "Zack and Andy do try to be careful but don't you think it's strange that we've got all these kids hanging around?"

"I thought you were a kid when I first met you but I was impressed because you had such an enquiring mind though I never imagined you as a scientist but you excelled yourself as an explorer." Brian said, "Andy and Zack are probably more curious because they're younger and don't forget, Billy's going his own way."

"So you don't think it odd then?" Stuart asked.

"I'd say that you need a youngster's imagination to take it all in." Brian said, "Tim saw it as a money making scam but teens are a blank book and see the whole picture."

"So I let Andy and Billy finish this time loop. The thing I

don't get is who thought it up in the first place?"

"I dare say that you could find an anomaly or a blister where it starts and ends. I wouldn't look though; answers usually result in more questions."

"I wish I'd just sneaked a base in their Antarctica like I did before on that other world." Stuart said.

"Are you worried about a Nazi invasion?" Brian asked.

"The thought's there." Stuart admitted, "I know it's silly but I couldn't help wondering."

"Not silly but probably not your best decision." Brian said, "And I hope that I don't have to eat those words."

"Okay then." Stuart said, "By the way, can we destroy the entire space-time continuum?"

Brian laughed, "I don't want to know but I suggest you play out this loop as it stands."

Stuart nodded contentedly, happier about the task ahead. He never did discover why Colonel-General Igor Vinokurov's car developed a puncture on a deserted country road near Moscow, neither did he discover why the jack was missing. Maybe he was just lucky being able to exploit the incident but he did wonder.

Igor was more annoyed that he was in a radio black spot and could not phone for help. It was definitely odd that two boys wearing Western type clothes should appear out of the woods carrying a jack. At first, he was concerned that it was a kidnapping or a hijack but it did not make sense. The sooner he was on his way again the sooner he would be safe so the jack was a godsend. He was suspicious enough to wonder if they were planting a tracker or a bug but he could have the car scanned as soon as he got to a base. It was a warm night, they wore t-shirts and jeans and apart from the jack they weren't carrying anything. There was no way that they could be carrying a bomb or a gun.

The boys knew what they were doing and quickly changed the wheel while Igor watched them, making sure that he never offered them his back.

"Thank you boys." he said as he took out his wallet and offered them money.

"We don't want paying." Andy said, "But will you do something for us. Don't worry, it's nothing bad."

"Tell me first." Igor said, now very suspicious.

"Keep this photograph until you need it." Andy said.

"Why would I need it?" he asked, studying it, "What's going on, who planned this and why fake this picture?"

"Please." Andy said, "We can't answer any questions now but will you keep it in your wallet? If you want to make sure it's harmless, you can show it to the person who's offering you a job but just keep it with you. You'll be busy with a project for a time and then an even more amazing one will come along and the photo will reassure you."

Igor was tempted to arrest the two boys but he hesitated. With or without them he could have been shot by a sniper. They did not act concerned, wary of him perhaps but not tense and ready for a fight so it was all very puzzling.

"Did you cause the puncture?" he asked.

"I don't know." Andy replied, "There's stuff no one can explain."

Clearly, the boy was telling the truth and it was a thoughtful answer, not the automatic, strong denial he was expecting. It was late, he was tired, he wanted to be ready for the meeting with Premier Chernekov and it was better to just get away from there.

"Do you want a lift?" he asked.

"No thanks." Andy replied, "Our ride will be here in a minute."

It was an extra reason to get away. They were waiting for a vehicle with an unknown number of occupants.

He nodded, "Thank you boys and I'll honour your request. Good bye."

The road remained deserted, no oncoming traffic and no sign of being followed. He reached a busier road and breathed a sigh of relief as he drove towards Moscow. Now that he was safe, he realised that he should have been more suspicious but he had felt vulnerable standing in those woods.

The next day, he listened with increasing amazement as Premier Chernekov described the space station project that he was being assigned to. He had not picked up on it at the time, but it occurred to him that the boys knew about it but they had mentioned an even more amazing project. Seeing the security threat he described events to the Premier and showed him the picture.

"They're no threat and I suggest that you do as they say. You'll be helping to bypass the two biggest rocket programmes ever conceived and that's enough for you to worry about now."

Igor was put in charge of building the station and recruiting crews, training them but with little idea of how it would be put into practice.

When Stuart asked him for help, Premier Chernekov

remembered the picture and selected Igor.

Now as Igor sat waiting for the mystery photo to be taken, it galled him that teen-aged boys should be able to cope with events better than him. He had to think it through and the photograph provided him with a logical problem. He knew that the picture would be taken and would be in Zack's possession until it was printed off. A copy would then be given to Andy and Billy.

He thought about the boys' reactions. Billy was as uncertain as Igor was himself. Andy just accepted it, no, he understood time travel and this was a minor incident. He glanced at Andy again who still seemed unconcerned.

Once the boys had the photo, they would take it back to the puncture and then give it to him. Igor would then carry it forward to the present day. Satisfied that he was catching up, he was confused again when Stuart asked about the boys' trip. Of course, it was the first time that they had met him, for them it was the start of the picture's journey so he explained and only then did Andy look worried.

"What's a jack? I don't know how to use one." Andy asked then grinned cheekily, "I can repair a spaceship and a reed boat but neither of them had wheels."

Igor assumed that it was some strange teenage joke but his sense of reality slipped again when Stuart replied, "At least there's no radiation."

Andy grimaced, leaving Igor to wonder just where did Andy come from.

"We'll show you." Stuart added, "Perhaps Igor would take a break from training cosmonauts and let you practice on the actual car."

At least teaching teenagers about car maintenance was ordinary and he nodded. He was adapting so when Stuart explained what he wanted and why, it almost seemed ordinary and he thought nothing of it when Stuart gave him a phone number to ring.

~~~

Stuart remembered setting up a temporary base in the US and expected considerable opposition from the base commander so he was startled when Major Borodin shook him warmly by the hand and personally led him to a hangar.

"Colonel-General Vinokurov says you can be trusted. There're all sorts of rumours about the work he's doing but he doesn't tell me, even if we were room-mates at Dzerzhinsky."

Stuart knew that he was referring to a military academy,

getting the impression that the two officers were close friends.

"This will do fine if you don't mind us beefing up the security a little." Stuart said.

"Of course. What can we do?"

"I'd like to seal up all the openings except for one." Stuart said, "Could you set up an outer perimeter, say ten metres from the hanger and clear anything where people could hide."

"That's routine. Anything else?"

"Once we're set up I'll show you what we're doing." Stuart said, "Then I can explain why I'd like military support in the background."

Major Borodin shrugged, "Igor says that I am to trust you and I trust him. You can phone my office when you're ready."

Major Borodin left Stuart to contemplate his new base and returned to his office. For the next few days, nothing seemed to happen. No equipment arrived, no personnel and to all intents and purposes Stuart was trapped inside an empty building.

It was only when Igor arrived and Stuart took them to the hangar that Major Borodin discovered that the hangar had been transformed. Part of it housed a peculiar tube like device mounted on gimbals, another part resembled a computer lab while yet another part consisted of a comfortable staff room. Stuart greeted him and invited him to sit.

"OK." Stuart said, "I can't tell you much at this stage but the key to the space station project is tied in with the technology that brought all this equipment here. For us it is a forward base where we can reconnoitre a potential enemy. There's a slight chance that this enemy could turn the tables on us and come pouring in here. I don't really expect it to happen but I like to feel covered."

"I should at least explain to Major Borodin what I know." Igor said, "A trip through your device may help. It'll make the threat seem more real."

"No problem. Once this particular project is complete then you won't have any more access to us, until your own people develop it."

"And that's being done in England." Colonel-General Vinokurov said.

Major Borodin started in surprise but Igor just grinned.

"That's a breach of Russian security not Stuart's." he chuckled, "I need Chairman Chernekov's permission to tell you more about that project."

Stuart was satisfied though, pleasantly surprised at the

friendly reception he had received. Finally, he felt ready and called his friends together.

"You know that I've wanted the dust to settle from Christmas before I tackled anything new. Visiting Dave-3's world is different. Ever since we started with clusters of universes I've wondered whether there's any sort of physical boundary. The best answer I have so far is that all the universes should be equally spaced but they exert a slight attraction to each other. They cluster together leaving gaps, each universe influences the others in the cluster so that the clusters have unique characteristics."

"You mean that Dave-3's cluster is one where Nazi Germany dominates and all the universes in it are variations of that?" James asked.

"I don't know about the Germany bit because it could be one where telepathy is more common and the lizard people could play a bigger part instead of being the exception."

"Okay so it's all too complicated even for you." Dave laughed.

"We're talking about an eleven – twelve dimensional continuum. I see the maths but I can't visualise it much beyond one dimensional universes in a three-dimensional box."

"Straws in a box, you've said before." Dave said, "And if they were standing upright and started sticking together then there'd be small gaps between the stuck together clusters. You're worried about jumping those gaps, right?"

Stuart nodded, "I'm not sure but I think every other universe that we've been to, has been in our own cluster and we're towards the centre of it. Our new base is in a universe near the edge. Again, I think of it as the water's edge and we've got to send a probe over the sea to a new land."

"But instead of being flat, the sea's ten dimensional." James said.

"It's working out to about eleven." Stuart said, "The maths is still tricky enough to boggle the human mind."

"The maths' not difficult anyway, is it?" James asked.

"Not once it's in the computers." Stuart replied, "It's interpreting the raw data that's difficult but once we've adapted the basic formulae, it's not easy but it's routine. Zack and Andy type in the coordinates, follow the safety procedures and don't care whether they're visiting Ancient Egypt, a distant galaxy or a parallel world. Brian says the same about me and it's true. I'd hate to be stuck in a single universe or a single time, let alone on a single planet. Oh, and

I don't want the boys visiting this site. It's too close to the frontier."

"Or the seashore because you're worried that they'll drown." Dave said.

"Only in the eleven-dimensional sense." Stuart chuckled, "Calling it the Continuum Sea does make it sound more real and more dangerous than an eleven-dimensional matrix or something. I know, I'm labouring the point but the Continuum Sea is something new even if it's only us that understands why."

"And you're worried about it." James said.

"The worst case for me, is that their Brians are all evil, trying to control universes. I'm not even sure if visiting is a good idea. That's why I keep putting it off."

"Supposing I said that Brian is basically good and responds to his surroundings." James said.

"That applies to all of us." Stuart said, "Except for me. I seem to be dead on a lot of worlds, I don't get a chance to be evil."

"Let's set up a probe." James said and Stuart reluctantly nodded.

Despite Stuart's obvious reluctance, entering the coordinates proved to be routine as they followed their normal procedures until the probe rested among some rocks near the top of the quarry.

"It's all wrong." Dave exclaimed, "There's no flagpole and no armed guards on the perimeter. Brian insisted on them being kept outside the quarry."

Suddenly an alarm rang and troops rushed out of a barracks. Stuart and the others were not worried until they lined up pointing their weapons directly at the probe but it was James who first sounded alarmed.

"Whoa!" he exclaimed, "Something's pulling the probe. If I de-materialise, I might drag whatever it is here. I'm blowing it."

The explosion was in the tip but was powerful enough to damage the compartment behind it which held the field generators. The remains of the probe reappeared, still smoking.

"It was me." Dave said, "I knew exactly where to look and what to do."

"You mean, Dave-3." James asked.

"No!" Dave replied, "Dave-4 possibly but not 3."

"God, more of you." Stuart exclaimed.

"Hang on." James said, "Something's showing on the instruments."

"How do you mean?" Stuart asked.

"Maybe it's that." Dave said looking at the landing area.

A probe or a portal had materialised. Stuart was not sure what to call it for it was bristling with guns and cameras. Even as the guns trained on them so their own portal shifted blocking it.

Stuart glanced at James who was concentrating on the controls.

"Everyone outside, get some troops in here." James yelled but just as suddenly the probe disappeared. Stuart breathed a sigh of relief.

"Stuart, get those troops and a bazooka." James commanded, "Move it."

Stuart jumped, recovered, and picked up a phone. Moments later troops poured in through the door followed by Major Borodin.

"Cover the portal." James ordered, "If anything appears in that area, open fire. Stuart, get over here. You too, Major Borodin."

James replayed a video of events from one of the cameras they had installed.

"OK, It's only a gut feeling but I reckon it was pretty crude compared to ours. Our portal started disrupting their fields as it moved in, that's why it de-materialised so quickly."

"How come you moved so fast?" Stuart asked, "It was almost as if you were expecting trouble."

"I used to be a soldier." James explained, "You don't think weapons or invasions but I've done some simulations. That blocking move is under 'jamesdef7'. 'Jamesdef1 runs in the background and looks for portal signatures. Remember I lived in a time that office mainframes took up a whole floor and I'm still not used to computers. I just wanted to be sure that the software worked properly before I told you."

"It seems that it does." Major Borodin chuckled, "You must be older than you look if you worked with that sort of equipment."

"Time travel." Stuart said tersely, "Can your programs analyse their fields as well as detect them?"

"No, it records it though and I've got our regular stuff working on it."

"I knew that we shouldn't have tried to cross the Continuum Sea." Stuart exclaimed, "I just couldn't put my finger on why."

"You know what you're talking about and I don't." Major Borodin said irritably, "If you'll excuse me, I'll go somewhere I can be useful."

"I'm sorry, Major." Stuart said, "This is new to us as well. There's a potential enemy who's just waved guns at us, and we need to learn more but they can detect our probes and I've just discovered that we have a similar capability. I'm not sure what happens next."

"Well the military response would be to send in a reconnaissance party. Whatever happens, we must have intelligence."

"It makes sense." Stuart agreed, "I'm not looking forward to it though."

"No, I said send in a team." Major Borodin said, "It's high risk and we cannot risk you being captured."

"The Major's right." James said, "I should go and maybe take Dave. Don't forget, you may be the objective."

"You may have to go, Major Norton." Major Borodin said, "But you need to brief your colleagues on the defences that you've created and that will take time. Would it be quicker to brief me on what to look for."

"Okay." Stuart said, "James, carry on with the analysis. Dave take Major Borodin's team to Mars then to our quarry. Make sure that they understand what they're looking for."

Dave nodded, "I could go with them."

"Definitely not." Stuart said, "I don't want to explain to Sally how you got wounded again."

"And I would not take you." Major Borodin said, "You are not a trained soldier. My men know how to respond, instantly."

Dave nodded in grudging agreement.

"How long do we have to train, Stuart?" the major asked.

"I don't know." Stuart replied, "Assemble your team, allow Dave to demonstrate our equipment and we'll take it from there. You've already got an idea of our capabilities but the rest of your team will need time to get used to it."

As Major Borodin hurried off, Stuart turned to James.

"How's the analysis doing?" he asked.

"For once it seems to be easy." James replied.

"Seems to be?" Stuart queried.

"Thermal emissions are high enough to suggest vacuum tube, I mean, valve operation. That indicates that the device was just a probe but was larger to accommodate much bulkier equipment. The CCTV cameras had copper wire feeds and not fibre optics like ours and may have had transistor technology so it was easy to pick up on the signal. I'd put their technology as about the sixties with some odd quirks. For the same reasons, their field generators were easy to read and they operated several levels below us. They were far cruder with considerable resonant problems. To be honest I reckon that they latched on to our probe and it towed theirs along."

"Is it one of the quirks that they could detect our probe and latch on to it?" Stuart asked.

"There was a gadget on their portal, it was bulky and took up enough space to be considered important and it had the right energy signals."

"So it was a weapon, do they confine their use to attacking other countries or does it have other quirks?"

"I don't think that it's much good for anything." James said, "Gravity causes time displacement. We've done some funny stuff with it but I don't think that they stand a chance of controlling it across a planet."

"The resonance problem." Stuart said, "You're also saying that they can't do controlled time travel which is a relief."

"You're the expert." James said, "You should be able to make more of it."

"Brian would never have considered operating a probe until the resonance problem was completely sorted." Stuart said, "It would leave too many variables."

As Major Borodin returned Stuart added, "There's three things that we need to know; one, their electronic capability, two their bomb making capability and three, their detection capabilities. James, make a start with a probe high over their site. Just look for any sort of activity. Major, we can do a lot with electronic surveillance but this is different. We need a close up look without any portal signatures. That means dropping you off some distance from the quarry and only leaving you a phone for contact."

"I understand." Major Borodin said, "I'll prepare a report for Colonel-General Vinokurov and send it before I leave. I will make it clear that you have genuine concerns and I agree that they need to be addressed."

Stuart nodded his thanks, accepting that he should not be involved in the operation. He expected Dave to be more excited though.

"How much time do we spend telling people about the portal and training them?" he asked, "It's just another intake. I wish I could go with them though."

"No way." Stuart exclaimed, "You jumped okay to Dave-3 but this new one is a complete blank. He may be so different that you've got nothing in common. You can't risk being captured by him."

Dave nodded in reluctant agreement.

"Remind me." he said irritably, "What's the Russian for 'Has it blown up'? I'm sure I'm going to hear it a couple of times."

Despite his complaints, Dave was very patient with newcomers and did not hurry the team that Major Borodin assembled. De-materialising portals, being weightless, the slow realisation that they were on Mars, all took time to understand. Even Major Borodin needed time to accept time travel.

As soldiers planning a covert operation, the strangest part was that they could explore the terrain, strolling across it as tourists, even visiting a pub while they compared notes, courtesy of trips to Stuart's world. Stuart and their friends often found their situation surreal or bizarre but the soldiers could not easily accept just how their perception of the universe had changed. However, if the soldiers were struggling with their new environment then they learned to respect Stuart and Dave who were completely at home with it.

"We have no idea why our coordinates were so far off." the Terzon scientist said to Stuart when he visited them. "It was a bad mistake and we have no idea of how it happened."

"Will you carry on looking for Earth-3, please." Stuart said, "We'll study Earth-4 then decide what needs to be done."

"Very well." the Terzon replied, "Do you really need to send a team there? Surely the probe will tell you everything that you need to know."

"If I knew what we were looking for, then probably not." Stuart replied, "I suppose I'm thinking about the stuff that we don't know about and you probably find that illogical."

"Curiosity is an emotion which we allow ourselves." the Terzon scientist replied, "Seeking something to be curious about, is a novel idea for us but it's too random."

"I call it fishing." Stuart chuckled, "We've got a pond, we know that there're fish in there but we need to see if they're a threat to other wildlife."

"An emotional description but a logical point. Covert operations figure in our history so seeing one being planned and carried out gives an insight to my own past. Who are you sending?"

"Just the soldiers." Stuart replied, "They're the experts."

"It would be logical to send Dave-1." the Terzon said, "He's more intelligent than he would ever admit to and with his knowledge, would see far more than the soldiers."

"It would be even more logical if I went." Stuart said.

"No, it wouldn't." the Terzon scientist responded, "You need to be where you can lead. Dave and James argue, Brian needs your insights you must think of all of them."

Stuart nodded thoughtfully.

~~~

Dave squatted with the waiting soldiers waiting for the scout to return. He was not excited any more, just frightened and wished that he had not impressed Major Borodin so much. Thanks to him, the surveillance team were as adept at deploying through the portal as they were from a helicopter. He had joined them on training exercises and, in his turn, had learned to work with them but instead of a gun, he carried equipment to study the quarry.

Once they had the all-clear from the scout, they edged forwards. He glanced at the gadget he was holding. It was about the size of a TV remote control but there were no buttons, just a screen displaying data that meant nothing to anyone except Dave.

"We're inside the field." he whispered, "It's weak but it's detectable now."

Major Borodin nodded, "I'll remind you one last time, if there's trouble, then drop down flat on the ground. We'll look after you."

Dave nodded and Major Borodin looked on approvingly. Despite his adventures, this was Dave's first combat experience where enemies were actively seeking to kill him and he was coping well, sensible enough not to start idle conversations to ease his fears. A couple of the major's soldiers were younger than Dave yet they had far more training than Dave so even they felt protective towards him.

Major Borodin's phone vibrated.

"There's a patrol about half a kilometre away. They'll cross your route a couple of hundred metres behind you." Stuart said, "There's a couple down in the lane, the patrol is probably interested in them."

It was a dark, moonless night, they were dressed in black, almost invisible, so they continued forwards and neither heard nor saw anything. Dave gave a deep sigh of relief, feeling a reassuring hand on his shoulder. They crept on and Dave was startled when they came up against the boundary wire. Briefly he thought of war films that he had seen or rather more of the clichés they contained. Their trek had been easy, almost too easy and he wondered if they had been allowed to walk themselves into a trap but it remained quiet and the others were waiting for him.

Cutting through barbed wire fences is also a common scene in a war film. Being able to weld the strands back together with a laser once they were all through, was different.

Also, what was different, they knew the location of every mine and were able to mark a path through the field without hesitating.

They were in the dip that they were aiming for before the regular patrol passed their entry point without noticing anything. They were not equipped to spot the ultra-violet light sensitive paint sprayed onto the grass.

Once in position, Dave began scanning the quarry. In his heart, he knew that the expedition was a waste of time, he was not seeing anything that the high level probes had not examined but he agreed with Stuart, they had to be sure. Suddenly Dave-3 was with him murmuring his usual 'heil'.

"Night manoeuvres." Dave-3 continued, "You do have fun."

"Less fun than you imagine." Dave replied.

"What did, you say?" Major Borodin asked.

"I was thinking aloud." Dave replied, "I was wondering if there was another Dave down there."

"There is." Dave-3 said, "And my Brian. That's how I found you."

"Major." Dave whispered, "I'm not going mad but someone's helping me. If it sounds as if I'm rambling then ignore it."

"Just keep it down." Major Borodin replied.

"Wait here." Dave-3 commanded, "I'll be back."

Dave-1 felt him leave but return almost immediately.

"Get out of here." he snapped, "Forget about secrecy, get that portal thing here, now."

Dave took out his own phone.

"Stuart, there's trouble, send the portal." he turned to Major Borodin, "Trust me, Major."

Major Borodin nodded, watching as a portal materialised just above the dip. He was the last to leave and stared briefly in the direction of two helicopters appearing above the ridge as he dived through the hatch.

As Dave-1 relaxed, he reached out for Dave-3 but he was gone. As the portal shut down, the soldiers gathered around Dave looking at him quizzically, seeking an explanation.

"How did you know?" Major Borodin asked, "We'd all like to know."

"Inter-dimensional travelling does funny things." Dave replied, "Another Dave warned me, but he was only here in my head. It happens because we break the barriers between universes down."

"It doesn't happen to us or is it something that grows?" the major asked.

"What do you suppose happened to your parents on that world?" Stuart asked, "If the Nazis are in charge what do you suppose Russia is like?"

"You mean we might not even exist there." one of the soldiers said and Stuart nodded.

"You should have told me of your abilities." Major Borodin said irritably, "It was not a good time for a surprise."

"I can't control it." Dave explained, "All I know is, I'm Dave-1, the Dave on your world is Dave-2, my friend, Dave-3 also happens to be a Nazi on Earth-3. While we were on Earth-4, Dave-3 said that he had found Dave-4. He also said that Brian-3 was there which makes it complicated."

"And the rest isn't?" a soldier asked.

"I know how you feel." Dave laughed, "Talk to Stuart, he's the expert in making things complicated."

"Everything seems to come back to Brian-3." Stuart said, "If he's also involved then it explains why we were led to Earth-4, if not how."

Dave turned to Major Borodin, "You might not want to work with us any more, Major but we have to plan operations as if it's just us. We can't plan around Dave-3 because we can't control his visits but if he does help then it'll be a bonus."

"I understand." Major Borodin replied, "He was certainly a bonus this time. Can I assume that the mission was a success and you got the information you needed?"

"We learned something and now we have a lot more questions." Stuart replied, "Would you say that they were expecting us?"

"Probably. Could this Dave-3 be a double agent?" Major Borodin asked.

"No. When he warned us, I felt his fear, almost panic." Dave replied, "There is something though, when he goes I sometimes feel Brian-3. I can't explain it unless... You know someone is hiding and watching you but you don't know where they are. You feel a bit uncomfortable but with this it only lasts for a moment."

"OK, something is going on. Brian-3 is at the bottom of it but what?" Stuart said. He might have said more but Dave fainted.

He came round clutching his head but as he took in his surroundings he smiled and muttered, "Heil. Wait."

He closed his eyes for a few moments.

"My Brian can force me here but I can't detect him this time," he said. "Have I slipped back in time because I've just been arrested by the Gestapo and I'm dressed for that recce you did. One of them remembered me from before and pistol whipped me. I hope your Dave is unconscious because it hurts like hell."

"It's possible." Stuart said, "Are you well enough to talk?"

Dave nodded.

"I'll tell you something about Brian, he doesn't think small. My colleagues talk about conquering the Japanese empire or finally invading America and ruling the world. He's planning on conquering universes but he needs your Brian and can't find him."

He paused, "No, that's not quite true. He'll be happy with our universe but he'll take the technology he needs from other universes."

He paused again, "No, that was his original plan but now he wants to transfer to another universe. I'm sorry but I'm not too sure what he's doing except that he sees himself as the ruler of an empire like no-one has seen before."

"Is Dave playing some sort of game or is something happening to him?" Major Borodin asked.

"We're used to it but this is Dave-3. I know it's difficult to accept because there's no physical difference."

"You're saying that the person who warned Dave in his head is here instead of Dave." Major Borodin asked and Stuart nodded.

"It's not your David who has gone quite mad?" the Major asked.

"No. Do you accept that you were saved because our Dave could talk with another Dave?"

Major Borodin nodded so Stuart continued, "Sometimes they also swap. Not physically, but mentally. It's an odd fact of portal travelling."

Major Borodin smiled, "Odd is not the word I'd use but I understand. No, I don't understand but I accept that somehow, someone helped us."

"In that case, this introduction is going to rank among the more interesting that I've made. Major Petrov Borodin, Soviet Army, may I present SS-Senior-Storm-Leader David Hilford."

Dave struggled to his feet to stand to attention.

"I'm honoured to meet you, sir." he said.

"And despite ancient animosities, I am fascinated to meet you." Major Borodin replied, "I'm grateful for the warning you gave us even if I'm still confused about who I'm talking to."

"We all understand crazed madmen seeking world domination." Stuart said, "Let's stick with that. Dave, or for the Major's benefit, Dave-3, I believe that you've something to tell us. Let's just sit down and listen."

"I seemed to pick up that you call the other world four." Dave-3 began, "Brian-4 is close to a nervous breakdown, it has something to do with someone he loved. He's vulnerable and my Brian, that's 3 is exploiting him. I need to jump around a bit and explain how I know all this. You see, when you escaped that trap, Brian-3 was furious, he dropped his guard and I saw nearly everything. I'm sure that there was something hidden in the background, but it was his quest for technology in the front."

Stuart nodded, "Go on."

"Those translators you have tune in on brain waves. Brian-3 has a similar device which he invented and he was also working on portals and somehow he put the two together. I don't know if this means anything to you but I caught a thought about tapping the resonance source."

"I'm not sure what that means either." Stuart replied, "For now, it gives him the way to transmit his mind."

"That's right." Dave agreed, "It also stopped him from building a portal like yours? Could that be right."

"Oh yes." Stuart replied, "Resonance is a real problem."

"How about he could look for minds and portals outside his universe?"

"Ah!" Stuart said, "That's new but it makes sense that he could detect typical energy patterns."

"If you say so." Major Borodin murmured. "If I understand Dave correctly, he used his mind machine to discover that a nearby Brian had a portal albeit a somewhat primitive one. Once he located the portal, he could use his machine to dominate Brian-4."

Dave looked surprised, "That's almost it. Brian-4 was working on detecting portals but his world is generally less advanced. We've discussed this before but I can confirm he knows about you, he wants your portal and for that he needs to make this Brian vulnerable so he's after you ..."

"Forgive me for interrupting." Major Borodin said, "Does he use the link between you and other Daves?"

Dave was silent for a time.

"If I said that he's used all of us in different ways? Even I can detect that Stuart has a powerful mind and feel the other Stuart on this planet. There's something else. You're Stuart-1, aren't you but it's Stuart-2 that he's after because I don't think he knows about you. No, he thinks you and Stuart-2 are the same person. Again no. He's confused and is trying to understand how Earth-2 is resisting him. Remember, his knowledge is confined to the people he can control."

"OK, we can't find your world or we'd try to get you and Robert out. Do you think that your Brian manipulated the Stuart on this world to involve me and bring me here?"

"Probably." Dave replied, "He recovered before I found everything and I'd let my guard down as well. He knows that we're helping each other."

"Helping each other?" Major Borodin queried.

"On my world, I'm loyal to the Fuhrer." Dave-3 explained, "Brian-3 is betraying him and he's a threat to you."

"I understand." Major Borodin said, "You do not think that this world is ready for Nazi domination then?"

"On my world, the Russian border with the Reich is about 500km west of Moscow and we struggle to maintain it." Dave replied, "I don't think that we could handle two Russias. Some things are just too big. "

"True." Major Borodin smiled, "Let's hope that your Brian doesn't get too big to handle."

Dave-3 nodded, "Brian-3 has got a lot of mind control but it is limited. I could hide from him, he can't force you to do anything and he can't slide into your mind unless it's open for some reason. I like your Dave and he likes me so we can cooperate but there's something about Brian, and I just shut him out. He put Robert in the machine and even then both Stuart and Robert fought it."

"If we destroy his equipment then he'll be trapped back on his own world." Stuart said.

"I think so, and so will I." Dave-3 replied, "I'll miss travelling."

"We're trying to find your world so don't start missing it yet."

Dave-3 grabbed a pencil and paper and wrote busily.

"These numbers are important." he said, handing the papers to Stuart, "Could they be addresses?"

Stuart looked at them, "They could be. It's the way my Brian writes them down but presumably they're places that he visits, we've got to figure out the origin. It's certainly a help though."

But David was staggering, clutching his head and falling to his knees. He recovered as Stuart and Major Borodin helped him up.

"God, Dave-3's in a bad way." he gasped, "I can't believe how his head hurts. It's OK, it's fading but I don't want to go through that again."

"Do I understand correctly?" Major Borodin asked, "This is your Dave back where he belongs."

"Yes. I'm sorry Major, it's something that's developed so we've had time to get used to it. You're being thrown in at the deep end but I'm getting worried about how easily you do jump, Dave." Stuart said, "It's time you had a check up."

"No, I'm fine." Dave said, "It's just that we're so similar, not only physically but mentally. Did you learn anything?"

"Clues about where Earth-3 is, and confirmation that Brian is doing mind jump experiments." Stuart replied.

"Not mind control?"

"No why?"

"A feeling but nothing tangible and nothing I can explain except, imagine something crawling around your brain trying to get in. What are we going to do now?"

"I'm going to tell the Terzons and the lizard people what we know, go through the Terzon lecture about interfering then go home and spend some time with my Brian. Maybe the military officers can come up with some sort of guard system so we're not all sitting around waiting for an attack."

Both Major Borodin and James looked at each other and nodded.

"Dave, I want you to see Dr. Tobias." Stuart said, "We won't be completely idle because we'll be looking for Earth-3. I'm going to ask my Brian to help. He prefers theoretical science but he'll be interested in Brian-3's work. That's new and not something he's considered before. He'd better stay on Earth-1 though. With luck, Brian-3 hasn't found it yet."

~~~

Despite his travels and the things that he had seen, the one thing that Stuart could not get used to was calling a conference. It was not that it would be held on Mars, or that his messengers were just fourteen or fifteen years old. Neither was it that he wanted to discuss an attack so bizarre that he scarcely understood it. It was that some of the brightest and most powerful scientists on several planets or even universes would be attending just to listen to him. It was far more a part of his normal life, that just before the meeting began Dave stumbled.

"Heil." he murmured, "Your Dave is here as well, and we'll try to keep the link open but I still have concussion and it might jam

195

the signals. Will that do for a description?"

Stuart nodded and stood up, "I believe that someone is trying to take over portal technology using mind jumps and that Earth-2 is the main target. We're hoping that the enemy is confusing Earth-1 with Earth-2 because the technology he needs is on One. The ship and space station project is safe enough because it's not what he's looking for. Even if there was a major effort to gain control of it, it would be easily stopped."

Stuart waited for the startled gasps to die down then added, "Myself and my personal team have been working from a secret base in Russia. However, since the enemy can locate it, there seems little point in hiding it from our friends."

It was an exercise in making sure everyone knew what was happening and Stuart felt happier that no-one from Earth-2 accused him of bringing trouble to their planet.

As Chairman Chernekov said, "We'd still be in trouble, but it would be far less interesting."

~~~

"I'm impressed, My Fuhrer." Dave said, "I don't know half of what's going on, do I, but you handled that meeting well."

"OK, you're welcome, and it's good to know which Dave it is but why are you here?" Stuart said.

"I don't know. My Brian is playing with his machine. There's something else, he's denounced me as a saboteur so I'm likely to be shot. Sabotage is something the Gestapo understands and they're not going to understand how he's the threat. I suppose I'm enjoying a bit of freedom before they start questioning me."

"Is Brian letting you?" Stuart asked.

"I think so." Dave replied, "But he already knows where you are, so what can he gain? Ah! Dave-1 says that he can feel something crawling over his mind again."

He might have said more but Stuart's phone rang.

"We think we've found Earth-3 again." Brian-1 said, "You've got Dave-3 with you and we were able to trace the link."

"Are you asleep back home, your body I mean?" Stuart asked.

"Dozing." Dave-3 replied, "I can hear noises outside my cell and this is like a powerful dream."

"OK!" Stuart said a few moments later, "I've got the coordinates. We'll get a probe to monitor you, then work out how to get you away. Dave promised to rescue Robert but he's in less danger."

Once again Dave-3 watched fascinated as most of the probe's

body disappeared. He jumped in alarm as he saw his body lying on the cell bunk but it was enough to wake him and suddenly he was back there staring up at the probe apparently embedded in the ceiling. He waved as Dave-1 stumbled then grinned at Stuart-1.

"He's certainly adapted well to this jumping lark." Dave-1 said, "It took me a few moments to realise that I was back. He doesn't say much but he's genuinely worried that he's being used to track you."

"OK! Let's take a look at the prison area." Stuart said.

They followed their well-worn routine and rapidly built up a picture of Dave-3's prison.

"It's the guardhouse at the entrance to the complex." James said, "There's only the duty guards. It's all wrong. Dave-3 warrants far more security than that."

"OK! It's another trap." Stuart said, "Maybe he's probing to see what we've got. Let's give him a display."

"Like what?"

"I don't know." Stuart hesitated, "Dave, you know that I trust you with my life but the enemy's nosing around your mind. I, er ..."

"I'm a security risk." Dave said cheerfully, "I'll go to the lizard planet and see if they've got any way of checking me out. Stu, I'm not offended but fetch me when they arrive. It'll be good to see Dave-3 for real and I'd like to see the Gestapo's faces when they see two of us."

As Dave disappeared through the portal Stuart said, "How about fitting generators to the whole building and taking the whole thing."

"It would never stand up to the stresses would it?" James asked.

"I doubt it... unless... it looks like a Portakabin type building. We could laser any foundation bolts and fit generators to the lifting points."

"OK!" James said, "Why something so elaborate?"

"Over two universes Brian-3 is working in different areas of dimensional technology. So far as we know he isn't working on field detection in Universe-3 but on mental effects. If we use probes to grab the building then there won't be any minds for him to grab. If he has fetched any field-detection equipment then we can blow the probes if necessary."

James nodded, "It makes sense. When do you want to try it?"

"When the Gestapo arrive to interrogate Dave-3." Stuart said, "Let them come for the ride, explain what happened then send them home. If Dave-3 tells them about a plot to take over the world, then they'll have some evidence. At least they'll know that he's not a traitor."

"It's still a bit theatrical, just like the Allen business isn't it?" James asked.

"No, well yes but in Allen's case, we aimed for something unreal and bizarre. In this case we're aiming at getting folk to accept the truth."

They only had a couple of days to wait. The Gestapo officers were not subtle. They filled a bucket with water, burst into Dave-3's cell, grabbed him and forced his head into it. Briefly Dave-3 felt himself drowning but even he felt the building shudder. The pressure on his head vanished and he knelt up. It happened so quickly that he was not even gasping and was aware enough to see that all the lights were out.

The senior officer signalled for his subordinate to go and investigate while he drew his gun aiming at David. He faltered as a loudspeaker rasped out in English then German, "Everybody out, we know there are seven of you in there. If you're not out in five minutes, we'll open fire."

A soldier hurried back, looking scared.

"Something's happened, come and look." he pleaded.

Handcuffing Dave-3 they made their way to the office, looked out and stared. The Yorkshire landscape had gone. Instead, they were inside a hangar surrounded by armed troops.

"Do you realise how crazy this is." Major Borodin asked Stuart as they waited, "An officer of the Soviet Army is waiting for Gestapo officers and SS soldiers to surrender. We don't usually treat them all that well."

"Make an exception this time." Stuart replied, "We do need to talk to them."

"What a strange world you live in, Stuart." Major Borodin said, "My grandparents will be furious that I didn't just open fire."

While Major Borodin was cheerfully accepting the situation, the four guardsmen and the two Gestapo officers were just as bewildered as Stuart had intended. Judging his moment it was Dave-3 who spoke first.

"They don't want to shoot us." he said, "If they did then we'd be dead by now. I'm hoping that they'll tell you what's really happening in the quarry."

"About your sabotage, you mean." the Gestapo officer snapped, "Just shut up or I'll shoot you myself."

"Haven't you noticed your chest." Dave-3 asked.

The officer looked down, only to stare at the red dot, then glance wildly around.

"How?" he spluttered, "It's impossible. There's no line of sight."

"They don't want to shoot you." Dave repeated, "They just want to be sure that you don't shoot them."

The senior Gestapo peered out of the window, took in the scene then nodded.

For a time it was confusion. Their captors spoke to them by loud-hailer, telling them of the guns, nightsticks and knuckledusters that they had in their pockets. The prisoners were still baffled at what was happening and how they could be so thoroughly searched without anyone entering the room so they duly removed the offending items and stepped out into the hangar. No-one seemed concerned that Dave-3 remained handcuffed while the prisoners were taken to a comfortable area and invited to sit.

"We can't tell you everything." Stuart said, "The main point is that SS-Senior-Storm-Leader David Hilford is loyal to your fuhrer. Did he try to explain that it was Brian Chapman who was behaving suspiciously?"

"He did, but who would believe his ridiculous story of alternate Earths…" he trailed off, looking around then just stared at Stuart.

"Is anyone going to release me?" Dave-3 asked, "Whose prisoner am I, anyway?"

"I'll let you release you when you get here." Stuart chuckled, "Would you mind us being a little cautious, I'd hate to discover that you're a plant put here by your Brian."

In fact, it was Major Borodin who arrived first. He stood stiffly then turned to Stuart.

"I'm sorry Stuart. It may not be my Russia but I still see them as enemies. I would prefer it if you moved them to another base. My men will help you."

Stuart nodded as Dave-1 clambered out of the portal leaving the Germans to stare in disbelief.

"What's up?" he asked, "Never seen twins before?"

"Your records make no mention of twins." the senior Gestapo officer spluttered, "Who are you?"

"Never mind that." Dave-1 said, "Why am I still handcuffed?"

As Dave-3 was released he straightened and gave his trademark 'Heil'.

"It's strange to see you alive." he laughed, "It's better than having you in my head though."

Inter-dimensional humour was lost on the Nazis; geographically they were probably British but politically they were Nazis.

"Enough of this nonsense." the senior Gestapo officer yelled, "I demand to know what's happening and that you release us now."

"Major Borodin wants you away from here and we have another base where explanations may come easier." Stuart said, "Dave-1 lead the way and Dave-3, bring up the rear."

The prisoners were still too disorientated to cause much trouble and it got worse when gravity changed. It took time and much flailing of arms to get them seated and then Stuart spoke to them though at first it didn't help.

"Welcome to Mars-1." Stuart said, "I don't know if you understand the concept of alternate realities or universes but it is what you are experiencing. You don't have to understand it all for now but I am Stuart-1, this is Dave-1, we're in universe-1 and on Mars-1. You gentlemen are from universe-3 including your ex-prisoner Dave-3 or as you know him, SS-Senior-Storm-Leader David Hilford."

"Ridiculous." the Gestapo officer snapped, "Tell the truth or it will be the worse for you."

"OK." Stuart said, "Take a walk across this cave and look outside. Better still, watch."

Stuart scrunched up a sheet of paper into a ball and gently tossed it so that flew in an impossibly slow arc over their heads.

"Take your time, and we'll try to answer all your questions."

"I read science fiction." one of the soldiers said, "I don't think that we have anti-gravity devices so something has happened but alternate universes? That is difficult to believe, and where is universe-2?"

"Our other base was on it but we were asked to move you."

"So!" the soldier replied, "Camps could be anywhere. You have a wonderful transport device, but across universes? Could you offer more proof?"

"Not dressed like that, I couldn't." Stuart said, "You'd be somewhat conspicuous. Dave, I mean Dave-1 he's about your size, can you help?"

Dave nodded, "What about the rest?"

"We'll take that guy as an experiment and at the same time, find some clothes for Hauptmann Fleischer."

~~~

It was a few days later that a far friendlier Hauptmann Fleischer, the senior Gestapo officer spoke to Stuart. The biggest shock was seeing how different Stuart's home village was, compared to the sealed off military zone where he had first arrived. He recognised the quarry, and later, the village church which on his world was a prison block but it was the every-day village life that was so different and the cheery welcome that they got at the pub.

Hauptmann Fleischer was fifty, unused to anything ruffling his ordered life so, even if he did not admit it to himself, he was badly affected by the gravity changes he had experienced, subconsciously needing Stuart's calm reassurance.

They were sitting in the pub garden only for the Hauptmann to be startled when Stuart asked, "So Hauptmann, do you see us as a threat to your Reich or as new lands to conquer?"

"I haven't thought about it." Hauptmann Fleischer replied, "It's not something that I could admit to, though."

"Why not?" Stuart asked, "You serve your Reich and you're duty bound to report anything that may affect security."

"Tell me about Brian Chapman. You would say Chapman-3, yes?"

"Yes." Stuart agreed, "There are a number of Earths, developing this sort of technology and Brian-3 appears to be trying to gain control of three of them. On your world, that's 3, he has developed it as mind transfer and I think that he's using it to find the Brian Chapman on this world."

"It's gone wrong because he was trying to control the wrong Brian but because of the political situation, Brian-2 hasn't progressed as far as he should have. However, he does have a link there. Brian-4 has developed detection and blocking fields, we've come across them before but not recently. Because of his activities, my Dave and your SS officer established a very close link and Dave-3 has been helping us to work out was happening."

Stuart paused, taking a sip of his drink, "So far as we know, mind jumps only work across universes because it breaks barriers between alternate selves but there're some quirks to that theory given what Brian-3 is doing."

"So you're claiming that SS-Senior-Storm-Leader David Hilford is loyal to the fuhrer and is serving the Reich." Hauptmann Fleischer said.

"I'm telling you what I know." Stuart said, "I don't like your politics but we're not going to interfere with your world, apart from

201

stopping Brian-3 though."

"Because he's a threat to all of you."

"All of us." Stuart corrected.

"What do you want from us?" Hauptmann Fleischer asked.

"Nothing from your universe but from you personally, I'd like Dave-3 officially cleared and released. You can refuse and I would accept it but should I make a threat on what would happen if you do agree then reneged on your promise?"

Hauptmann Fleischer grinned, "I would threaten you anyway but I understand. It's not your way. It's going to be difficult to explain our absence and a disappearing guardhouse though."

"As an academic exercise, imagine that we can travel in time." Stuart said, "We can take you back to just seconds after we took you, what would be the most favourable plan for you?"

"In other words, you do have time travel and you want to prepare me."

Stuart shrugged so Hauptman Fleischer continued, "We're dealing with state security. The Under Storm Leader is suspected of treason and sabotage. To be cleared, he either needs to die in the line of duty or he needs the patronage of a highly placed official. Without them he's likely to be held indefinitely, just in case."

"Fair enough." Stuart said, "Do Gestapo officers have a sense of humour? We could try for something dramatic to make everyone think."

Gestapo barracks were designed to be intimidating. Even a witness shuddered as they stepped out of a car into a courtyard surrounded by high walls punctured by tiny windows. Steel barriers closed behind the car as the Gestapo's *guest*, be they visitor, witness or prisoner was led to the appropriate door.

Hauptman Fleischer's base was typical and it was five days after the guard-house's disappearance that it reappeared with a crash in the courtyard. Officer's poured out of the main building to stare as Hauptman Fleischer stumbled out of the wrecked guard-house followed by his subordinate and guards. Whatever the panic following Hauptman Fleischer's disappearance, guardhouses do not crash-land onto car parks. Everyone looked on in stunned silence while Hauptman Fleischer sought out the commanding officer.

Once order was restored, one by one, they were called in to report and each began, "I cannot tell you what really happened but my perception of events is as follows."

Human nature is strange. If you tell a person not to touch wet paint then he'll touch it to see if it's dry. Ask them to test the paint and they'll refuse, not wanting to get paint on their fingers. By admitting that they may have been brainwashed so their interrogator's found their explanations easier to accept.

It did not stop them from being held in solitary confinement and questioned in detail, It did encourage the questioners to look at their stories very closely only to find them interlocking and without any inconsistencies. Even the coins found in one of the soldiers clothes fitted in with their incredible tale.

Dave-3's file was pulled and studied closely. As Hauptman Fleischer predicted, he was no longer suspected of sabotage but of something else though no-one was quite sure of what.

Brian-3 was called in to examine the guard-room but was unable to contribute anything though trained interrogators like the Gestapo could see that he was furious or frustrated by something. However, his anger did help Hauptman Fleischer and Dave-3 as it bore out their story that Brian-3 was up to something but he was being blocked.

Higher and higher ranking officials visited to examine the guard-room and baffled, left it to their superiors to sort out. Those higher and higher officials accepted that they were dealing with powerful forces that they did not understand so hesitated. Hauptman Fleischer, his subordinate and the four guards were sent on extended leave, with orders not to communicate with each other, go anywhere near the quarry or to speak of their experiences. They were all happy to oblige, accepting that it was only everyone's confusion that was keeping them alive.

While Brian-3 was away, examining the guard-house, the quarry-3 had been deserted with Robert left alone inside the barriers. Dave-1 kept his promise by dematerialising a portal as Robert was running his laps. He recognised Dave, was used to strange events and scarcely broke his step as he ran into the portal.

In one respect, the Reich Chancellor was alarmed enough to act. There was an outside chance that Hauptmann Fleischer had stumbled onto something which had to be dealt with.

Dr. Darren Barker was summoned to explain events. What they did not know was that Stuart had met a Darren Barker on another world and thought that his only skill was being adept at taking the credit for other people's work. Fortunately for him, the guardhouse had disappeared while he was in Berlin briefing the Reich Chancellery. He emphasised the results of work that had been done under his supervision and the progress that had been made towards inter-planetary travel. He also made it clear that SS-Senior-

Storm-Leader David Hilford had been assigned to him against his will and put in charge of security so he could hardly be blamed if Hilford was a traitor. The Fuhrer had instigated a visionary line of research which was in danger of failing because of the treachery of others and he would be honoured to serve in future projects.

It was enough to save the Reich Chancellor's face, and for Darren to be relegated to a remote Arctic station and forgotten unless he was needed but the project itself was still an unknown threat.

Brian-3 was on the couch and attached to his machines when a slow transport plane droned overhead. He had no idea that its only cargo was a bomb, often called a daisy-cutter, designed to explode just above ground level, creating an enormous blast. The quarry walls would contain the blast, magnifying its effect. Brian-3 was incinerated in the blast, obliterated along with all the other evidence.

From Stuart's point of view though, it was too late, Brian-3's consciousness was elsewhere. For now though, he was more concerned with what to do with ex-SS-Senior-Storm-Leader David Hilford.

"Dave-1's parents would ask too many questions if he came home with us." Stuart said.

"And you'd like me to make him welcome, here." Major Borodin said, "What about the boy, Robert?"

"He's only half me." Stuart said, "Same mother, different father so we can pass him off as my cousin. It's Dave-3 who's the problem."

"He did save us on that recce and I agree, he's more like your Dave than a typical SS officer. Very well, he's welcome and we'll find officer's quarters for him but he'll be called Lieutenant rather than Under Storm Leader and he can't wear that uniform."

"No, I suppose not." Stuart agreed, "It's a long story but he does have some clothes on our Earth, assuming that he and Dave-1 are about the same size. It's a story that he can tell you though."

For a time, Stuart monitored Earths 3 & 4, watching, shocked as everything in quarry-3 was destroyed by the daisy-cutter. It was something of a shock to realise that Brian had been killed. Admittedly it was Brian-3 and not his Brian – Brian-1 - but it was still too close for his liking, making him realise that they were all vulnerable.

The blocking field continued to operate on Earth-4 so Stuart could not observe too closely but there seemed to be increasing activity there.

To Stuart's surprise he was welcome to continue operating his base in Russia-2 despite the Soviet Union's innate suspicion of anything Western. They trained Major Borodin's men to monitor the portals and use James' defensive software though their access was highly restricted but it allowed Stuart's team to relax more and spend time at home.

Chapter 10

It seemed more of an inconvenience when Major Borodin asked them all to return and invited them to the officer's mess where a large TV had been set up.

"The Chancellor of Christian Crusaders is making a special broadcast." Major Borodin explained, "We're getting confused reports from Washington that President Jackson is under virtual house arrest and American forces are manoeuvring for an attack on England. All of their forces are on high alert and we're responding. It doesn't sound good."

"No. James, how about launching that probe you've been working on. We may need it."

Major Borodin looked at him quizzically.

"We've been caught up in a nuclear war before." Stuart explained, "Let's just say that it's not going to happen again."

"That's comforting," Major Borodin smiled, "Let's hope we don't get that far."

"Agreed, but you do understand that we'll stop Russian rockets as well as American ones, don't you."

"I must see the medic." Major Borodin replied, "My ears are playing tricks on me. It sounded as if you were threatening to sabotage the Soviet Defence system but you'd never do such a thing, would you?"

"Of course not." Stuart smiled, "I should visit Premier Chernekov, will you excuse me?"

Major Borodin watched Dave-1 and Dave-3 quietly chatting. It was easier to think of them as twins but enough had happened for him to accept the reality of the situation and he had enough respect for them to be mildly pleased that his own Earth had Dave-2.

Premier Chernekov was surprised to see Stuart arrive.

"It's not a good time to visit, my friend." he said, "I've warned Zack not to return until you say so."

"Thanks," Stuart replied, "I wondered if you were concerned at all."

"I am." Premier Chernekov said, "Perhaps we could watch his speech together."

They waited in a companionable silence until the broadcast began.

"The one thing that true Christian believers have in common

with Islam is a belief in one god who created the universe. It is the Soviet Union that is truly the evil empire since it denies belief in anything but its own transient glory. It is with considerable sadness and shock that I have to announce that those who you trust to lead you into His glory are in fact, betraying you. They have accepted the same vainglorious aspirations of the evil empire. They are planning to betray you, and hand you over to God's enemies."

The Chancellor paused to stare sternly into the camera, "True believers are rallying to our cause and taking steps to eradicate the evil that has appeared like a canker in our midst. I now call on all of you to prepare for the sacrifices that are to come."

He paused again, this time relaxing, "There is still hope. If the sinners admit their transgressions and allow true men of god to destroy their evil then all will be well. Let us pray that they see the error of their ways and repent."

Premier Chernekov turned to Stuart.

"We appear to be on the brink of war." he said quietly, "Whatever happens, the three-way stand-off is over. I think that we are too late."

"Why not make your own statement." Stuart said, "We'll make sure that it's heard."

"And say what?"

"That British and Russian scientists have come up with the means of exploring space but to ensure that it was truly for peace other nations were invited to participate. Although others may see it as a way of exploring God's realm the Soviet Union sees it as a way of discovering peaceful cooperation and developing man's potential."

Premier Chernekov nodded slowly.

"I make the announcement unilaterally." he said, "Will the Crusaders' followers believe it, though?"

"I can't help feeling that Brian-3 is behind it, but he's supposed to be dead." Stuart said.

"Is it important for now?"

"I don't know. We were never certain what he was doing except that he wanted a portal."

They were interrupted by the premier's phone ringing. He picked it up and listened.

"I have my staff demanding my attention and I must deal with them before they panic."

President Jackson sat in the Oval Office in the White House. Communications had been mysteriously cut to the outside world but he was still president and to all intents and purposes Commander-in-Chief of America's armed forces. That was the dilemma for the Crusaders; he still retained full command unless he was legally removed. While many were willing to limit his powers believing that a legal investigation was under way, few were willing to cross the line into mutiny and rebellion.

Like Premier Chernekov, President Jackson was familiar enough with probes and portals to be relieved rather than worried when a probe materialised in front of him. He listened carefully as Stuart repeated his discussion with the Russian Premier.

"He's right." President Jackson said, "We're ready to fit the drives to the prototype ship. Can you get it done ASAP? If he makes that speech then makes a flight to Washington, he could land on the White House lawn. That should be a good enough stunt. What about Prime Minister Shanks? We should include him."

"Agree to name the ship the Queen Elizabeth and he'll get the credit for the project. You claim the credit for stopping a war."

"That doesn't sound like you, it's too cynical."

Stuart shrugged, "My Brian invented the thing and he's respected by people who are important to him. He doesn't need political recognition. You, Prime Minister Shanks and Premier Chernekov exist for it. That's cool, but stopping the war is more important."

"What happens next?"

"I'm going to see Chuck." Stuart said, "The plan always was for us to fit temporary generators to the ship and bring it to our world to fit the main engines. We can still do it but I need to warn Chuck that if we're going to do it overnight then he's going to see something that might even blow my mind."

There were four recesses for the engines, two on either side of the ship. Chuck was puzzled at being asked to set up canvas screens to hide each recess from the others but he complied.

Nothing seemed to be happening so he poked his head around a screen to see James, Stuart and Dave at work on an engine already in place.

"I told you that we could do it." Stuart said then paused thoughtfully, "I'm going to tell you that we could do it."

Puzzled, Chuck looked behind another screen only to see James, Stuart and Dave at work installing an engine.

Stuart looked up and smiled, "We've never done anything like this before but I reckon that we can do it."

Someone tapped on Chuck's shoulder. He turned to see Stuart

standing there, smiling.

"That was me, four nights ago in there." he said, "The first one you spoke to was me last night in my time-line."

"You're jumping around in time to fit the motors." Chuck said slowly.

"Installing the motors will take several weeks." Stuart said, "These are our own generators. They're rated for a single trip but they won't last much beyond that."

Chuck shook his head. "Haven't you seen the news? Things are hotting up now."

"The ship will be collecting Premier Chernekov from Red Square tomorrow morning, Washington time. The Crusaders have been fed various launch codes though I don't know the details of how it was done. I suppose enough high up officials were more loyal to the Crusaders than the government. The Chancellor of the Crusaders is already in his nuclear bunker. He intends attacking our primary base in Yorkshire and claiming that it was Russia turning on its new allies. He's probably planning on calling for a reprisal attack on Russia but he may hold back from that."

Chuck stared at Stuart.

"We're that close to war?" he gasped.

Stuart took out a phone that was vibrating in his pocket and hurried away from the ship before beckoning Chuck over.

"I don't remember hearing us talking on my previous nights and I didn't have my phone on those nights but I want to be sure." Stuart said, "An American warship is just about to launch two nuclear tipped missiles at our base. Watch."

It was dark in the Atlantic but the probe that James was operating had enough light to pick up the warship. Suddenly the picture became white but fading to a bright red flame engulfing part of the forward deck. The light continued fading until the ship was just visible together with the two rocket trails shooting up into the sky.

The probe was also picking up on the conversations in the control room. At first all was calm but as the course readings came in so the tone of the voices changed. The crew was too well-trained to show panic or fear but tension definitely increased.

They heard the officer in charge give the order to destroy the missiles but the missiles continued resolutely for New York and Washington.

Despite the earlier Daves helping earlier Stuarts to fit the generators, their convoluted time-line reached the present. While

Stuart-1 was talking to Chuck, Dave-1 was standing with Major Borodin as news of the launches filtered in.

"Your work?" the Major asked and Dave nodded.

"I'm not sure what Stuart's planning but he said something about scaring them."

"Apparently our satellites show them as attacking two American cities. Do you suppose that they will blame Russia?"

"Maybe in the press." Dave replied, "Washington will see the Crusaders attacking them. It could prove interesting."

"You call nuclear war interesting? And when they reach their targets?"

"It depends on what their targets are." Dave said, "James is the expert on this sort of stuff but I don't know what his plan is."

"We're on full alert of course but we're a couple of levels from launch." Major Borodin said, "The last command that we can expect is to take cover. Before that regular TV and radio stations will go off-air and they're still running."

Dave nodded and shuddered.

"I sat out an attack once before. It was a sort of Siberia where dissidents were sent. A city about two hundred miles away was hit and that was bad enough."

Dave shuddered again, "Sorry, I was rambling."

"It sounds as if you're entitled to." Major Borodin said, "Does your security permit me to speak with James at a time like this?"

"It's your base." Dave said, "Come on."

To their surprise, they found Dave-3 already with James. He straightened when he saw Major Borodin but, just in time, refrained from giving the Nazi salute. Instead, he watched the monitors while James explained.

"The missiles lack the range to hit any American city." he said, "It should still give them a scare because if two missiles can veer so completely off course, what else can go wrong?"

James paused, "However they will veer off and crash into the Laurentian Fan. It's an area of canyons 3-4000 metres deep and there's even an abyss that goes to 6000 metres. They won't arm so they won't detonate and they'll be incredibly difficult to find. That means that in any time frame that we need, neither the Crusaders nor the Pentagon will have any idea what happened. With their control of the missiles so suspect, what would happen if the Crusaders launch a missile attack from American soil?"

"In other words they'll wonder whether the launch codes that the Crusaders got, have been tampered with?" Dave asked.

"Whatever else he is, the chancellor loves a good conspiracy." James chuckled, "He's bound to make something of it. I bet he's sitting working out who in Washington is betraying him and who they're working for."

In an age of satellite surveillance, where no-one trusted anyone else and spying was a major industry, others wondered as well.

Abu al Khayr Naṣṣār's earthly master flew into a mighty rage at the news. Considering that he was frail, almost senile, his rage seemed even more terrible and out of all proportion to the consequences. After all, if the Christian infidels were tearing themselves apart then Islam could appear as the calm face of reason. Why should the loss of an obscure English village be so important?

Being neither Christian nor Muslim, the Chinese premier disliked being an outsider. Only his communist counterpart, the Russian premier had really benefited by events. He was definitely in a stronger position at home even if he appeared to be remarkably friendly with the American and British leaders but what if his new allies were tearing themselves apart? Russia would be even stronger and it was a fellow communist state, a more natural ally than the Warriors of Saladin.

Around the world, reactions were mixed as the two missiles powered into the sea. They broke up with the impact, some lighter debris floating back to the surface. The cores of the fission bombs they carried drifted on down resisting the immense pressures.

"It should have delayed things." Stuart was saying to Chuck as they watched, "A lot of people are going to wonder what's just happened. We've found our cave on Mars-2 and we've been fitting it out. It's not been easy because we usually have the portals set so that we can only materialise in strict chronological order. Fitting the generators have broken that rule and I got some sort of odd rapport with the others back there. I remember feeling it while we were installing them as well and it's odd even knowing that we'll succeed because I've got four memories of what we're doing in your now."

"What would happen if you stepped through one of screens and spoke to yourself?" Chuck asked.

"I don't want to know." Stuart retorted, "Now is not the time to experiment either."

"No, I suppose not." Chuck chuckled, "Look, there's a lot of scuttlebutt flying around the yard but they've all kept it secret. They're not stupid though, there's some who've been calling it a spaceship but it's also a time-ship isn't it? I understand that now but the crew's not going to understand how it was under construction today and is flying around fully operational tomorrow."

"OK." Stuart said, "We're working to a schedule just now and we've only delayed the war. If we don't stop it, nothing else matters but I'll see what I can do."

Of all the things that Stuart and his friends valued, it was working to a regular routine. The portal reduced all of time and space to a walk through an air-lock. However, they could still be 'home in time for tea' which gave them all a chance to digest the most extraordinary of events. It also allowed their body clocks to stay in synch with a twenty-four-hour day thus preventing jet-lag symptoms on a chronic scale.

For once, they couldn't work that way. The ship had to be fitted out, tested and the crew trained in just a few hours. Time travel could stretch those hours to a few months or more. The problem was that the if they 'went home for the night' then a day would elapse which would make events hopelessly confused elsewhere.

The cave where they worked had already been fitted out, again they had done it before so it was straightforward. It had been harder attaching generators to the guardhouse where Dave-3 had been held because the stresses had needed careful calculation to avoid ripping the building to pieces. The ship's motors were heavy and seemingly complex but the design was modular. Computer controlled cranes did the lifting, lasers, also computer controlled, welded them in place and even more computers guided them as they made the connections.

Saying that a device is computer controlled makes a job seem easy. A film clip lasting a minute has 3000 pictures, each one slightly different. The computer cannot choose the scene, decide what elements should be added or how they should move. The director has to give the computer directions. Once the directions are right, the computer can manipulate those 3000 frames.

The same principle applied to Stuart and his team. They used simulations to programme their equipment so that it worked to the tightest of tolerances, putting up with each other's frustration and increasing irritability when things went wrong.

They weren't completely trapped. They had friends in 3000BC Egypt who they could visit. That was the thing about their lives. The most ridiculous sounding trip was routine, a step through the portal yet, at that moment, a trip to their local pub would cause paradoxes that might never be sorted out. The crux of the problem was continuity or ensuring that events happened in the right order, otherwise there was a danger that one of them could install a part and then forget to order it. It would leave the question, where did the installed part come from?

Ships powered by multi-dimensional generators don't need big crews. Again, *it's all done by computers.*

As Stuart once said, "I'm an are-we-there-yet type of traveller. That's when the fun starts."

However, the crew who were being trained to fly it were not seasoned portal travellers. Stuart Johnson-2, Terry Stevens, Sergeant Charlie Pernell, Viktor Levkova and Colonel-General Igor Vinokurov were learning but nothing came automatically any more, not even walking.

Even in an ordinary corridor, Igor would look for a handrail and wait for his legs to start drifting upwards. An experienced jet pilot he worried about the lack of flight plans and air traffic control. He insisted on pre-flight checks and Stuart agreed that they were relevant to a ship but Igor never liked that they were lines of green writing scrolling up the screen. Only in simulations did it ever stop with a red line indicating an open hatch or something.

~~~

Ever the showman, Premier Chernekov decided to make his response to the chancellor of the Crusader's speech in Red Square. Nobody understood why but the Premier insisted the Square be cleared except for his own podium and an enclosure for the press which represented media from all over the world, even the Crusader's own TV station. Premier Chernekov arrived, then leaving the other dignitaries on the dais circulated amongst the press apologising for the cramped space but asking if they all had a good view of the deserted square.

He returned to the dais and turned to the microphone.

"Comrades." he began, "Comrades of the international press, you are about to either witness me becoming the biggest fool in human history or the dawn of a new age for mankind."

As all the planning came together, the Premier's timing was perfect because at the precise moment he finished speaking, so the ship materialised.

"It appears that I am not a fool." he said quietly but he made sure that the microphone and of course, the media managed to pick it up.

Premier Chernekov stood impassively watching the shocked chaos that the ship's arrival provoked. The press recovered quickly, they were professionals and whatever else was going on they had been presented with one of the biggest stories imaginable.

Security recovered next trying to hurry the members of the cabinet away. A few allowed themselves to be moved but Premier Chernekov stood his ground just along enough to yell, "I was expecting it, you fools."

The security staff's reaction was much slower that time. They could react to apparent danger but could not believe there was none. For a moment the scene was farcical. Premier Chernekov grabbed the podium, refusing to be moved while the security staff tried to surround him.

Eventually the premier's calm determination seeped through and the security men calmed down and he was able to speak into the microphones.

"It seems that the honour of officially naming Earth's first true space ship falls to me. Before you, is the *Terrestrial Space Ship Queen Elizabeth* and it is named in honour of the country that developed the technology then offered it to the world."

"In an ideal world, this event would have been staged in London but there is no time. Already shots have been fired to destroy the peace, unity and cooperation that is being offered to us. To prevent more, I am visiting Washington and providing my security staff can stop pulling on my coat sleeves, I will be there in ten minutes."

Security finally got the message and relaxed allowing Premier Chernekov to stride away.

Reaction around the world was just as confused as the premier's security staff. For most there was relief that suddenly, there was an alternative to the war that had seemed to be just days away.

In the UK there was also anger that the Government had surrendered a major military asset. George Rosswell hoped to exploit it but events were moving too fast. From positioning himself ready to take on a prime minister losing Crusader support, Prime Minister Shanks was suddenly the world's saviour. Even the hawks, angry at the surrender of such powerful technology, were aware of how close to nuclear war they had come so were uncertain as to how to react.

In America a tremendous schism appeared between those that supported the Crusader's rigid fundamentalism and those that finally had the chance to speak for a more liberal approach. Military reaction was far simpler. Where there had been doubts about President Jackson's loyalty, nothing had been proved and they needed their Commander-In-Chief when faced with a sudden completely unexpected threat.

For the first time in days, there were no obstacles when he announced a press conference. His statement was terse but to the point.

"America's contribution to the world's exploration of deep space was the building of the *TSS Queen Elizabeth*. The launch of the *TSS Abraham Lincoln* will take place in the next few weeks. They and their three sister ships will supply the deep space station *Lenin*.

"The *TSS Queen Elizabeth* will be landing on the lawn of the White House in a few minutes. Security has already cleared the area. My next statement will be made in London."

The Chancellor of the Crusaders watched, seething in helpless rage. Control of events had switched to those who knew about the ships. Within seconds of the broadcast, private lines to loyal military personnel closed. Within minutes, ships, planes and troops that had been quietly diverted to bolster his position were returning to their proper station.

The ship's sudden appearance on the lawn of the White House was as just a big a shock as its arrival in Red Square. Security looked alarmed but at least they had received some warning so did not react. Assorted advisers, generals and admirals stood uncertain what to say as Premier Chernekov descended from the ship to warmly greet President Jackson and with his arm around the president's shoulder, guide him into the ship which promptly disappeared.

Stuart-1 and his Earth-1 team were watching from their own base in Yorkshire-1 as the ship landed in Horse Guards Parade, London-2. Until then no-one knew why the Prime Minister had asked for the area to be cleared, why he had called a press conference there or why he was just accompanied by an obscure civil servant and a young boy. As events in Red Square and then the White House unfolded so observers versed in body language watched Prime Minister Shanks relax, and in his turn he watched impassively as the ship arrived. Guided by his associates, the Prime Minister boarded the ship.

The reaction around the world was stunned silence, followed by a sense of relief, followed by an almost hysterical demand to know what was going on.

Different groups had their own take on events. The military quickly saw an incredible new weapon. Politicians struggled to find their position in the new reality. For most, it was relief that persisted, aided by the only point that reporters understood; the obvious friendship between the three leaders.

There was some consternation when the ship disappeared from Horse Guards Parade because no-one knew where it had gone, at least not until news feeds from an obscure village in Yorkshire took up the story.

The three premiers may have considered themselves seasoned travellers but it was something of a shock to realise that people who had accepted them as just visitors now saw them as important strangers. It was the difference between visiting Earth-1 and Earth-2. The exception was Zack-2. He had been questioned about a visit to Canterbury that he did not make. He had met his alternate self and found himself as an unofficial guide to all the visitors coming and going yet he just accepted it all as part of his widening world.

From the moment that the team installed themselves in the village, Zack-2 had been welcomed into the group. By now, he was at home dealing with important strangers, completely at ease standing next to the prime minister and a Mr. Eric Stevens. However, he was surprised to be so cordially greeted by the premier of the Union of Soviet Socialist Russia who seemed to know so much about him. However, he was on a spaceship. That was so much more cool and exciting.

Emotions and reactions remained confused for some time. Old enmities would take time to fade but the picture shoot where all three leaders stood together before the space ship became a symbol of unity, together with Prime Minister Shanks' speech.

"The universe is bigger than we can imagine." he began, "For those of us that believe in a creator and worship him then, we can only feel more humble and marvel at his greatness. As a Christian, I pray that he might guide us to use his gifts of curiosity and intelligence wisely for the benefit of all. For those that do not believe, may they still dedicate their lives to the same end. Today we are standing at the centre of this great project. Looking around I see the representatives of many nations, beliefs and religions. All will be invited to take part.

"There are those that would see us wallow in ignorance, limiting our knowledge of God's wonders for their own aggrandisement. They have dragged us to the brink of war and it is only through the extraordinary efforts of those involved in this project that we present an alternative, exciting and peaceful future."

The real impact of events stemmed from the world-wide

shock, amazement and relief that most people felt. Many had been frantically building shelters; churches, mosques and temples were full of those expecting the end of the world. Ordinary life had faltered because many had chosen to wait with their families, so close had they come to disaster. Suddenly, instead of conflict, they were witnessing cooperation on a scale never before imagined and a project that stretched the imagination to the limit.

There were still plenty of hawks who were alarmed at trusting those who had been enemies just hours before and had the project gone through normal channels, they would have done their best to stifle it. However, for once, they were ignored.

Reporters struggled to make their questions heard.

"Do you regard NASA as obsolete?" an American reporter asked.

"No, NASA and other space agencies are still vital." Prime Minister Shanks replied. "Our civilisation depends on the communications, surveys, and the general advancement of knowledge that they provide. For that sort of work, our ships would be as useful as an articulated lorry would be for going shopping. Your government may well consider it a suitable organisation to handle your part of this great venture."

It took a few days for the story to become clear. The village was sealed off except for anyone authorised by Stuart-2's team. Mrs Perkin's daughter was allowed through on Dave-2's authority to visit her ailing mother watched enviously by George Rosswell who could not get clearance.

The residents of the village were the first to be shown around the ship. Among them were Lau Cheng and Daniyal Lone and a number of other spies. Initially their masters were delighted at the success of their agents but delight gave way to confusion as it transpired that were wearing badges depicting their country's flag.

None of the old assumptions were working and it was unclear which country broke ranks, surrendered to the situation and passed on their agent's mobile number to the media. In their haste to become a player they tacitly approved, and it became harder for them to backtrack. Unusually for communist Russia, it enjoyed favourable media attention and enjoyed its own moment of glory when it launched the Space Station Lenin.

Chapter 11

"I'm assuming that you want to check out Earth-4 before you're ready to leave." James asked when they gathered a few days later on their base in Russia-2.

Stuart-1 hesitated.

"I'm not sure." he replied, "Major Borodin, are we outstaying our welcome?"

"Not at all." the major replied, "My orders are that you're to have everything you need. Unofficially my government regrets that it cannot recognise your contribution but there again you are not here officially."

"OK, none of the Daves jump to each other any more, I'd guess that they're too much of one world now. I'm not sure if that made sense but they're living separate lives here and diverging naturally. I mean ..."

"We've got the gist of it." James said, "I don't know if you can be clear and succinct describing it all. What's your point?"

"They report seeing Brian when they're asleep."

"And you're going to struggle to explain what that means as well." Major Borodin said, "You're saying that a strange portal could appear again."

"I don't know." Stuart said, "Stuart-2, his Alan and his Brian now have a world that they can live in. The Nazi regime on Earth-3 seems to be mellowing but it'll be a long time before Dave-3 can go home. It's stable, it's rejected Brian's work, it's not a threat here, so we couldn't interfere even if we wanted to."

"He's been accepted by my men but elsewhere?" Major Borodin said, "Feelings do run deep and he'll never be fully welcome."

Just then Dave-1 and Dave-3 arrived, Dave-1 noticing the sudden silence.

"Still not trusting us?" Dave-1 asked, "Is that why you didn't tell us about this shindig?"

"Do any of your thoughts get passed on to Brian-X, the one you dream about?" Stuart asked, "Sorry Dave, both of you but I don't know what we're dealing with, even after all this."

"No, neither do we." Dave-1 said, "If you want a clear, objective report then I don't know what's going on. My feelings say that it's the same nasty version of Brian but he's a lot weaker. This'll sound stupid, but when he crawls over my brain his claws have gone. He can't dig his way in."

"I'd be on a charge for making a report like that to my superiors but I can't put it any better." Dave-3 said.

"We've always assumed that Brian-3 was the dominant force." Stuart said, "Supposing it's Brian-4?"

"What do Brian-1 or Brian-2 say?" James asked.

"They're both of this cluster." Stuart said, "They can block Brian-X easily because nothing's made them vulnerable. I doubt that Brian-X has much in common with them so I'd say that they're not the target. Supposing that he could have persuaded Dave-3 that one of our Brian's was a threat to the Reich or that the Reich needed his expertise. If Dave-3 then jumped, he would see it as his duty to kill me or Stuart-2 to make Brian vulnerable. It's weak as a plan but consider the different parts of it, Maybe the different elements could be put together in different ways."

"As you say, it's a weak plan." Major Borodin said, "It doesn't allow for Dave-3's own experiences or observations. It's not clear whether Ones or Twos should be the target. It also over-estimates his equipment's capabilities. However, if this Brian-X is as paranoid as it seems, he may believe the problems can be overcome. Why do you call him Brian-X?"

"Because I don't know which one he is. On some worlds, Brian broke down completely because I died. Apparently something similar happened to Brian-4 and he was unable to block Brian-3. The timing's a bit confused and how did Brian-3 start jumping?"

"And how can he fish around and find compatible minds?" James said.

"Maybe it's a feature of jumping clusters." Stuart said, "It doesn't make sense though. Unless … Dave, both of you, do you ever pick up on Dave-4?"

"Pick up on?" Dave-1 queried, "Now that you mention it, no. Dave?"

"Not so much. I can feel Dave-1 when he's around but Dave-4, not even when I jumped to him. I'll have to be as poetical as you. I homed in on his signal but it was fuzzy and blurred. So was I. The dominant feeling was about a trap being sprung, but it wasn't like visiting you. I'm sorry, there's just not the words for it."

"Not to worry." James said, "What do you make of it, Stuart?"

"Nothing useful. I reckon that there's a Brian-5 who started it all. He developed a portal or a probe that crossed universes, and found Brian-3. Remember that Robert jumped to another world; he didn't come here but he mentioned the Crusaders. My Brian nearly blew himself up once, maybe Brian-5 did or he was shutdown by the Crusaders. Brian-3 saw the jumps before tackling the resonance problem which led to his machine. World-4, developed a primitive probe, saw the military potential and focussed on blocking fields. As I said, none of it helps except that it may explain why Brian-X is so desperate to get control of another Brian."

Stuart paused, "What may help is that Dave-1 and Dave-3 were pushed together and are closer mentally. Dave-2 is more violent and presumably Dave-4 is too. Could they establish links between each other but not these two? Remember, Brian-X tried to push Robert and Stuart-2 together and it didn't work properly because they both fought it."

"For all practical purposes Robert and I are half-brothers." Stuart continued, "Leaving out the inter-dimensional bit, we have the same mother. The lizards talk about imprint. Everyone is different but supposing some are similar, you know, like tissue matching for transplants, strangers can be compatible. Our alternate selves in other universes are most likely to be compatible yet Dave-1 is compatible with Dave-3 but not with Daves 2 or 4. Now Robert is not a full-blown Stuart yet he found one to jump to so if the conditions are right, can we jump to complete strangers? Was Brian-3 jumping to strangers helped by that machine of his?"

"Ever heard of doppelgängers?" James asked, "There are all sorts of myths and legends about them but some say we've all got a double. It doesn't help much except that it ties in with what Stuart said."

"Myths and legends are often based on something but as you say, it doesn't help." Stuart said.

"Do you have any thoughts?" Major Borodin asked.

"Only one." Stuart replied, "Kidnap Dave-4 or someone similar. Ask him what's going on."

"Isn't that interference?" James asked.

"Yep." Stuart replied cheerfully, "It's easy enough to learn about Earth-4, basically it's Nazi dominated, even harsher than Earth-3 and technologically, it is comparable to our sixties or seventies. We can't find anything out about Brian-4 but we know that there's a Dave there."

"No weird and wonderful theories to do my head in?" Dave-1 asked.

"Not really." Stuart replied, "We know that Brian-3 intends conquering a world. Earth-4 could be the easiest target using this cluster's technology and Earth-3's mind control."

"Go on!" Dave-1 exclaimed, "I understood that, now make it complicated."

"Brian-3 should be dead but we're not sure if his mind is. Supposing he's on Earth-4, pulling Brian-4's strings and he's already built himself a power base because of the technology he's introduced." Stuart asked, "Their records aren't computerised so it's going to be far harder, but how about getting Brian-4's files. Let's do that before we kidnap anyone."

"Should you be discussing it with us?" Dave-3 asked.

"I don't know." Stuart replied, "You're right, I didn't tell you about this meeting but now, I'm glad you're here. Both of you."

"OK, I've already done some checking." James said, "Dave-4 has quarters in Howkbury. It's called Heßstadt now, apparently after Rudolph Hess. The detection field at the quarry is similar to a distortion field that we came across once before but with the limitations in technology it's also very limited. Our probes interfere with it enough to cause ripples which can be detected so if the field is a kilometre wide, then probes can be detected up to 10 kilometres away."

"You have been busy." Stuart said, "How did you figure it out?"

"Every time the field is disturbed, they call out the guard." James explained, "I started with a probe at 100 kilometres and lowered it until there was a reaction. I then used a second probe to check the perimeter. Now there's one interesting point, the guards search at random; that first time, Dave-4 knew exactly where to look."

"They knew the details of our recce as well." Dave-1 said, "Dave-4 was involved both times, could he have detected me?"

"With a bit of help from Brian-3, it's possible but I don't know." Stuart replied.

~~~

On Earth-2 the quarry became the world's first Inter-Planetary Shipping Centre. It was less prestigious than it sounded because it was mainly an administrative centre. Space-ships using warp drives needed very little in the way of maintenance and used hastily improvised landing fields near capital cities. However, any shipping line needs to be organised and it was there that movements were planned. To sound less military and emphasise the peaceful uses of the venture, words that suggested missions and operations were studiously avoided. Announcements on web sites and in newspapers were on the lines of:- TSS Mao Tse Tung. Departs: Beijing 5th April. Destinations: Mars Colony 1, Space Station *Lenin*. General Cargo, Crews on Rotation. Just another shipping line going about its business. However, it was novel enough to fascinate everyone and they gathered at the landing sites to watch departures and arrivals. They forgot about the quarry where nothing ever happened.

What tourists there were, had left as it was getting dark and staff had already gone home when the contents of the quarry disappeared. The force of the explosion broke windows miles away, and dislodged roof tiles in the village.

For a time there was complete chaos and confusion. What security there was, was geared to the daytime tourists. The most senior officer able to take control of the situation was Superintendent Jenkins but his half dozen or so men were unarmed. As a mushroom cloud formed over the quarry, satellites could not see what was happening on the ground for the timing could not have been worse. The explosion happened an hour before nightfall on a dull, overcast day so that visibility remained poor.

Superintendent Jenkins had learnt enough to believe that the explosion was a conventional one. If it had been nuclear, it would have badly disrupted electrical supplies and radio communications. Even so he sent a car, equipped with radiation monitoring devices, towards the quarry. Superintendent Jenkins' phone rang. It was one of the policeman sent to investigate.

"There's no sign of radiation, sir." the policeman reported, "There's a fair amount of dust but that's all. Hang on, there's someone there. What the ..."

The sound of gunfire was unmistakeable, followed by a groan. The last sound was the crack of a smaller explosion, a grenade Superintend Jenkins guessed and the connection failed.

Something was badly wrong and for the first time he used his direct line to the Prime Minister. He then sent for Lau Cheng and Daniel Lone glad that such a peculiar situation, where he had resident agents, had developed. He explained what he knew.

"Any thoughts, gentlemen?" he asked as he finished his explanation.

"I don't believe that it's my government." Lau Cheng replied, "My brief now, is to monitor our involvement in the Ganymede project."

"I need information and I should be more tactful but you gentlemen are spies." Superintendent Jenkins said, "I don't want any more casualties so I need someone who knows what's needed."

Both Lau Cheng and Daniel Lone nodded.

"Excuse us," Lau Cheng said, "I don't think that I'm ready to discuss my methods in front of a counter-intelligence agent."

"Just do what you can, please." Superintendent Jenkins smiled.

The agents left and it proved to be just in time for moments later he heard shouting. Incredibly it sounded like German.

'What, the … 'Jenkins cried out getting to his feet as suddenly the pub door banged open and a troop of Nazi soldiers rushed in to cover the bar and the terrified customers.

'Stay where you are! All of you,' demanded the Officer in charge wielding a pistol and glancing around the room.

Superintendent Jenkins stood out from the rest in his uniform and the Nazi officer pointed his weapon at him and squeezed the trigger. The gunshot in the confined space was deafening but Tom did not hear it. He died staring at the Swastikas that adorned the soldiers' uniforms.

Satisfied that there was no other threat present, the officer holstered his pistol and removed his helmet. The regulars gasped as they recognised David Hilford, or another double. The Hauptsturmführer looked around before glaring at Bill the landlord.

"Sie, was ist falsch?" he rapped out but Bill just looked, terrified and uncomprehending.

"I asked you, what is wrong?" he said in a thick accent, menacingly resting his hand on his holster.

"You look like a village lad." Bill replied, "That's all."

"You call me sir, and stand at attention when you speak to an officer. Don't you scum have any manners?"

"We don't have many soldiers around here and they come in here to relax just like the rest of us."

"We're not here to relax but I'll allow you that." Dave grinned, "Now where's Stuart Johnson?"

"I've not seen them for a bit." Bill replied, "Not since they got on that ship."

David leant across the bar and slapped Bill's face.

"Last chance. Show more respect."

"You want respect, lad, then buy a drink and you'll get the same respect as any other customer." Bill replied, "If you don't then for the record you're barred."

Bill was terrified, shocked at the policeman's murder, aware of the body lying on the other side of the bar and the spreading pool of blood but violent customers were an occupational hazard for any publican. He was instinctively trying to control the situation without becoming confrontational. He knew something about Dave Hilford or at least his local one, and thought he had detected something of the same sense of humour in the intruder. His instincts were proved right as Dave laughed out loud.

"I'll shoot you when I have the time." he said, "Tell me about this ship."

"It just appears then disappears again. I don't know how it works except that it travels regularly to Pluto or a space station out that way. You need to speak to Stuart-1."

"Stuart-1?" the Hauptsturmführer queried.

"They talk about alternate Earths. Stuart-2 comes from here. You're about the fourth or fifth Dave Hilford if that's your name. I take it that's what you meant by a double."

SS-Hauptsturmführer David Hilford might have asked more questions but he was interrupted by the sound of gunfire. He frowned as he listened, sure that he could hear his troops returning fire, but the enemy fire sounded professional, rapid and powerful. His briefing had said that there were no armed troops nearby and that he would have time to establish a strong perimeter around the village not expecting anything more deadly than a farmer's shotgun. He frowned.

"What troops are stationed here?" he asked, "How many defend your quarry?"

"None." Bill replied, "So far as I know, the nearest army base is fifty miles away but there's been some funny comings and goings these last few weeks."

Dave looked suspiciously at Bill but a soldier burst in raising his arm in a Nazi salute.

"The TDT has been destroyed, sir." he reported, "We're trapped here. There's a boulder hovering a thousand metres above the quarry and it has been evacuated."

"What about the interference field?" Dave snapped.

"Smaller rocks were just falling out of the sky and smashing the generators I left to report, sir."

"Who's attacking us?" Dave asked.

"We don't know, sir. Communications are reporting Russian intercepts on the radio."

"Russian?" Dave exclaimed, "Very well. Suggest that the Standartenführer falls back to the village."

"The Standartenführer is dead, sir." the messenger replied, "So is Sturmbannführer Weiss. The first boulder hovered over the TDT as if it was giving troops time to clear the area. The Standartenführer said something about getting the TDT closed and ran towards it just as the boulder started to fall. He didn't make it and there's broken metal sticking out from under the boulder, sir."

"If you have a radio, order all units to the village."

Dave was thinking fast when the pub's phone rang.

"Make it sound as if everything is in order and hang up quickly." he commanded.

Bill picked up the phone and answered then turned to Dave.

"Are you SS-Hauptsturmführer David Hilford?" he asked, "Because it's for him."

Confused but not knowing what else to do, he took the phone.

"Yes." he snapped.

"This is Major Borodin, of the Russian People's Liberation Army. Will you surrender to a fellow officer who can offer your men safe conduct home?"

"But not for me." Dave replied, "My mission is to capture one Stuart Johnson and get the coordinates of your second TDT base. I assume that you are speaking from there."

"It would not help you even if I was. The Stuart Johnson you need is not on this planet and you lack the technology to find his base. I'm afraid that your mission has failed."

"Not with a village full of hostages, it hasn't. I'll shoot the first ten at dawn then another ten an hour later and so on. You know what I want, their lives are in your hands."

David jumped, startled as his team who were covering the customers in the pub, collapsed to the floor.

"We are not fighting the Great Patriotic War so we are trying not to kill you or your men, but believe me that it is a difficult order to obey."

David put the phone down, then studied it, only then realising that it was a wireless handset. He was thoughtful as he walked over to check his men's pulses, surprised to discover that they were still alive.

He picked up the phone again.

"Now do you believe that we're trying not to kill you." Major Borodin asked.

"How did you know ..." David trailed off, "Why the gunfire then? Why not just knock all my men out."

"We're limited in what we can do." Major Borodin said, "By the time we stunned the last of them, the first would be coming round. If we can arrange a cease-fire until British troops arrive, then

225

we'll maintain a sense of order but I'm afraid some of my men stumbled into some of yours. We're not used to inter-dimensional warfare either so the odd skirmish was inevitable."

"If I still have communications then I shall order my men to hold their positions but to take no further action." Hauptsturmführer David Hilford said, "Since the mission has failed then I'm probably heading for the Eastern front if I'm not court-martialled and shot but I'd prefer to surrender to the British."

"Very well." Major Borodin agreed, "It would be better if you surrendered to the British on British soil anyway. I'm not sure how welcome we are."

"How did you get here so quick?" Dave asked, "We didn't expect any organised resistance before dawn."

"It's a long story." Major Borodin chuckled, "I'm sure someone will explain but for now, shall we get back to the war?"

At that moment, no-one fully understood what had happened. Those trapped in the pub correctly assumed that Lau Cheng and Daniel Lone were involved. For once, they were tackling an enemy that was actually hostile. Odd as it may seem, it was something of a relief because it was a situation that they understood. It was easy to reconnoitre because they had studied the land before. Lightly armed, lightly clad individuals could move more quietly and easily than squads of men. Lau Cheng and Daniel Lone observed troops pouring through a portal, out of the quarry to take up defensive positions around both the quarry and the village.

They saw the Hauptsturmführer's group hurrying to the village. Lau Cheng took out his phone and dialled a number then spoke in Chinese. Daniel Lone looked at him quizzically.

"It's too late to phone Superintendent Jenkins." he said, "I've phoned my embassy in London. They're contacting the British authorities and the Russian embassy. Maybe Stuart's base there can help. They'll pass on my number if we can help."

It was just five minutes later that Daniel who was looking towards the quarry gasped, "Ya khabar abyad!"

Lau Cheng did not need a translator as Daniel stared wide-eyed and with his jaw dropping towards the quarry. He uttered his own equivalent of 'Oh my god' as he stared at the rock hovering over the quarry. They stared unbelievingly as the rock just hovered until finally it crashed down, creating its own plume of smoke and dust. Moments later they felt the ground tremble.

They watched as other rocks fell around them. They recovered their composure as none fell near them but the last of the twilight was fading and they could see no more.

"I assume that was Stuart's work but how did he get here so quickly?" Daniel whispered.

In fact, it took the Chinese embassy two hours to get permission to pass the message on and it was several more hours before Chairman Chernekov was informed though he immediately contacted Major Borodin. The British government, already alerted by Superintendent Jenkins were getting reports but initially decided that a communist government was too much of an enemy and would not want to be that helpful. Without Stuart's help, the invaders from Earth-4 would have secured an advanced foothold that, short of using a tactical nuclear weapon, would have been difficult to destroy.

Fortunately Prime Minister Shanks had received a phone call from Stuart as he headed for a meeting with Joint Chiefs of Staff but it was not going to make the meeting any easier.

General Pritchard's briefing was little more than an admission that they did not know what was going on.

"We're programming drones but that takes time and the Americans are shifting the orbits of their satellites." he said, "In the meantime, helicopters are being shot at so we don't know what's going on."

Prime Minister Shanks leant forward and looked at the map before pointing to the quarry.

"An hour before sunset, a large daisy-cutter type bomb was detonated in this quarry." he said pointing at the map. Immediately afterwards enemy troops began arriving through a device that uses similar technology to our new space ships. Enough troops came through to establish a strong foothold before the device was disabled. Friendly troops also arrived using their own devices and are a strong enough presence to deter further advances."

He paused, "I would like you to send a rapid response force to liaise with our allies. As more of our troops are deployed, so our allies will quietly leave. I understand that the enemy is willing to surrender and if we can avoid a bloodbath, then we stand a good chance of containing the publicity."

"Yes sir." General Pritchard said, "That appraisal ties in with what intelligence we do have so may I ask, who's briefing you?". Do you know who's attacking us and who's helping us."

Prime Minister Shanks took a deep breath. It was not going to be the easiest of answers.

"I am not mad, and I trust my sources." he began, "Accept for the moment that my information comes from the same source as our new technology. Our allies are troops of the Soviet People's Liberation Army led by a Major Borodin. Our enemies are troops of Waffen-SS Brigade *Saxon*. Its surviving senior officer is Hauptsturmführer David Hilford."

General Pritchard stared at the prime minister.

"I'll accept that at face value for now." he said, "Is there anything else that I should know?"

"There is something that may be relevant but it will be straining my credibility even further."

"Try me!"

"Major Borodin has two officers on attachment. One is a civilian but he has been given a temporary commission. His name is Lieutenant Dave Hilford. The other is SS-Senior-Storm-Leader David Hilford, late of the Waffen-SS Brigade *Halifax*. Both SS officers come from Nazi occupied Englands but they do things a little differently to each other."

General Pritchard stared again.

"It sounds like sci-fi babble to me but you're serious, aren't you?" he said bluntly, "There's been a lot of speculation about the meteor that hit Salisbury. I also read the report on the tank that was mysteriously sliced in two. Is there any connection?"

"Yes."

"And it's all tied in to the new technology that we so mysteriously developed. What about the rumours of alien involvement?"

"I would have thought the attached officers I mentioned might have given you a clue. They're not aliens in the sense that they come from outer space though. Can we get on, please? I feel that we're wasting the advantage that we've been given."

General Pritchard had already ordered a reconnaissance unit forward, so modifying its orders was simple. At first Lieutenant Blanchard thought that he was involved in some sort of instant readiness exercise. He was the duty officer but fully expected to pass a quiet night in the mess playing snooker. He had enlisted as the best way of getting a university education and he succeeded although for now, it worked to his disadvantage. His colonel was suspicious of a soldier who thought too much.

Like everyone else he was relaxed, off guard after the events of the previous month or so and at first, he was more annoyed at leaving his game just as his opponent needed snookers to win. It was as he checked his orders and saw where he was going that he began to wonder. He recognised the place as the sleepy Yorkshire village that had suddenly become the world centre for space travel. Even so, the idea of space travel was too new. When he had visited the place, he had been disappointed; it was just a collection of portable cabins, hastily assembled to deal with administration. He became more concerned when the radio operator adjusted the controls and a new voice crackled over his headphones.

"This is General Pritchard. You are not on exercise and you are entering a front-line situation. I have the prime minister with me, radio silence is not an issue so keep us informed at all times. You are to report to a Major Borodin. His position will follow. He is an officer of the Russian army and his troops are containing an incursion by a foreign power. Remember, we now see Russia as a friendly power so when you arrive, since you're on British territory, you will be the senior officer present."

General Pritchard paused before chuckling, "I don't suppose you understand. Report to Major Borodin and take it from there."

"Yes sir." Lieutenant Blanchard replied, "That I do understand."

Bewildered, when he arrived at the coordinates given he found a well-established command post. He noted a lack of vehicles but one tent bore red cross markings while another was full of radio equipment. A Russian soldier grinned at him and beckoned him to follow.

He found himself in the command tent, snapping to attention and saluting as he recognise a senior officer.

Returning the salute, Major Borodin smiled, "Relax lieutenant, you are now in charge. We are only here to help. What do you know of the situation?"

"Nothing, sir." Lt. Blanchard replied, "Will you brief me please?"

As Major Borodin complied, indicating locations on a large scale map, Lt. Blanchard tried to follow.

"Yes, but what is this Greater Reich you mentioned. Is it a Neo-Nazi terrorist group? You say their leader is British. I'm to arrest him as a traitor. Is that it?"

"A raid by an enemy nation has gone badly wrong and you, my friend, are here to accept their surrender and clear up the mess. Their commanding officer, Hauptsturmführer David Hilford is not British as you understand it and he is not a traitor. He and his troops will be repatriated as prisoners of war. Just accept that they are enemy troops for now. Believe me, it's more than enough to deal with. Now, do you have any orders?"

229

"Er, no. Would you carry on as you are, please?" Lieutenant Blanchard replied, "Would this German surrender to me, do you think?"

"He's already agreed to surrender to a British officer but be warned, his Britain is a province of the Greater German Reich."

"So you keep saying but there's no such thing. It doesn't exist."

"Lieutenant. We do not have much time. Will you at least accept his surrender to avoid further bloodshed?"

Confused, not understanding anything of the situation, Lt. Blanchard nodded, "I'll talk to him."

Once the surrender was agreed, Lt. Blanchard drove into the village. The Earth-4 soldiers were paraded on the village green awaiting his arrival. The uniforms, the orderly parade smartly at attention convinced Lt. Blanchard that he was dealing with a regular army unit though he desperately hoped that the main contingent of British troops would arrive soon and a more senior officer would take over. Lieutenant Blanchard, already confused by friendly Russian troops operating in Yorkshire, and phoning the enemy to negotiate a surrender, forgot the essential part of accepting one; disarming the enemy. It was the Hauptsturmführer who reminded him.

"I've got two lightly armed reconnaissance vehicles." Lieutenant Blanchard replied, "If you ordered your men to scatter, I could take out a good few before the rest got between the houses but then the Russians surrounding the village would deal with the rest of you. Your men would be cut down if you ordered them to make a direct attack on the Scimitars. If I spread my men out to disarm you then I wouldn't have enough to operate my own guns and I'd prefer to keep my men under their protection."

As Hauptsturmführer Dave Hilford nodded in agreement Lieutenant Blanchard relaxed, allowing his confusion to get the better of him.

"Just what the hell is going on?" he asked, "Who are you? Where do you come from?"

"I'm only required to give my rank and name." Dave smiled, "I'd prefer others to give the explanations especially since I appear to be less than well briefed on the situation."

"Fair point, but normally I would at least know which flag you serve under. What are the Russians doing here."

"That is something that I'd like to know." Hauptsturmführer Hilford answered, "You haven't been occupied, have you?"

For Lt. Blanchard the situation remained bewildering. He was relieved at the sound of approaching lorries, assuming that they were British but not completely sure until they came into view. He recognised Colonel Freeman and hurried over to give his report.

"I've asked everyone to stay indoors until we get the situation under control. Hauptsturmführer Hilford has agreed to surrender providing we can send his men home."

He turned and beckoned Dave-4 over.

"This is now a military zone, so you order civilians to stay indoors and you don't negotiate with traitors and terrorists." Colonel Freeman snapped

"Sir, according to Major Borodin, they are regular soldiers of a bona fide country. I accepted their surrender as the best way of avoiding bloodshed." Lieutenant Blanchard exclaimed.

"Yes, Yes, I've received these crazy reports as well. However, you exceeded your authority and I refuse to call some terrorist enclave a nation. What is it, a communist cell or an Islamic one?"

"A Nazi one, sir." Lieutenant Blanchard snapped, pleased to see a startled look flash across the colonel's face."

Colonel Freeman turned to look at Dave-4 who came smartly to attention. It was not long after midnight and in the glow of the street lights and the vehicle headlamps the colonel could see enough to recognise Dave-4's uniform before turning to one of his officers.

"Major, send a squad to disarm those men, secure them and get them into the lorries. That is something else you failed to do, Lieutenant. You, hand over that pistol and remove your helmet."

As the major hurried off to obey so the loud clattering of a helicopter landing at the far end of the green prevented further conversation.

They waited as General Pritchard hurried over, accepting the salutes from the other officers before turning to Dave-4.

"Hauptsturmführer David Hilford of the Waffen-SS Brigade *Saxon* I presume. Your men will be treated with full military honours but you will be held as a civilian and tried for the murder of Superintendent Jenkins and two other civilians. You will also be held under a false name. I find the reason almost unbelievable but those are my orders."

"I understand." Dave-4 replied, "Look after my men, please."

General Pritchard turned to Lieutenant Blanchard.

"You did well. I've checked your record and I don't want another officer becoming involved so I'm promoting you to acting-captain to ensure that the Hauptsturmführer is accompanied by an officer of equivalent rank. It's been a long time since an officer received a battlefield promotion so we'll have to sort out the procedures to confirm it but your first task is to provide an escort to the Hauptsturmführer."

"Sir, I must protest." Colonel Freeman interjected, "Lt. Blanchard exceeded his authority, failed to act decisively in securing the prisoners and did not even send a patrol to check the area. He hardly warrants promotion."

"Perhaps not but his negligence is helping us contain an awkward situation. When I was talking to Major Borodin yesterday, he seemed to think that the Lieutenant did everything right."

"You spoke to Major Borodin about me yesterday, sir." Lieutenant/Captain Blanchard asked, understandably confused.

General Pritchard smiled, "I'm still getting used to the idea that it's not insane to say that I was on Mars yesterday though that is becoming more common thanks to our new ships. Where it becomes incredible is that I only think that I was still in this universe but I was chatting to this SS-Senior-Storm-Leader David Hilford."

"Sir, we've never met before, I'm a Hauptsturmführer so why would I translate my rank into English?" Hauptsturmführer David Hilford exclaimed angrily.

"Apparently different universes do things differently. I'm authorised to debrief you, Hauptsturmführer, however, once your usefulness ends then our civilian authorities will want a piece of you. You'll help your country but you're heading for the noose."

"I understand that I'm to be hanged and it's hardly an incentive to betray the Reich so why would I help?"

"Excuse me, sir but I'm confused." Colonel Freeman interrupted, "I just don't understand what you're talking about"

"It's my fault." General Pritchard, "Time travel has left me disorientated and almost as confused as the rest of you but I'll try to explain. The Hauptsturmführer comes from an alternate Earth which is designated *four*. The SS-Senior-Storm-Leader that I mentioned comes from *three* while we're designated *two*. The people that the Hauptsturmführer was sent to kidnap come from *one*. Someone has been trying to gain the technology that he needs to conquer universes. This madman is a threat to all worlds which is why Hauptsturmführer, you'll be helping your own world by helping us. I hope that's clear."

"No-one's going to believe a story like that." Colonel Freeman exclaimed, "Surely we can provide a better cover than that."

"Oh, the cover story is that our Hauptsturmführer here is a spy for the Warriors of Saladin by the name of Daniel Lone and in cahoots with a Chinese spy that went rogue. They caused the mayhem, Daniel Lone was caught and will stand trial while Lau Cheng unfortunately escaped. They're real people and real spies yet they were instrumental in stopping the assault. Out of gratitude we're suggesting that they retire and quietly disappear."

Dave-4 nodded, "I'm to provide the body to prove the tale."

"I'm afraid so." General Pritchard said softly.

"But it's all so preposterous." Colonel Freeman exclaimed angrily.

"You're an excellent officer, Colonel so I was pleased that it was your regiment that would contain any incursion." General Pritchard said, "However, Captain Blanchard may adapt to the rest of the situation far more readily. You will hold the prisoners and offer them every courtesy due to fellow soldiers until we can arrange their repatriation. I don't intend allowing the Russians to have all the fun so you will remain at instant readiness."

"Yes Sir." Colonel Freeman replied, "Congratulations, Captain Blanchard. It seems that you understand the situation better than I do."

"I doubt it." General Pritchard grinned, "Captain, do you trust the Hauptsturmführer to show you the way to the quarry where your transport awaits. I warn you now, you're about to meet an SS-Senior-Storm-Leader David Hilford who is not a prisoner and neither is Lieutenant David Hilford of the Russian Peoples Liberation Army. It'll be a unique family meeting for you Hauptsturmführer."

As they headed for the quarry, Captain Blanchard said, "Sorry about the cuffs but SS officers are supposed to be pretty ruthless and I think that you may be more used to unarmed combat than me."

"I would have just opened up on your men if you had been my prisoners, neither would I be treating you like a fellow officer. You're right, you're nowhere ruthless enough."

"I'll take that as a complement." Captain Blanchard laughed, "You looked out for your men though."

David shrugged,

"Just my own weakness." he shuddered, "I hope that I'm stronger when I face the noose."

They trudged on in silence only stopping to stare at the portal. For the Hauptsturmführer it was surprise at the size and the much smaller space for the field generators. For Captain Blanchard it was just another shock to his system.

"What is it?" he gasped.

"A TDT." David-4 replied then seeing the Captain's blank look, "A trans-dimensional transporter but I don't see how it can carry all the generators it needs."

"No, I don't suppose you do." Captain Blanchard replied irritably.

"Sorry. Your world doesn't have them yet, does it?" David-4 said, "Here's another mystery, you see that officer approaching? If I'm not mistaken, he's Russian."

"It's Major Borodin." Captain Blanchard replied, "Of course, you've only spoken on the phone."

Major Borodin accepted Captain Blanchard's salute before turning to Dave-4.

"You're the second Nazi that I haven't shot on sight." he said, "I'll try to be polite but it's not easy."

"I understand." Dave-4 replied, "I've seen action on the Eastern Front so I'm not that happy about being your prisoner."

"I have a great deal of respect for Dave Hilfords in general so I'll try to accept that you're just doing your duty. I suggest that you remove his handcuffs, Captain. Dave, I still want to shoot you so if you want to fight, go ahead. Make my day."

It was still Captain Blanchard who was the most bewildered as Major Borodin led the way through the portal to their Mars base. Although both of Major Borodin's guests accepted the idea of inter-planetary travel, it was academic rather than a practical understanding. Again, although they had been warned about the other David Hilfords, it was still a shock meeting them. Most were relieved when Stuart-1 arrived and they all settled down for a briefing.

"OK!" Stuart said, "Earth-4 has a portal and it's controlled by Brian-4 who wants to conquer the universe. My Brian can think big but the 4 is something else."

He paused, "Inter-dimensional navigation is tricky and Brian-4 lacks the attention to detail that my Brian has. That works to our advantage as does the fact that the Reich-4 devoted more of its energy to invading Russia and a number of key research projects dried up due to lack of resources. Hitler-4 loved his rockets but they weren't much use against a highly organised guerilla army."

"I know what you're going to say, Dave." he continued as Dave-4 stood up, "I'm not respectful enough of the Fuhrer, but the fact is, electronics development slowed considerably. That is relevant and to our advantage. On Earth-3 Nazism relaxed more while on Earth-4, it tried to exert more control over everything. Dave-4 is more used to speaking German and speaks English with a distinct accent while Dave-3 has lost any trace of Yorkshire and speaks er, I suppose you call it London English."

Dave-4 nodded and sat down again.

"Are you sure that it's Brian-4?" James asked, "You were calling him Brian-X because you weren't certain."

"I'm still not." Stuart admitted, "He seems to be based on Earth-4 so I guess it's near enough. I could call him Brian-E for enemy if you like but as long as you're clear who we're talking about it's not that important."

"You really do believe that he's a threat to the Reich, don't you?" Dave-4 asked but instead of waiting for a reply, added, "I'll help if you'll let me."

"Thanks." Stuart acknowledged, "For the record, we reckon that your world is near to collapse. Your Reich is bleeding to death on the Russian front. Your America is trying to remain isolationist and relies on selling wheat to Europe across the Atlantic and arms to Russia across the Pacific. It might still be at war with Japan but it's more of an uneasy truce than actual hostilities. Breaking the Japanese codes, discovering about the Pearl Harbour attack in advance and defeating it, made the American government more complacent. There's more to it but now is not the time to go into detail."

Stuart paused, "That's our estimate, and they're usually pretty reliable. Now, we don't interfere unless a society is collapsing and then we offer an alternative but in Earth-4's case, no-one would accept it. However, if Brian-4 succeeds in importing technology from alternate worlds then he'll be interfering in his world, big-time. Dave-1 and Dave-3 still report Brian-3 crawling around their brains so he's still around though he died on Earth-3."

Stuart paused again, "Physically he's dead so we come back to Brian-4 and we need to stop him or them if you prefer. Brians tend to keep key points about their work in their head so it's unlikely anyone else can build a portal on Earth-4 but if he's got a couple of sites then we need to know about them."

"Are you saying that you believe in ghosts and that this Brian-3 is haunting Brian-4?" Dave-4 asked.

"No, at least not in the supernatural sense. If he found a compatible mind that was receptive to him, then he could be there. Brian-4 is a good candidate because he's the only one we know of but there could be others."

"But it only happens across universes and only because you cross them."

"That's right." Stuart agreed.

"And the Fuhrer doesn't know anything about it?"

"I doubt it." Stuart said, "Brians do not discuss their work with the authorities."

"I understand but you may be wrong about Brian-4." Dave-4 said, "There is another site and it's much larger. He's done enough to convince the Reich Chancellery that he has a new super weapon. I don't know where it is, though."

"I'd guess the moon." Stuart said, "Small rocks dropped from a great height causes massive explosions. The portal at quarry-4 could supply it while he threatens to bomb, Berlin, Washington and Tokyo."

"The moon! That's quite a jump." James exclaimed, "Why think of that?"

Stuart turned to Dave-4, "Do the names Darren Barker or David Bradley mean anything to you?"

"Herr Bradley is Gauleiter of North Britain province and Darren Barker is in overall charge of the TDT, sorry, portal."

"Ah!" James exclaimed though this time in understanding, "That makes sense."

"It doesn't to me." both Dave-3 and Dave-4 snapped in unison, then looked at each other in surprise.

"People have a habit of coming up with similar ideas in all the universes. The Reich-1 was full of intrigue and political infighting. If it's the same on Earth-4, then maybe Brian-4 is playing off one faction against the other so that no-one really knows what's happening. Bradley and Barker have a history of dropping rocks off the moon."

"Come on, Dave." James commanded, then hesitated, "I meant Dave-1. Stuart, you're going to have to do something about the other two."

"Excuse me, sir, but the Haupsturmfuhrer is my prisoner." Captain Blanchard interjected.

"I understand." Stuart said, "You would confine him to quarters while I'm content to confine him to a planet or a universe. Besides, I'd like you to report to Major Borodin. I think that you'd be more useful helping with any military operations we might need."

"The Major does not want me involved." Dave-3 said, "He tries but he cannot see beyond my uniform."

"Living in one third gravity isn't healthy so you can't stay here for long either." Stuart paused thoughtfully before grinning, "Brian has a friend who will help. He'll see that you're comfortable and provide you with minders who'll see that you don't get into trouble."

Brian was not keen at first but eventually he agreed, so before long, Brian-1, Dave-3 and Dave-4 were seated in Mr. Allen's office, waiting while Mr. Allen flipped through a dossier of all his activities. Apart from being concerned that the shadiest of his deals were known, even to the location of a number of bodies, he was rattled by the presence of the twins – the two Daves. One of them had thoroughly humiliated him during their previous encounter so two were intimidating. However, he sounded calm enough as he said, "I am to find comfortable accommodation for your colleagues and to provide them with minders. I don't see why, one of them handled himself well enough at our last meeting."

"They can handle themselves too well and now need to be discreet and unnoticed. Their guides will remind them to stay in the background."

"And do you offer a fee for these services?" Mr. Allen asked.

"You'll get the money back that we destroyed and any extra expenses."

"OK, but why me. Surely you've got all sorts of contacts."

"Their electronic trail stops in Yorkshire and you're the last person that we'd do business with. No-one will link your two new associates with us and since the new electronic trail will be yours then they'll be untraceable."

"So there's a price on their heads."

"You might think so, but you wouldn't live to collect. Our enemies have methods way beyond yours."

"So why aren't they after you?"

"Why do you ask so many questions?" Brian felt as if he was back in a bad film but it seemed to work with Mr. Allen. "Let's just say that the more that they can be assimilated into society, the more grateful some very powerful friends will be."

"I see." Mr. Allen did not see at all, "That dossier will disappear?"

"No," Brian said, "We don't normally involve ourselves in planetary affairs but unless you consider a career move, we may reconsider."

Although he didn't say anything, Mr. Allen picked up on the word, 'planetary'. It tied in with what Tim had said about their activities but it didn't help. Like Brian, Mr. Allen always felt as if he was in a bad film when they talked and the idea that he was expected to shelter two alien fugitives was just too much. He needed to get back to normality.

"I'll help if I can, perhaps you should introduce me."

Brian smiled, "One is SS-Senior-Storm-Leader David Hilford of the Waffen-SS and the other is Haupsturmfuhrer David Hilford of a different Waffen-SS. The Haupsturmfuhrer is the one with the thicker accent."

"So it's the SS that are after them?" Mr. Allen asked knowing just how stupid it sounded but he could not stop himself being led further into the film.

"I know how this all sounds but it should tie in with events from the last time we met." Brian said, "You can refuse to help us and take your chances with the authorities, help us and, as I said, use the time to consider a career move or try to betray us. That would be a bad mistake."

Mr. Allen shuddered, remembering how he lost control, the last time they met. He agreed that crossing Brian would be very unwise, "I'll find them a flat and see that they have spending money. I've got a minder, he's mainly a bouncer in one of my clubs. He's also studying with the Open University. I'll assign him to you and you can help him."

Mr. Allen caught Brian's look of surprise. "I do nicely enough from the lowlifes. How is Tim, by the way? Still under your protection?"

"No." Brian replied, "He never has been, just his ex-partner and son."

"They're safe from me though I can't say the same for Tim." Mr. Allen said, "It's better to have honest folk on side. Instead of grassing to the police, they feel grateful and tell me."

"Very well," Brian said, "We'll help your friend if we can. In return, you'll help my two friends to assimilate themselves into our society. It's a good start that you're Jewish."

Both Brian and Mr. Allen caught the startled looks on both Daves. Dave-3 recovered first. He held out his hand, "I was well treated by the Russian People's Liberation Army. That was a first and this is another."

Dave-4 chuckled, visibly relaxed but did not follow suit.

~~~

Later when Brian met up with Stuart he said, "You could be right about them being vulnerable. Dr. Tobias should write a paper on the psychological effects of suddenly being weightless or in a different gravity field. It could be adapted to help earthquake victims."

"It's just lucky Mr. Allen considers himself a cultured man." Stuart said, "He's also used to people not having the right paperwork so we don't have to create false identities for them. Was it wise to say that they were aliens though?"

"He's got no proof, it makes us more powerful and it suits his ego to feel involved in something so big."

"Once he got used to the idea it appealed to Captain Blanchard's sense of humour." Stuart laughed, "He's never heard of a prisoner confined to a universe before but he sees the logic now. Dave-4 can hardly resume hostilities and it's in his best interests to learn about our world."

"How come you knew Allen would be so useful?" Brian asked.

"I didn't know." Stuart replied, "I just wondered how many gangland bosses would have listened to Tim's weird tales. He should have simply left Tim for dead as a warning."

Brian nodded, "Good point. How's the war doing?"

"We've found a defensive shield on the Moon so we seem to have guessed right. Quarry-4 has been beefed up. Dave-1 is happier being separated from Dave-3 and he doesn't think that Brian-4 is prowling around so much. He says his mind feels as if it's his again. Believe me, I can understand that."

"So do I." Brian said, "So the mental attacks are getting weaker which presumably means that he's not got another mind machine but the military situation is as bad as we expected."

"That's about it. We're sending the prisoners back a few at a time and scattering them across the Reich. That's just in case they were planning a reception committee for us. Major Borodin's men seem to like handling Nazi prisoners and showing off as if they were seasoned travellers. I don't mind, it gets a bit monotonous seeing people react the same way all the time."

"I thought the prisoners knew all about the portal." Brian said.

"It's where we've got the advantage." Stuart explained, "They stripped their portal out to allow the soldiers through, and the power supply is massive compared to ours because theirs is all valves and what have you. Apparently they saw it dematerialise once during their training and then they practised deploying through it. The downside to that is that they concentrated on the protective shields. They're static and can be larger."

"And the problem is, Earth-4 has attacked us, but we're

limited in what we can do because of this interference nonsense."

"Do you really think that it's nonsense?" Brian asked.

"Not really." Stuart replied, "I had to keep Stuart-2 out of my head otherwise I'd have left Earth-2 alone. They tolerated our meddling and don't want to revert back so that's OK. Earth-4 is very militaristic, and the Reich is trying to expand but all we can do is to confine their activities to their own world. To do that we've got to stop Brian-4 only we've got to do it very gently."

"Any thoughts?" Brian asked.

"No, except that we've got to take over the moon-base. The problem is if we do, then we'll demonstrate just how effective portal technology is for delivering weapons."

"So you don't want to demonstrate what they could do?" Brian asked, "Not even on their equivalent of Salisbury plain?"

"No. Before we started on Earth-2, we got the idea that everyone there wanted to break the tension. They're already squabbling between themselves and there's a bit of tension between countries but it's more sabre-rattling and threats to look good to their people than anything. There's enough real action for everyone to have a piece of it, so things are stable."

Stuart paused, "On Earth-4 we're only dealing with one country and one we don't like very much but we have to remain neutral."

"You've taken over a moon-base once before." Brian said, "What's so different, apart from a protective field and last time, you were trying to stop aliens destroying the Earth."

"That's the key aim." Stuart exclaimed, "We're trying to stop Brian-4 from attacking other Earths. We've weakened him but he could recover and start again. There's another problem, I know that he's not you but it feels as if I am going against you."

"You could never do that." Brian whispered, "You give my life so much meaning. Be careful because I couldn't bear losing you. Go and find James. He's your military expert, talk it over with him."

Stuart complied and found himself talking to James, Major Borodin and Captain Blanchard.

"We've not been idle and you seem to be right." James said, "Most of their records are on paper so it's harder checking them. We've got a couple of probes that can handle it and it seems that the Reich Chancellor knows that he has a moon-base. The good news seems to be that there's little detail on record. Various departments want to take over and try to find who has the information. We reckon the best plan would be to occupy quarry-4 but do it in such a way

240

that the portal is not obvious or too visible. We destroy the portal that they use for communications then offer to evacuate the moonbase. The thing is, both Dave-3 and Dave-4 could be useful. 3 because he saw more of the mind jump equipment and would recognise it if there was anything similar there and 4 because he knows more of the site."

Stuart breathed a deep sigh of relief, "That's good news so far as I'm concerned; no-one need get killed. The only question is, what do we do with Brian-4 when we have him?"

"The lizard planet." James suggested, "They do have rules about telepathy and the like. Well not rules, guidelines? Anyway, they agree that Brian-4's behaviour is unacceptable and will try to reason with him."

"They have a protective shield so you need to send an advance team in to disable it, then the main force can capture this Brian-4 and destroy the quarry." Captain Blanchard said.

"Do you want my men involved?" Major Borodin asked.

"They already have field experience." James replied, "It would save time if we didn't have to train a new squad."

"So you're asking us to take part without trying to impose yourself and I'm offering without wanting to impose." Major Borodin laughed."

Stuart grinned, "Diplomacy's weird but yes, if your government is still willing to have us on Russian soil then we would be grateful for your help."

"In which case, I'd like your Dave along." Major Borodin said, "On my Earth, it was my grandparents who fought the Nazis and they never forgot what they did. I need a Dave who is not a Nazi and who understands the full picture. Stuart, I know that you dislike being left behind but you are still our commander and we suspect that you are the main target. If the operation goes wrong, we cannot afford to have you captured. Again, if anything does go wrong, then I can think of no-one I would rather have planning a rescue."

"Yes but…" Stuart began.

"No buts." James said, "Major Borodin is right. If something happens to you, Brian-1 will become vulnerable and we can't risk Earth-4 getting his knowledge. Besides, we need you in charge of the defence garrison while we're gone. "

"No." Major Borodin snapped, "Not you either, James. I'll take Captain Blanchard but only if he agrees to command the assorted Daves and any specialists that we bring along. That's assuming that he volunteers of course, but you proved your worth defending us from invading portals."

James nodded in reluctant agreement, "Does the fact that I'm American have anything to do with it?"

"I'm trying to accept Nazi help without feeling ashamed when I think of my grandparents. I've spent most of my career, preparing for war with our America. I'd rather not take on too many new ideas before going into action. A man's got to know his limitations."

"I shouldn't have introduced you to films from my world." Stuart chuckled, "You're beginning to sound like Clint Eastwood."

"I like your westerns." Major Borodin grinned, "They make life seem so simple. Not like your life, eh?"

"Fair enough." Stuart acknowledged, "Oh yes, there's just one more thing, I don't want any casualties."

"I took that as read." Major Borodin laughed, "I wonder if it's why you won't just drop a rock on the generator building even if you say it's to hide the portal's potential. You work out how to disable the field and we'll plan the land operations."

As Stuart already knew, the defensive fields at quarry-4 relied on valve technology. It made equipment more bulky, caused heat dissipation problems and limited the complexity, which made it difficult to generate the higher field levels. Because of the limitations, it was unable to be used for exploration much beyond the solar system but Brian-4 or was it 3 had been confident that he could obtain more advanced equipment. Whatever the limitations, Brian-4 had built smaller generators that could be hauled through the portal and set up in quarry-2, not as effective but able to make dematerialising in the area very hazardous.

The plans were simple. The advanced party would get as close as possible but when the guard was alerted, a probe would drop dummy parachutists on the wall opposite them. It should ensure that the entire guard was called out and then the probe could drop stun grenades to disable them. The probes would have to operate within the outer limits of the field but they could get close enough to stun any guard not disabled by the grenades. The plan worked well that far. Without being able to probe for Dave, the guards did not learn of the advance party until they reached the quarry wall. They had abseiled down, were safely hidden amongst the rocks and it was not even a guard dog that found them. It was the garrison commander's pet poodle.

As the SS-Standartenführer strolled over to see what had caught his dog's attention there was a bright flash and an explosion behind him. He swung round to stare at the parachutes drifting down. Apparently they had drifted off course and were landing in the minefield surrounding the quarry. While the poodle contentedly licked Dave-1's face, the Standartenführer recovered his wits as the klaxons sounded and troops poured from the barracks.

Dave-1 was vaguely embarrassed as he turned to protect the dog from the concussion blasts and the rest of the team chuckled quietly, briefly forgetting the developing battle. As the grenades reigned down, the advance party donned protective hoods.

The poodle whimpered in terror at the noise but in moments, the party was charging across to the buildings with Dave-4 leading the way. Stuart was watching, worried about his friends. As a shot rang out, Dave-1 crumpled to the ground while Dave-3 staggered briefly. Stuart stared in horror gripping James' arm so tightly that blood dripped down.

"He was in full protective clothing." James whispered, "Let's not expect the worst until we know."

To James' relief, Stuart nodded and relaxed his grip.

"It was a straggler." James said, "He was late out of the barracks and missed the blasts. I got him and he's out for the count."

Inside the building, the remaining party paused, they were all trained in various ways to accept the death of friends but it should not have happened.

"You two other Daves. Fetch him in. We'll cover you." James ordered

"There's no need." Dave-3 said quietly, "That body is quite dead. Stu will hate us for just leaving it but I'll make him understand later."

"Your special link with him?" Major Borodin asked quietly and Dave-3 nodded.

"Very well, if this is the field-generator room, where do we plant the explosives?"

Dave-4 nodded but it was Dave-3 who gave the directions as confidently as Dave-1 would have done.

"Why hasn't anyone checked on Dave?" Stuart snapped over the radio.

"Dave-3 says that he's dead." Major Borodin replied, "I'm sorry. I trust his opinion."

There was a long silence.

"Stuart has fainted." James said quietly, "It's OK, I'm monitoring the enemy. It's all quiet."

Major Borodin nodded in sympathy, "He deserves a hero's funeral."

"We're done." Dave-3 said, "Let's get clear before the charges go off. Stu won't take any more deaths."

Major Borodin looked at him quizzically but did not say anything as they hurried out.

"We need to recover the body, now it's safe." Dave-3 yelled, "If we leave it then they'll think that it's Dave-4. He'll never get home then."

The others nodded and Captain Blanchard hoisted it over his shoulder. They hurried past the poodle who was now licking his master's face.

They watched as the building that they had been sabotaging disintegrated in a series of loud thumps. Windows and doors burst out as the roof lifted then crashed down, the walls collapsing on top of it.

Paper in book form or in files is notoriously difficult to burn and there was no time to separate each page. Filing cabinets were wheeled outside, probes picked them up and dropped them into the sun.

Captain Blanchard had enough regard for Major Borodin to leave him to complete the clean up operation and took his charges back through the portal. The whole operation had taken just ten minutes. They had little time because diversions, including more dummy paratroopers, would not keep Nazi forces distracted for long but everything was working to plan including probes sounding like helicopters and giving the right radar emissions. However, Dave Hilford could not be seen aiding the enemy.

They found Stuart, ashen faced with tears staring at the body.

"You'll find that we're looking for Brian 3+4, Stu." Dave-3 said quietly, "I need time to understand but I'm not just Dave-3 any more."

"I don't understand." Stuart whispered.

"Neither do I yet." Dave-3 said, "Captain Blanchard, it was Dave-4 who was killed wasn't it. You can have Dave-1's body, but we don't want one of us hanged."

Captain Blanchard nodded in understanding, "As long as he never steps foot on my Earth again."

"I really don't understand." Stuart said, "Who are you?"

"I told you, I don't know yet. I can tell you that a bullet hurts like fuck when it passes through your neck. I can also tell you that when you're as close as Dave-3 and Dave-1 it hurts almost as much seeing him die."

Stuart might have said more but Major Borodin called.

"We've got Brian Chapman." he said, "You'd better take a look."

Stuart seemed happier as he turned to the monitors then the blood drained from his face again. James hurried round to see what was happening. The monitor showed Brian-4 standing, holding – Stuart could only assume that it was Robert Downing-4 by wrapping one arm around his neck, holding a pistol in his free hand.

"I want to go to your Earth." he yelled, "I can help you. Your country will control the world."

"Thank you for such a generous offer." Major Borodin replied, "Unfortunately it seems that it's also your ambition."

"Of course it is." Brian-4 screamed, "Why not. You can't imagine where I can lead you."

"Just drop your gun and let the boy go." Major Borodin said quietly, "Believe me, he's not keeping you alive."

Brian paused thoughtfully.

"You're probably right." he said, "I'm too valuable to kill."

He pressed the gun against Robert's head and fired. Stuart just managed to turn away from the controls before he was sick on the floor. He staggered and was caught by Dave-3.

"Easy Stu." he said, "Sally won't know that I've been killed but your Brian will certainly notice if you cough your insides out."

He was distracted by the sound of another shot as Major Borodin shot Brian-4 through the heart. He slumped to the floor and those watching, could see the look of amazement as he fell.

"I'm sorry, Stuart." Major Borodin called out, "My finger twitched. Premier Chernekov would have understood that he was insane but others would have used him to gain a political advantage. They would not have understood just what he was capable of."

"I've got to find my Brian." Stuart yelled pushing James' out of the way.

"Easy Stuart." Dave-3 said quietly, "He really is dead. Neither Dave-3 nor your Dave really understood how he used his mind machine but we could feel him. I can't any more."

"Let him through but be quick." Major Borodin called across the radio, "He'll be no use until he calms down."

James nodded and reset the controls. Stuart hurried through to his world, running faster than he ever had before down the lane to find Brian-1.

Brian was in his study, and alarmed by the state Stuart was in as he burst through the study door, leapt up to grab Stuart as he collapsed, yelling for Demetrius.

"What's happened?" he asked, "Are you hurt?"

Stuart shook his head, "No. Is it really you, Brian."

"I assume so." Brian chuckled, "What's wrong?"

"Dave's dead but he's not. Brian-4's dead and I don't know where he is. I'm so worried about you."

"We'll go to the lizard planet." Brian said, "They'll help you and you'll know that he's not here. How's that?"

"Yes please." Stuart murmured, "I'm already sure but please can we go."

Epilogue

It took time before anyone really understood what had happened and no-one ever fully understood how Brian-3's mind machine worked or the side-effects it produced. For a time, Stuart remained in shock only slowly accepting that Brian 4 was truly dead and wanting to stay close to his Brian, Brian-1.

Theories remained confused and uncertain, not even the lizard people or the Terzons could fully explain what had happened but there was no doubt that Dave was happy. The best idea was that even for *images* of each other across dimensions, Dave-1 and Dave-3 were unusually close. *Spillage* from Brian's mind machine allowed them to *bond* even closer. Dave-1 was fortunate in that the bullet did not kill him instantly. As always happened when one was stressed, he could jump to another. When Dave-1 *died*, the closeness took one last step and they became one.

"Judging by Dave-3 memories, he could have refused but he wanted Dave-1's gentleness." Dave said on one occasion, "Dave-1 was panicking and in pain but I think he also admired Dave-3's military skills. There's no way of describing it. We could wrestle and horse around like we always did but now I'd have to hold back all that military training so that I didn't snap your neck. You might get to win once or twice."

"You wish." Stuart retorted then grinned, "You sound like my Dave. Full of bull."

"I've got Dave-1's admiration for you but I could always thrash you at pool." Dave grinned, "Now I've got a soldier's coordination, you won't stand a chance."

There was one odd incident and that was the first time that Dave went home. His step son, Aidan looked at him and asked, "Have I got two daddies now?"

"What a silly question." Sally, Dave's partner exclaimed, "This is your only daddy."

"Yes, he's there." Aidan replied, "Can we go to the swings today?"

Aidan never mentioned it again and never treated Dave differently than before so it was still Stuart who was most affected by events. He took to joining Brian on his trips to Terzon where he worked with their scientists. Otherwise, Stuart avoided all portal travel and his friends, and despite the few moments banter, he became steadily more morose and lethargic. Although concerned, his friends accepted that he needed to rest.

Earth-2 had been given their future back and now that all threats had been eliminated, wanted to get on with it. Stuart's friends sensed that they were overstaying their welcome. Earth-2 did not want another Earth looking over their shoulder, though individually there were some sad goodbyes and it was Zack-1 who was most affected. He got on well with Chairman Chernekov, enjoyed his visits and it had been his first major project with minimal supervision so felt the end more acutely than the rest.

There was nothing that the others had not done before and soon, for the first time in ages they all found themselves back on Earth-1 with nothing to do.

On Earth-2, Captain Blanchard had the most contact with Russian troops, he had engaged in off-world military adventures but had apparently allowed a prisoner under his care to be killed. He was something of a hero for his actions but he was also an embarrassment as no-one wanted to admit to Russian troops operating on British soil. It was suggested that he leave the army and join the deep space programme. He found himself with a knighthood and a good start to his new life. He was well out of the way when the enquiries began, which suited the authorities.

Only Dave-4 was lost, with nowhere to go. They had obliterated the last of Brian-4's work in the now abandoned quarry with their own daisy-cutter bomb and the moon-base proved to be no more than a slowly deflating, pressure dome in a cave. Without Earth-1 type technology, the portal on Earth-4 proved inadequate to maintain it. They monitored investigations in the Reich-4 and Dave-4's name kept cropping up. The attack on the quarry was put down to a highly organised, Russian backed, terrorist group and the authorities spent a great deal of time hunting down collaborators.

Like other Daves he found himself responding to his unusual surroundings but he was an experienced killer and far harder than the others.

Dave-1 and Brian considered giving him false papers and letting him work as a bouncer at one of Mr. Allen's nightclubs but he was too violent. It was even difficult for him to accept that he was being employed by a Jew though he adapted. The lizards might have helped but they were not sure that he wanted to change.

The lives of parallel images of people tend to follow patterns and it was a young single mother who caught his attention. She was struggling with a ten-year-old boy who kept playing truant and she faced court and a fine.

She was one of Mr. Allen's favoured clients and Dave-4 was sent round to collect her weekly payment.

"She does her best but she struggles." Mr. Allen said, "When she's not nervous, she listens and knows what's going on around the estate. She pays what she can and she'll offer it without being asked. Speak gently if she can't pay. Let her offer you a cup of tea and listen. She'll pour out her problems but listen to the gossip. Don't force it, just listen."

Naturally, Dave-4 followed Mr. Allen's orders and was still there when the boy, Craig, burst in marching straight for the fridge without acknowledging his mother. Dave-4 actually understood the situation. He was intelligence gathering and his informant needed help. He leapt up almost standing to attention.

"Halt!" he snapped, "Get back here now!"

Craig jumped in alarm and started to obey only to recover and stare defiantly.

"You can't make me." he retorted, "I'll report you to social services if you touch me and say that you tried to feel me up."

"If you're going to report me, then it had better be for something worthwhile." Dave was removing his belt and doubling it over as he spoke, then yelled, "Greet your mother properly, now."

Craig could see Dave's military bearing even if he did not know what it was. He was also aware of Mr. Allen's shadowy presence which made Dave's confidence more believable and his own threat much weaker. He surrendered to the situation and meekly walked over to his mother and kissed her on the cheek then stood looking nervously at Dave-4 as he replaced his belt.

"Where I come from boys like you get sent to a punishment camp. They sleep in tents and spend their time doing drill and physical training. They don't leave until they can find their way out by a map and compass doing a route march across country. The boys here are too soft for that."

"I'm not." Craig said, almost before Dave had finished speaking. He was the sort of boy who relished a physical challenge and Dave recognised something of himself in the boy.

"You act tough but real tough guys don't have to prove it. You're content to add to your mother's problems and you can't acknowledge what she does for you."

Craig was silent. This was the direct opposite of what his mates on the estate said, yet it was Dave who commanded respect and exuded authority.

"So you say, I bet you're the one who's all talk and act tough. I bet you wouldn't take me camping."

Dave-4 knew that if he let himself get riled, he'd say something like, 'You're talking like a Jew' which would not go down well so he had to keep calm.

"It's your mother's decision, but if you attend school and show more respect to her then we'll go on your next holiday."

"Yeah, I bet we don't."

Craig's mother was twenty-five, attractive and with minimal financial help from Craig's father, just about managed. Dave felt as if she was appraising him, just as much as Craig was. Dave glanced around, the flat was a little shabby but it was clean and tidy. Comfortable was the word that came to mind. Suddenly, he wanted to impress her.

"Have you got any running gear?" he asked Craig, "Mine's in the car. If I could change in the bathroom then we could go for a run in the park. I wonder if there's somewhere nearby where we do a proper cross-country run instead of this silly jogging."

None of them were thinking properly. A sexual tension was building between Dave and Craig's mother and he was showing off to her. She should have been far more careful about letting her son go off with almost a complete stranger while Craig found the physical challenges that Dave was offering, more stimulating than he could have imagined possible.

When she agreed though, their lives changed for ever. Dave-4 knew that he would have to learn to treat his partner as an equal rather than a dutiful wife indoors. She never learned where he came from, with Mr. Allen involved it was better not to know. However, she understood that it was from a very different background and appreciated his efforts to change while Craig came to love the man who taught him the physical skills that he craved to learn.

Dave continued working as a bouncer as well as an enforcer. However, he also took training classes, learning to deal with troublemakers by using more diplomacy than force and they worked because he now had an incentive to settle down at home. To everyone's amusement he took cookery lessons showing a real talent so that eventually they took on a country pub in the West Country, paid for by Mr. Allen who was still wary of Dave and his friends.

Only Stuart remained withdrawn and miserable, refusing all help at least in his immediate circle though there was another who had lost everything.

Abu al Khayr Naṣṣār stood also feeling lost, deflated and

defeated. His master may have been old and senile but at times he displayed a sharp incisive mind that seemed to reach out to him. He vaguely understood that his master's plans involved creating a coalition that would force the Western empire to share vital equipment, knowledge and personnel. Abu al Khayr Naṣṣār did not understand why inconsequential youngsters were so important, but it seemed that his master could actually understand it all. The old man's periods of intellect became fewer and less powerful until he just rambled on about defeating those jumped up little German fuhrers. The collapse had happened quickly especially after the announcement of the new spaceships. Abu al Khayr Naṣṣār could see that with Russia, Britain and America offering space travel to the world their own coalition was obsolete but he could not see why the ships 'ruined everything'.

Stuart and his friends never even got to hear of Abu al Khayr Naṣṣār, let alone learn anything of his problems. They only knew that Brian-3 visited Earth-2 but the details remained a mystery. Only Stuart remained a real concern.

The others laughed outright and Stuart managed a half-hearted grin as Dave took to acknowledging every instruction from James by clicking his heels and rapping out, "Jawohl, Herr Major," but they were all worried about Stuart.

"He won't talk to me. Until he does, I can't help but I'd say it was post-traumatic stress. He feels responsible for those deaths. If you say he's not sleeping then together with his loss of appetite and general listlessness, it could be depression." Dr. Tobias paused before continuing, "Taking in all the mind jumps he's done, he could just be exhausted from processing too much information or a combination of it all. I don't know but let's give him a couple of weeks and see what happens. Complete rest may be all that he needs."

It was Stuart's mother who began to break through Stuart's despair when she called on him and Brian.

"Sue and Demetrius want to get married." she said, "She can't understand why he needs your permission and why his past is such a secret. It's time to tell her about the family business."

"NO!" Stuart yelled, "I'm not letting anyone else get hurt. The less she knows the better. Sally manages without knowing what Dave-1 did."

"I know the story but I can't believe it." Mavis said, "Dave is a loving partner and a brilliant father. Sally doesn't want to know what Dave does at the office as she calls it. You straightened Dave out and he's a fine young man."

"Was. I got him killed." Stuart sobbed.

Instinctively Mavis knew not to argue so instead she said, "The point is, Sue is not Sally and is not prepared to have another partner whose life is full of secrets. She needs to know. Demetrius will not disobey you so you've got to help them. Unless Brian intends shutting everything down, I'm taking her to meet Tanya and Chloe. Did you know that they're biologists? It seems that our world has a far more complex bio-system than Terzon and they're keen on studying it. I'm picking up quite a bit but I still prefer cooking fruit to analysing them."

"You can't go, Mum." Stuart sobbed, "It's too dangerous."

"Given the way some idiots drive, so is walking here along the lane. Zack and Andy want to visit Andy's parents for that festival so are you going to stop them?"

"If I tell Zack's mother where he's been then she will."

"Do you realise just how childish that sounds?" Mavis exclaimed angrily, "Let's see, he helped you rescue villagers with nuclear bombs going off around him. He watched Christopher Columbus set sail, and he was arrested on another world because of the way he was dressed and that's just his first year with you. Once I took her to Terzon, Zack told her everything. She knows that there are risks and won't let him out of the house unless he's got the phone you gave him and a translator. Oh and she can't resist saying, 'mind how you go'."

"Then his father will stop him." Stuart said desperately.

"He sees how Zack has grown up over the last year. He was more worried about him hanging around with you and Brian because you're gay, but now he only sees Zack's prospects improving."

Mavis hesitated, worried by the hysteria in Stuart's voice, fearing that he was near breaking point.

"Your Aunt Maria can't stop singing your praises now." she said, "The rest of the family's sick to death hearing about how well her nephew's doing. That's you; you make people happy. You just don't believe that Dave can be happy but I'm sure that he is. So Brian, can I show Sue what goes on here?"

"I was always keener to stop and dismantle the portals than Stuart but not now though." Brian said, "You're right that if we stay on the well trodden paths, it's safe enough. It's when we get dragged deeper into the forest that we get into trouble. I'll ask James to arrange it."

"That's all right." Mavis said, "I've asked Dave to take us. He can show Sue around while I chat to my friends."

"He's never been…" Stuart tailed off uncertainly.

"You really need to talk to him." Mavis said, "He misses you."

"That Dave is dead and I'm to blame." Stuart sobbed, "He's not Dave."

"I don't know what gives you that idea." Mavis exclaimed, "Just go and talk to him."

Stuart just shrugged and eventually it was Dave who knocked on the door. Stuart glared angrily at Brian who ignored his protestations and let Dave in.

Dave stared at Stuart in shock, taking in that he was unshaven, unkempt and just sitting around in boxers but was more alarmed at how Stuart had lost weight.

"I was so very lucky as Dave-1." he said by way of greeting, "If we hadn't been so similar I'd be dead."

"Yes but…" Stuart began.

"No, just shut up and listen." Dave interrupted then grinned, "I should say, ve haf vays of making you listen. I have Dave-1 and Dave-3's memories and they do cause conflicts. I remember things I did as a Hitler youth and Dave-1's revulsion seeps through. I also remember you and me bunking off school and Dave-3 is irritated that we wasted our opportunities. For most of the time I'm one because they agree on everything and I also now have my own memories. If you like, I'm the consensus between them. I am *not* one of them with the other struggling to hang on.

"Yes I must sound confused because I do have both sets of memories and sometimes I'm focussing on just one set. I love Sally and Aidan and I can't distinguish Dave-1 or Dave-3 in that. I did have an urge to prove that I belonged to the master-race when I played Abraham Isaacs at pool but even you think that he's a big-headed twat so Dave-1 liked the extra edge it gave me. I was just one when I bought his brother a drink."

Dave paused, turning to Brian, "I'm just one when I say that I'm worried about Stuart. I think that Brian-3 saw how close the two Daves were and saw it as a way to get here but he couldn't control us. He saw Stuarts as Brians' weak point so targeted them. He found Stuart-2 who was already reaching out. Possibly, because you and Stuart-2 were already linked, he only saw one of you and muddled Earth-1 and Earth-2 together. The whole business started because the barriers between worlds are weakest with Stuarts and we come a close second."

Brian nodded, "Are you sure that you're coping? Those conflicts you mentioned could drive you mad."

"No they couldn't because our experiences are merging. Remember I said I now have my own memories so we agree more not less. "

"Interesting." Brian said, "It's fascinating listening to you switching 1st person to 3rd and still make sense."

"There's something though." Dave said, "I've got four parents. There's two in this village, which I get on with now, my father on Earth-3 who I betrayed to the Gestapo. I've always felt bad about that but now I can't even tell myself that it was my duty. Then there's my mother on Earth-3. We've not got on and I'd like to make my peace with her but I'm not sure how to do it. I do want to talk it over with Stuart when he's feeling better."

"It would be dangerous if you visited." Stuart said, "Do you really want to do that or could we arrange a letter or a phone call?"

There was an alertness in Stuart's eyes as he turned and looked at Dave.

"I'd like to see her." Dave replied, "But I can keep in contact by writing for now because Spock's got a problem. They've found a Terzon that never discovered reason and they want to help. The trouble is they will not interfere, will only observe and they're hoping that you'll do some meddling."

Although Stuart shook his head, Brian was sure that briefly, Stuart's eyes were even brighter but the excitement passed and they dimmed again.

With Thanks to
James Apps (no relation)
for his help in editing this book.

I would also like to acknowledge the artists who provided the
elements of the cover.
Unfortunately I found myself travelling in circles around
Pinterest and Google trying to find them.
My thanks to them and perhaps they would contact me.

Peter Apps

Peter Apps lives in England, and The Long Way Round was his first novel to be followed by Time Askew and Deja Vu To The Nth.

He was born in 1948 and has lived in Sheerness, Kent for most of his life. The Isle of Sheppey where Sheerness is situated has a long, rich history has always fascinated Peter. History might seem a far cry from Science Fiction but imagining life in a Roman settlement is imagining a world just as alien as a distant planet.

Although he worked in a series of routine jobs, he likes to do his own thing when he can. For example, all his computers are Microsoft free zones and prefers to use Linux. He has always had an interest in science, especially Astronomy. Now that planets have been discovered around other suns, he feels that the time is coming when we could discover intelligent life out there.

Other interests include classical music and jazz. He also likes to settle down in the evening watching a good film and enjoying a nice glass of bitter or occasionally visit his local for a chat over a friendly drink.

The author is just a click away by email, peter@sjtales.uk.

Science Fiction
By
Peter Apps

The Stuart Johnson Chronicles

The Long Way Round
Time Askew
Deja Vu To The Nth
Earth Against Earth
Across The Continuum Sea

Worlds Beyond

The Growing Universe
Consolidation (2018)

Other Science Fiction

Disastrous Science (Short Stories)
Fracture Point
Meanwhile In Time (2018)

Non Science Fiction

Contributions to
Quirky Humans And Others
Flash Fiction
(Anthologies by the
Sheppey Writers Group)

www.ingramcontent.com/pod-product-compliance
Lightning Source LLC
Chambersburg PA
CBHW071135260626
47162CB00003B/802